THE SLAB

Borgo Press Books by MICHAEL R. COLLINGS

THE SLAB

A NOVEL OF HORROR

MICHAEL R. COLLINGS

THE BORGO PRESS

MMXI

THE SLAB

FIRST EDITION

Published by Wildside Press LLC

www.wildsidebooks.com

DEDICATION

For the past quarter-century, three masters of modern supernatural and psychological horror have been virtually constant companions in my life—in my academic studies and publications, in my private reading, and in my creative imagination.

Although I have previously responded to their works in the form of books, articles, and reviews based on their works, in which I endeavored to explore some of their widespread influences on contemporary American literature and culture, *The Slab* hazards treading the harrowing, sinuous paths they pioneered, and follows them into the deepest recesses of fear and terror.

For so many years of fascination, enlightenment, and pleasure—albeit frequently of a darkly gruesome sort—my heartfelt thanks to Stephen King, Dean R. Koontz, and Robert R. McCammon.

—Michael R. Collings
Meridian, Idaho
November 2010

…there is something so strange about this place and all in it that I cannot but feel uneasy. I wish I were safe out of it, or that I had never come.

—Bram Stoker, *Dracula*

…but whatever walks at Hill House, walks alone.

—Shirley Jackson, *The Haunting of Hill House*

CONTENTS

CHAPTER ONE
THE HOUSE ALONE,
29 OCTOBER 1991

A Time of Reckoning

1.

It was a day made for death.

Brittle shards from the slanting October sunset stabbed at the quiet street. Brassy gold stained shaggy lawns a murky, coppery brown. The dying light fingered naked limbs of rain-blackened elms and fruitless mulberries and peaches and skeletal jacarandas. It rested heavily on the drooping branches of the occasional valley oaks that had survived construction of the subdivision two years earlier. It tinted vibrant stucco walls not yet faded to earth-mud brown by interminable summers of suns, not yet hidden behind luxuriant passion vines or junipers or the creeping jasmine so popular in this part of Southern California.

In the odd, quirky light, the Charter Oaks subdivision became an enigma of striated shadows, dead black pinioned against muted October color in the late evening of a day that had been more cloud-ridden than otherwise.

Ace McCall squinted. The sun sliced through a bank of clouds low over the horizon, as if day were pleading for one last chance at life before giving up and dying painfully into night. Blinking and cursing under his breath, McCall slapped the sun visor down. This place was bad enough in the summer, he grunted to himself, when the sun would sear a man's naked eyeballs in their sockets like eggs frying on a hot garbage can lid in the hundred degree heat, especially when the glare billowed in waves off the glistening white finish of his year-old Lincoln Mark VII. But you'd think that by this time of year, the damn sun would let up.

He blinked a couple more times, the movement of his eyes unconsciously echoing the rhythm of his turn-signal indicators as he swung off Mariposa Way onto Oleander Place. He didn't stop, even though the intersection was clearly marked with the standard red octagon. Almost as an afterthought, he slowed just enough to scan the cross street. A California rolling-stop came as close as anything to describing the maneuver—illegal by any account, but Ace McCall didn't give a damn. There wouldn't be any cop cars on watch, not here in the middle of Charter Oaks. And there wasn't any cross traffic, anyway. He wasn't dumb enough to just pull in front of some snot-nosed kid's dilapidated Beetle and get sideswiped. There wasn't a nick on the Linc anywhere, and he'd been driving it for over a year. Even into LA two or three times a month.

If he could survive that cannibalistic traffic, this piddling street counted for less than nothing.

He knew how to handle machines. He straightened the wheel and followed the gentle arc of Oleander Place as it rose gradually to crest the tallest of the small hills that dotted Tamarind Valley. The top marked one of the boundaries of Charter Oaks. The end of Ace McCall's responsibility.

Responsibility.

He grimaced. He was beginning to hate that word. He glanced at the passenger seat beside him. An issue of the *Tamarind Valley Times* lay open, accusing him with a white-eyed, blank stare. He caught the edge of a headline and tore his eyes from the roadway just long enough to register three words—"Construction Fraud Charged"—before he crumpled the top page and tossed it over his shoulder and returned his eyes to the road.

There was a flicker of movement. McCall glanced sideways, across the lane to one of the tract houses. A solitary ghost stood forlornly in a recently landscaped front yard. It gazed wistfully at the street and clutched a white bag decorated with silhouetted black cats and witches in its sheet-draped hand. Clutched it as tight as death itself.

You're gonna have to wait kid, McCall thought glumly, oddly touched by the sight. Sorry, kid, no spooks for two more days.

Saturday.

Halloween.

He clenched his teeth in anger.

The day he had to turn over his books to the shyster that paraded as his attorney. The sleazy bastard had offered him a day's grace. Out of the goodness of his heart. His cast-iron heart that had no more human warmth in it than a lump of rotting, frozen graveyard-clay.

"But they'd better be on my desk by noon Saturday," Alberts had intoned officiously over the phone in his best intimidation voice. "I'll wait for you in my office. And I'm going to have to make a special trip to pick them up, so you damn well better be on time."

McCall grunted. It was pretty rough when your own side started figuring you for a cheat and a thief.

He crumpled another leaf from the *Times*, tossing it over his shoulder into the back seat as well.

Shit.

He glanced in the rear-view mirror. The ghost was gone. For the moment, the shadowed length of Oleander Place was deserted. Cut-outs of bats and pumpkins and witches dangled here and there, construction-paper corpses that festooned door frames and window sills. Scattered clumps of drying leaves whispered beneath bare trees. But he saw no other movement, no people.

Where is everyone? McCall thought. He glanced at his watch.

Dinner time.

He pulled the Lincoln to the curb and jammed the shift into park. The engine roared, then settled into an uncomfortable idle. Everyone was inside—Momma, Poppa, the statistically proper two and a third kiddies—all tucked away from the crisp October wind and the crisp October darkness, shut safely away from the outside world in their safe new homes. Homes *he* had maneuvered and finagled. Homes *he* had busted his ass to get approved by the County board. Homes *he* had built. Homes *he* sweat for and bled for and even....

He twisted in his seat. Now they were trying to get him, trying to take away everything he had worked for, just because he had cut a few corners, made the places a little cheaper than he should have. Hell, in fifteen or twenty years, nobody would even remember his little scams...or so he had figured two years before.

And even now—even after it had all come out and the County was dogging him, slobbering for a head—in a decade the shoddiest house in all of Charter Oaks would still probably sell for at least two hundred thou—twice what they were going for now. He crumpled another sheet of newspaper and pulled away from the curb.

He drove slowly now. He studied the houses as he passed, remembering each one, recalling a sticky problem with the plumbing in that one, a shattered plate glass window in this one. In each, he saw the glow of lights behind closed draperies echoing the sheen of the dying sun.

He felt alone. Miserable and alone.

Slug-like, the pale Lincoln crawled up Oleander Place. To the top of the hill.

And stopped.

In front of 1066 Oleander Place.

The last house.

2.

Even a cursory glance showed that 1066 differed from the rest. It was dark, for one thing, inside and out. No lights gleamed warmly through draped windows or reflected on a tidy, well-tended lawn. Its shadowed stucco was scarred and pitted in half a dozen places from peltings with rocks and sticks. A necklace of broken glass circled the foundations where hot-rodders had tossed their beer bottles on Saturday nights. The lawn was a lawn in name only—instead of grass, dusky grey-green weeds that looked jaundiced in the fading light clustered in harsh knots and hillocks. Even the weeds were scrawny and half-dead from lack of care.

1066 Oleander Place.

McCall angled the Lincoln into the driveway, fully intending just to turn around and get the hell away from the place. With everything else he had on his mind, the last thing he needed was to start thinking about 1066. He closed his eyes. His forehead furrowed as if he had just felt the first hammering assault of a mind-shattering migraine. He shook his head and stared ahead. He refused to let those memories through.

But the next thing he knew, his hand rested on the key dangling from the ignition. In spite of his better judgment, he twisted it and throttled the engine into silence. He opened the door and stood, an angular silhouette with one foot propped on the Lincoln's glossy frame and the other crushing a strag-gling weedy morning glory that had wandered halfway across the drive.

He glanced over his shoulder. The sun was gone. The sky still glowed, but now it was mostly an unhealthy yellow glow that was part cloud, part lights from the businesses cropping up like toadstools along the Ventura freeway, just like he figured they would when he started planning the Charter Oaks project five years ago.

Just like he figured.

He shivered and pulled his jacket tighter. After a couple of moments, he almost slid back into the Lincoln, was halfway crouched into the doorway when he stopped. A sound from the house startled him.

Craaack! Like breaking glass.

"Shit," he muttered. "Kids again."

He swept the yard with his eyes. The blood-red McCall/ Sidney Realty "For Sale" sign was canting again—how the hell had he missed seeing that. He shook his head. "Gotta get a clean-up crew out here."

This was a prime lot—probably the best view in all of Charter Oaks, perched as it was at the top of the rise. From the front yard, you could follow the downward sweep of Oleander Place across the northern half of the shallow valley. From the back yard, the southern half opened out, dropping abruptly—almost precipitously—to survey vista on vista as the valley lengthened, then wrinkled to become the foothills of the coastal range. The asking price was good, McCall knew—an easy five thousand below list.

But the "For Sale" sign remained staked steadfastly in the front yard, standing sentry over emptiness and darkness.

Client after client said they liked the deal. They liked the view. They liked the floor plan and the generously sized lot. They liked the quiet neighborhood, with its handy shopping centers a short drive down Bingham Boulevard, its handful of churches of varying denominations scattered nearby, and its three schools almost within walking distance. One after another, they sauntered through the place and *hmmm*-ed and *maybe*-ed approvingly.

But they didn't buy.

The house at 1066 was the last of the original Charter Oaks subdivision. The only one that had never sold.

McCall shivered again. He listened intently, but the cracking sound wasn't repeated. "Imagination," he said to himself. "Too close to Halloween. Too much stress."

He bent again to slide into the Lincoln. A slit of light, suddenly visible when his head turned to just the right angle, glimmered beneath the garage door. He straightened. As his head moved, the glimmer disappeared. He scowled. There wasn't supposed to be anyone there. No one had shown the place for a month.

Irritated, he slammed the car door, fumbled in his pocket for a set of master keys, and walked to the side garage door. His feet crunched dried weeds that needled through his socks and prickled his ankles where his slacks pulled up from his shoes. He slid the key into the door, then stopped, listening.

Nothing.

Wait...what was that?

No, it was just the wind in the naked branches of an elm in the corner of the lot. Or the whisper of cars on the freeway.

Somewhere down the block, a woman's voice wailed "Mikeeee," and another voice, high-pitched and piercing, replied with a drawn-out "Commiiinnng Mommm."

But the house at 1066 lay silent as a white-stucco sepulchre.

3.

McCall's hand trembled as it held the key. He steadied his fingers with his other hand and thrust the key home. The lock was stiff, tight. When he turned the key, the scrannel grating of metal on metal sent shivers coursing up his spine. The door creaked opened.

Welcoomme, to Inner Sanctumm.

"Gotta get a crew up here," he said loudly, as if to push the creaking echo away. "The place is going to hell fast."

The garage smelled musty in spite of the fact that it had never been used. No ground-in grease droppings from split gaskets stained the concrete, no spatters of paint, no stench of gasoline from leaky power mowers. But still the place smelled...bad.

There was no light visible now.

McCall paused. He glanced back at his car. He could just see the edge of the white front fender gleaming against the rapidly darkening sky. He thought about the flashlight he always carried in the trunk. But he didn't go back for it because just then, *craaaack*!

The sound repeated somewhere inside and he stepped into the garage before he was aware he had and carefully shut the door behind him. It seemed important at the moment that the door be closed. Fatally important. He just didn't know why.

The place was dark but not pitch black. A hazy light penetrated from somewhere. The kitchen door must be open. He shuffled across the garage. Even though he knew where everything was, including the as yet unused water heater hunkering in the corner to the left of the door, he instinctively held one hand out from his side, the other in front of him, as if he were afraid of running into something unexpected, something sharp that would jab his eyes or gut his stomach. His heart thumped. He smelled the rankness of his own sweat overlaying the stale air. He slid forward. The sound of leather against smooth concrete—a grating *ssshhh, ssshhh, ssshhh*—made him nervous. He almost wished to hear the sound of breaking glass again.

He stopped.

"What's going on?" he said out loud, startling himself as the sound echoed from empty walls. "I'm no kid afraid of spooks. This is shit!"

He took a long stride, another. Two more and he would be at the kitchen door and he would....

His toe caught and he went down. He sprawled, stretched out on the concrete. His knee cracked on the smooth surface, then his chest, and then his chin. His teeth snapped together and he came *this* goddam close to losing half an inch of his tongue. The pain in his knee was sharp, burning, moist. For a long instant, he didn't dare move.

Broken bones, fractures, sprains—all sorts of possibilities flickered through his imagination as he lay sprawled in the darkness. Something hot dripped along his chin. He raised his hand to touch it. It was sticky as well.

Blood.

Shit, he'd probably sliced his chin open. He rolled onto his side, ignoring pain like a shard of ragged glass slashing his elbow, and sat up. So far so good. He rubbed his knee. His fingers came away stained dark. The thin gabardine of his slacks was shredded along the knee. He flexed his leg and tried to stand. Wobbly but apparently all right, he made it to the doorway separating garage from house.

As he passed through the door way, he instinctively palmed the light switch just inside the kitchen, even though he knew in the back of his mind that he had had the power shut off weeks ago. One of his men had found signs that some bum had been camping out in the back bedroom. No lights, no water, no free hotel, McCall had figured.

With a spine-chilling snap, a light flickered on.

He threw his hands over his eyes, as much out of surprise as out of pain...then winced as the movement twisted his body and his knee threatened to give way.

"What the...?" he began. There shouldn't be any lights.

There weren't. The three bulbs in the ceiling fixture stared down, blank and dead. The same with the fixture in the ceiling of the dining area in front of the double windows that looked over the valley.

McCall breathed a tremulous sigh of relief. The pull-shade over the right-hand pane was up. It should have been down. McCall nodded. That explained the sharp snap and the sudden light—the remnants of daylight streaming through the window as the shade popped loose at the instant he touched the light switch. Coincidence, yes. Certainly nothing more.

He swiveled on his good leg and peered into the darkness of the garage. With his body between the jaundiced light and the garage, all he could see was his bulky, dark outline where it had bled across the concrete. He moved to one side.

Even in the dimness he could see clearly the jagged line of a break in the concrete slab of the garage. It looked like it was at least three inches across, but he realized almost immediately that he was seeing a shadow, not the break itself. The concrete was probably offset only a fraction of an inch, but that was enough to send him reeling when he stumbled over it. The crack started along the outer wall, perhaps a dozen feet in from the double-width wooden doors, and twisted like a shadowy rattlesnake across the floor until it disappeared beneath the inside wall that connected with the entryway. Directly in front of him, the edge of the crack glistened wetly.

Blood. His blood. Caught on a crack in the glass-smooth garage floor.

McCall's mind snapped back to the headlines on the day's papers, to the calls from investigators and engineers and attorneys. To the threats. And to....

"*Ace.*"

His head jerked up and he whirled around, almost pitching himself headfirst across the kitchen floor. It was a whisper that might have been only the passing wind. Or it might have been something more.

No. It can't be.

He's dead!

4.

"Who's there?" Ace McCall yelled, his voice midway between a scream and a shriek of anger. "You better get the hell out of here. I'm armed!"

He clenched his fist—not as effective as a gun, he knew from a lifetime of experience, not even as good as a nice, heavy white-ash bat or a long sturdy length of two-by-four, but it was all he had and he knew well enough how to use it.

"Who's there?" He strained to hear any movement.

Nothing.

He crossed the kitchen slowly, uncomfortably aware of the layered shadows of cabinets and alcoves designed to hide nothing more threatening than crockery and silverware but that now had become abysses of darkness and fear. He crossed the dining room as well, angling his body so that the dim light through the open shade fell just to the right. He wasn't about to give whoever was there a good glimpse of where he was. He glanced out the window. The lights of Tamarind Valley glittered coldly, like bits of silver ore shattered from a larger piece. Further out, strings of white and red from the freeway cut through the valley like twin, thin coping saw blades.

Craaack!

This time, he knew he had heard it. Deeper in the bowels of the house. A window, perhaps, or a door panel shattering beneath a hammer blow. Something hard and violent. McCall shivered even though beads of sweat stood out on his forehead.

He moved into the living room, skirting the double sliding door that opened onto a small covered patio. In most of the houses in Charter Oaks, the patios were already hedged by pyracantha and hibiscus or half-cloaked with newly planted wisteria or grape vines. But the one behind 1066 Oleander Place was stark, awash with white moonlight that turned shadows into prison bars.

McCall breathed deeper as soon as he was on the other side of the doors, safely in the darkness along the living room wall. He followed the smooth plastered surface with one hand as he crept toward the front of the house. At the entryway, he stopped again. He wanted to yell, could feel a screaming "Get the hell out of my house!" billowing over his tongue and pressing against his teeth, but he forced himself to keep still. To his right was the skull-blank wall separating the entry from the garage. To his left and about a foot in front of him was the black mouth of the hall that led past two bedrooms and a bathroom before it made a right angle and continued into deeper darkness, where it opened onto three more bedrooms and the second bath.

Seven rooms.

In the darkness.

For a second, McCall almost took three strides straight forward, where he could wrench the front door open and burst out of the house and run to his car and get far enough down the hill to stop at some nice safe Mr. and Mrs. Suburbia's place and call the cops.

Almost.

"McCall."

The voice was still less than a whisper. But, he realized, it was far more than just imagination. It chilled Ace McCall to the bone. He recognized it immediately. He knew whose voice it was, and he knew, dammit he *knew* that the throat that made those sounds was crushed and dead and buried where no one *no one* would ever find it.

"McCall."

Now the whisper was less than a breath.

He turned into the dark hallway. Even during the middle of the day, this part of the house was always gloomy. Windows in the bedrooms were offset from the doors just enough that only filtered light penetrated to the hallway even at noon. After nightfall, the blackness was absolute. He literally couldn't see his hand in front of his face.

For a moment he heard himself thinking, *This can't be. This isn't happening. It's a trick or something.*

The best thing to do would be to get the hell back down the hall, rip off the chain lock from the front door and explode out into the night and climb into the waiting Lincoln and drive away from 1066 Oleander forever. Never look back. Never come back. Never think about it again.

"McCaallll."

With that single, guttural sound, the last moment of clear thinking for Ace McCall passed unnoticed into oblivion.

"No!" he shrieked in fear compounded with a fury that drove rationality from him like brittle-dry, skeletal October leaves whirling dervish-like before a madding hurricane.

No one does this to Ace McCall no one tries this kind of game and gets away without broken bones.

He plunged deeper into the darkness of the hall, crashing into the closed door at the corner. His shoulder screamed with the pain of his two hundred and fifty pounds. The door creaked, threatened to give way but finally held and rebounded enough that he fell backwards and slammed into the opposite wall. He shook his head. Kaleidoscopic red stars and yellow lightning bolts and blue whirlwinds appeared, disappeared, re-appeared. Then disappeared again. But not entirely.

He shook his head again to clear his vision, rubbed his hand across his face, and stared down the right-hand branching of the hallway.

The bathroom door was a black abyss, so was the bedroom door opposite and the last door on the left. But the door on the right, at the far end of the hall—the door to the back corner bedroom...that door was open and through it spilled a feeble light tinged pale, gangrenous green, like things once living but now dead and slowly, silently rotting into a putrid luminescence.

McCall swallowed and, more automaton than thinking man, he moved forward.

Get out of here Ace get the hell out of here now! part of his mind screeched over and over, but his feet weren't listening. His fisted hand relaxed and dropped to his side, limp and useless.

"No no no no no," he repeated endlessly, his voice hoarse. It can't be.

He reached the edge of the doorway and stopped just out of sight of what waited beyond.

"McCall."

And now it seemed as if the whisper were nearer, monstrously intimate, as if corrosive words were filtering through the mad rush of fevered blood in McCall's ears. "I've been waiting," it seemed to say, each syllable echoing with horror and threat. "A long time."

Ace McCall's face blanched white, although in the hellish light his stark, fleshy features were stained the sickly, mottled red-grey-green of an oozing wound, suppurating and inflamed. His heart thudded. He pressed his back against the wall, the light spilling over his right shoulder and reflecting on him from the wall opposite.

"I didn't...," he began. Answering the sound suddenly made it worse. It was as if his acknowledging it out loud had enfleshed what might just have been imagination. Suddenly, he felt the presence coalesce into something more, felt a sudden, pressing, frightening physicality, felt it with a surety that stunned him and left his limbs as weak as unwanted newborn kittens destined to be drowned in a dank, fetid gunnysack before too many more minutes of painful life had passed. His voice choked off as if invisible hands had constricted around his throat. He tried again.

"I mean, I thought.... It was an accident!

"Noooo!"

The unseen presence whipped out and grasped McCall's mind and yanked. He stumbled into the back bedroom, fell hard on the carpet-shrouded concrete. His knees scraped against rough carpet and the blood flowed freely again. His shoulder banged against the door casement, and then his head struck something rough and cutting and he vaguely felt the skin on his temple slice away as the thing (*can't be can't be you're not real*) spun him around with the ease of a child playing with a Christmas toy and raised him effortlessly to his full height and stared him in the eyes and laughed.

Ace McCall tried to speak, tried to cry out, had to struggle even to breath. His eyes narrowed with pain. The loathsome green light faded to coppery, dusky brown and then to blood red.

Or perhaps it wasn't so much a change in the light as it was the fiery blood...his own fiery blood...shrouding his eyes and gouting onto the carpet at his feet not six inches from the faint shadow that marked the sinuous twining of yet another crack in the foundation slab in the house at 1066 Oleander Place.

"*McCall.*"

From the *Tamarind Valley Times*, 15 June 1989:

HOUSING STARTS SCHEDULED

Construction will begin by the end of June on a proposed 60-site development to be called Charter Oaks, reported a County Planning Commission spokesman today. The development, bounded on the west by Bingham Boulevard and on the north by the newly completed Reynolds Avenue, represents the single largest housing project in the history of Tamarind Valley.

Ace-High Construction submitted the lowest bid and was formally awarded the contract at last night's Council meeting. The homes, when completed, will form the heart of what is envisioned by some as a new city nestled in the foothills of the coastal range, with easy freeway access to....

CHAPTER TWO
THE HUNTLEYS, 21/22 DECEMBER 2009

Moving Day

1.

Catherine Huntley stiffened. She turned her head slightly, angling toward the sound she thought she had heard. She relaxed...marginally. It was nothing, she argued with herself, as she had been doing most of the night.

Just your silly imagination.

She dropped her head back into the pillow's embrace and tried to persuade her over-active mind to accept sleep. But she knew that it was useless.

She felt her legs beginning to twitch nervously, a sign she easily recognized. She wouldn't get to sleep for a long time tonight.

At her side, Willard snored lightly—not enough to have awakened her if she had been asleep but enough to help keep her from getting there.

The snore stuttered into a muffled snort as he turned onto his side, flopping heavily on the mattress and pulling most of the last of her grandmother's hand-stitched quilts—a delicate Wedding Ring pattern in rose and palest blue—with him as he turned.

She smiled.

As if he were awake to her smile, he snuggled against her, his curving back and buttocks nestling against her side. His spine caressed her ribs. She smiled again. Part of her felt warm and tingly tonight, in spite of the light rain that had begun late that afternoon, in spite of the prediction of near freezing temperatures by morning—a rarity in near-tropical Coastal Southern California.

The faint draft from the windows touched her cheek with a chilling briskness, and the air in the bedroom was both cold and faintly damp, almost musty, even though the previous owners had only been out three days before the Huntleys began moving in.

That morning, in fact.

Willard had put the bed up first thing, with a grin and an unspoken promise that he had more than fulfilled tonight.

Catherine smiled again.

She still felt his fluid warmth inside of her.

She still tingled with the memory of his touch, his body pressed against hers, his lips seeking hers, his tongue penetrating. Loving Willard had always been special. But tonight it seemed even more so.

Because they were doing it in their house.

Their very own.

Catherine raised her head, the tendons in her neck straining and streaking her flesh with knife-sharp shadows.

There it came again.

A low murmur.

Like water rustling through pipes.

Or the toilet tank in the back bathroom running.

Or....

Get a hold of yourself, she thought sternly, it's nothing. Remember the first night in the apartment in Riverside, thirteen long years ago, when you made poor Willard get up and tramp through the house barefoot, not even letting him have enough time to throw a robe over his nakedness, then him stubbing his toes on every box and carton in every room, all because you *knew* you heard someone pounding on the back door.

Well, she thought in her own defense, there had been a pounding.

Right.

And she remembered how embarrassed she was when they drove away from the manager's office first thing the next morning.

"Pounding," the woman had said, leaning back in her chair. "Probably just the pipes. You turned the hot water on, right?"

Willard had nodded.

"Just the pipes expanding and contracting." She had turned away, the action eloquently expressing her mixture of contempt and humor at the couple sitting stiffly before her, already complaining after only one day in their apartment.

She seemed to have known that it was also the first apartment for either of them, that they had only been married a week and were just returned from their honeymoon.

She must have imagined the two of them....

Catherine's cheeks flushed in the darkness.

Her hand strayed over Willard's shoulder. She turned on her side and moved against him, spoon-fashion. She didn't know when she had first heard that expression, but it was right on. Spoon to spoon. Her hand strayed further now, along the lines of his chest and stomach, still taut after thirteen years of marriage, and down to his hips. She nuzzled the back of his neck, not really caring whether he was awake or not, half hoping he was, half resigned to the fact that he almost always fell asleep—no, she corrected herself, he always *crashed*, that was more like it, tail-spinning, out-of-control, earth-shattering *crash*—right after they made love.

At first it had bothered her.

She would come back from the bathroom, still warm with passion, her skin alive and so sensitive that the faint movement of the silent night air against it made her light-headed. And Willard would be lying there, stone-still.

Asleep.

Oh well, she sighed, repeating herself for the umpteenth time in thirteen years.

If that's all I have to worry about, I'm better off than....

Her head snapped up again.

This time she was certain.

She *had* heard something.

She sat up, dragging the covers with her.

Willard shifted and one hand reached back and tugged on the edge of the quilt her grandmother had given them as a wedding present. In his sleep, he burrowed further under its warmth. But Catherine couldn't ignore this sound.

It was definite.

Not really loud, but definite.

And she couldn't quite identify it. But it was *something*.

Just the house settling, stupid. Old wooden joints do creak, you know.

She listened more intently. She turned her head from side to side, trying to fix a location for the sound.

There it was. A muted *thump, thump..., thump*, too irregular to be the winter wind splaying a naked branch against a window. Too random for anything else she could imagine.

She slipped out of bed, pulling on her long flannel robe, the high-necked white one Willard hated because he claimed it made her look like someone's great-great grandmother out of another century...and because (although he would never admit to it) it was infinitely harder to remove in the dark than her others. But it was warm and thick, and the night had promised to be a cold one.

She slipped her feet into scuffs and padded from the room, stopping at the door into the hall. Directly in front of her, the hallway extended past the bathroom and the front bedroom she had requisitioned as a combination sewing-room/all-purpose escape-from-the-children-when-things-got-too-hairy room. Beyond that lay the blackness of the entry and, to the right, the living room and from there the kitchen.

Straight ahead, she could dimly see a reflection through the door the previous owners had built to join the entry hall with what had once been the garage but was now a large, comfortable family room. It was presently chock-full of unopened boxes, but it promised to become the focal point for their lives for years to come.

She strained her eyes.

The reflection focused into a small orange glow, like an unblinking eye studying Catherine Huntley from the darkness. For a moment her skin crawled and her breath halted. Then she exhaled in a long, relieved hiss that echoed in the silence.

Stupid, she thought, not for the first time that evening. Stupid stupid stupid.

It was only the clock. Right.

The electric clock with the luminous dial that she had carefully set to the exact time then placed on a stack of cardboard boxes along the far wall. Not the glowing eye of the cannibal goddess Kali, or anything so exotic.

A stupid clock.

She felt her heart slowly creep back to its steady pace. Her arrested breathing resumed as well, and her goose-fleshed, crawling skin crept coldly back to its rightful place on her arms

Thump thump...thump...thump.

A long pause, then...*thump.*

It was definitely coming from her right, from somewhere along the darkened hallway that led to the second bathroom, past Suze's room and dead-ended by the doors to the boys' room on the right and what would probably end up as Willard's office on the left.

They had intended for Will, Jr., to have his own room— finally, the twelve-year-old's dream had come true—but both Burt and Samuel (Sams to everyone since the day he had come home from the hospital and Suze tried to say his name and tripped up on the syllables, and everyone laughed and from then on it was just Sams) had unaccountably refused to sleep in the back room without their older brother.

So, for now at least, all three boys were together, the older two in the bunks, Sams in the little box trundle-bed that each of the boys had slept in until they turned four or five. She stepped down the hall.

Thump.

She stopped, waiting for the sound to return and give her some idea of what it was, where it came from. When it didn't she continued. There was no sound, no movement in Suze's room. Catherine flicked the light on, just long enough to see the top of the six-year-old's head sticking out of a bundle of quilts, blankets, stuffed animals, and favorite clothing that somehow had not gotten hung up that evening and that—Catherine knew ruefully from past experience—would somehow never quite make it to a closet or dresser drawer. Suze was short for Susan; the Huntley's first girl-child had been named after Catherine's grandmother.

Catherine breathed in relief.

Suze was fast asleep. And safe.

Catherine turned the light off. The sudden darkness seemed deeper, colder. She shivered. Even though the forced-air furnace was on, the house still felt damp, unlived in.

It would probably be all right in a couple of days, though, she reassured herself.

Thump.

The sound jerked her from her stasis and reminded her that she had a job. Mother's responsibility number 483—investigating strange but undoubtedly harmless noises in the dead of darkness on cold December nights.

She paused by the bathroom door but heard nothing there. Again she flicked on the light.

And again everything was normal.

The storage bedroom was next to the bathroom. Enough moonlight filtered through the dusty but curtainless windows for her to make out most of the shapes—again, boxes and cartons, things they wouldn't need for the next few days, pushed into this room as soon as the boys announced their decision that

Will was going to have to sleep with them for a while. The room was silent.

That left the boys' room. She swallowed tightly and looked across the dark hallway. To her imagination, the open door into the back corner bedroom seemed unaccountably threatening, like an open mouth of impenetrable darkness against the faint gray of the hall.

For a frightening instant, she didn't want to walk through that opening—it would be too much like stalking down a demon's throat.

Don't be absurd, Catherine Huntley, she told herself sternly. You've play enough mind-games tonight already. It's just a room.

She crossed the hallway and entered.

2.

A shard of moonlight glowed in the room.

It hadn't seemed this bright from the hallway, she thought with a tinge of wonder. Then even that suggestion of strangeness disappeared and she returned to the business at hand—being a mother, protecting her boys from..., well, to be honest, she thought, from funny noises in the night—like funny noises in the car, she added mentally, that in the comic strips only wives hear but that husbands must eventually pay for when the funny, imaginary noises suddenly transform into reality and become cracked blocks or stripped brakes or exploding radiators or expiring transmissions.

She stopped.

She didn't like the direction her thoughts were heading. She looked around.

She could define the outlines of the bunk beds, the box bed against the far wall, the dressers. She crossed to the dresser and turned on a small Mickey Mouse table lamp. It had been Will's, but he had recently announced that it was "baby-stuff," and Burt had inherited it by default. In the soft golden glow of the

40-watt bulb, she studied the room.

Sams was curled up against the wall, swaddled in his favorite blanket, the satin edging stuffed into his mouth like a surrogate thumb. It *was* in fact a surrogate thumb, and sometimes he sucked on the edging until it was so wet and filthy and smelly that Catherine wanted to burn it. But each time it went into the wash, Sams would stand solitary guard over the machine until it came out, then transfer his attention to the dryer.

Somehow, she never quite found the courage to get rid of the thing.

She leaned over and pulled the edging out of his mouth, shivering when she felt how clammy the material was. But she knew that even asleep Sams would have it in his mouth again in a matter of seconds.

Sure enough, before she had straightened, his hand flailed for a moment, made contact, and retrieved the grungy satin.

Oh well, she sighed silently.

She turned her attention to the other boys.

Will, Jr., on the top bunk, was nothing more than a heap of bedding. She knew that he must be in there somewhere, but it took a bit of probing to find a scrawny, warm arm connected to an equally scrawny shoulder that led to neck and head. His forehead felt a bit warm, but Catherine put that up to the excitement of moving.

On the lower bunk, Burt presented an opposite picture. Most of him was exposed to the cold. His legs were clearly visible, encased in flannel pjs that had pulled up almost to his knees; his stomach was similarly exposed almost to his chest. But his head was covered. For Burt, that always seemed enough, no matter how cold it might get. She shook her head, tugged his pajama tops to his waist, and pulled the pant legs to his ankles. She unwrapped the mound at his head, straightening the blanket and tucking it around his body and wondering as she did so how the kid had managed to avoid a fatal case of pneumonia during any of his eight winters. But he never even had so much as an ear infection or a light case of croup.

She shrugged.

There was no understanding kids. But then, that was something she had learned long before. She leaned over and planted a kiss on Burt's forehead, knowing full well that before she was out of the room the bedding would begin its inevitable trek upward, past shin and knee and tummy and chest, to wrap like a friendly serpent around his neck and head. Oh well, as long as....

Thump.

She straightened so suddenly that she cracked her head on the edge of Will's bunk. This thump echoed the other ones, the mysterious sounds that had drawn her from her bed and sent her on this nighttime search. She pulled herself away from the bunks and stood in the center of the room.

Eyes closed, ears strained, she concentrated. After what must have been minutes, she heard it again.

Thump thump thump.

It was coming from the roof! She was sure of it. She crossed to the window. The moon glowed faintly through a break in the cloud cover. The rain had stopped, but the wind was still high enough to rustle the elm in the corner of the lot.

Behind the tree, through its December-naked branches, she saw the lights of traffic on the freeway. Even at this hour, she thought, still as busy as ever.

Thump.

Now she had a handle on the sound.

She left the boys' room and went into Suze's. She slid the newly hung curtains open and watched as the wind fingered through a line of black yew trees bordering the property next door. The branches seemed dipped in silver and sable, at once intriguing and subtly frightening in the intensity of light and shadow. Catherine shuddered.

Thump.

Yes, that had to be it.

She left Suze's room, with a final glance at the mound that hid her daughter, and returned to her own bedroom. Willard hadn't moved. She stepped out of her scuffs and, still wearing the flannel robe, slipped beneath the covers, feeling their clammy chill where they had been turned back, the lingering warmth of her own body further down. Willard seemed to be radiating waves of heat, but Catherine knew that it was only because she had become chilled from her little trip. She put her feet on Willard's calves. Part of her wanted him to wake up, at least enough to reach for her, perhaps enough to want to do more.

But another part urged him to remain asleep. She didn't want to tell him what she had done.

She didn't want to admit that the thumping of seedpods dropping from the yews onto the roof had nearly freaked her out as badly as had the hot water expanding pipes over a decade before. She didn't want him to know that she had been nervous and upset her first night in the house...in *their* house. She snuggled against him.

Mentally she thanked the previous owners for being so desperate to move to their new, custom-built house in Newton Park, at the eastern edge of the Valley, that they took a deep cut in their asking price. After all, escrow had fallen through on two previous attempts to sell the house, and if it fell through a third time, Chuck Maxwell had explained, the other family stood a real chance of losing their new place. They *had* to sell.

And she thanked Chuck as well, with his creative approach to real estate that had gotten them just past the money requirements for the house. A five-thousand dollar landscaping allowance for the bare back yard, paid by the Merricks as part of the deal, had given them just the edge...and the house at 1066 Oleander was theirs.

Theirs.

The word made her feel snug and safe. She nestled against Willard's back and, her arm resting across his shoulder, finally drifted into sleep.

From the *Tamarind Valley Times*, 5 November 1989:

SEARCH CONTINUES FOR
MISSING VALLEY BUSINESSMAN

The investigation into the disappearance of Bryan Sidney, the Tamarind Valley realtor and construction executive missing since last Friday, expanded today to include county agencies. Sidney, 47, senior partner in Ace-High Construction and co-founder of McCall/Sidney Realty, was reported missing on October 30 when he failed to appear at a meeting of the County Realtors' Association annual meeting in Santa Barbara, at which he was to deliver the opening address. A full investigation has been launched, said a County Sheriff spokesman today, although there are no substantive leads as yet.

A long-time bachelor, Sidney was last seen by his secretary when he closed his office Thursday evening. He had no scheduled appointments for that night, she claimed, but it was possible that he might have gone....

CHAPTER THREE
THE HUNTLEYS, JANUARY 2010

Settling In

1.

Catherine Huntley jerked awake. She shot a glance at the luminous dial of the digital clock by her nightstand.

It read 2:37 AM.

"What...?" she began, and then her sleep-numbed mind registered two things.

Sound...and movement.

The sound was a constant muted roar, an irritating rumble that vibrated on her ears like the approach of a heavily loaded eighteen-wheeler careening out of control down a city road, distant as of yet but drawing closer and closer. The movement was more subtle but for all of that infinitely more frightening. The bed quivered. The windows above her head vibrated tightly in their aluminum frames. The silver slats of the Levelor blinds rattled against each other, clicking like dozens of dice being rattled in a metal cup. Old hand that she was to Southern California's geologic vagaries, Catherine Huntley recognized the signs.

Earthquake!

The shade on the lamp by her bed was swaying now, back and forth, back and forth, as if someone had jostled it in passing.

The movement of the bed had intensified to a clear shaking. The roar grew.

The Big One!

Without thinking, Catherine punched Willard in the shoulder. "Get up!" she yelled, then she was out of bed and pulling on her robe as she swept through the door, calling over her shoulder again to Willard, "Get up! It's an earthquake!"

By the time she was halfway down the hall, the sound had stopped, the motion had stopped. The concrete slab again felt solid and stable beneath her feet.

Her bare feet.

She grinned in momentary embarrassment—she had broken rule one of Earthquake etiquette: NEVER WANDER AROUND BAREFOOT. There might be broken glass, broken tiles. All sorts of things that would not go well with bare feet. She could tell from the lack of sound behind her that Willard had remained dead to the world. As usual. Still, getting up at 5:00 AM Monday through Friday for the commute into L.A. wasn't easy on him, so she shouldn't complain.

Anyway, the immediate crisis seemed to be over. She went down the hallway, straightening a favorite oil painting of a grey-and-brown rabbit huddling in unbelievably vivid green grass, done by a college friend years before. The nightlight in the bathroom shed enough light for her to see that the picture had been jostled well out of plumb by the temblor. With any luck, there wouldn't be much more damage. Thank God they were still unpacking some of the moving boxes stored in the back bedroom. Grandma's china and crystal were still safely crated away. If they had been on the shelves....

She glanced in at Suze. Sleeping as usual. The kid could sleep through fire, flood, and famine. Catherine envied her daughter that ability. Since moving into the new house, she had slept restlessly, lightly. She was easily awakened by the slightest sounds. Her cheeks reddened as she remembered the yew trees and the wind less than a month before.

The boys were also asleep. It seemed as if only Catherine had even felt the earthquake, let alone reacted to it. She was about to leave the room and make her way back to bed when one of the boys—probably Will—groaned. It was a long, fitful sound guaranteed to strike a chill up any certified mother's spine. It was echoed by another moan, this time from the lower bunk.

She bent over Burt's bedding-swathed head. She touched his bare stomach. The skin was cold and damp, sweaty almost. She pulled the blankets away from his face and was startled to see that his hair was plastered to his forehead, thick and dark even in the filtered light from the bathroom. He tossed his head several times, his eyes flickering up and down beneath their lids.

"Mmmnnhhh," he murmured, as if trying to articulate a word.

"Burt," Catherine said, whispering so as not to wake the others. "Burt, honey." She shook him gently. "Wake up."

"Mommy?" His voice was dark and thick with sleep, deep and disturbing, not at all like his usual boy's treble. "Mommy?"

"Did you have a bad dream?"

"Dream?"

Catherine recognized the signs. He was awake and not awake. But she hoped that she had roused him enough to dispel whatever was frightening him in his sleep.

"It's okay," she said, putting as much motherly soothing and reassurance as she could in her voice. "Go back to sleep."

"'Kay," Burt murmured, then: "'Night."

"Goodnight, honey." She kissed him and, careful to avoid the edge of the upper bunk, stood up.

And gasped.

Will was staring straight at her.

For an instant, the dim light in the room had caught his face, sharpening planes and ridges and reflecting from eyes so dark as to seem black even in midday. For an instant he seemed a stranger, piercing her with eyes that burned cold and deep. For an instant, he looked dead.

"Mommy?" he said, and the instant faded and it was just her son watching her from his bed.

"Yes, dear."

"I dreamed I was at Disneyland. On the roller-coaster."

Catherine smiled. Let him think that it was a dream. Tomorrow would be time enough to discover—in the reassuring light of day—that he had just experienced an honest-to-goodness California quake. If she told him that now, he would probably want to stay up all night waiting for the inevitable after shocks.

"Just a dream," she said.

"And the man tried to pull me out of the car," he continued, slowly but without a noticeable break, as if he was finishing his thought without being aware that she had interrupted. "And then I tried to run away but he chased me."

She rubbed his arm the way she knew he liked. "It was just a dream. Go back to sleep."

He closed his eyes. She felt a twinge of relief when the blackness disappeared beneath eyelids drained of color by the dim light. She tucked the covers around him, noticing for the first time that his skin seemed cooler than usual—just the opposite of Burt's. She shivered. The room was cold as well. There was no cloud cover tonight, and that meant that there was a real chance of temperatures dipping to the teens.

Welcome to sunny California, and turn on the hot-air fans in the orange groves, folks. Come to think of it, turn up the heater as well.

Willard insisted that they set the thermostat as low as it would go at night. On the twenty-year-old furnace in this house, that meant somewhere in the forties. If it dipped below that, well, there were always more blankets and quilts, he insisted. But at around nineteen degrees, even quilts and blankets had a limited usefulness.

So in spite of the probability that Willard would wake up grumpy and complaining of a mild headache from the heated air (they were real headaches, she knew, and she usually tried to accommodate to his need for cool air at night), she decided to turn on the heater. After all, it was nearly 3:00, and Willard had only another couple of hours of sleep. And anyway, she thought as she made her way down the hallway, she could always open the window in their room a crack and close the door and turn off the vent. At least that way the kids would sleep a bit more warmly.

She followed the turn in the hall, already familiar with the feeling of the stiff-piled carpet beneath her bare toes. Their last place had been tiled, with only occasional throw rugs that rumpled so easily that were more bother than they were worth.

In the living room, she turned on the lamp by the thermostat, gave the circular dial a twist that re-set it to fifty, waited for a second to hear the reassuring *whoomp* of the gas heater kicking in and, with a clarity that made her mouth convulse, suddenly realized how extraordinarily good a cup of steaming hot Sleepy Time tea would taste.

It was the last time she ever associated Sleepy Time tea with pleasure.

She wrapped her arms around herself to ward off the chill, wishing that she had thought to put on a robe, wishing that the heater was more efficient, wishing that the press releases for Southern California would include the fact that on the rare occasions when it got really cold—sub-freezing cold—the humidity coupled with the woefully insulated housing made it seem much worse than winter had been when she was a child in Montana. At least there, she thought ruefully, the cold was honest, and everyone knew it was coming and what to expect, and dressed warmly and built sturdily to keep the cold out and the warm in. Here the houses were cracker boxes, with no insulation to speak of.

But wishing didn't make it so. At least with a cup of hot tea in her, she would be a little warmer when she returned to bed. At the closed folding doors that separated the kitchen from the living room, she could have reached out and turned the dimmer switch on the living room wall next to the switch that controlled the patio light. She could have done so, and then pulled the folding doors open, and the kitchen would have been well lit and what happened next might never have happened, or if it did, it might not have been so horrifying.

Or perhaps it would have happened anyway.

But regardless of the infinite *maybe*-s and *perhaps*-s that infest and destroy so many lives like God-sent plagues, she did not touch the dimmer.

The dimmer was connected to a four-bulb light-and-fan affair in the dining room half of the kitchen, and she was still worried about the electrical costs in a house this size. Heaven knew that Willard's salary was undergoing enough trauma with the sudden pressures of a mortgage frighteningly larger than their apartment rent. She was sure that they would grow into it eventually, just as she was sure that the way rents were spiraling in the area their house payment would seem increasingly small in comparison over the next couple of years. But right now, after only a little less than a month as homeowners, she was trying for frugality, systematically replacing 100-watt bulbs with 60-watters wherever possible, trailing after Willard and the kids to turn off lights left burning in empty rooms.

So instead of simply reaching out and turning the dial and flooding the kitchen with light, she decided to cross the dark kitchen. She knew where everything was, and anyway there would be some spillage from the living room lamp. If necessary, she could always turn on the swag lamp Willard had hung over the sink. She started to open the folding doors.

Most of the kitchen was still cloaked in darkness. She had drawn the curtains over both windows before she turned in the evening before, hoping that the thin material might help keep out even a bit of the cold. She blinked at the pocket of darkness that opened before her. For an instant, memories of dank cellars and musty attics in her Grandmother's place flitted through her mind. Memories of childhood fears of things in the dark, of things that go *bump-thump-thump* in the dark almost overcame her good resolves to be a conscientiously cost-aware house-holder.

For an instant she trembled with a fear that froze the marrow of her bones, a terror triggered unaccountably by the angular wedge of light that cut across the table. She blinked, and the complex of light and shadow resolved into hauntingly familiar forms. In spite of his promise to clean up after himself, Willard had left his late-night snack things out for her to take care of.

Again.

The mundanity of a small white plastic cup, a plate and butter-and-jam-covered knife crossing it, and a loaf of bread with its plastic sleeve still open to the air penetrated her fear.

She shook her head in a gesture at once accusatory and forgiving and stepped into the kitchen

At the same instant, she realized with a panicky *thrummm-ing* in her veins that there was something wrong with the table. It was a relic from Willard's family's pioneer past, purchased by his great-grandparents at the turn of the century and handed down from generation to generation since, and finally officially his on the day of their wedding. But now, the once solid oak planking wavered and heaved as if it were undergoing its own California temblor.

And then her foot touched the cold linoleum floor...or rather, what should have been cold linoleum but was in fact even colder, frenetic and scuttering and dry and husky and cold and moving *moving* and the floor rose up to brush the sole of her foot and lap over like an incoming wave at Zuma Beach and rise higher, onto the arch of her foot, and then the foot was down before her mind could assimilate the shock and the horror, and her weight was on it and something *somethings* crushed beneath her and the floor was frenetic and scuttering and husky and cold and slimy-wet.... And Catherine Huntley screamed!

2.

For Willard Huntley, getting to sleep had become a real chore lately. Even with the younger kids in bed by 8:00 and Will, Jr., down by 8:30, even by staying up half an hour or so later than Catherine and watching the 11:00 news and then getting something to eat before padding down the hallway, even by consciously trying to wear himself out at work each day, he was finding it harder and harder to get to sleep. Except, he would have reminded himself wryly had he been awake at the moment Catherine screamed, and languidly contemplating his life, *except* after he and Catherine made love

But those occasions were rare enough. She was often tired nowadays, and there was always the chance—no, make that the high probability—of one of the kids waking up and calling "Mommy" at just the wrong moment, like they were all endowed with some kind of alien your-parents-are-having-sex radar. Or, worse, either he or Catherine might glance up at a moment of passion and see a pair of wide, dark eyes staring at them in sleepy bewilderment. That had already happened at least once (that they knew of), and now Catherine was wary of simply indulging in raw passion.

She had to check the kids first, she had to close the bedroom door (that always made Willard feel slightly constrained, slightly confined, slightly guilty), she had to remind him half a dozen times to be quiet, she had to do this or that. And the upshot was that since moving in, they had really made love only once—passionately, wildly, satisfyingly, that first night. Since then, a little touching, a little playing around— hell, he had seen more action in the back seat of his '73 Chevy convertible when he was a kid than he had seen in his own bed for the past few weeks.

One consequence was that he had been sleeping less lately, growing more exhausted, more touchy with each passing night... lying awake, listening to the subtle noises of the house, listening to the less subtle sounds of Catherine breathing beside him. But the good part, if there was a good part, was that once he finally made it to sleep—whether on his own or through pure, physical, sexual exhaustion—he slept, sometimes jaws agape, like *the mouth of one newly dead*, until his alarm clanged him awake at 5:00.

He had been known to sleep through minor household catastrophes that included tummy aches and croup and ear infections and the million other ailments that set kids from infants to teens wailing in the night. He had heard about them often enough from Catherine, more than often enough from his mother-in-law who, after thirteen years was still not sure her daughter had chosen either wisely or well enough. So he didn't notice when the bed shook a little, or when the mattress shook substantially more as Catherine slipped out of bed.

He might have registered hearing her yelling at him to get up, but the part of his brain responsible for timekeeping and schedules seemed to realize intuitively that the hour was wrong, so it shunted her voice to another part of Willard's brain, and in the next ten seconds he endured a nightmare of cries of terror and weirdly surrealistic situations that in the cold light of day would seem totally unfrightening as they swiftly passed from experience to memory to intimation to simply a feeling of slight discomfort. He didn't hear the whispered conversations between his wife and his older sons. He didn't hear Catherine pass by the bedroom, and he certainly didn't hear the faint click of the living room lamp or the inaudible scrape of plastic against plastic as she turned the thermostat up.

He did, however, react to the soft *whuump* when the gas heater kicked in. He winced slightly, and his closed eyes flickered. Within a moment or two, the first wisps of heated air emerged through the vent above the open door and feathered into the coolness. In spite of Catherine's sometimes lax, sometimes almost aggressive attitude about his responses to heated air at night, Willard was not simply being contentious. Within seconds of the heater's firing up, his head began to feel sluggish, heavy, the blood to pound fractionally more stridently against his temples. Even in his sleep—no longer quite as deep or as complete as a moment before—he was preparing to wake sick, edgy, slightly nauseated.

But finally, of all the sensations that conspired to destroy Willard Huntley's sleep that night, one succeeded where all else had failed.

Willard jerked fully awake, sat straight up in bed, and then was out the door and down the hall, wearing only an old, faded T-shirt and his boxers in spite of the iciness heavy in the air, before Catherine's frantic scream had even begun to die away.

3.

Catherine was not afraid of many things. Oh, she cringed at the occasional snake or lizard or frog Will or Burt might bring home. But generally she handled the zoological traumas of motherhood with amazing aplomb. She had somehow even found the reserves—deep, deep reserves, to be sure—to hold up a nearly complete lizard skin shed by some long-forgotten denizen of an overgrown vine that crept along the back fence in their apartment in Riverside. Burt had found it one July and brought it to her with all the pride and triumph of Sir Francis Drake presenting the treasure-laden *Golden Hind* to Her Majesty the Queen.

"How nice. How interesting," she had murmured to Burt's breathless, "Gosh, Mom, isn't this neat" as he dropped the thing into her hand. Somehow she managed not to crush the monstrosity...at least not until Burt was long out of sight and she could safely deposit the treasure in the garbage. Fortunately, he had never wondered why she was not wearing the paper-thin, transparently scaled skin as a brooch to church or as a hat on special days.

No, she could handle most things.

But not this!

Her scream echoed even louder in her own head than in the silent air. Long and harsh and painful. Her throat felt on fire. Her lungs screamed their own counterpoint, demanding air air air.

For a moment—a blessed moment that she hoped would come but feared even more because then she might lose control and fall to the cold tile floor and become one with the rustling, scabrous, heaving movement—she nearly fainted.

She caught herself at the last instant and thrust her hand out to the counter to steady herself. And felt more dryness and frenetic movement. She passed beyond startlement and fear into horror as the things crossed her fingers, their legs burning into her skin like infinitesimal points of acid.

She jerked her hand away, the action simultaneously rousing her out of her threatened faint and intensifying her disgust and revulsion.

They were climbing her hand and arm!

Shuddering beyond conscious control, she screamed again and sliced frantically at her arm with her other hand, fingers stiffened into knives, palm slapping viciously against her own flesh, oblivious to pain, oblivious to anything but a burgeoning horror.

Roaches.

Roaches!

She might have been able to handle one. Perhaps. But even one was generally enough to send her screaming for help— please Willard get it out of the tub please Willard flush it down the sink please Willard please Willard.

She might have been able to handle one. On an extraordinary day, two.

Three? Never.

But now the floor seemed alive with them, flooding in and out of the darkness to scuttle with their hideous dry, raspy *click* from darkness to the eerily distorted square of light from the living room, then back again to the darkness. They jittered across the white plate on the table, they danced in mindless pagan circles around the white plastic cup, they slithered like animated nightmares in and out of the red-and-blue printed plastic bread wrapper that should have been tied with the little yellow metal twist-tie but that Willard had left open. In and out. In and out.

Feeling the hot press of vomit in her stomach, Catherine moved. Unthinking, responsive only to her body's single command *get out of here now!* she stepped back into the safety of the living room. Her foot touched carpet, reveled in the sudden sensation of shag loops tickling the sensitive skin. Her hand slapped the dimmer switch and unconsciously twisted it to full. The four bulbs in the kitchen's overhead fixture glared down balefully, and Catherine took a single long look and screamed for a fourth time and closed her eyes.

4.

By the time Willard reached the living room, Catherine had screamed three more times, each cry short, sharp, pitching upward into registers he had never heard from her. Only seconds had passed, but from the sounds coming from the other end of the house, Willard understood at once that an eternity of subjective time must have separated them.

He careened around the corner.

Catherine was standing on the coffee table—impossibly, *on* the coffee table, and she wouldn't even let the boys put their school bags there for fear of scratching it.

Dressed only in her nightgown, dancing barefoot up and down, she flicked at her arms, her neck, her breasts. Willard flashed to a scene he had seen as a child of some English actress—Dame Someone-Or-Other—playing Lady Macbeth in the throes of madness. Her bony fingers had seemed to stretch for miles as she held them rigidly, like radiating spokes from the central hub of her palm, and rubbed hand to hand trying to remove imaginary blood. The image had disturbed him as a child; he had dreamed of it for days. Seeing the image made flesh in his own wife chilled and horrified him.

He rushed to her, grabbed her arms, and tried to lift her down from the table.

She screamed again, flailing out at him and staring with unseeing eyes at the wall behind him. One hand connected with his cheek, hard, and his head rocked back and he saw bright flashes of stars and comets.

Then suddenly, as if someone had turned off a control switch, she slumped. Her dead weight almost threw him off balance, but he managed to stop her from falling. Half carrying her, he swung her around the end of the coffee table and laid her on the sofa. He reached down and lifted her legs onto the cushions as well. For a moment, he thought she had fainted, but when he looked back at her face, her eyes were open. Her lips were bluish, her skin whiter than he had ever seen it. She was clearly in shock of some kind, but at least she was conscious.

"What's wrong with Mommy?" piped a small voice behind Willard.

He whirled.

The kids—all but Sams—were lined up across the entryway. At any other time, Willard would have been bemused to see that they had automatically arranged themselves by size—Will, then Burt, then Suze. But right now that was the last thing he noted.

"Nothing. Go on back to bed," he said, trying to keep his own panic out of his voice. No use getting the kids more frightened than they already were.

"But...."

That was from Will. He considered himself pretty much a man, and all too often irritated Willard by offering to help in situations he would do best to stay out of.

"Now," Willard said.

"Yes, Dad." The boy's voice was low and frightened, but Willard was too concerned with Catherine to pay much attention. Her skin felt cold and papery, and she was starting to shake. Willard suddenly became aware as well that he was bare-legged and bare-foot, that the air was frighteningly cold in spite of the *hummm* that told him Catherine had turned the heater on.

He twisted his head around. The kids hadn't moved.

"Wait," he said quietly. "Will, get me some blankets from the linen closet."

Will nodded and ducked into the darkened hallway. A second later, a light glowed from somewhere, and a second after that, Willard heard a door open with a hollow squeak.

"Burt."

"Yes, Dad."

"Get me Mommy's pillow."

Burt disappeared as well. Suze took a step or two closer. Her thumb was in her mouth, and her wide-staring eyes seemed the size of quarters, large and innocent and frightened.

"It's okay, sugar. Mommy's just...she's just real tired."

"Daddy?"

"Yes, hon." He answered absently, not taking his eyes from Catherine's face.

"What's that?"

"What's what, hon?" After living for so long with four children, Willard could handle this kind of question-answer dialogue without even hesitating.

"There."

"Where?"

"There." Suze's voice had that oh-Daddy-you-can-be-so-silly-sometimes lilt that he liked to hear when they were teasing each other but that now seemed horribly out of place.

"Where?" he repeated, not taking his eyes off his wife's still face, her sallow cheeks, her dry lips that had begun moving as if she were trying to murmur something.

"There. On Mommy's foot."

Catherine screamed. She sat bolt upright, her foot extended so stiffly that Willard half believed he heard tendons and bones shatter from the pressure. Suze screamed as well, and Will and Burt burst into the room as if they knew Nazi hordes had descended on the Huntley home and only they could combat them...with maybe just a little help from Superman or Spiderman or Iron Man or even Indiana Jones. Willard grabbed at Catherine's foot.

There was a sticky-looking smudge of something dark and crushed and partly fluid pasted on her instep.

An insect.

No, he realized with a flash of understanding that answered Suze's question as well as many unspoken ones of his own. It was not an insect, no.

It was a cockroach.

He grabbed a tissue from the box on the end table and swiped at the sole of Catherine's foot, wiped again and again to remove all of the squashed guts he could, then folded the thin white tissue in on itself to hide as much of the oily dark brown stain as possible, and thrust the soiled mess at Will.

"Toss this." Will took it gingerly between finger and thumb. Willard watched his son disappear into the dark kitchen, all the while holding Catherine tightly.

He whispered reassuringly to her, "It's all right, baby, it's all right. Everything's under control. Relax."

He felt weirdly as if he were coaching her through the Lamaze births of each of their four children—all the stress and fear and pain compressed into a single trauma that he was only now beginning to comprehend. "Relax, Catherine," he whispered soothingly.

"But..., " she whimpered once. Her eyes had lost their fixed, glazed-over look. Her breathing sounded more regular. Normal color was returning to her face.

"Shhh," Willard whispered. "Not now. It was just a bug. Don't worry."

She closed her eyes and allowed her head to slump against his shoulder. Then she jerked rigid again. "No, there were...."

Will, Jr., emerged from the kitchen. She saw him come through the darkened doorway, saw him move with a maddening slowness that more than anything convinced her that whatever she had seen in there—had *thought* she had seen in there—was no longer visible.

"...More," she finished lamely. "There were...more."

"Shhh."

Burt and Suze moved closer. Burt handed Suze Catherine's pillow—it was almost bigger than she was, and in other circumstances it would have been comic to watch her struggle with it. Burt picked up the blanket Will had dropped and began spreading it over Catherine's legs.

"Mommy." This was a new voice. Sams stood alone in the entry hall, one hand balled up and wiping sleepily at his heavy-lidded eyes. His voice stirred Catherine out of her shock.

"Come here," she said, sitting up and opening her arms to all four of the children. Will stepped closer but didn't try to get too near. Burt and Suze crowded alongside Willard, their small hands touching their mother's legs tentatively as if to make sure she was really there, that the white screamy thing that had only sort of looked like Mommy was gone and that Mommy—the *real* Mommy this time—was back again, leaning on the arm of the couch and reaching out to touch their hair. Sams crawled onto the end of the couch and made his way up Catherine's legs, as he always did when she was lying down. He couldn't seem to get near enough to her any other way. He perched cross-legged just below her stomach and studied her, a blue-eyed, tow-headed Buddha staring innocently at her and absently sucking on the matted, stained, sour-smelling satin edging of his blanket. He didn't speak.

No one spoke.

Finally, as if he had abruptly decided that things were somehow wrong and that only he could take the one action that would set them right, Sams moved. He took the blanket in one hand, careful to grasp it so the damp satin ribbon was folded out, and extended it toward Catherine.

"Here, Mommy," he said slowly, in his most solemn, precise, toddler-almost-a-little-boy voice. "This will make you feel better."

From a yard away, Willard could smell the stench of the thing; his stomach roiled with a sharp, nauseated twist that cut like a dagger thrust. No matter how often Catherine washed it, it always smelled like a dishrag wadded in a corner and left to ripen for a week. He shuddered at the image as much as at the smell. But Catherine only smiled, a weak smile to be sure, but it was a smile.

"Thanks, Sams," she said, accepting the outstretched blanket just as solemnly as the boy had offered it. She took it and laid it, satin edging out, against her cheek. "Thanks, Sams," she repeated. "I'm sure this will help."

From the *Tamarind Valley Times*, 15 November 1989:

DISAPPEARING VALLEY
BUSINESSMAN STILL A MYSTERY

A spokesman for the TVPD confirmed today that, in spite of every effort, investigators have no new leads in the disappearance of Tamarind Valley realtor Bryan Sidney, 47, who disappeared over two weeks ago. The TVPD source did reveal that Sidney's partner, Andrew McCall is no longer considered a person of interest in the case.

According to the spokesman, "Sidney may have panicked at the prospect of facing...."

CHAPTER FOUR
HALLOWEEN 1991-JUNE 1992

The House in Waiting

1.

"Chicken!"

"Am not!"

"Chicken!"

"Am not!"

"Chicken...shit."

With that single syllable, Brady Wilton crossed the invisible line that defined the boundary of off-handed squabbling and escalated the stakes immeasurably. There was no backing out now. Kyle knew it and stood ready to face the consequences.

"Chickenshit," Brady repeated slowly, his tongue savoring each syllable as if he were trying to infuse as much authority into his boyish treble as his big brother Frank had in his sometimes warbly, mostly teen-age bass when he used that word.

"Chickenshit."

"Am not!" Kyle Jantzen yelled, painfully aware of how lame that retort was next to Brady's sudden explosion into near-adult near-obscenity. Of course, Kyle could easily have spiced his own phrasing up—he heard the F-word often enough from his Dad to know that nothing, *nothing* could top that one. But he also knew what his mother thought of the F-word, and the fatal sounds choked in his throat when he tried to slip them in between the two words. (He knew from close scientific observation of his father's speech patterns that the F-word worked best like that, slipped in between two other words that weren't that bad at all).

"Am f...—am not!"

"Then ya gotta do it." Kyle glanced up the long stretch of street bordered by glowing porch lights and dotted at irregular intervals by an assortment of juvenile ghosties and ghoulies shouting ear-splitting choruses of "Trick or Treat" at each open doorway.

He let his gaze wander further upward, finally stopping at the dark house outlined in the evening light. Then he turned his attention back to Brady, at this point in his short life bravely disguised as a gory mummy trailing shrouds of ragged, dusty, pukey mummy-stuff (otherwise known as one of Mrs. Wilton's old white sheets ripped into long strands and stained with mud and ground-in ketchup that Kyle could smell a dozen feet away—the odor threatened to break the illusion but somehow he didn't care).

"Now?" Kyle's voice took on a whining pitch that contrasted with his All-American-hero's black and silver cowboy outfit, complete with hat, holster, and twin silver six-shooters.

Brady nodded. "Now...or you're a chickenshit for life."

Kyle nodded in return. That was the way it would be. Once branded, always branded. It didn't matter that Brady was Kyle's best friend in the world, or that they had lived their entire nine years side-by-side in two of the dozen or so homes that had dotted this part of the valley before new houses started cropping up all over, covering favorite fields with asphalt and concrete and boringly tame lawns, enclosing wild bike trails and impromptu baseball fields with faceless slump stone fences, appropriating for faceless new people the scattered oak trees just made for small boys to climb on lazy, sunny, summer afternoons. Kyle and Brady lived across Bingham Boulevard from the Charter Oaks, and even though Kyle would have died for Brady and

Brady would have died for Kyle—they had actually promised *in blood* to die for each other—Kyle knew that if he chickened out now, Brady would be honor-bound tell all the guys at school on Monday. That was the way the world went.

"Kyle wouldn't do it," Brady would stage-whisper to Bobby Marx or Jimmy Sanderson or one of the other kids. "He was too chicken."

Out of deference to the decorum of school—or more likely, out of fear of Miss Robinson's sharp hearing, capable (as most of the boys knew to their sorrow) of penetrating like radar to even the farthest corners of the schoolyard—Brady would probably leave off the offending *shit*, but what was left would be enough to make life a living torment for Kyle. So in spite of his hesitation, he was already dismally aware that he really had no choice at all.

2.

In fact, Kyle knew that had already used up his quota of choices for the night when Brady suggested that they cut short their Trick-or-Treating.

"This stuff's for babies," Brady announced after only ten minutes of raiding outstretched bowls filled with little squares of Dubble-Bubble gum and glittering, cellophane-shrouded lollipops. "And besides, I found out where Mom hid our stuff this year." He reached into his mummy-bindings, fumbled in a hidden jeans pocket, and pulled out a handful of paper-wrapped candies. "I got lots more in my room."

Kyle really wanted to Trick or Treat some more. His white pillowcase was nowhere near full—in fact, he could still see part of the bottom seam when he angled the impromptu cloth bag just so. And, unlike Brady, he had never quite been able to figure out where his mother hid the small packets of Sugar Babies she was handing out this year. He knew from past experience that the piddling collection of sweets he had garnered wouldn't last until tomorrow night. Kyle wanted to keep on.

He wanted to find a group of little kids and tag behind them, gleaning the rich benefits when all the adults would gush "Oh, how cute" or "Isn't she an angel" at one of the kids and then hand out double helpings to all the other Trick-or-Treaters at the door as well. He had tumbled onto that trick the year before and was eager to try it out again.

But no, Brady had decided otherwise. Brady had bigger ideas, Brady was the one who made the rules, and who was Kyle to argue?

3.

"Let's check out the haunted house," Brady said abruptly as the boys finished the fifth house on Oleander Place.

It was just past sunset, with enough light to see the grey-white gleam of sidewalks sandwiched between swathes of green-black lawn and the darker asphalt.

"There isn't one."

"Sure there is." He pointed up the road at the new houses. "We can Trick-or-Treat until we get to the top." He lowered his voice to what he hoped was a menacing tone. "To the haunted house."

"It's not haunted, just empty," Kyle said, knowing as he did so that the truth wouldn't faze Brady's imagination.

Brady shot Kyle a withering glance and Kyle felt his head nodding, distantly, as if it were someone else's head nodding *yes* to someone else's best friend's question.

"Okay," the fearless cowboy sighed. "Let's go."

That was it. The decision was final.

For a couple more houses, Brady went through the motions of little-kid Trick-or-Treating. He even grinned outrageously when one old guy pretended to be horrified by Brady's mummy costume and acted like he was going to barf in Brady's candy bag, hunching his shoulders over the opened bag and *whoop-*ing like he was about to spew his guts up. But Kyle could tell that Brady's heart was somewhere else, and he waited apprehensively for the moment when Brady would look at him and say, "Come on, let's ditch this stuff."

And all too soon, Brady did.

So, without really knowing why, certainly without wanting to, a lone black-and-silver suited cowboy trudged up the hill behind a tattered, shambling mummy. His head bowed, his feet dragging, Kyle was the only kid on the street no longer excited by Halloween.

4.

The empty house stood dark and ragged-looking in the end lot. The yard angled away on either side to form a truncated wedge, like a piece of pie with the house in the center and the point nibbled away by the sidewalk. The houses on either side were lit with yellow porch lights and haphazardly carved Jack o' Lanterns grimacing wickedly along the walkways. But the house at the end seemed to swallow, not reflect, the light. In spite of the brightness and the activity along the rest of Oleander, it remained aloof, distant, coldly unaffected.

Kyle stood in front of the house and looked at it. The two windows visible from that angle stared blankly and blackly at him.

Eyes, Kyle thought, unaware of how stereotyped the image was. Eyes glaring at me, waiting to open, *wanting* to open and get me. He shivered.

"Hey, Brady," he began, but just then a troupe of clowns and fairy princesses cut from the house on the left across to the house on the right. Kyle noticed that the kids avoided the dark stretch of sidewalk in front of 1066 and dashed straight across the road instead. As they passed a dozen feet away, silhouetted by the house lights from below, Brady grabbed Kyle's arm and pulled him into the shadow of a huge tree on the corner of the lot.

From there, the house looked even worse, more sinister. It swelled up at the crest of the hill, seeming to grow larger and larger as Kyle stared at it. A long, white car stood in the driveway, a ghostly hearse waiting patiently for whatever haunted inside the house.

"Come on," Brady whispered. "The coast is clear."

Kyle risked a quick glance down the street. Amazingly enough, Brady was right. There wasn't a kid in sight for three or four houses on either side. The group that had just crossed Oleander was hidden behind the swelling bulk of a garage, and even though Kyle could clearly hear their happy laughter and the ringing echoes of "Trick-or-Treat," he couldn't see them.

"Now's our chance," Brady said. He slipped from the shadow of the tree, crossed the weed-infested yard, and crouched by the darkened left headlight of the long, white car.

"Hurry."

Kyle hurried. Bent over as if he were running against a strong headwind, he followed Brady's trail until he too crouched on one knee in front of the car. The silvery-gleaming grill loomed over his shoulder like a tooth-filled mouth, and Kyle suddenly wanted to join the clowns and the fairy princesses and hold his pillowcase out for packets of Milk Duds and maybe even some of those little Mars bars that he considered the ultimate pay-off of the evening. But Brady was moving again, running low, dodging invisible shadows and phantom enemies as he skirted the corner of the garage and disappeared. Kyle swallowed hard and followed. He was running so hard as he rounded the garage that he almost rammed into Brady.

"Look," Brady whispered, his finger pointing toward the side of the house. In the faint light, his skin seemed dead-white, his finger more bone than flesh. The mummy wrappings seemed distressingly real, and even the rank smell of old ketchup seemed to have disappeared, replaced by something heavier and hotter and darker.

Kyle looked.

The side garage door hung open.

"Cool," Brady said. "Come on."

"Hey...uh, I mean...."

Brady turned and looked coldly at Kyle. "Chickenshit?"

"Uh, no, I...." But there was nothing to say. Brady shook his head. The message was clear. Come with me and be my friend, or stay out here in the dark and you're on your own.

Kyle wasn't too familiar with the term *blackmail*, but at that moment he understood the panic and terror of its victims. Brady was blackmailing him. At stake was a lifetime's friendship. He didn't want to go into that house. He would have been willing to do almost anything rather than go into that house. Go to bed at six o'clock for a month straight. Eat lima beans and spinach. Study his spelling words for hours on end. Do dishes. Wash windows. Clean toilet bowls.

Anything.

But given the way Brady was acting, given the stakes Brady had established, Kyle had no choice. He followed Brady into the darkness.

5.

The garage was pitch-black, but Kyle had expected that. Everything about the old house was dark and grim and gruesome

"Wait a minute," he said softly. He dug in his back pocket and pulled out a small red and silver metal flashlight. When he depressed the switch, the bulb flickered. It was only a penlight bulb, and the batteries were obviously weakening, but it gave out enough light for the boys' shadows to dance grotesquely behind them as they moved. And enough for Brady to whisper, "Watch out. There's a big crack here."

Kyle stepped cautiously, letting the light play for a moment on the ragged edge of concrete. It looked like a miniature cliff when the dim yellow light spilled across it. Brady knelt by the crack and touched a dark spot with his fingertips.

"Blood," he intoned in his best Bella-Lugosi-as-Dracula voice. "*Blooood!*"

"Stop it," Kyle said. "It's not blood. It's probably just...just oil or dirt or something."

"Aw, come on," Brady answered, punching Kyle lightly on the shoulder. "Get into it. This is a Haunted House, see, and this is the blood of a crazed axe murderer who slices his victims' throats with a rusty knife and drinks their blood. Only he got nervous and spilled some. And I'll bet if we looked around we'd see the white, blood-drained bodies hanging on great big hooks on the walls."

"Don't," Kyle began, but almost instinctively he swung the tiny beam of the penlight in a wide arc.

Both boys screamed.

The penlight clattered to the floor, blinked twice, and died.

The boys screamed again, Kyle's voice higher and sharper than Brady's. Something filmy, cob-webby, and slightly sticky flickered against his cheek. He yelped and slapped at the thing with his free hand.

"Oww!" Brady yelled as Kyle's open hand caught him on the shoulder, right where a long strip of mummy wrappings had become unraveled and flapped back and forth. "Oww! That's me."

He grabbed Kyle's arm. Kyle let out a small screech, then a whimper before he understood that it was Brady. Only Brady.

"I...I saw...something," Kyle said finally, his breath still catching in his throat. There was a moment of silence. Something rustled in the dark. Brady's feet, Kyle decided.

Hoped.

"Yeah," Brady admitted, his voice echoing hollow and frail. "Yeah. I did too."

"What was it?"

"I dunno."

"Should we...."

"Where's the light?" Brady's whisper had dropped almost to inaudibility.

"I...dropped it."

"Shit." There was another long moment. Nothing moved in the garage. There was no sound.

Maybe, Kyle thought frantically, maybe if we don't move,

it won't know we're here. We'll be safe. Something shuffled to his right. "Brady!" He grabbed out and found Brady's arm—or what he hoped was Brady's arm. It was swathed in stiff bits of cloth that in the dark depths of Kyle's imagination hung fetid with mold and clotted with long-rancid mummy-sweat.

"Here. I'm trying to find...just a sec."

The arm wrenched away and Kyle was left alone in the darkness. He scrunched his eyelids so tightly closed that blue lightning streaked across the darkness. He concentrated on every sound. A small scrape. A smaller flick. And Brady's laugh, harsh and hollow.

"Gotcha."

Kyle jerked his eyes open. He was staring into the pale yellow eye of his own penlight. He held his hand over his eyes. Even the dim glow seemed too bright. The light disappeared. As his eyes adjusted to the near darkness, Kyle saw Brady sweep the closest wall with the beam. There was so little illumination that he could make out no details—just a broad stretch of yellow-grey drywall. And a hint of white. He drew in his breath with an audible hiss.

Brady laughed again and walked toward the thing apparently hanging in the corner. As the light spread across its smooth surface, even Kyle felt a flood of relief.

It was not a blood-drained corpse after all. It was only a water heater. Brady touched the slick enamel surface with his free hand. The mummy wrappings hung like dead moss from his arm.

"Cold," he announced, as if he had discovered an important clue. He bend over and peered into the darkness under the heater.

Kyle's arms shot out, as if to grab Brady and pull him back, away from there, away from the darkness that might hold...rats, snakes, spiders, anything at all.

"No pilot," Brady said. He straightened up and turned the penlight toward Kyle. For the second time in moments, Kyle's eyes took the full force of the light and he blinked against it

"Come on," Brady said, motioning with the light. Their shadows bounced crazily from the ceiling and the walls and the shiny white water heater. For an instant, Kyle felt dizzy and sick. But there was no time to worry about shadows. Brady was already through an open door—open?—and playing the light across dark wood cabinets.

The kitchen.

Kyle shuddered and followed.

6.

He caught up to Brady and put his hand on Brady's shrouded arm.

"We been inside, okay. Now let's go."

Brady flicked the penlight off for an instant. When he turned it on again, he was holding it against his chin, the light spilling upward across his face, half swathed with wrappings, the other half scarred and shadowed with his mother's best lipstick and eye shadow.

Kyle yelped, knowing all the time that he was being silly, that it was only Brady showing off, but frightened nonetheless. He fingered his silver six-shooters, wishing that they were real, that he was a real Texas Ranger and not afraid of anything.

Brady turned the light away and started moving through the kitchen.

"Hey Brade, how 'bout it? Huh? Let's go."

Brady swiveled and thrust the light beneath his chin again and spoke in a low whisper that almost made Kyle wet his pants. "Velcome to my castle. My name is Drrraaacuuula!"

It was the wrong line, given Brady's choice of costume, but neither boy cared. Kyle was too frightened by the darkness and the eerie shadows and the coldness and the sense that he had better get out of there right now. Brady was just having too much fun to worry. He disappeared into the living room.

Kyle watched for a second, debating whether or not to back

on out through the garage and head down Oleander toward the welcoming lights. But as the cabinets and fixtures in the kitchen disappeared and matching shadows began bobbing on the bit of the living room wall he could see through the walkway, he knew that he wouldn't, couldn't go back, not alone. Not without the light, puny as it was. There was that water heater, after all, that just might not *really* be a water heater, not any more. And the blood on the concrete that just might really *be* blood. He started after Brady.

By that time Brady was turning another corner into the hallway. The living room was empty, its blank walls and high, open-beam ceiling looming as vast as an aircraft hanger in the darkness.

Kyle half-ran across the room, noting vaguely the shuffling sound of his feet on unworn carpet. He caught up to Brady just as the other boy was shining the light into the first opening along the hall.

A bathroom. The toilet and sink glowed ghostly pale. The shadow line on the tub wavered and quivered, and it didn't take much for Kyle to imagine the porcelain half full of something dark and thick and oily that wasn't oil and that might hide....

He backed out, pulling Brady with him. The door opposite opened into a bedroom. It was empty. Kyle was relieved to see that the closet door was tightly shut. No shadows. No bogeymen hiding in there. A bit of light from the houses down the hill came through the dust-caked window, dimming the tiny penlight even more. The corner room was another bedroom. It was empty too.

Brady flashed the light along the final stretch of hallway. Three...no, four doors. Two closed, one open just enough for the difference in colors to suggest a slit of black caught between two larger surfaces. And one wide open.

"Brady," Kyle said, not caring how much fear came through in his voice. "Come on. Let's go!" He was whining, he knew it. He heard the childishly petulant tones he used (not always successfully) on Mom and Dad when they wanted one thing and he wanted another. And right now, he wanted another thing more than he had even thought possible. He wanted to leave.

But Brady didn't, and Brady had the light even if it was Kyle's light to begin with and the...the *creep* wouldn't give it back.

"Just one more room," Brady said over his shoulder, already partway down the hall. His mummy-strips trailed a foot or two behind him.

If he had thrown his weight a bit to the left or right and dragged his other foot in the lurching gait both boys knew instinctively that mummies had to use, Kyle would have broken away. He would have run for the front door, the bedroom window, anywhere to get out of this place.

But Brady didn't. He hunched over slightly, his shoulders rounded enough for the light to reflect off the top of his bandages. But he walked straight and true toward the open door on the right at the end of the hall. He was nearly there when Kyle did finally break out of his panic and run to catch up. So they were standing nearly shoulder to shoulder when Brady thrust his arm out, penlight clenched in his fist, and arced the light through the room.

The two boys shrieked as one, a long, breathless eruption of high-pitched, squealing sound.

This time there was no question about what they saw.

The air was heavy and cold. Both of the boys caught the dank odor and, even without having smelled it before, at least not in such quantities, certainly not smeared like thick, clotting paint on the walls and doors and windows and carpets—even with their limited experience with it oozing out of nice, neat little cuts on shins and fingers or rough scrapes on elbows and knees, they recognized it.`

Blood.

Everywhere. Walls, floor, window, closet doors.

There was even a spattering of drops on the white ceiling. They looked brown, almost black, in the yellowish light.

Kyle's mouth dropped open. Brady's opened as well, closed, opened, closed. Finally he squeaked out a faint, "Holy shit." He started to step into the room, but Kyle caught his arm in a vice-like grip that approximated a dead-man's grasp.

"No," he whispered hoarsely, as if the inside of his throat had been sliced away and then scabbed and scarred and distorted, and he would have to learn to talk all over again. "Don't."

"But we gotta...."

"We gotta get someone. This ain't play. This is real," Kyle said.

For once Brady didn't argue, didn't try to have the last word. He nodded. But instead of retreating down the hall, he took a long step...inside the room.

He turned the penlight to the windows. No light penetrated from the cars on the freeway only a mile or so away. No lights penetrated from the houses that dotted the valley floor. The window was painted over with crusted blood, all except for a corner of the farthest pane. There, the night lights glimmered faintly through a jagged break that might have been made by a small rock or a carelessly tossed elm branch...or a balled-up fist.

Brady dropped the beam to scan the floor beneath the break. A few shards of glass glinted back at him but nothing more. He could see no pieces large enough to fill in the hole in the pane. He moved one step closer to the glass, then turned enough to play the light on the walls. Great swathes of dark stuff spattered the smooth surfaces. They weren't regular—no letters in blood or anything like that. Just spurts of dripping stuff.

He backed away, swallowing. Kyle wanted to call out something to remind Brady that they were going to get out of there, but before he found his voice, Brady took one step too many. His shoulder bumped the closet door. Something inside shifted with a hideous thump and the door swung open, knocking Brady to his knees just as something heavy and huge and matted and stinking struck him.

Kyle screamed as the thing erupted from the closet and enveloped his friend. Part of him wanted to run shrieking down the hall, but most of him found himself rushing forward, screaming anyway but at least trying to help Brady. Kyle slammed his fists at the unyielding shape. Underneath its monstrous bulk, he could hear Brady's helpless whimpering—so unlike Brady, so chilling that this time nine-year-old Kyle did wet his brand-new black-and-silver cowboy suit. He felt the sudden warmness on his legs and smelled the stench of ammonia, but neither sensation penetrated his terror.

He wrenched his six-shooters from their holsters and smashed them butt-end first against the thing that was pinning Brady to the floor, again, again, again. His exposed wrist passed by the thing's shadowed shoulders, and suddenly there was a sharpness and a bright pain and a liquid warmth that smelled coppery and thick.

Kyle screamed, his voice already hoarse but now re-animated by pain as well as fear. He dropped his six-shooters, not hearing as they thumped against the thing and fell softly to the crusted carpet. He didn't hear Brady's whimpering die away to hitching sobs, then to nothing more than painful breathing and unconsciousness. He only knew that if he didn't get out *now now now* he would never get out at all.

7.

The front door was latched but not bolted. That saved Kyle's sanity, perhaps his life.

With fingers that felt as thick and cold as frozen hot dogs fresh from the freezer, he fumbled with the pin in the center of the round knob. Two, three, four times he tried to swivel it just so. Finally, he succeeded.

The knob turned, the door swung open without so much as a *creeeeak*, and Kyle stumbled into the cold night. He grabbed his wrist with his good hand and stumbled down the sidewalk, blinded by tears and terror, faster and faster until he ran full-tilt into the front fender of the Lincoln. He bounced like a ragdoll, striking his shoulders and head on the rock-hard soil of the weed-choked front yard.

For a long while, he lay there, staring at the stars that whirled faster than stars had any right to. Finally, he remembered.

Brady.

He struggled to his feet, his good hand still clasped around his sliced wrist. His fingers felt stiff, as if the clotting blood had married flesh to flesh and his two arms were now one. He stumbled down Oleander, so light-headed with shock that the incline of the asphalt was enough to threaten to topple his precarious balance. He should have run for one of the porch lights on either side but he didn't. He simply staggered down the center of the street, a small figure in silver and black that nearly disappeared into the night.

He might have run to the end of Oleander, he might have run until a careless driver crashed into him and killed him, he might have done a number of things. But what actually happened was that he slipped on a discarded candy wrapper, a bit of cellophane innocuous by itself but just enough to twist his right foot and throw him onto the asphalt. He yelped as he went down, crying out again when his cheek struck rough pavement.

Instantly—or years later, he didn't know which—someone was pulling at him. He cringed away, trying to huddle into a corner of a darkness that wanted to consume him.

"Who is it?" one voice said.

"He's hurt," another said.

And then there was a babble of voices calling out and hands plucking at him and cold things pressing against his cheek and his wrist, and after a long while, red lights flashing, flashing through the darkness and a deep voice speaking to him.

"What happened?"

"His name is Kyle, Kyle Jantzen," a shrill voice piped.

"What happened, Kyle?" This time the deep voice penetrated far enough to touch something quiescent and waiting in Kyle. He looked up, blinked.

"Brady," Kyle finally said.

"He must mean Brady Wilton. He was out with the Wilton kid," the shrill voice said. "I saw 'em together not twenty minutes ago."

"What about Brady?" The deep voice continued uninterrupted, as if the shrill voice had not spoken at all.

"Dead!" Kyle squealed without thinking. He felt his own life withdraw as he uttered the dreadful word.

"Where? Come on, Kyle, where?"

The boy looked around long enough to understand that he was lying on a thick pad, probably from someone's chaise lounge. He was in the middle of a front yard perhaps three-fourths of the way up Oleander. He raised a shaking hand and pointed one finger at the dark outline at the top of the hill.

"There."

8.

The police found Brady only a few minutes later.

In spite of their fears, after what the Jantzen kid had cried out, he wasn't dead. But then he wasn't exactly alive either.

A short hospital stay would probably be enough for Kyle, already safely in the back of a County Hospital ambulance waiting for his father to arrive when the police entered the back bedroom at 1066 Oleander. It would take a longer stay—a *much* longer stay—to do the other boy any good.

He wasn't hurt physically. Not much, anyway. A man's mutilated body had toppled onto him and bruised his shoulder and his hip. But the carpet had cushioned most of the weight. If he was hurt much, it didn't show. But when the police pulled the body away, he was staring straight ahead, as if he were examining on a microscopic level the shard of blood-encrusted glass still embedded six inches deep in the corpse's throat, not three inches from the boy's own throat but miraculously (it seemed then) not touching him.

He was still staring straight ahead half an hour later, an hour later. Days later.

Three weeks after Halloween night, the Wiltons put their house up for sale, and before Thanksgiving they had gone.

Kyle never saw Brady again.

9.

It was easy enough for the authorities to identify the body. Ace McCall's blood-soaked cowhide wallet was still buttoned securely inside his back pocket. Whatever had happened to him, it wasn't a robbery. No one had disturbed the California driver's license, the half dozen credit cards, or the five hundred dollars in cash tucked into the back flap.

The white Lincoln parked outside the house on Oleander carried additional identification in the form of a registration slip and a leather briefcase crammed with documents attesting to the identity of its owner.

It was far more difficult to determine precisely what had happened in the back bedroom of the house.

Officer Mark Riehmann's first impression of the carnage in the back bedroom was simple: homicide. After calling for back-up on this one—a gnawing gut instinct honed by fifteen years with the County Sheriff Department told him that this case was going to be a bad one—he made sure that the Jantzen kid was going to be all right, then approached the house at the top of the hill.

He moved tentatively, slowly, alert to the sounds of sirens racing in response to his call. He was not quite to the sidewalk in front of the house when the first back-up car arrived. In spite of a sense of urgency amplified by the knowledge that there was still a kid in the house, perhaps trapped there with a homicidal maniac, he hesitated long enough to be joined by two other figures, shadowy in the darkness. He whispered instructions, then the three of them approached the house.

The front door gaped open. Other than that, there was no sign of life. Still, it took almost five minutes for them to penetrate the house and turn their flashlights onto the scene in the back bedroom.

McCall's body lay sprawled across the floor, the feet still in the closet, the head angled toward the window opposite. The body was awash with blood, most of it crusted and brown, some still vividly scarlet and dripping. Beneath him lay another body. For an instant all three officers thought the boy must be dead, too. Then they realized that what they assumed to be a deathly pallor was actually smudged cosmetics and that the boy's open eyes were not rigid with death but deep and dark and secret.

They pulled the body off the boy, and one of the other officers knelt to carry him outside. The boy shrieked once—long and loud and piercingly shrill. Then he lapsed into a silence so absolute that Riehmann wondered for a second time if he weren't dead.

"Get him out of here," Riehmann instructed softly. "Quick." As soon as the other officer disappeared into the hall, Riehmann knelt beside McCall's corpse. The face was distorted with pain and fury. Even after fifteen years witnessing death and destruction in all of their guises, Riehmann knew that this one was different. He trembled when his light played across the tight, drawn features

And the blood.

There couldn't be a pint left in the guy, Riehmann thought, not with what's spattered all over the walls and the carpet and the ceiling, not with the fact that the front of McCall's clothing was stiff with it. Not given the fact that his chest and belly and groin and thighs were slashed and that a wickedly sharp, massive shiver of glass was still embedded in his throat.

Homicide, Riehmann decided almost immediately. And he was rarely wrong. But this time, as the evidence unraveled, he seemed to be. True, it looked impossible for it to have been suicide, for McCall to have inflicted some of the gaping wounds—at least impossible for any man in a healthy state of mind.

But the crumpled newspapers and the documents locked in the briefcase ultimately suggested that McCall might not have been quite sane. He could easily have been on the edge of desperation, seeing the company he had built on the verge of total collapse with himself the sole responsible agent for what eventually amounted to millions of dollars in alleged fraud.

Beyond that, much of the money involved was linked to individuals and organizations whose financial dealings were at best questionable. It looked increasingly as if Ace McCall had swum too far beyond his depth, discovered that he was doomed, and instead of struggling to get back, simply took a deep breath and sank beneath the waves. Figuratively speaking, of course.

In addition, an examination of the room—especially the blood-splattered door jamb, the razor-sharp shards of glass, the small red and silver flashlight found beneath the Wilton boy—revealed three sets of finger prints...and only three. Brady Wilton's. Kyle Jantzen's. And Ace McCall's.

Of course it was possible that the killer or killers might have protected themselves by wearing gloves. But as the days became weeks and the weeks turned into months, the County investigation team could not discover one shred of evidence that anyone else had been in that room for at least a month before McCall died.

Riehmann kept up with the case as much as he could. He read reports and followed up leads. But everything led to the same conclusion. There was no evidence that McCall had died at the hands of another person. And, given the at best ambiguous nature of his wounds, it was just possible that he did kill himself.

Just barely possible.

10.

The house was barricaded until well past Thanksgiving, its front yard fenced off by a strip of yellow warning tape. The Lincoln remained on the front driveway. It grew dustier and dustier; an early November rainstorm transformed the grainy dust to grey-black muck, and by the time it was hauled away behind a Bingham Boulevard Shell towing truck, it no longer gleamed white. No one had bothered writing "wash me" on any of the windows so thickly caked with grime that the interior had long since become entirely obscured. Perhaps no one had dared. A large oil spot on the driveway marked where the car had been sitting.

By mid-December, the yellow tape had disappeared as well. The week after Christmas, a work crew appeared early one morning and silently disappeared into the bowels of the house. Ladders and tarps and rolls of carpeting and cans of paint and panes of glass disappeared into the house as well.

The neighbors on both sides of Oleander were curious, of course. After all, how often does one get to live right next to an honest-to-God murder house. But none of them ventured up to the front door. None rapped lightly on the wooden door-jamb where, for a long time, a bloody, smudged handprint had lingered untouched until one kid on the crew, a part-time helper from the High School, couldn't stand it any longer and washed the whole doorway down. No one asked what was going on inside.

But by the end of January, it was pretty evident. The construction truck disappeared, replaced the next day by a landscaping truck. Over the next weeks, a deep-pile green lawn appeared, along with a line of yew trees along the eastern edge of the property and a similar row of hibiscus along the western. The sidewalk leading from the drive to the front door was bordered with annuals that by the middle of May would become a solid bed of scarlet and pink and purple and yellow and blue—petunias, pansies, puffs of sky-blue ageratum, masses of purple and white Royal alyssum.

"Alyssum," the woman next door snorted when a weekend visitor from San Francisco later commented on the vibrant white mounds blooming in the yard at the top of the hill.

"Alyssum! That's called madwort where I come from—and rightly so!" And then she invited her visitor to share a cup of tea and began telling the story of the Murder House.

By April, shiny new cars with magnetized realtors' signs on the doors began parking on the drive. Couples, occasionally accompanied by a child or two, would get out, survey the view from the top of Oleander, then disappear into the house. It might have seemed unusual that none of the families were ever outside without a realtor hovering around as well...that none of the prospective buyers ever actually talked to the neighbors on either side.

It might have seemed unusual, except for the fact that no one really wanted the house left empty. Things happened in empty houses. So the neighbors peeped from behind drawn curtains at bright shiny faces that entered the house. The realtors spoke persuasively of increasing property values and spectacular views and convenient schools and the brand-new shopping center going up not half a mile away.

And on a bright sunny day during the first week in May, 1992, almost three years after the house at 1066 Oleander was begun, the For Sale sign stuck in the front lawn was plastered over with another sign that simply read "Sold."

From the *Tamarind Valley Times*, 1 November 1991:

SAFE HALLOWEEN REPORTED

Tamarind Valley safety officials announced today that yesterday a long-standing record was not just broken but shattered—Halloween, 1991, was the safest in Valley history.

At a time when pranks can sometimes get out of hand, when so many little ghosties and beasties are on the streets, when parents are urged to accompany their children as they Trick-or-Treat just to be on the safe side, last night was exceptional in the few number of incidents responded to by the TVPD.

No injuries, other than tummy-aches from too much candy, were reported, and no significant property damage resulting from over-enthusiastic revelers....

CHAPTER FIVE
THE HUNTLEYS, JANUARY 2010

Settling In (Cont'd.)

1.

It took more than an hour for everyone to settle down. By the time Willard looked at the children with his unmistakable "time to get to bed" expression, even Will, Jr., was red-eyed and nodding. Sams had fallen asleep curled against his mother's shoulder. Willard roused the older children and herded them shuffling and sleepy down the hall, waiting to tuck in Will and Burt in spite of Will's muffled objections that he was too old for baby things like that. Suze was already asleep when Willard slipped into her darkened room and looked down at her. He returned to the living room and picked Sams up out of Catherine's lap. He grunted at the sudden weight.

"He's growing up, isn't he," Willard said quietly as he shouldered his youngest son and made a second trip down the hallway to deposit Sams on his bed.

By then the other two boys were fast asleep also. Willard paused for a second outside Suze's door, his hand poised over the switch for the hall light. His first inclination was to turn the light out; even Sams was used to sleeping without a night light, and there was enough filtered light from the full moon and cloudless skies should any of them wake.

Then he dropped his hand without shutting off the light. The kids had been startled from sleep once tonight. Best not to take any chances.

His shadow preceding him like a sentry, he headed out for the living room. Catherine was almost asleep as well. For a second time, he was tempted to leave things as they were, to cover her with an additional blanket or two and let her finish the night on the couch. It was comfortable, she would be warm enough, and she really needed the rest she was already getting.

But after a couple moments of thought, Willard crossed the room and gently shook her shoulder.

"What!" she yelped as she startled awake. Her voice was midway between normal tone and scream, and Willard immediately took her in his arms to calm her. "Hey, hon, it's okay. The kids are in bed. Everything's all."

"The bugs!" Catherine's eyes were wide open and darting around the living room as if they could penetrate the solid patches of darkness behind and beneath furniture. "There were thousands...."

Willard patted her shoulder. His back ached from the awkward position he found himself in, neither standing nor kneeling but halfway between, his arm around Catherine's shoulder and supporting much of her weight. He dropped to one knee and shifted his arm. "They're gone, too. Don't worry."

She sat upright and turned her glance on him. He was startled by the depth of fear in her eyes.

"But...."

"Shhhh. Don't think about it."

She relaxed against his arm.

"I was so frightened, Willard," she said finally. Her voice sounded hollow and lonely in the echoing room. A moment later, the furnace flicked on with its usual low *whuump*. He felt her body tense beneath him. Her breathing stopped, held, then finally resumed—ragged, shallow, and much faster than normal.

"Look," he said, "give me a minute and I'll take care of things." He got up, aware of her hand trailing along his arm, as if unwilling to relinquish his physical presence. He turned on the light over the kitchen table, waiting in the living room until the glare flooded through the open kitchen door. He thrust his head into the kitchen and made a clear show of looking it over.

"Nothing here now," he said over his shoulder. Catherine breathed a sigh of relief. "Just to be on the safe side, though," he continued, "I'll give the place a shot of Raid."

He crossed to the pantry and took down an aerosol can from the top shelf—carefully stored out of reach of the children, and as far away from foodstuffs as possible. Chattering all the time—not saying much of anything but fully aware of how important it was to Catherine that she hear his voice—he sprayed the baseboards in the kitchen.

He glanced around. A body or two remained on the tile floor, and a couple more were squashed on the counter where Catherine had apparently pressed her hand down on them. He shuddered, knowing the intensity of her fear of roaches and how she must have felt when she realized that she had actually crushed several beneath her bare hand and feet.

"No wonder she freaked out," he said under his breath. "A few would seem like a hundred to her under those conditions."

He ran hot water over a cloth and washed down the counters and the table, then threw the cloth in the garbage.

"Okay, now for in here" he said, returning to the living room with the can of Raid. As much as a precaution as to further reassure Catherine, he sprayed around the baseboards there as well.

By the time he was finished, Catherine looked more her normal self. Her color was better. She was sitting up, her feet squarely on the carpet. Still, Willard was taken by the sheer magnitude of her terror and horror and, doing something he had not even though of trying since the first year of their marriage, he leaned over and gently picked her up. She curled her arms around his shoulder and allowed him to carry her down the hall toward their bedroom.

Under any other circumstances, the action would have struck him as unbearably if not idiotically romantic, but tonight it just seemed the best thing to do.

"Wait," Catherine said as they passed the open bathroom door. "Let me take a shower before I get back into bed."

Willard started to argue, fully aware of how late it was, how soon he would have to get up and head into LA. But he thought better of it and nodded.

Catherine waited outside in the brightly lit hall while Willard stuck his head into the bathroom and checked things out.

"Just a minute," he called to her as he yanked a wad of toilet paper from the roll and used it to trap an inch-long roach skittering around the bottom of the tub. He cringed as he felt the horny carapace crush beneath his fingers, and again he felt a shudder of empathy for what Catherine must have experienced.

He flushed the wad of paper—and the remains of the roach—down the toilet and turned the hot water on in the shower, drawing the curtain enough across the tub to prevent water from spattering onto the floor.

"Okay, everything's ready."

Catherine entered without speaking and, even though the bathroom was really too small for two people, said nothing as Willard waited just inside and watched her undress. He wanted to reach out and touch her body—her breasts and thighs and stomach, the cool softness of the skin along her shoulders. But he knew instinctively that it would be a mistake. Instead, he watched as she ducked around the half-drawn curtains and disappeared.

He returned to the bedroom and waited, his head propped on the pillow. It was a long time before Catherine finally reappeared, her hair matted against her head and her skin red and flushed. Apparently unconcerned that the door was still open and one of the kids might conceivably rouse and come in at the wrong moment, she dropped the towel she was wearing and pulled on a fresh nightgown from her drawer. As she got into bed, Willard noticed that the skin on the soles of her feet and the palms of her hands was roughened and inflamed as if it were just this side of bleeding.

He reached up and turned the overhead light out. The light from the hall spilled into the room. Catherine shivered—whether from cold or a residue of her terror, he couldn't tell. He circled her with his arms and held her without speaking until the smoothness of the rise and fall of her breasts assured him that she was finally asleep.

Only moments after that, Willard was asleep as well.

2.

Briiinnnggg.

Briiinnnggg.

Willard slapped at the alarm button and stared groggily at the luminescent face confronting him.

Five o'clock.

He sat upright in bed, staring from side to side, wondering why five o'clock seemed so much earlier than it ever had before. Then he remembered. All told, he had gotten maybe four and a half or five hours of sleep.

He groaned.

That wasn't enough any more. When he was in college, he had thought nothing of staying up until two or three a.m. shooting the bull, then rousing at six to head out for a full schedule of classes. And when he and Catherine were first married, they might have gotten to bed by eleven or twelve each night, but that didn't mean that they went right to sleep—and somehow he had made it up each morning, bright and ready.

But now....

He groaned again. I'm too old for this kind of thing, he thought as he forced himself out of bed and into the bathroom.

Half an hour later, showered, shaved, dressed for the office, he stuck his head into the bedroom to check on Catherine.

"Willard?" Her voice sounded ghostly and thin as it emerged from the relative darkness. He switched on the lamp by the door—it was far enough away and low enough wattage that it shouldn't bother Catherine's eyes.

"I'm just getting ready to head in to work."

"Don't."

"But...."

"Please don't. I need you here today. Please."

He wanted to refuse. There wasn't really anything he could do to help her, other than stand around and reassure here that everything was all right. And he did need to get going on a couple of projects that had come his way over the past couple of days.

"Honey, I really have to....

"Please."

The third *please* did it. There was an unfamiliar note of pleading in the word that Willard could barely connect with his mental image of his solid, competent wife. Catherine rarely asked for anything; she never begged. But that was what her voice was doing now. Begging. The sound made Willard feel even more uncomfortable

"But...."

"Please."

He had no choice.

"Okay, I can call and say I'm sick or something. Okay."

"Hmmmm," came Catherine's voice, dulled by sleep and now incoherent.

He crossed the room and looked down at here. Her eyes were closed, and she seemed much paler than usual, even in the dim light. He pulled the covers tighter over her, remembering her constant joking whenever he did that with one of the kids.

More covers cures all sickness, huh? Well, this time it might.

He slipped out of the room, turning off the lights and shutting the door behind him. He stood for a moment, then walked a few feet toward the kids' bedrooms and shut off the hall light, too. The hall was lit only by a reflection from the bathroom, where he had left the light over the sink burning.

The house was silent.

He listened intently but could hear nothing beyond his own breathing and the beating of his own heart.

After a long while, he went on into the living room, switching on lights and turning up the furnace as he went. To all appearances, the living room was unchanged, except for a used tissue lying in a lump a few feet from the sofa.

He picked it up, feeling his back creak as he bent over. He checked to make sure that there were no roach-remains embedded in the folds—that it was just damp from Catherine's hysterical tears—then he wadded it more tightly in his fist and went into the kitchen to toss it away.

As soon as he turned the light on, he saw the bodies. There must have been two dozen roaches lying feet up on the tile floor. The smallest was a field roach, barely more than half an inch long and thin, looking more like a large grain of wild rice than anything else. The largest, half hidden in the shadow cast by one of the dinette chairs, came close to measuring an inch and a quarter—maybe an inch and a half, but Willard was in no mood to worry about particulars.

Grimacing, he gingerly crossed the kitchen, cringing when he inadvertently stepped on one of the corpses. The dry crackling crunch seemed to echo throughout the room. He noticed that not all of the things were dead. Maybe every fourth or fifth one was flailing its legs wildly, as if trying desperately to right itself and scuttle for the safety of cracks and darkness.

He grabbed the broom from its niche between the refrigerator and the wall by the family room—formerly the garage—and began disposing of the remains. Usually a sloppy housekeeper on the rare occasions when necessity called on him to fill that role, this time he took sedulous care to sweep beneath all of the counters, to remove the trashcan and push the bristles into each corner. He swept the debris to the center of the room and, masking his disgust at the pile of quivering husks, brushed the roaches into the dustpan and dumped them into the trash. Before the last one hit the bottom of the plastic garbage can, he had the Hefty-bag liner out, cinched at the top, and tied with a connected twist-tie. And a moment later, the bag—only half full of Huntley garbage, with a thin sprinkling of roach-remains scattered throughout—was stuffed inside one of the big brown outdoor garbage cans that lined the fence between the backyard and the garage.

Only then, when Willard stepped back into the kitchen, his nose frosted by the January chill and the sudden discovery that he had forgotten to put on a jacket—only then did he breathe easily.

He gave the counters and tables a quick once-over with a steaming hot washcloth, then looked over at the clock.

Six-fifteen. Time to get the kids up.

Waking Will and Burt was every bit as frustrating as he had feared it would be. They were deeply asleep, and when they finally sat up in bed, they were cranky and sullen.

"I don't feel good, Daddy," Burt whimpered, trying vainly to slip back between the inviting covers.

"Are you bleeding or throwing up?" Willard asked, echoing his mother's litany, remembered from almost three decades before.

"No," came Burt's reply.

"Then up and at 'em. Breakfast in fifteen minutes." He swatted Will, Jr.'s rump and yelled out a final, "Out of bed, right now," before he left the boys' room and went into Suze's.

Suze always woke more easily than the boys—Willard didn't mind trying to get her out of bed on the rare days that the duty devolved onto him. This morning was no exception.

Apparently he had made enough commotion that when he opened her door a slit and stuck his head in, she was already sitting up.

"I'm awake, Daddy," she said quietly

"That's my girl," he answered. "Breakfast in fifteen minutes. Don't forget to make your bed."

"Okay, Daddy."

Just as a matter of course, Willard retraced his steps and glanced into the boys' room.

Will was up and staggering around the room, his eyes half closed as he struggled to pull on shirt and pants in the crisp air.

Burt was snuggled back in bed. Willard yanked the blankets off the bunk bed, pulling so hard that they ended up a mash of rumpled blankets and quilts at his feet.

"Up and at 'em, I said."

Burt sat up groggily and rubbed at his eyes with his knuckles.

"If you're not out in fifteen minutes, you go to school without breakfast."

Willard surreptitiously monitored the progress in the back bedroom for the next few minutes and was not particularly surprised to see how slowly his second son could move when he wanted. But somehow, miraculously, Burt actually made it up within the required time. Even more amazingly, from Willard's admittedly biased perspective, all three of the older kids managed to get through breakfast, get dressed, instruct him in the intricacies of making lunches—"ya gotta put the peanut butter first, Dad, then the jelly," that was Burt's contribution to fine cuisine—do a lick and a promise cleanup job on their rooms, and present themselves ready for his inspection beside the front door by twenty minutes after eight.

In spite of the frequent flurries of "But Dad, Mom never does it that way" and "Why do we have to do that?" the kids were finally ready, buttoned into heavy coats and scarves, each carrying a thin plastic raincoat just in case the volatile January weather decided to shift before the end of school.

"Now you keep a good eye on your little sister, Burt," Willard instructed as the younger two shuffled through the front door to confront the wide outside world once more. Burt and Suze went to Charter Oaks K-6 Grammar School less than three quarters of a mile away. Catherine had walked the route with them for the first weeks after Christmas vacation ended; today they were on their own for the first time.

"Go straight to school and no playing around. You've only got twenty minutes to get there."

"Yes, Dad," Burt said. His voice was low and muffled, as if he were still upset that his father had had the temerity to insist that Burt actually smooth out the wrinkles in his bed. After all, the whole thing would just get wrinkled again as soon as he slept in it tonight, so why waste the time. Willard grinned to himself at a recurrent memory—that had been precisely his attitude toward bed-making when he was about eleven.

"Bye, Daddy," Suze chimed.

Willard leaned over and kissed the top of her head.

"Bye. See you this afternoon."

"Are you going to stay home today?" she asked, her eyes wide in surprise. "Are you sick?"

"No, hon, I'm just staying here so Mommy can get some rest after last night."

"What happened to her?"

For a long moment, Willard was stumped. He didn't want to mention the dead roaches he had swept away this morning, for fear that he would reinforce Suze's incipient fears of the vermin. He noted that Will and Burt were watching intently as well, as if his answer to that question were the single most important event of the day.

"She probably just had a bad...dream," he said finally, aware of the weakness of the excuse.

"Just like me," Burt said.

"Yeah, after you watch one of those monster movies," Willard said, tousling the boy's hair. Burt ducked his head and escaped; Willard knew how the boy felt about that kind of display of parental affection and reminded himself to watch it in the future. The kids were growing up. They weren't all that little any more. Still, his answer seemed to satisfy Suze, who took off across the damp lawn, her plastic *Toy Story* lunchbox thumping heavily against her legs. Burt followed, shoulders slumped, as if he were marching on his way to certain execution.

Will, Jr., stood just inside the doorway. He walked a mile or so to the junior high—a squat stucco structure bearing the highly original name of Ronald Reagan Junior High. Still, it had a good reputation in the district and so far Catherine reported that Will was doing all right—working hard, and not too far behind from the trauma of starting mid-year at a new school and settling into new routines. Classes there started twenty minutes later than at the elementary school, so Will's departures had gradually become more leisurely as he became familiar with the way.

Willard noticed a pack of five or six kids Will's age gathering on the front yard of a house several doors down.

"Those guys look like they're about your age. Do they go to Reagan?" Willard asked, motioning toward the knot of giggles and laughter.

Will, Jr., glanced down the street. "Yeah," he said noncommittally.

"Do you know any of them. From classes or anything."

"A couple."

"They seem like fun kids?"

"I guess."

"Have you talked to them at all."

"Some."

"Why don't you catch up with them and walk with them to school?" Willard was growing impatient at the boy's apparent inability to take a hint any faster.

Will shrugged, an eloquent gesture in a twelve year old that carried meanings impossible for the boy to put into words. "Dunno."

Willard looked closely at his oldest son. There was a look in the boy's eyes that bothered Willard. They were hooded, masked, downcast, as if the boy were afraid that Willard would see into his soul and ferret out whatever problems he was trying to conceal.

"Well?"

"They said...."

"They said what?"

"Uh...nothin', Dad. I just like walkin' by myself. It gives me time to think."

In spite of himself, Willard smiled at the sudden adult tones in the boy's voice. Maybe there was even a hint of a crackling basso beginning to emerge.

"Well, don't stick to yourself too much or it'll get even harder to make friends."

"Okay, Dad."

"Now get going."

Will, Jr., got going, trudging down the sidewalk, gripping the rolled-up top of his brown paper bag lunch. He had steadfastly refused the offer of a new lunch pail, arguing vehemently that such things were kiddie and no one else at school *ever* took a lunch pail.

Willard watched until his son disappeared at the bottom of the hill. He didn't notice that Will, Jr., had carefully timed his progress so that in spite of the fact that the other kids paused occasionally to wait for other children to emerge from houses along the way, Will never quite caught up with them, never quite drew close enough for them to spot him lagging behind.

Willard closed the door with a sigh and slumped against it. Made it, he thought. Got them all off and didn't wake either Sams or Catherine.

"Daddy?"

He looked down. There was Sams, the discolored satin edging of his blanket stuffed into his mouth, the rest of the blanket trailing him like a softly graying ghost. His night diaper hung askew, so sodden that it threatened to pull his printed Iron Man pajama bottoms down to the child's knees. Willard smelled the pungency of urine and realized that he was not finished yet. One more child to get started this morning.

3.

By the time Sams was changed, dressed, and fed—dry Sugar Crisps and a glass of milk, both of which Willard assumed would get mixed properly during the course of digestion—Willard felt as if he were ready for bed himself.

He carried Sams down the hall, wondering to himself how Catherine managed this day after day. No wonder she was tired and drawn.

He left Sams in the bedroom, happily engrossed with spreading colorful wooden building blocks all across the carpet in random patterns that sent him into fits of giggling.

Willard set the spring-action child gate across the door. There, that would keep him happy and out of the way for a while. Nothing in there can hurt him, Willard thought as he glanced over the room crowded with piles of toys. It's been completely kid-proofed.

Willard returned to the front bedroom and looked in on Catherine. She was still asleep, but from the way the covers were twisted around her and pulled from the bottom of the bed, it had not been an easy sleep.

He slipped over to the side of the bed and touched her forehead with his hand.

"Huh!" She startled awake immediately.

"It's okay," he said quietly.

"What time...oh no, it's late and I...."

"I took care of everything. The kids got off to school okay. Sams is up and dressed. He's playing in the bedroom."

"But...I...."

"You needed to sleep. So I let you sleep."

She dropped her head back onto the pillow and smiled. "What about work?"

"You wanted me to stay home today and help out a bit."

"I...did I ask you to? I don't remember."

"Well, you were pretty much out of it when I got up. Anyway, there's nothing at work today that can't be handled tomorrow, and you really did need to get some sleep. And besides, it was... uh...interesting to see what goes on around here on school mornings. I finally learned the proper way to make a peanut-butter-and-jelly sandwich, compliments of Burt."

He grinned. Catherine smiled back, but the movement seemed strained. There's still some carry-over from last night, Willard decided, like the half-remembered echoes of a particularly bad nightmare that linger well into waking.

"Are you okay?" he asked gently.

Catherine seemed to understand that he had subtly shifted the topic of conversation. He was not asking about how well she had slept since he got up at five, or whether she felt better for the additional rest. As obliquely as possible, he was asking about last night.

"I...I don't know. It was so horrible. They were everywhere. I touched...I felt them....." She shuddered.

He hugged her reassuringly. "I think I got most of them with the Raid. There were a...a couple of dead ones this morning. I cleaned them up."

She shivered again—and Willard realized that in spite of the exertion of the morning, in spite of being fully dressed, in spite of the furnace roaring away in the living room as it combated the mid-thirties outside, he was chilly, too. He pulled off his shirt (the tie had disappeared long before, about the time Suze grabbed it and smeared a long streak of cinnamon butter on it, a permanent reminder of her breakfast of choice) and toed his loafers off. His pants followed, and then he slipped beneath the covers next to Catherine. They lay together, snuggling in the warmth of their body heat.

Distantly, they heard Sams laughing to himself, following by the occasional click or thump of his building blocks as he devised new shapes and arrangements.

Somehow, without quite being aware of the direction of their movements, Willard and Catherine moved from passive cuddling to more active, more directed movements. Willard was momentarily surprised by the fervor and passion of Catherine's embraces, aware that she had never felt quite comfortable with making love during the day—a hold over from her rather rigidly traditional upbringing. But this time there was an unusual fervency in her movements, a fevered sense that communicated itself to him as she held him and her hands ranged over his body as if seeking solace...or protection.

Afterward, they lay back, their bodies still intertwined. And as gradually as they had passed from comforting to loving, they passed from loving to sleep. Sams' cries woke them.

This time Catherine was up before Willard. He was just pulling on his shirt when she returned, swathed in her robe, carrying Sams. The sunlight glinted in the boy's eyes. His cheeks were flushed as if he had been running, and a couple of glistening runnels marked the track of tears down his cheeks.

"Did he fall down or something?"

"I don't know," Catherine said, setting Sams in the middle of the bed and tickling him. Sams looked solemnly at her for a moment before letting down his reserve and falling back on the covers and laughing. The sound was light, tinkling, infectious.

"He was just sitting in the middle of the room, crying. I didn't see anything wrong."

"Maybe he was just lonely," Willard said as he sat on the edge of the bed and pulled his loafers on.

"Or maybe he was frightened by those horrible sounds?" Catherine said, a small smile curving her lips.

"What? What sounds?"

"Coming from this room. The moans and groans and...."

He rolled across the bed, careful not to lay on Sams, who was watching them wide-eyed. "I'll show you moans and groans, woman," he said, his voice dropping to a threatening growl.

Sams laughed as Willard grabbed Catherine and pulled her down onto the bed with him, and suddenly there was a free-for-all of arms and legs and tickling and unbounded laughter. Will felt a flood of warmth as he lay with his wife and baby, in his own house. The day was theirs, and all was well with the world.

4.

Catherine seemed completely recovered from the shock of the night before, although even after she was dressed and moving through the house on the innumerable tasks a mother must endure, he noticed that she hesitated fractionally before entering each room. It was as if she were checking things out, scanning the floors and walls for any signs of the phantom intruders of the night before. Fortunately, Willard had already made sure that the bathtub and sinks and kitchen were free from infestation.

Catherine visibly relaxed as they finally sat together at the kitchen table and ate a light breakfast of juice and toast together—fashionably late, but the more pleasant for that. Sams was strapped into his chair, enjoying a second helping of dry Sugar Crisps, most of which ended up on the floor or stuck in his hair.

On an impulse, Catherine reached over to the small radio on the counter and turned it on to KNWS, the local news station she had discovered a day or so after moving in. The station could be counted on to repeat weather and local updates during the morning, giving her a better sense of how to dress the kids for school.

The newscaster's voice murmured largely unnoticed in the background as she and Willard sat without talking, enjoying the muted quiet, enjoying each other's presence.

"Cath," Willard said after a while, as he stood to set his plate in the sink. "How about a drive? It's cold outside but it looks like it's going to be a beautiful day. We could pack up Sams and head up the coast toward Santa Barbara. Maybe we could...."

"Wait," Catherine said suddenly. "What was that?" She leaned over and turned the volume on the radio up.

"...Struck just after 2:30 and registered only 3.0, with its epicenter five miles off the coast of Malibu. There have been no reports of any damage from the quake, although a number of Valley residents were awakened by the jolt. No aftershocks have been reported." The newscaster's smooth voice robbed the announcement of any of the terror Catherine had felt the night before when the temblor had shaken her awake.

She turned the radio off. "There was an earthquake," she said, her voice quiet.

"What?" Willard tore his eyes from the spectacle of his youngest son, mouth speckled with stray bits of cereal, sipping milk from his Scooby-Doo cup so carefully that not one of the strays dropped off.

"That's what woke me up. Before I saw the...before I came into the kitchen. There was an earthquake. I felt it and got out of bed and went to check on the kids, then I came out here to get some tea and...."

"Her face grew white at the memory.

"Sit down, hon," Willard said.

She dropped heavily into the solid oak chair—one of six that surrounded the equally heavy oak table.

"I woke up from the quake, and I went in to see if the kids were all right," she repeated, her voice calm and even, as if she were repeating instructions on how to bottle boysenberry jelly or how to change a tire on a car. "Then I went into the living room and turned the furnace on—it was really cold, and you would be waking up in only an hour or so anyway," she added, looking slightly discomfited at the admission of her guilt.

Willard shook his head and said, "Don't worry about that. No problem."

"Anyway," she continued after a long pause, "Then I came into the kitchen and saw.... There were hundreds of them. Thousands."

Willard almost shivered at the raw horror, the open revulsion in her voice. He reached over and touched her arm.

"Come on, honey, that's impossible. Thousands?"

She whirled to glare at him. "I *saw* them. I know how it sounds. I know that sometimes I freak out pretty much when I see one or two of the filthy things. But I know what I saw." She glanced around her—at the table, the counters, the floor. "They were all over everything. They were on the table, in the...." Her eyes flew open, and what little color there was in her cheeks bleached out. Her throat visibly constricted, so convulsively that Willard felt a pang of sympathetic pain. For a moment it seemed as if Catherine was choking.

Suddenly she burst from her chair and crossed the kitchen in two strides and doubled over by the sink. He heard the sounds of heaving, smelled the pungency of vomit, and rushed to her side.

He held her tightly, one hand on her forehead—hot and damp. She vomited explosively again, and once again. He twisted the water taps and ran a stream of water into the sink. It curled around the clotted remains of Catherine's breakfast, barely able to wash away the bitter-smelling stuff.

Catherine heaved once more, but this time nothing came. She was trembling beneath his hand, her muscles quivering and tight.

"Are you all right?" he asked, feeling like a fool—of course she's not all right, all-right people don't toss their cookies in the kitchen sink in the middle of the day, all-right people don't shake like their insides have been vomited loose. But he couldn't think of anything else to say. "Are you okay?"

She nodded weakly

He helped her back to the table and lowered her into the chair. She sat with her head in her hands for a long time. Willard watched her carefully, alert for any signs of recurrent nausea. Sams was silent, watching as well.

Finally, Catherine looked up. "Sorry," she said quietly. Her voice still shook. Her breath stank. Willard could smell the sourness on her breath and felt his own stomach twist momentarily. She sipped at the orange juice in her glass. That seemed to help.

"I just remembered...." She paled again, and Willard was afraid that she was in for another bout of vomiting, but she visibly controlled her reflexes, swallowing hard a couple of times. "They were in...," she began, seemed to choke again, then she continued, her voice breaking, "… in the bread."

Willard understood. His stomach convulsed again at the image her words conjured. "It's okay. There were only a couple of pieces left in the wrapper this morning. I had a piece of toast before I went to bed last night, and I left the wrapper open. Like always."

The last was a play for humor.

Catherine didn't laugh.

"Anyway, when I got up this morning and cleaned up in here, I could tell that the rest of the bread was all dried out. I tossed it.

And got a new loaf from the freezer." He could trace the relief as it blossomed in her face. For a moment, it seemed as if she was struggling to say something, then her expression crumbled and she burst into tears, long and hard and frightening.

"I know I saw them. I know it. I *know* it."

"Come on," Willard said finally, not really knowing how to handle the situation. "Let's go into the living room and sit down. Relax."

She allowed herself to be led into the other room. She dropped heavily onto the sofa. Willard returned to the kitchen and lifted Sams out of his high chair and set him on his feet. The boy toddled across the carpeting, clambered slowly and awkwardly onto the couch, and settled himself next to his mother. He carefully spread his blanket over his own legs and across part of his mother's lap. Catherine took no notice.

Willard knelt next to her, forcibly reminded of the night before. "Look," he said, "you two stay here and I'll check things again. Okay?"

She nodded without speaking. Her passivity was more frightening to Willard than anything else. Catherine was nothing if not self-reliant, independent, strong. She might have an aversion to crawly, squirmy things, but Willard was well aware of how much she struggled against those weaknesses. For her to collapse this completely....

He was baffled.

Still, he began carrying out his promise. Armed with a now-familiar, half-used Raid can noticeably lighter than it had been the night before, he re-sprayed the baseboards in the kitchen. He felt Catherine's eyes on him as the repeated the process in the living room.

Then he concentrated his efforts on the metal frame of the sliding door that opened from the house to the patio. There, it seemed to him, would be the logical place for vermin to enter. The doors might not meet exactly. Possibly there was some dirt in the tracks that....

"What the hell?"

Catherine's head jerked up at the sound of his voice.

Willard dropped to his knees and began tugging at a loose flap of carpeting that had been tucked into the corner where the wall between the kitchen and the living room abutted against the back wall.

"What....?" he repeated.

"Willard?"

"Look at this."

Catherine got up slowly and crossed the room.

Willard was still on his knees, slowly pulling the thick carpet back a foot or so. He glanced over his shoulder at her.

"This isn't even tacked down. It's just laying on top of the padding." He leaned further over and peered into the corner. "Shit." He leaned back and held something out to Catherine.

It was a splinter of wood, perhaps ten or eleven inches long and just over an inch wide, with needle-sharp nails protruding every half inch or so, the tips just long enough to catch in the backing of the carpet.

"This is supposed to be set into the concrete. It keeps the carpet stretched. Something broke it off."

He turned back to the flap of carpet. Catherine looked over his shoulder. They could both see the remains of twisted, broken strips bordering the carpet pad. Willard caught the edge of the pad between his thumb and index finger and peeled the half-inch-thick green foam pad away from the concrete flooring.

Catherine screamed and nearly fainted.

5.

A three-inch-wide crack in the concrete slab roughly paralleled the back wall, perhaps an inch and a half in from the baseboard and extending from the corner until it disappeared beneath the protective covering of carpeting and pad where Willard had not yet pulled them up. The crack was rough, edged with crumbling concrete.

That was bad enough.

But worse was the rippling, glistening black-brown roiling that surged inside the crack.

Roaches.

There might have been thousands—certainly hundred of the vermin swarming over each other, legs and feelers quivering as the things skittered like a repellant, oily wave breaking on grey sandy shores.

Then the edge of the wave broke over the top of the slab. First one or two, then a handful, then a dozen—the roaches spread from the crack onto the smooth but stained concrete exposed when Willard had stripped both pad and carpet.

Catherine screamed again, but Willard stared transfixed. Only when the vanguard of the wave reached him, and the lead roach crawled onto the toe of his loafer did Willard finally act. Galvanized by the presence of the thing, he reacted convulsively. His thumb jammed down on the spray nozzle of the Raid can, directing a killing jet onto the roach. The thing scrabbled helplessly at the soft leather of Willard's shoe, then fell backward, its legs twisting frantically.

Willard shot the contents of the can across the concrete, catching all of the roaches on the slab. The force of the spray at this close a range was so strong that it spun several of them back into the crack. He followed up, spraying continually until he was at the edge of the crack. He thrust the nozzle directly against the crumbling concrete and sprayed, not looking, not wanting to see the seething mass as it contorted beneath the poison. He could hear the *hisssss* of the spray; he could hear Catherine's harsh, ragged breathing—at least she wasn't screaming any more—he could hear his own breathing, his heartbeat, the *creeaak* of shoe leather as he shifted his weight from one foot to the other, and somewhere behind him Sams own snuffling cries, vague echoes of Catherine's.

But above all of that, he could hear the dry, horrible rustling of the roaches as they scurried frantically downward, tumbling over each other in a tumultuous mass, seeking the safely of darkness and dampness and distance from the hideous stuff that was coating their bodies and systematically destroying them.

Finally, with a sputter and spit, the Raid can ran empty.

Willard kept his thumb on the nozzle, though, shaking the can, and spraying, shaking the can and spraying, again and again even though nothing seemed to be coming out except an unsettling dry *hissss*, until the last possible drop of poison had penetrated the crack. Then he lifted his thumb.

His hand hurt from the strain. The plastic nozzle had impressed its serrated form deeply into the flesh of his thumb. His knuckles were white, and he was scarcely breathing. He looked into the crack.

Nothing.

Except for a few feebly struggling bodies, the mass of roaches had disappeared.

He stood, his foot crushing one of the dead roaches on the bare slab. He winced, then carefully stepped on each of the roaches in sight. He shoved the crushed remains into the crack with the edge of his shoe, unmindful of the viscous smears they left on the concrete.

He turned to face Catherine.

"Come on."

He picked up Sams, still crying softly, retrieved Catherine's purse from its usual place on the end table by the couch, grabbed three coats from the closet, and was out the door, yelling "Hurry" over his shoulder, almost before Catherine could move to follow him

6.

The clerk at Builder's Bargain Barn looked askance when Willard slapped his Mastercard down on the counter next to the twelve aerosol cans of Raid and ten room foggers.

The clerk was an elderly woman with faintly bluish hair and a perpetually confused expression on her rather pinched face. She looked as if she should be home spoiling grandchildren rather than tending to a behemoth computerized register that usually required her to enter each purchase at least three times before the machinery would accept it. Her neatly blue bordered plastic name tag announced simply that she was "Marge."

Fortunately, Marge did not say anything about Willard's unusual purchases or about the harried expression that haunted Catherine's eyes. She stolidly passed the electronic scanner over the pricing bars on one of the cans of Raid and looked curiously pleased—not to say surprised—when the register tallied the purchase price plus state tax times twelve...and on the first try.

As if on a roll and afraid to spoil her good fortune, Marge repeated the process with one of the home foggers. Her luck didn't hold. Glancing up at Willard, she diligently re-keyed the necessary information—department, function code, quantity— and passed the scanner over the pricing bars again.

Still nothing.

She sighed and began the procedure one more time.

"Hurry it up," Willard said, his impatience finally bursting through. He immediately regretted the outburst and tried to make what amends he could. "We got a real crop of roaches sprouting in the...." He faltered, realizing that the subject was not quite appropriate for the tone that was coming out.

Marge ignored both his initial comment and his explanation. For the fourth time she patiently and methodically entered the information. With all of the intent determination of someone not quite certain how to proceed next, she passed the scanner over the home fogger. This time, finally, the data jelled and the computer rang up price plus tax times ten.

Marge punched a final button and the LCD screen announced the total. She carefully bagged the cans while Willard swiped his card and scrawled his name at the bottom of the charge sheet. He jerked the bag from her almost before Marge had dropped in the last canisters, and took off for the door. Catherine, almost clutching Sams against her, followed close behind.

Willard did not see the odd look Marge sent after him. Instead, he concentrated on backing out of his parking spot, speeding down the narrow lane toward the highway, then driving home as quickly as possible.

Even so, by the time they arrived at the crest of Oleander, Sams had fallen into a restless sleep and Catherine had had enough time to read out the directions for the home foggers.

"You wait in here," Willard said as he cut the engine in the driveway. "I'll go set these and we'll take Sams out for a couple of hours. When we get back, everything will be all right."

"No," Catherine said. "I'll come help."

She carefully lifted Sams from his car seat and carried him into the house, laying him in a makeshift bed of afghans and pillows on the living room sofa. While she was doing that, Willard emptied two Raid cans in the crack along the back wall, spraying until the fluid dripped stickily on the rough concrete of the fractured slab. He pulled more of the carpet back, from the portion of the back wall adjacent to the kitchen wall, across the room to the sliding patio doors, then on to the far wall—the one separating the living room from the fifth bedroom.

To clear the full width of the living room, he had to push an end table and a small corner cabinet toward the center of the carpet.

The crack continued the entire span of the wall—varying irregularly from one to four inches wide, and at least as deep as the foundation slab itself. Some places had sheered cleanly away; others were rough and crumbling.

He saturated every inch of exposed concrete with Raid.

When he was finished, he turned his attention to the kitchen.

The vinyl floor tile seemed unbroken along the outer wall, but when he knelt down and looked closer, he noticed odd ripples in the tiles next to the baseboards. On a hunch, he grabbed a sharp paring knife and punched the wall-edge of one of the tiles near the middle. The blade easily broke through. He wiggled the handle. The blade moved freely, swinging an inch or so forward and backward before grating against concrete.

He tried another spot midway between that one and the far corner of the kitchen. Same result.

"Shit," he yelled, reversing the blade and slamming the end

of the handle against the brittle, yellowing tile. The vinyl shattered, revealing a foot-long crack. He struck the next tile. The crack continued beneath it as well. Increasingly frustrated and angry, he grabbed another can of Raid and emptied it into the exposed opening.

He could see nothing at the bottom of the crack—the sunlight was too bright through the windows and cast too sharp a shadow at the base of the wall, but he wasn't going to take any chances.

In the meantime, Catherine had resurrected half a dozen old packing boxes—not yet discarded—and was haphazardly stacking dishware, silverware, cooking utensils, and linens in them, emptying every closet and drawer in the kitchen. Fortunately, some of their things had not yet been unpacked; she was angry enough as it was and didn't need the added aggravation of breaking china or glasses.

Finally, though, the kitchen was ready—prepared according to the explicit directions on the back of the fogger package.

"Get the pets," Willard instructed, "while I get these ready."

Catherine went back through the house and grabbed the double cage containing Yip and Yap, the boys' hamsters, threw a heavy towel over the cage, and ran it out to the car. On her second trip, she carried Sams out and strapped him into his car seat.

Inside the house, Willard slid the removable plywood door into the doggie door, making sure that Will, Jr.'s dog—officially named Richard Beagle but mostly answering to "Crud," Will's favorite expletive—was safely blocked outside.

"A few hours in the cold won't kill you," Willard said when he heard the dog scrabbling at the plywood insert with his sharp nails. "It's not as if you don't have a perfectly good dog house out there. You just never use it."

Ignoring any further complaints by Crud, Willard checked the rest of the house: interior doors open, windows closed.

Everything okay.

His last act before leaving the house was to set up four of the foggers: one in the kitchen, one in the family room that had started life as a garage and had been converted by the last owners, one in the intersection of living room and entry hall, and one at the end of the hall by the back bathroom door.

Holding his breath as he activated each of the foggers—and understanding all the while that it was not necessary to do so— he retraced his steps through the house and finally left, locking the front door securely behind him.

In the car, Sams was whining and restless. Yip and Yap were huddled beneath a pile of cedar chips in the corner of the cage. Already the car was assuming the bitingly ammoniac stench Willard associated with hamster cages at least two days beyond scheduled cleaning time. He wondered if he would ever get the smell out of the unpholstery.

Without speaking, he cranked the key and backed out of the driveway. He glanced at his watch.

Eleven fourteen. About two hours until Charter Oaks released classes. Another hour before Will's school was out for the day. They would have to pick up the older kids from the school yards and find something to do for a good part of the afternoon.

Maybe a quick visit to a park, if it proved warm enough. Or a surprise early dinner at Carl's Jr. or Burger King. The boys would love a kids' meal, complete with toy treat. It was an inconvenience to have to stay away so long, Willard thought, but better that than the alternative. Better that than the unending colonies of roaches that seemed suddenly to have infested their house.

Squaring his shoulders and sternly reminding himself to ignore the increasing odor emanating from the hamster cages— now accented by a hauntingly similar odor from Sams—Willard drove away.

7.

By eight thirty that night, the house had returned to a semblance of order. The padding and carpet had been folded back in place, minus the splinters of tackless carpet strips. Willard wasn't too happy with the slightly rumpled texture the carpet had taken on near the baseboards, but there was little he could do about that. And a few ripples were the least of his problems at the moment.

He stood up and surveyed the carpet, then turned away and began staring at the walls and ceiling, probing in the cracks along the interior baseboards.

"What are you looking for?" Catherine said as she came in from the bedrooms. She sounded worried, as if she were afraid that their attempts to eradicate the roaches had failed. "Are there any more....?"

"No," Willard said. "No sign of wildlife." He grinned, trying to lessen Catherine's lingering horror over the experience.

She grimaced.

"No, I'm just curious." He pushed the thin blade of a small screwdriver into the back corner, along the juncture of the rear wall and the common wall between the living room and the back bedroom. The plaster resisted for a moment, then the blade disappeared.

"Shit," Willard muttered as his knuckles scraped abruptly against the plaster.

"What's wrong?"

"Look."

He sliced downward with the screwdriver—the blade slit through the plaster as neatly as if it were warm butter. He gestured to the dark opening.

"I'll bet this whole damn back wall's separated from the house. The gap's been plastered over and painted."

"Willard," Catherine said sharply. "The children might not be asleep. I don't want them to hear that kind of...."

But he wasn't listening. He was already in the kitchen, rummaging through the utility drawer until he came up with a small hand flashlight. He carried it through the living room, knelt in the entry hall, and began examining the shiny Solarium tiles.

"Look," he said after a few moments. He held the light at a

sharp angle to the floor. Small as it was, the bulb was sufficient to cast hairline shadows that zigzagged faintly but definitely from wall to wall across the entryway. "See that." He pointed with his free hand to the shadows.

"What is it?"

"Another crack. In the foundation slab." He rose to his feet with a grunt and disappeared into the hallway, the flashlight throwing a faintly orange glow in front of him.

It took less than half an hour to discover that the house—walls and slab alike—seemed laced with cracks, major and minor, each of them carefully retouched with plaster and then artfully repainted to disguise the flaws. The worst of them seemed to be in the northwest corner of the master bedroom, where the plaster split the entire length of the juncture of the two outside walls—another hairline crack, so fine as to be virtually invisible unless one searched for it. In addition, the line separating wall from white popcorn-textured ceiling was ragged and rough.

Obviously the entire side wall of the house was shifting

The more he discovered, the angrier Willard became.

Curiously, he was not so much distressed at the fact of the structural flaws as at the equally obvious fact that the previous owners had clearly known about them and had done everything in their power to hide them. Fresh paint, new coats of texturing, re-plastering in strategic corners, new tiles on the entryway floor—all with the express purpose of hiding the serious problems in the house. Without a word, he stalked back through the house to the wall phone in the kitchen and began ruffling angrily through the phone

"Ma…Mar…Mat…Max—here it is," he said, more to himself than to Catherine. "Maxwell, William. Realtor." He punched the numbers, allowing his growing fury to communicate itself through his fingers. He tapped on the receiver as the phone rang once, twice, three times.

"Maxwell." The voice on the other end sounded confident, sure of itself. Willard recognized it immediately, remembering the ease with which Maxwell had worked the deal for the house.

I wonder how much he got from the scam, Willard thought, even as he was speaking.

"Mr. Maxwell, this is Willard Huntley."

"Sure, Will. How's the new homeowner?"

Faced with the easy assurance in the voice, Willard suddenly found himself stalled for words. He was still angry—furious and upset—but he wasn't quite sure how to begin. "Well," he said after a long pause, "actually that's what I'm calling about."

There was another long pause. He was half waiting for Maxwell to ask for particulars, but the silence on the other end of the line remained deafening.

"I, uh...I've found some problems."

"Yes?"

Apparently Maxwell wasn't going to make things any easier.

"Well," Willard took a deep breath. "The walls and foundation seem to be cracked to hell and gone, and I want to know what you're going to do about it."

There, it was out. He felt better already. After all, there were such things as local ordinances, required inspections, things like that.

"Me?" Maxwell sounded honestly surprised. "What makes you think that I can do anything?"

"Well, you helped us with the house. You must know how to begin...."

"Begin what?"

"For starters, I want the previous owners...."

"The Merricks," Maxwell added, as if he were trying to be as helpful as possible.

"The Merricks," Willard repeated, nodding as if Maxwell could see him. "Anyway, I want to know how we can get the Merricks to make good on the problems. We haven't even been in here a year yet—hell, we haven't been in here more than a couple of months, and already the place is falling apart."

"Don't exaggerate," Catherine whispered.

"And besides," Willard added, her presence reminding him of the immediate cause of their problems. "Besides, the place is overrun with roaches."

"Sorry to hear that, Willard," Maxwell said, "but there's really nothing I can do about the problems. There was a clearly stated 'as is' clause in the contract, remember?"

Willard was stunned. He searched his mind but could dredge up no mention of any such thing.

"Just a minute," Maxwell said, his voice ebbing gradually, replaced by the sound of shuffling papers. "I've got a copy here somewhere," he continued, again speaking more to himself than to Willard. "Yeah, here it is." He fell silent, except for a murmur as he scanned the contract sheets. "Right, here it is. Page seven of the original contract. 'Summary of county inspection, specifying items anomalous to original construction, accepted and countersigned by purchaser(s).' A couple of other items, but the gist is that any such problems become the responsibility of the new owners.

"That's you."

Willard opened his mouth to speak, but the words stuck in his throat. "But...but," he finally sputtered. "But I didn't know, I mean, it's our first house and everything. I thought, I figured that you would let us know if there was anything wrong."

Maxwell laughed. "Huntley, do you know that your house was the least expensive one in the entire Tamarind Valley? By a factor of several tens of thousands of dollars?"

"No, I didn't. But what...."

"My commission on any other house listed with this agency would be almost double yours. And over the past six months, I've had seven houses in escrow."

Willard was beginning to understand.

"So maybe I might have let a few details slip. But you got the house, didn't you? And the property values will probably go up two, three thousand a month when real estate gets hot again. So you're not really out anything. And it's not as if you were planning on selling tomorrow or anything, is it?" Maxwell laughed.

Through the phone lines, the laughter sounded tinny and hollow.

Willard sputtered a few sounds, then fell silent. Everything Maxwell said was true.

"And anyway, the house isn't going to fall in any time soon. Maybe in forty or fifty years, but not tomorrow." He paused, then said, "Good to hear from you, Mr. Huntley. Have a good day.'"

And then the line clicked and Maxwell was gone.

"Damn," Willard swore softly as he hung up the phone and looked quizzically at Catherine.

"Damn."

From the *Tamarind Valley Times*, 29 June 1991:

STRONG QUAKE FELT, LITTLE DAMAGE IN VALLEY

One person died in Arcadia and one person died of a heart attack in Glendale as a result of yesterday's 5.6 earthquake, centered near the San Gabriel Mountains. Although extensive damage was reported in Pasadena, Sierra Madre, and other near-by communities, Tamarind Valley escaped with minor damage.

Several local stores reported overturned shelves but....

CHAPTER SIX

THE WARRENS, APRIL
1992-NOVEMBER 1997

Living the Dream

1.

At age thirty-two, Daniel Warren could surely be counted a success, in his own eyes if not in the eyes of his mother. He owned his own Ford dealership—one of the most lucrative in the entire San Fernando Valley. His apartment, snuggled in the dense greenery of the Santa Monica Mountains just off Sepulveda, was well furnished with antiques that even his mother recognized cost more than she had ever had to spend on furniture, Heaven knew, and more than she would ever feel comfortable spending on furniture. His clothes were always immaculately tailored, his shoes always expensive continental brands.

All in all, he was a success.

But success is as success does, as they say. And no amount of money could atone for what Amanda Warren considered her only son's greatest failure.

"You should be thinking about getting married," she would repeat every Sunday afternoon as Daniel Warren sat at the family table, surrounded by innumerable bits of bric-a-brac from his mother's sixty-seven years of life. The faded black-and-white pictures of Alfred Warren—none showing a man beyond his late thirties, and several of the later images eerily reminiscent of Daniel Warren as he sat at the side of the table—served as silent reminders that thirty of those years had been spent in patient widowhood and selfless, focused motherhood, days and months and years devoted to seeing that her Daniel had only the best she could offer. Now it was her turn, she had thought more than once. Now it was her turn to have what *she* wanted.

And what she wanted was simple.

She wanted grandchildren.

"You're not getting any younger," she would argue as she ladled gravy onto the flawlessly creamy mashed potatoes mounded at precisely eleven o'clock on her son's plate. It didn't matter that she knew he was watching his cholesterol count and that he had warned her that the gravy would probably send the numbers skyrocketing. She'd served gravy for Sunday dinner every day since she married Daniel's father thirty-eight years ago this September, and it certainly hadn't killed anyone yet.

"What about that nice young thing who lives on your floor, what's her name again, oh yes, Rita. Have you asked her out?" she would say as she set his huge wedge of cherry pie in front of him at the end of the Sunday meal, in spite of the fact that he had just announced that he was full, thanks Mom, but no dessert for me. And while she listened to him explaining how Rita was engaged to a construction foreman that weighed three hundred pounds and would probably snap Daniel's spine in two at the first sign that Daniel even knew Rita walked the face of the earth, Amanda watched each heaping forkful of pie disappear into Daniel's mouth, watched, almost not breathing until the entire wedge was gone.

Daniel was used to her obsession. For the past seven years, the litany had altered only fractionally. Sometimes it was "that nice young thing Rita," then it would be "that nice young thing Ellen." Always one "nice young thing" or another. Always after him to marry.

Daniel Warren was not particularly interested in marriage. He worked hard and he lived well. He could get what sexual companionship he wanted whenever he wanted it, and if that particular companionship was not precisely what his mother might have imagined—or approved—well, that was her problem not his, wasn't it.

After thirty-two years of Amanda Warren, thirty of those without even the questionable buffer of the father who had so inconsiderately keeled over from a heart attack on Daniel's birthday, just after Daniel had puffed out the candles on the cake and held out his plate for the first, special, birthday-boy slice, Daniel knew when to nod and smile, and when to answer Amanda's questions with just the right touch of ambiguity to assuage her for a while longer at least.

And he knew when to keep his mouth shut.

In April of 1992, however, on the Sunday following his thirty-second birthday, Daniel Warren broke his cardinal rule about keeping his mouth shut. He spoke out, and in doing so came as close as he ever would to killing his mother.

He didn't do it intentionally, of course (although he might perhaps have considered such an action more than once), but even without meaning to, he almost killed her.

On this particular Sunday afternoon, he sat for a long time, staring at his nearly empty plate as if the single smudge of pie filling (peach this time, not cherry—he had grown to hate both) along the floral edging concealed the intricate answers to an infinite universe, he removed the carefully ironed napkin from his lap, folded it just the way Amanda expected him to when he was finished with his meal, laid it precisely across the top edge of the empty plate, sat back in his chair, and looked at his mother for another long time.

When she began to shift uncomfortably under the weight of his gaze, he grinned at her, a foolish, little-boy grin, as if he already knew that he had done something wrong and was trying to figure out the best way to break the bad news.

And finally said simply, "I'm getting married tomorrow, Mom."

2.

Like all service organizations, the Helping-Hands Club was always on the lookout for volunteers. It had to be. Cash for paying a professional staff was scarce, especially here in the San Fernando Valley where even the most reasonable-seeming rent rates were punishingly high. Even though the Helping-Hands Club inhabited part of an antiquated school closed the year before when the new high school opened a couple of miles away, the marginal break on rent offered by the Sepulveda Basin School District did little to counter the fact that electric costs were high, heating costs were high, maintenance costs were high, everything was high…except the interest of most of the people in the area.

So when the well-dressed man appeared out of a cold, grey drizzle and walked into the office at Helping-Hands late one January afternoon and asked if the club needed volunteers, Marty Franco literally jumped at the chance.

"Sure thing, Mr…?" he said, out of his seat and hurrying around the cluttered desk before the man had stopped speaking.

"Warren, Daniel Warren," the man answered curtly.

"Hello, Mr. Warren. Marty Franco." Marty held out his hand. The other man's grasp was firm and warm in spite of the chill outside. Marty could feel a comfortable strength in Warren's wrist and fingers.

"Sit down," Marty said, pointing to the other chair in the small room. The chair was almost hidden beneath a flurry of manila folders. Warren carefully stacked the folders on the floor and sat down.

"So," Marty said after a short silence, "what do you know about the Helping Hands?"

"Not much," Warren admitted. "I saw an ad in the GreenSheet at a grocery store the other day. It didn't say much, just that you're a service club and that you work with young people. Kind of like Big Brothers, I guess."

Marty grinned. He'd written that ad himself. Nice to see

that it was pulling in some responses. "That's pretty close. We handle maybe forty kids at a time here, mostly kids with no fathers who need to be around a man some of the time. You know. Bonding. Role model. Like that."

Warren nodded.

"We're not a day-care center or anything. We run limited hours, but we do post a pretty good schedule of activities. Basketball, swimming, baseball. Some weekend hikes and camping trips. That sort of thing."

Again Warren nodded.

"And of course we appreciate any help we can get. Most of our funding is through private donations. We know that our volunteers are doing a lot just by being here, but sometimes it helps if...."

"I understand. I have no family myself and I make a pretty good living. I'm willing to cover some costs where necessary."

Marty broke out into an even wider grin, relieved that *that* hurdle had been successfully negotiated. "Well, Mr. Warren, then if you'll fill out these forms, we can get started."

He handed a sheaf of papers to Daniel, who skimmed through them before removing his pen from an inside jacket pocket. The form looked like fairly standard stuff. Name, address, age, marital status. Occupation. References. General backgrounds.

He began writing.

Three weeks later, Daniel Warren met Miles Stanton for the first time.

During an impromptu basketball game pitting four adult volunteers against half a dozen pre-teenagers (who severely and definitively trounced the old-timers), Daniel first noticed the skinny kid sitting alone on the sidelines, elbows propped on bony knees. Once or twice, he had even waved for the kid to come over and play, but the boy had just stared ahead as if the game, the other kids, Daniel himself simply didn't exist. As if the wall opposite didn't exist and he could see clear through it to the Santa Monica mountains and beyond.

After the game, while the others were heading sweating and

laughing into the shower room to clean up and change, Marty entered the gym and, standing by the boy, motioned Daniel over.

"Daniel, I'd like you to meet a new fellow here at Helping Hands. Miles, this is Mr. Warren. Daniel, meet Miles Stanton."

At a nudge from Marty, the boy stood. He seemed even skinnier standing up. His basketball jersey was at least two sizes too large for his shoulders and chest and threatened to engulf him. His baggy shorts hung well past his knees, as full as if the boy were wearing a skirt.

Daniel stifled a smile, leaned down stiffly, and solemnly shook hands with the boy. At least now the boy—*Miles*, Daniel reminded himself—was looking up at Daniel, but he still seemed no more interested in the man towering over him than he had been in the basketball game.

"This is Miles' first evening here, Daniel," Marty said by means of explanation.

Daniel noted that the man spoke about the boy as if the kid were not present. The fact grated on him. He squatted down until his eyes were level with the kid's. He heard his knees cracking; as always, he hated such physical reminders that his body was growing older.

"Hey, Miles," he said, smiling and watching for any flicker of interest in the kid's grey eyes. "You like basketball?"

Nothing.

"How about baseball?"

Still nothing.

Daniel glanced up at Marty. The other man shrugged, as if to say sometimes it takes a while, don't give up, just keep trying and something will break.

Daniel pulled away a bit and examined the boy. He looked to be about ten, perhaps an inch or two taller than average, thin but certainly not malnourished. His light brown hair was unruly but had been recently trimmed. His eyes still seemed empty, though.

"How about swimming? Do you like swimming?"

There...finally, there was something.

The boy glanced up, for an instant his face a flash of eagerness. Then, as if afraid that he had given himself away, and that by doing so he had lost any chance of ever going swimming again, he looked down to the floor. His thin shoulders rose, lowered in a shrug.

But Daniel had caught the glimmer of interest. He swiveled around until he was sitting on the bench next to the boy. He was sweaty from the basketball game. His T-shirt clung clammily to his back and the nylon of his sweat-stained shorts felt sticky and uncomfortable. But he sat there for a few moments anyway.

Finally he glanced up at Marty and nodded. I'll take it from here, the gesture said. Marty left.

"I liked swimming a lot when I was your age," Daniel continued, as if there had been no break in the one-sided conversation. "But I didn't get to go very much. We lived in Maine and it was pretty cold most of the year. And we didn't have heated pools back then. My mother didn't let me swimming out much—she was always afraid I'd get polio or something from the water."

The boy looked at him questioningly.

"Polio," Daniel said, "that was a real kid-killer when my Mom was younger. They had a vaccine for it by the time I was born, but Mom still worried. You know how Moms are."

The boy nodded gravely.

"Anyway," Daniel continued, "sometimes I would sneak away to a creek a couple of miles away and my buddies and me would strip down and go skinny-dipping. It was great.

"Now I can swim anytime I want, though. There's a great pool back there." He gestured to the doorway that led through the changing room and from there to an indoor pool.

The boy stared at the floor.

"Want to try it?"

Again, there was a slight movement.

"Well, I don't know about you, but I'm going to go in for a swim. We just played a hot, tiring game, and a cool dip sounds perfect right now." He stood and walked a few steps toward the changing room. "Come on if you want."

Daniel didn't bother to look back, but by the time he entered the changing room, he could hear the boy's soft tread only a few steps behind him. Daniel reached into an open cabinet just inside the door and pulled out a suit. Boy's medium. He tossed it to the kid. The kid caught it with one hand, his fingers snapping like small wires around the fabric.

"You guys change over there." He pointed to a partitioned section of the changing room. "We older guys have to use that side. Meet you right here as soon as you're dressed." He grinned at Miles, and for the first time Miles grinned back. It was fleeting, but it was an authentic grin.

"Okay." The kid's voice was a little deeper than Daniel had expected. "Okay...Mr. Warren." He disappeared around the partition, already tugging at his jersey top.

Daniel went to his locker on the adults-only side of the partition and changed into his trunks. He moved quickly, stuffing damp gym shorts, T-shirt, and socks into the basket at the bottom of the locker, then slamming the door and spinning the combination. He grabbed his towel from the bench and hurried back to the center of the room.

The boy was already there waiting. He looked even thinner in the trunks, which were large on him, barely hanging on his narrow hips, it seemed, and so full in the legs that they made Miles look as if he were perched on two knobby stilts instead of on legs. But the kid was still smiling, and in his eyes Daniel saw intelligence, eagerness, and interest.

"Come on, Miles. Last one in's a rotten egg."

They swam for nearly an hour, doing laps at first, then just horsing around in the water, ducking and splashing each other and playing a kind of two-man tag in which Daniel always seemed to be 'it', leaping in the water and trying to tackle Daniel, who would twist and spin and swivel away. To Miles, it seemed like only moments before Marty came in to yell at them through the noise that Miles' mother was waiting in the foyer to pick him up.

3.

By the end of February, Miles Stanton and Daniel Warren were officially partners at the Helping-Hands. They swam together for at least an hour two or three times a week. They played basketball and racquetball and handball. They went on an all-day field trip to the L.A. Zoo on one Saturday that was unseasonably warm and too perfectly glorious not to be doing something outside. They had shared hamburgers and fries at McDonalds and pizza with everything at Straw Hat.

And sometime during that interval, Daniel Warren had met Miles' mother, Elayne.

Divorced for eight years, Elayne was bright, vivacious, intelligent, witty. And beautiful. Once free from a husband who had turned alcoholic and vicious at the same time, she had struggled hard to provide for her son and herself, and had done a remarkable job. She had waitressed at half a dozen restaurants, sometimes working two shifts to bring back enough money to keep their small household going. She had taught Miles self-reliance and responsibility—he had to have both in unusual concentrations, she knew from the beginning, because sometimes she had to be gone for hours at a time, even when he was only seven or eight years old.

He was self-reliant and responsible, all right. He also had no friends to speak of. He preferred staying in the apartment and reading or watching TV to rough-housing with other guys his age. Guys who had Dads that blustered through the door in the evenings and gave them hugs and tickles and took them neat places. Guys who had Moms that baked cakes and cookies and played games with them when it was too rainy to play outside or when they didn't feel good.

In spite of Elayne's best efforts to be both a Mom and a Dad, Miles effectively had neither. He was a true latchkey kid, and he responded to his enforced isolation by withdrawing into his own world of imagination. It was safer there than on the outside. No one could hurt you there.

For a long while, Elayne Stanton wasn't particularly aware of how withdrawn her son was becoming. When she did finally notice, she didn't know quite what to do. She was working double shifts again—the rent had spiraled another $75 a month, and the car was making funny noises that in her limited experience with mechanics usually translated into major bucks, and Miles was starting to outgrow his clothes almost before she could get them home from the store. He needed help, she realized, but she couldn't give it to him.

Then, just after Christmas the previous year, she heard about Helping Hands. She checked it out, was pleased with what she saw, and decided that the Club might be just the thing for Miles. But it took a while for her to convince Miles to leave the apartment and try it out

When he went into the Helping-Hands building that first afternoon, his eyes were fixed on the ground and his shoulders were slumped so much that it looked like his raincoat would slide right off and lay in a bright orange puddle at his feet. To Elayne's worried mother-eyes, he didn't look like a little boy on his way to an exciting afternoon of male bonding; he looked like a condemned prisoner on his way to be involuntary guest of honor at an electrocution.

When he came out that night, though, everything had changed. His hair curled damp and tousled against his head. His cheeks flushed red with excitement. His eyes snapped with an electricity that she could not remember ever having seen before. And all he could talk about was Daniel Warren.

Daniel did this. Daniel did that. Daniel said this. And Daniel said that. Miles chattered so constantly about Daniel Warren that by the time they entered their tiny apartment that night, Elayne had both a headache and an frighteningly yearning desire to meet this man who had so abruptly become the solitary focus of her child's universe.

Elayne met Daniel for the first time two weeks later. They had their first official date in the middle of March—they took Miles to a dollar-a-car drive-in to see *Home Alone*. Even though it was raining so hard that neither of them could see through the front window, and Miles fell asleep fifteen minutes into the film, they counted the date a huge success.

And a week after Daniel Warren's thirty-second birthday, accompanied to the Chapel of the Roses in Las Vegas only by Miles and by a still stunned Amanda Warren, Daniel and Elayne were married.

4.

The new family lived for another couple of weeks in Daniel's apartment, but it had been clear from the beginning that that arrangement was only temporary. The apartment was spacious enough, but there was only one bedroom, and even though Miles insisted repeatedly that he thought sleeping in the living room on Daniel's overstuffed sofa was "real cool," both Daniel and Elayne realized that the boy needed a home, a *real* home.

They began looking at possibilities.

From the beginning, Daniel had insisted that they not even consider anything right in the San Fernando Valley.

"It's already too expensive to buy here, too crowded for a family," he explained to Elayne late one evening. "In another few years, it will be like living in the middle of a fishbowl. There're some new places going up farther north, between here and Ventura, that look pretty nice." Besides, he continued, he had begun negotiations to take over an ailing Ford dealership in a rapidly developing area called Coastal Crest. So far there wasn't much there, but what there was had been building up fast. Daniel could imagine it as it would be in ten years or so— an exclusive, high-priced neighborhood where the people would have plenty of money to spend on things like second or third cars.

So they began looking near Coastal Crest, in the hollow tucked comfortably into the Coastal Range that was generally known as Tamarind Valley.

It didn't take long to find the perfect place.

On a beautiful, summery day early in May, Daniel took a day off from work. Miles was still in school, but Elayne had already quit her jobs, so the two of them drove the thirty minutes by freeway out to Tamarind Valley. The further they went, the more Elayne liked what she saw—gently sloping hills crowned with bright green grass and patches of vivid yellow, thigh-high mustard. They met the realtor at his office on Tamarind Boulevard, just off the 101 Freeway between one knot of developments that was Coastal Crest and a second, maybe five miles further north, that was Tamarind Valley.

Half an hour later, they were comfortably seated in the back seat of a brand new, air-conditioned 1992 Ford Taurus wagon and heading out to look at listings.

Elayne fell immediately in love with the third house they viewed. It was certainly big enough for the three of them. "And for more children, if you want more," she added in a whisper to Daniel. Diplomatically, the realtor chose that moment to turn on the kitchen tap and blither on about the high water-flow.

The house had five bedrooms, a huge open-beamed living room that looked even larger than it really was, and a comfy kitchen/dining room combination overlooking a deep back yard and beyond that the Coastal Range further to the south. The two-car garage was roomy as well, and even though there was a small crack in the cement slab that threaded its way aimlessly on a rough diagonal from one corner to the opposite—recently sanded down so that it was less obvious and, more importantly, presented less potential for tripping—the place seemed just right. The yard was beautifully, professionally landscaped, with trees and shrubs and blossoming geraniums that nodded brightly in the sunlight.

"I just love it," Elayne whispered to Daniel as Fred Land ushered them back to his waiting Taurus and drove them past the long lines of houses on Oleander. "It's a great house, and there are lots of kids for Miles to play with."

That at least was true. There seemed to be three or four kids per house all along the block.

"How about it?" she asked again an hour later when Fred Land stepped out of his office at Lyons Realty for a moment to get them coffee. "Please."

"We should check things out a little more, first, shouldn't we?" Daniel said. "We should talk to some of the neighbors, find out about the area. We should...."

"Please," Elayne repeated.

And because there was a certain texture to her voice that for an instant sounded startlingly like Amanda Warren's, and because the exact details of the house were less important than the simple fact of who would be living in it with him... and because he recognized that land values in Tamarind Valley could only go up, he agreed.

Elayne never quite noticed that Daniel had not said anything at all about the house itself. When Fred Land returned with tray supporting three cups of steaming coffee and a half a dozen doughnuts on a paper plate, Daniel Warren said simply and directly, "We want it. Get started."

The deal closed thirty days later, on June 17, 1992. The next day, June 18, Daniel Warren, Elayne Warren, and Miles Stanton moved in (they hadn't gotten around to legally changing Miles' last name, although Daniel assured Elayne and Miles that he intended to—Miles giggled happily at the idea). They rented a U-Haul truck and began moving from his apartment just off Sepulveda to the house at 1066 Oleander.

To *their* house.

That night, Daniel Warren waited until his wife of just under two months was soundly asleep, worn out by the rigors of moving and nudged further into deep sleep by medication that he knew she took nightly...only this time she didn't know that she had already taken another pill carefully pulverized and mixed with a glass of fine white wine after dinner.

Then he got out of bed, careful not to disturb her just in case, and left the room. He closed the door silently and securely behind him.

For the first time—but not for the last time—Daniel Warren

tiptoed naked down the hall, trying to calm his racing pulse and steady his shaking hands. He had waited for so long, planned so carefully, put up with so much, just to reach this moment.

He stopped at the closed door at the end of the hall, breathed deeply two or three times, then swung the door open and stepped into the early summer-night warmth of the back bedroom where his ten-year-old stepson Miles lay sleeping. He stood next to the boy's bed, his legs almost touching the bed clothing that had fallen halfway to the floor, his toes digging nervously into the carpeting.

In spite of everything he had felt for all of his adult life, for a long time he dared not move. Then he silently drew back the single sheet that covered the boy's bare chest and bare legs. Holding one hand ready to clamp tightly across the boy's mouth if Miles should wake up screaming, he extended his other hand, trembling with anticipation, and began tugging at the inch-wide elastic waistband of the boy's stark white underpants.

5.

By the time Miles Stanton turned fifteen, he still had not changed his surname from Stanton to Warren. He adamantly refused to allow the change, even though his mother pressured him again and again to do it. She could get no reason from him, simply his stony rejection of the idea. Daniel never pushed the issue.

In addition, the boy had learned a number of important things.

He had learned how to keep frightening secrets from everyone, even—*especially*—from his mother. He had learned to pretend that he loved someone that he did not love. He had learned to keep to himself just in case he should let something slip during an idle moment of play or relaxation. He had learned to accept pain without making a sound. He had learned to give pleasure that was, for him, torture. He had learned fear.

Yes, he had learned much.

But most importantly, he had learned one more crucial thing. Hatred.

Hatred of himself.

And hatred of the monster that Daniel Warren had kept so carefully hidden during the months he and Miles had been partners and friends at Helping-Hands, during the weeks the three of them had lived lovingly together in Warren's apartment. Those few weeks were now the only time Miles could remember feeling like part of a family; he felt a nostalgic, yearning warmth for that cramped apartment and his lumpy bed on Daniel's sofa that sometimes frightened him with its intensity.

When he had first seen the house at the top of the hill, first chosen which of the four smaller bedrooms would be his very own, first carried his brand-new suitcase (a gift from Daniel) packed with his clothing across the threshold *his* house and into his very own room and hung his things in his very own closet, it had seemed as if his wildest dreams were coming true. He would live there with his mother, the woman he loved more than any other person in the world. He would live there with Daniel, his only buddy, his only real friend, and now—unbelievably— his father as well. They would be a family, together forever. For a lonely, often frightened ten-year-old, it truly was a dream come true.

The dream became a wildly distorted nightmare that very night, when Miles woke from a deep dreamless sleep to feel a hand constricting over his mouth and nose. For a horrifying instant he wondered frantically if someone—robber mugger thief murderer—had broken into the house and was trying to suffocate him. But at that instant, his numbed, terrified mind registered the movements of another hand, and then more horrifying movements, and in the hour it took for his brand-new Big Ben alarm clock on the nightstand next to his bed to *tick tick tick tick* slowly through the attack and *tick tick tick tick* even more slowly back into reality, he learned more about Daniel Warren—the *real* Daniel Warren, the repulsive, brutal skeleton hidden so carefully beneath the smooth, handsome skin—than he ever wanted to know.

Daniel's did not visit the back bedroom every night. That much the boy was spared. Sometimes Miles would lay in his own bed, straining to hear the first faint sounds of steps on the carpet in the hallway outside, and he would hear other sounds instead, muffled moans and murmurs coming from the master bedroom at the far end of the hall. Sometimes he could hear them even though the doors to both bedrooms might be closed. He could hear them even though the intervening room sat empty except for Elayne's sewing machine, stacks of patterns and folded material waiting to be transformed into clothing, and her dressmaker's form standing on its single leg in the corner like a headless, deformed, shrouded corpse. He could hear them even though the heater might be on in the winter, or the air conditioner in the summer. In spite of everything, sometimes he could hear the panting, animal gasps his mother made when Daniel did to her willing body what he also did to her son's unwilling one; and then, only then, Miles could relax slightly, maybe even fall asleep without staining his pillow with tears or grinding his teeth in impotent fury and humiliation until his jaws ached.

No, Daniel did not visit nightly. Not even weekly. But somehow the stuttering irregularity of the boy's nighttime degradation ultimately made the situation worse rather than better.

As Miles grew older—reaching eleven, twelve, thirteen— there would be erratic breaks in the sequence of Daniel's visits. Each might last as long as a week or two. Once Miles enjoyed a respite of almost a month; by the end of the third week Miles had nearly convinced himself that he could believe (although it took little forcing) that the visits were finally over...that the "games" Daniel wanted him to play were finally, mercifully over forever. That Daniel had finally decided that he preferred playing the games with Elayne's body.

Almost-a-month extended with a frightening slowness into a full month. Then to six weeks. Seven. For the first time since he moved into the house on Oleander Place, Miles found himself drifting easily to sleep. It became gradually easier to keep the secret—he had promised Daniel that first time that he would never tell anyone what they did, what games they played, partly because Daniel had made him promise and Daniel was an adult, but mostly because Daniel had made it frighteningly clear what would happen to Elayne's love for her shameless, deviant son if she should ever find out. If Daniel treated Miles like he did (and Miles instinctively knew that most fathers—even most step-fathers—did not treat *their* sons like Daniel treated him) then there must be something wrong with Miles as well, something twisted and deeply, deeply perverse. The boy's inner fear and terror and humiliation that someone might discover exactly what *he* was became more of a guardian over the secret than Miles' naive boyhood promise had ever been.

Then, at the beginning of the eighth week...the whispered movement of the door, so quiet as to have been almost silent but even so more than enough to awaken Miles to a panicky tightness in his chest and a clammy sweat oozing through his pores. Then he felt the familiar, hated hand tightening over his mouth. The other hand (even more familiar, even more hated, if that were possible) scrabbling at the waistband of his pajamas.

Miles had refused to wear only underpants to bed for nearly three years, regardless of how hot it might be. No matter how much Elayne had argued about it as she bathed swathes of prickly heat rash along his shoulders and stomach during the frequent 100+ temperatures of July and August, he refused to sleep in anything lighter than full-length, long-sleeved, winter-weight flannel pajamas. Elayne could not understand why. Miles himself could probably not have explained why. Perhaps somewhere, deep in his mind where the horror remained submerged hour upon hour, he held out the frantic hope that the thick flannel might somehow protect him.

But it never did.

Now, after almost two months of blessed loneliness, when the soft, damp hand touched his quivering skin he knew that everything he had hoped to believe had been a lie. The visits were beginning again.

Only now, it was much worse for the boy. Since turning thirteen, Miles' unwanted but undeniable physical reactions to Daniel's depredations had intensified. He didn't want them to; God knew that he despised himself more each time, condemned himself to a deeper level of his own private hell every time his body leaped from his conscious control and responded wildly, almost eagerly to the man's filthy touch.

But it did respond.

Now even his always fragile sleep was infected by the nightmare visits. He would awaken to hear Daniel closing the door. Knowing that this was real, that he could not awaken from this nightmare, Miles would look up to see Daniel glowing ghostly in the leaden moonlight, leaning over his bed. He would feel Daniel's rapid touches like a million insects crawling across his naked skin.

And then later—hours later sometimes, each tolled second by wearisome second by Miles' Big Ben alarm clock ticking metronomically on the nightstand—Miles would finally stumble into fevered sleep....

And in that sleep, something new, a phantom Daniel, ghastly and loathsome in the stark shadows of slanting moonlight in the corner bedroom, would return.

6.

Age thirteen shaded imperceptibly into fourteen. There were few changes in the Warrens' lives, mostly superficial. Daniel contracted for a company to come in and convert the two-car garage into a wide, roomy family room, and to construct an adjoining garage along the side of the property. The garage held Elayne's aging station wagon, sitting sedately next to an series of new, sporty vehicles for Daniel. Miles had a bicycle that was new when they moved in but that was now covered with a thick layer of dust and rested rather sadly against the far wall on two long-flat tires.

Elayne never complained that her car still stuttered sometimes, or that it continued to make unpleasant noises. She was far too content with her life as she was leading it to let minor inconveniences interrupt. She spent much of her day time in the sewing room making clothing for friends' children and amassing a wardrobe for the babies she was still sure would eventually come to her and Daniel.

Evenings the three of them spent in the new room, to all appearances a happy, stereotypical Southern California family. They watched television, or read, or played games…usually two-handed card games between Elayne and Daniel. Miles never seemed interested in cards.

And if occasionally Miles chose to huddle morosely at one of the sofa or curl up bonelessly in the recliner, well, wasn't that usual for teenagers, especially teenage boys? Moody, temperamental, unpredictable?

Neither Daniel nor Elayne knew—or perhaps would have cared to know—that at night Miles was beginning to inhabit a twisted never-never-land that felt as real as the waking world he shared with his mother and Daniel. In fact, the ugly phantasms of his dream-world became incrementally more vivid, more frightening than the painful, mortifying midnight visits he endured. As the months and years passed, Miles slept less and less each night. Most of the time he lay huddled beneath the covers, his eyes little more than black points in the night. In his desperate struggles to avoid the spectral world of sleep, he came almost to welcome the flesh-and-blood Daniel.

Almost.

Elayne finally noted with some concern that the boy seemed too thin and drawn. She saw that he was almost as tall as Daniel and his voice was cracking and dropping more every day, and that a skiff of what just might become whiskers had darkened his cheeks and chin—but in spite of these physical evidences of increasing maturity, he remained strangely childlike. He was increasingly withdrawn, introverted. She tried to talk with him one day.

"Are you feeling well, Miles?" she asked over breakfast. He was supposed to leave for school in a few minutes.

"I'm okay," he answered, staring into a bowl of rapidly disintegrating Cheerios.

"You don't look well. You look...tired."

He looked up at her. At his mother, this woman who bore him and then who married that bastard and even now didn't know (*couldn't* know!) what was going on in another bedroom in the darkness of midnight. For an instant his vision blurred and a voice said *tell her, she's your mother, she loves you, in spite of what* HE *says she'll understand that it wasn't your fault, that it was never your fault, that you didn't know any better back then and that now you do and you want him to stop to stop to stop-stopstop.*

"Mom," he said. His voice crackled from bass to treble and back again. "Mom, I...."

Daniel Warren swept into the room. Five years had changed him little. At thirty-seven, he was still successful. His two dealerships had split to become four; he now spent much of his time on the road traveling from San Fernando to Coastal Crest to Ventura to Santa Barbara checking in with the managers at each location. He still dressed expensively, and his tailored clothing complemented his body well. He took good care of his body. It was taut and muscular, younger looking than his age. His mother was proud of how well he had kept himself, even though he no longer came over every Sunday afternoon for dinner. And he smiled a lot, a secretly self-satisfied smile that most people seemed to enjoy but that filled Miles' throat with bile that burned like acid.

The man kissed Miles' mother on the lips, then crossed around the table to run his hand through Miles' hair. Miles tried to duck away and felt the fingers tighten momentarily on his hair, not much, not enough for his mother to notice but enough for him to feel and to understand that Daniel was still in charge.

Totally in charge.

"I won't be back until later tonight," Daniel said softly to Elayne. His voice betrayed none of the pent-up tension that communicated itself like an electrical current through his fingers to Miles' scalp. The man sounded for all the world like a normal father talking to a normal mother.

Elayne looked up sharply and opened her mouth as if to speak. Daniel cut her off without appearing to do so.

"Sorry, hon. We've got a manager's conference in Ventura this afternoon. It may take a couple of hours." He walked away from the table. "Love you," he added as he took his briefcase and slipped out the kitchen door into the garage. The door closed behind him.

A moment later the whine of the electric garage opener—the first installed on Oleander Place—served notice that Daniel Warren was preparing to leave. Elayne toyed with a wedge of toast in front of her. Miles' Cheerios were drowned beyond redemption, but he forced himself to eat a soggy spoonful anyway.

The garage door opener whined again as the door dropped, and the tiger roar of Daniel's brand-new electric blue Corvette died away down Oleander before Elayne spoke again.

"We're so lucky, Miles." She concentrated on stirring her cooling coffee. "Daniel takes such good care of us."

Considering what Miles had been about to say to her, he could only stare at his mother. She lifted her eyes and looked directly into his.

"I don't know if I could take it...you know, having to be alone like that again. Working all the time. Wondering if we were going to go hungry next week, or where the rent payment was coming from. If I thought something, or someone was coming between us"—meaning herself and Daniel, Miles understood at once—"I'd do anything, *anything* to keep him. *Anything.*"

She rose and set her empty plate and coffee mug in the sink. Her jelly-and-butter-smudged knife rattled a long, clattering dirge as it fell onto the porcelain. When she turned and stared at her son, her eyes held a strange expression that struck Miles as coldly across the face as a physical blow.

"What did you want to say to me, Miles?" she asked sweetly.

"Mom...," he began. Then: "Nothing. I'm all right." They never spoke of his looking tired again.

But as his fourteen year closed—the fifth since they had moved into the house on Oleander Place—Miles slept less and less.

7.

The *real* dream—the dream beneath the dream, the one that nearly drove Miles mad with terror each time it began—started shortly after that discussion with Elayne, in late October of 1997.

The first time it came, Miles was not asleep in his bed. He lay naked on the floor of his room, his body curled into a tight ball, with his knees touching his chest, nearly touching his chin. His hands were clasped tightly over his shins, as if by holding on to each other they could create a lock against pain and fear and self-hatred and despair.

Daniel had just left. Miles knew that he should get back into his bed, that he should pull on his crumpled flannel pajamas and climb between the sheets that for almost every other fifteen-year-old in the world would mean warmth and comfort and peace but that for him had become synonymous with horror. He knew that if Daniel found him lying naked on the carpet in the morning, the next visit would be worse—Daniel had already warned him about such things.

No use taking any chances that your mother might happen to drop in early and see something she shouldn't and get worried, right.

Miles knew that Daniel was capable of inflicting exquisite pain without leaving visible marks. The thought of punishment from that man chilled the boy. But tonight, the coldness sweeping over his spine felt uniquely right. Maybe he would catch pneumonia and burn with fever and cough his bloody lungs out and die. Maybe....

He lay with his head against the rough carpet. A thin line of blood trickled from the side of his mouth. *Tell your mother you slipped going to the bathroom and hit the door jamb*, Daniel had warned just before he left, *She'll believe that. She knows you're a clumsy little shit.*

It wasn't the first time that Daniel's visits had left Miles bleeding, but such occurrences were blissfully rare. Usually Miles tried to remove any evidence of blood—and so far Elayne had not noticed anything untoward. Tonight, though, he simply didn't care. Let the bastard find me like this and kill me. Let her come in and see me naked and bloody on the flood and then try to pretend that everything's just hunky-dory, her and Mr. Perfect.

His anger warmed him, even as he realized with a distant, almost disconnected part of his mind that the temperature in the room was dropping precipitously. His exposed skin crawled into goose bumps and he shivered violently. The movement caused a ripple of pain through him.

The blood thinned to a viscous drop that hung suspended at the corner of his mouth before dropping heavily to the carpet. Already the thick pile of the dark brown shag had absorbed most of the blood. Miles realized dimly that no one would even notice the stain by the time the blood dried.

No one but him.

His tongue brushed a cut in the inside of his cheek. The movement stung, but he chose to ignore it. For a moment, he stiffened. He thought he heard something in the hall. He raised his head an inch or two from the carpet and listened. It could be Daniel returning to make sure Miles was "safely in bed." It might be his mother, although he could count on the fingers of one hand the times she had awakened during the night and come in to check on him. He wasn't sure which prospect was the more inviting, which the more terrifying.

After a long moment, he decided that there had been no

sound. He must have imagined it. He dropped his head to the carpet again. His ear rested on a rough, slight, unseen ridge only partially buffered by the thickness of carpet and pad.

The crack in the slab started in the corner of his room and arced across the center to disappear beneath the closet door. Miles had discovered the irregular edge only a few weeks after they had moved in. He spoke to no one about it. Sometimes he would spend long hours running his fingers along the phantom crack; sometimes he half believed that he could see the precise place where the floor started angling oh so marginally downward toward the far wall.

Tonight, he felt an odd comfort in lying against the crack, feeling its shadowy reality as a jagged line beneath his body. He lay without moving, his eyes closed, his heart thumping.

And finally he fell asleep.

The nightmare intruded almost immediately. It began like all of the others—a phantom Daniel silently opening a phantom door. The phantom-not-phantom hands. The roving and clutching and groping, and the pain. But then...suddenly there was someone else with them in the darkened room. At first Miles couldn't tell anything about the shadowy figure—not its age or its sex or its size. He just knew without knowing how that someone stood behind Daniel.

At the critical moment in the dream-Daniel's frenzy, the dream-Miles saw something glistening in a white-lightning arc, and Daniel's head jerked back as a soundless scream of unutterable agony exploded from between his teeth. A jet of burning blood followed. Daniel threw his head forward, eyes wild with a terror that kindled joy like a raging flame throughout Miles' whole being. For an instant. Then the dream-Daniel's head struck the dream-Miles' forehead, and there was an eternity of exquisite pain and Miles thought he would die for certain, and then Daniel's head exploded, nearly suffocating Miles in a flood of red blood and grey tissue.

The dream-Miles felt Daniel's body twisting on top of him, writhing in an intensity of bleak sensation that had nothing to do with sexual passion. Out of one blood-curtained eye, Miles saw a glinting, silver-white thing rise and sweep downward again. Daniel's body quivered. Another rise and fall. Another quiver, like the legs of the dead frogs Miles galvanized for an experiment in science class earlier that fall. Another sickening rise and fall—this time less silvery white than mottled red...and now Miles felt the first slice of pain across *his* abdomen.

The dream-Daniel fell away like two halves of a dead, rotten husk, parts of his body propped bloodily on each side of Miles. Now the boy could see clearly the curve of the long knife suspended at the apex of its swing directly above his groin. And he could see the thing that held it.

The blade descended with a deliberateness that must have been the dream equivalent of slow motion but that served only to prolong the terror, the anticipation of the sharp pain it must bring. Miles brought his hands together. They moved in normal time, two fluttering white-stained-red birds rubbing wing to wing as his dream-self pleaded with the monster above him... pleaded for one more minute, one more second of life.

The blade continued inexorably downward. The movement was still horrifyingly slow, but the dream-Miles intuited at once the hideous force behind blow. His dream-hands flew faster and faster, his skin abrading as his palms scored each other, as his fingers flickered long and white, in and out of shadows.

The blade was almost to his groin. The steel glinted wick-edly in a light that seemed to come from everywhere at once. Then the light transformed from silver to red and he screamed in an agony that transcended any he had ever imagined—his throat tore open with the intensity and blood washed into his lungs and added its fire to his gasping breaths. His hands flared liquid flame, a beam of living fire that scored the blade just as it severed his flesh. His hands flew apart and the raging flames spilled over him, over the rotting remains of the dream-Daniel's body, over the blood-stained carpet.

He felt tongues of flames licking at his flesh. He twisted his head in anguish as the fire consumed him. Above it all, beyond all the pain and the terror and the torment, the nightmare figure retreated, laughing silently.

Noooo! the dream-Miles screamed, one final burst of life...

...and Miles shuddered violently awake, his skin soaked and sticky with his own sweat, and his arms and legs as rigidly cold as blocks of ice. For an instant he heard the lingering dream-scream. Then he rolled slightly and felt the stiff nap of carpet against his back—even stiffer where his blood had soaked into the fibers and was now part of the carpet itself, perhaps had even filtered through the pad beneath and oozed thickly into the crack and from there descended to the waiting bowels of the earth itself.

He sat up. Big Ben said 2:15. Barely half an hour since Daniel—the real, flesh-and-blood Daniel—had left. Miles struggled to his feet, his body stiff with cold and pain. He shuffled over to his bed and dropped heavily onto the mattress. Still awash with sweat that stank of fear, still naked but for once uncaring, he burrowed into the covers and slept as if dead.

8.

From then on until the end, that nightmare repeated itself nearly every night regardless of whether Daniel visited or not, regardless of whether Miles lay asleep in his bed or (as happened more frequently) curled fetus-like on the carpet. As bedtime approached, Miles would shower, dry off, and dress in his long pajamas, brush his teeth, and then—irregularly at first but with an increasing consistency that even he realized bordered on sheer obsessiveness—walk through the kitchen and the living room before going to his bed.

"What's the matter?" Daniel asked as Miles walked through the living room early in November. Daniel and Elayne were sitting side by side, his arm over her shoulder, reading. Elayne was reading a Harlequin romance. Miles couldn't see the cover of Daniel's book but the volume was thick and the open page crowded with print.

Miles ignored him. He saw in Daniel's darting glance something that might have been an unspoken threat, might have been a burgeoning fear as the bastard looked up into the eyes of his stepson and perhaps saw intimations of the man Miles was rapidly becoming. Miles straightened his shoulders. After all, he was nearly fifteen, and he already had a couple of inches and possibly even a few pounds on Daniel. Maybe after all this time, Daniel was beginning to worry. The thought was pleasantly exciting.

"Yes, honey," his mother added. "You've been wandering around like this every night for a while now. Is something wrong?"

"No," Miles said. "Just checking. Making sure I turned the stove off after dinner." It wasn't a lie. Dinner had been over for three hours already, the dishes washed and dried and stacked away, the counters and cabinets cleared. But Miles knew that he would not be able to sleep (if he slept at all) until he was sure that the four rings of blue flame were safely extinguished. Until he was sure that the house was safe from a sudden fire that might tear through its bowels burning and destroying and consuming.

"But....," his mother began. Daniel laid his arm on hers and she fell quiet. Miles stared at the two of them for a moment, then left. As he turned the corner into the hallway, he heard Daniel say, in a voice he probably assumed Miles would not be able to hear, "It's just a phase. You know, teen-age jitters. I was just like that, always wandering around when I should have been in bed. Worrying about nothing."

Miles waited in the hall for a moment to see if he could hear anything more.

"Elayne," Daniel said suddenly, softly, "you almost forgot your medicine."

"I don't think I need to...."

"You know you do. I think that if you ever really did forget to take it, you'd have as much trouble sleeping as Miles does."

The boy heard Daniel get up. He hurried down the hall,

reaching his bedroom only an instant before he heard the click of the bathroom light and then Daniel opening and closing the medicine chest.

Standing in the darkness, his back again his door, he watched and listened until he heard the bathroom light flick off and then the unintelligible rumble of Daniel's voice from the living room.

That night (and every night thereafter), Miles did not even look at his bed. He walked into his room, careful not to touch the light switch. Feeling his way in the dark, he meticulously unplugged every electrical appliance in the room: stereo, lamp, even the electric clock his mother had given him for Christmas when she decided that the loud *tick tick tick* of the Big Ben might be keeping him from sleeping. Satisfied that nothing remained that could be a fire hazard—remembering even in waking the intense pain as flames blossomed from his hands—he pulled the cast-off Big Ben from the nightstand drawer, wound it as tightly as he could with fingers that felt corpse-like, cold and stiff and awkward. He wound it so tightly that he could feel the tension in the spring. He sat it on the nightstand and dropped to the floor, curling up on the carpet and hoping not to sleep.

From Daniel's insistence about the medicine, Miles knew that this would be a hard, difficult night.

The visit was indeed rather longer than usual. And substantially more painful

9.

By November 20, Miles knew that the situation was coming to a head. Daniel was subdued but Miles could detect a smoldering anger in the man, a volcano of violence waiting to erupt. Miles knew now that his mother was deeply asleep each night in the corner room at the far end of the hall, heavily drugged. Daniel was taking no chances.

But Miles also knew that Daniel was not impervious. Daniel was not longer the towering, distanced adult telling the innocent child what to do, how to act, what to say...and what *not* to say.

Daniel could be hurt. The dream had told him that.

On the night of November 20, Miles went through his normal ritual. Shower. Dress. Brush teeth. Check stove. Unplug everything in the room. Drop exhausted to the floor and hope against hope that the door would remain closed, that the dream would not come that night.

But in spite of his efforts at staying awake, including stabbing the palm of his hand repeatedly with a needle taken from his mother's sewing room, he slept.

And, irresistibly, the nightmare came.

This time it was different. This time, the dream-Daniel did not appear. Instead, Miles seemed to awaken to a frightening greenish glow in his room. It made his hands and arms look swollen and dead where they thrust from the long, thick sleeves of his pajamas.

The room was hot. That fact alone startled the dream-Miles. Usually the dream-world was cold, freezing at times, growing steadily colder until he was forced to move his hands faster and faster, and the air heated and burst into flame that consumed and destroyed. But this time, even though it was foggy and cold outside, with the temperature hovering around 40 degrees, Miles dreamed that he was stifling. Sweat furrowed along the crease of his spine, oozed beneath his arms, down his back, and in his groin. He blinked constantly to keep the burning moisture from his eyes. His hair was matted against his forehead and temples and neck, thick curls of heavy, sodden darkness.

He slid the window open. Whispers of fog roiled through and blended with the subtle green glow until the room was awash with light that seemed to have no single source but rather to emanate from every possible surface—walls, ceiling, furniture, even the rough, shadow-dark carpet.

Opening the window made no appreciable difference in the temperature, however. Miles was hot, boiling. He felt as if his brains were frying, his skin curling from his body in long strips like fresh bacon. He ripped his pajama tops off without bothering to unbutton them; the small white, pellet-like buttons shot across the room with the force of bullets and clattered against the wall.

Now the tendrils of greenish fog brushed against his naked chest like icy fingers, burning with their coldness, but still the room seemed to grow hotter and hotter. He unsnapped his pajama bottoms. They dropped unnoticed to the floor. And still the air was stifling. His lungs were about to explode. The agony intensified as he writhed against the volatile air; his body would combust in an instant and incinerate himself and his room and Daniel and the house and....

Something moved in the closet.

His heart thumping with panic, Miles watched as absolute darkness-within-darkness swirled and coalesced into the shadowy dream-figure. This time he knew immediately that it was male, knew it was old—older than himself, older than Daniel.

And he knew it was evil.

The figure glided like a shroud into the room. Miles stood naked before it, his body a sheen of greenish light as the shadow figure moved closer. It was taller than Miles, bulkier, dark with dread and horror.

It carried the knife.

Faster than thought, the blade slashed toward him. This time, the dream-Miles saw the blade coming. No Daniel lay atop him to intercept its deadly edge. The tip caught the flesh on his upper arm and sliced to his elbow. The wound, while not especially deep, was deep enough that the blood flowed freely and the pain coursed like an electric current through his body.

He tried to jerk back, tried to raise his other arm and cradle the wound, but he could not move. The blade returned.

Swish.

It sliced like liquid fire the length of his other arm.

Again. His belly this time. Then his thighs. And then....

He closed his eyes, expecting the fatal thrust...and a distant, abstracted part of his mind wondered absently—with the objectivity of a scientist observing the progress of a particularly interesting lab experiment—whether the real-time Miles would die at the same instant the dream-Miles died.

The point of the blade touched his chest, directly over his heart. The metal was icy; his blood was hot. The point touched, pressed. He felt it puncture the top layers of flesh, felt the first drops of blood as they wandered like errant streams down the contours of his chest and abdomen. He waited for the final thrust.

That never came.

He waited, waited, and finally opened his eyes.

The shadow-man stood so close that Miles could see the horror that remained of its face. The flesh heaved and writhed with a life of its own. His cheeks were flayed away to reveal twisted knots of muscle and blackened stumps where teeth might once have been. Light burned through the shadow-man's eyes, a green and baleful and poisonous light that reflected on the sheening blade.

So abruptly that Miles felt as if the breath were being ripped out of his own body, the blade tip withdrew. The shadow-man deliberately reversed the knife, mesmerizing the boy with the flickering of light across its blood-stained metal until finally Miles realized that the haft was pointing at him, that the shadow-man held the gory tip piniuned against his own rotting chest.

For an eternal instant, Miles stared into the hollows where putrescent remnants of eyes glittered coldly, invitingly at him

And somewhere deep in the horror-stricken, fear-raddled recesses of his mind, the boy understood the hideous offer. Tears streaming down his cheeks, he understood and he accepted the final gift and closed his eyes again—willingly descending deeper deeper into the bottomless abyss of the dream-world—and with a sharp intake of breath that rippled pain through his own lungs and heart, he gripped the blood-slick haft with all his strength and thrust the blade home.

10.

Daniel Warren usually slept lightly. Unlike Elayne, who could rarely be raised by anything less than a 10.0 earthquake once she fell asleep (assisted, as always, by a pill or three), Daniel roused easily. And he never dreamed.

Which was why he was so startled when he suddenly became aware that he was dreaming of a ghostly hand clamped tightly over his mouth and nose, suffocating him.

Eyes wild and staring, he struggled to sit up and wrench himself from the grip of the nightmare. Then the nightmare took on entirely new orders of terror for Daniel Warren, when he understood that it was not a dream at all. And that he hadn't wakened when the bedroom door had opened, in spite of the slight squeal that always *always* awakened him. His mind spun for a second, then his eyes flew even more widely open and his breath caught in a painful, ragged gasp that left him reeling. Even in the near darkness of the bedroom, he knew at once what he was seeing. He just couldn't believe it.

He saw the hot blood streaming from wounds all over his step-son's naked body—arms, shoulders, chest, gut, thighs. He saw with a shudder that threatened to twist his spine the hideous light in Miles' staring eyes, the flicker of hideous light on black-stained blade, and the single eye of brilliant white that was the tip of the knife as it slid into his belly as easily and as wetly as a red-hot branding iron would slide into a block of ice, consuming as it destroyed.

11.

The instant he finished what had to be done in the master bedroom, Miles' body began to shake with an intensity that jarred his teeth and blurred his vision.

This is no dream!

He stared at the blade hanging limply from his outstretched hand, at the carnage of what had only moments before been a chastely intimate bedroom scene, husband and wife sleeping side by side. They still lay side by side. But no longer sleeping.

Hardly registering that fact that he was covered with gore—not all of it his own—and naked and bleeding from a dozen wounds ranging from superficial to near-fatal, the boy fled the room, throwing the knife away from him with such force that it spun dervish-like through the open bathroom door and shattered the mirror over the medicine chest.

He ran through the silent house. His feet left a trail of moistness blacker than black behind him. In the kitchen, he paused only long enough to grab a set of keys from the homemade key rack next to the garage door—a cunning bit of his own work in the shape of a large key cut from plywood and painstakingly stained redwood and polished to a flawless gloss as a Mother's Day gift nearly four years before.

Then without realizing what he was doing or where he was heading, he found himself in the garage and jerking open the door to Daniel's Corvette. He sank into the seat, numbly registering the icy coldness of leather against the blistering heat of his naked back and legs. In the darkness his right hand scrabbled in the storage compartment between the seats, blindly, frantically, for a long moment before he felt a flood of relief as his hand struck something small and oblong, with two studs protruding from one end. He grabbed it and aimed it over his shoulder and hit the left stud, grateful that Daniel had at least taught him that bit of technological magic.

The garage door whined as the heavy plywood doors ascended on their well-oiled hinges. Cold night air billowed into the garage. There was no fog, not even any clouds. The sterile stars prickled coldly, malevolently against a midnight sky.

The boy jabbed the key viciously into the ignition and cranked it so hard that the key nearly broke in his hand. The engine turned over once, twice, coughed ominously, then with a screaming roar, caught. He jammed the gear into what he hoped was reverse and hit the gas pedal, hoping against hope that all of the time spent watching Daniel manipulate the gears would help him now. The engine roared unevenly and the car jackrabbited out of the garage, tires squealing against the concrete driveway as the boy struggled with the wheel, finally managing to spin the car around on the circle of pavement directly in front of the house, until the 'Vette was facing directly down Oleander.

He jammed the gear shift into another position and depressed the accelerator again. The car jumped forward a dozen feet, shuddered, then jumped forward again. All the time the engine roared as if it were a mob of hungry lions. Or merely an echo of the bloody *thrummm* behind Miles' eyes. His head ached horribly, and he felt as if he were going to throw up all over Daniel's genuine leather sport seats.

In one of the houses just down the street, a light went on and a curtain wavered, but the boy paid no attention to the face that appeared, stared, then abruptly disappeared again. The light flickered out.

The boy slammed the accelerator again, and the car leaped forward. He didn't try to shift gears—he was in second, which was why the car had started with such difficulty, but at least he could keep going. He let gravity take its course, and the car rolled faster and faster down Oleander. At the far end, where the street dead-ended onto Mariposa, he swung wide, barely trying to see through eyes almost blinded by blood and tears.

He didn't know if any other cars were coming or not; he didn't care. He was beginning to chill now. The heat was evaporating from his body in great waves that steamed over the windows, cutting his visibility even more.

A stuttering left onto Reynolds, then a quick right onto Bingham. He grappled with the gears and the clutch again, just enough to jump from second into fourth. Again the car almost stalled, but he managed to keep it going, building up speed as he slipped through the night.

Thirty-five, forty, forty-five, fifty, sixty, sixty-five.

The speed limit was a well-posted thirty in this part of town. He didn't care. He slammed through two red lights without braking. Neither time was there another car in the intersection, but Miles didn't bother to look. He was escaping at last. He had the man's car. He wore the man's blood (and his own—and his *mother*'s) crusting on his body like a badge of honor...or disgrace. Like armor inviolable and protective, seamless and corrosive. He wore the man's life encasing his own. And he was escaping at last.

The car slowed slightly as it began the final ascent out of Tamarind Valley toward the north. From there, Reynolds Boulevard's four wide lanes shrank suddenly to two, pitted and badly in need of repair. What had been a major artery became instead little more than a twisting, rutted roadway that connected Tamarind Valley with the Santa Reina Valley on the other side of the foothills. That part of the road was known simply as Norwegian Grade.

He took the crest of the hill at seventy—somewhere around fifty miles too fast for safety, fifty-five too fast for comfort. For an instant, the front tires left the pavement, then the 'Vette was flat on the roadway again, squealing as Miles yanked it to the left, then sharply to the right in a frantic attempt to keep on the asphalt.

A quarter of the way down the grade, his right front tire slipped off the splintered tarmac and slewed through loose gravel. Prickly pear cactus with spines six inches long scraped the side of the 'Vette from bumper to bumper. The sound touched something deep in the boy, something that had been suffocating and lay nearly dead. He grinned wildly. Then he blinked—and in an instant of horrifying clarity, understood that he was naked and bleeding and shivering with cold and with shock, and in a car he could not drive, hurtling down Norwegian Grade at impossible speeds, fleeing through the night from....

He remembered everything. His mind froze. And with it, his hands.

The steering wheel twisted like a captive serpent beneath his grasp as the roadway dished up on a nearly ninety-degree curve halfway down the grade. If he had jerked the wheel an inch, even half an inch, there might have been a chance.

But the images of what lay behind him stunned him. He held the vibrating wheel in a death grip and opened his mouth and screamed, long and piercing and desperate, as the 'Vette ripped through the woefully inadequate barbed wire fencing and arced over great patches of ghostly cactus. The car flipped once and almost completed a second flip before it smashed into an outcropping of ragged burnt-brown stone and with a soft *whuuump* that instantly became a hurricane's roar, exploded into flames.

From the *Tamarind Valley Times*, 21 November 1997:

ANOTHER TRAGIC DEATH ON KILLER CURVE

The still-smoldering remains of a late-model sports car were discovered at four o'clock this morning by a passing motorist. The driver had apparently been racing down Norwegian Grade, notorious as one of the most dangerous roads in the entire Tamarind Valley. Because of the inaccessibility of the wreckage at the bottom of the canyon, police investigators were unable to reach the scene of the incident until well past seven o'clock. At this time, the identity of the driver has not been released.

The incident, the fifth fatality on that section of road in less than two years, will likely spur increased controversy in the City Council over whether or not to widen the pavement, at an estimated cost of....

From the *Tamarind Valley Times*, 22 November 1997:

NORWEGIAN GRADE MYSTERY INTENSIFIES

In a bizarre twist, the driver of the late-model Corvette destroyed by fire along the Norwegian Grade two nights ago has been identified as an unlicensed fifteen-year-old, Miles Stanton, of 1066 Oleander Place. Attempts at notifying his parents led to the grisly discovery of the bodies of his mother, Elayne Stanton Warren (35) and his stepfather Daniel Warren (37), in the bedroom of their home on Oleander Place. Both had been stabbed repeatedly. One informed source reported unofficially that the circumstances surrounding the deaths were particularly vicious.

"It was like a slaughterhouse in there," the source noted. Officers present at the scenes of both incidents refuse to make any additional statements, other than that a preliminary investigation suggests the youth first killed his stepfather, then his mother, and then attempted to escape in the car owned by his stepfather. Elayne Warren leaves no immediate relatives; Daniel Warren, owner of four automobile dealerships in the area, is survived only by his mother, Amanda Warren, of Woodland Hills.

Funeral services for all three are pending.

CHAPTER SEVEN
THE HUNTLEYS, FEBRUARY 2010

Cracks

1.

The good news was, for several weeks after that night, neither Willard nor Catherine saw a single roach.

The bad news…in the middle of February, it began to rain.

The first few days of February were fortunately clear, relatively warm, and dry. The skies were the deep blue portrayed in the more touristy postcards that touted Southern California as a perpetually green, perpetually blooming paradise. One of the neighbors down Oleander Place even had a beautiful large tree in the front yard that was laden with bright, ripe oranges. From a certain angle it was silhouetted against the Coastal Range across the freeway and could itself have been the star of just such a post card.

Once school resumed, the neighbor kids—occasionally including the Huntley four—were able to play outside wearing only light jackets well into twilight. Not that Will, Burt, and Suze seemed drawn to any of the *pro tempore*, shifting gangs that formed and re-formed along the short street. The older three Huntleys stayed pretty close to home, satisfied with brief forays into the backyard for tag or wildly awkward attempts at badminton…played mostly without the benefit of nets—or rules.

Sams, however, seemed delighted by the limitless prospects from the front yard. His favorite Christmas present had been a brand-new, battery-powered, ride-on car. The thin plastic body was molded in bright-red with mock-chrome details, then finished in the general outlines of a classic 90s Chevy Corvette, sleek, low to the ground, looking like it was racing even when standing still, with the promise of infinite, lightning-fast speed.

Well, perhaps *very* slow lightning.

"Willard, he's too little for something like that," Catherine had protested when Willard caught her arm and guided her over to where a floor model sat gleaming on the top shelf in a Wal-Mart display. "He'll get hurt."

"Nonsense, he can probably walk faster than that thing can go, and anyway it has seatbelts. Safety first, you know." He laughed and pointed at the specifications on one of the boxes.

"And it's *way* too expensive," Catherine responded, not willing to give up the battle just because of a little laughter.

"Yeah, it's more than the bikes we got for the other kids," Willard agreed, "but not that much more. And besides…"

"And besides, you always wanted something like that when you were a kid, didn't you?" This time Catherine laughed.

"Okay, you caught me. But they didn't make motorized cars then. The only thing we had were clunky, pedal-driven sedans and fire-trucks. One of the kids on my block had one when I was six or seven and it broke my heart that I didn't.

"Of course, when he let me try once, I was almost too big and the pedals stuck and I ended up pushing it along with my feet, which wasn't all that much fun. But it was the principal of the thing."

Catherine was silent for a second before she sighed and nodded. "All right. At least we live in a safe neighborhood now. No one racing up and down the streets."

The car came home with them that day.

The moment he opened the huge box on Christmas morning, Sams seemed possessed by the car. He sat in it through all the morning festivities, even though the battery hadn't been connected and not even the horn would work. He sat in it mock-steering and making his own hooting horn sounds while the rest of the family trooped out to the garage to be surprised by their own sets of wheels, bicycles in a variety of styles, colors, and sizes. He wanted to sit in it when Catherine called everyone in for the traditional Christmas breakfast of freshly baked cinnamon rolls and hot chocolate.

"No you don't, buster. No spilling on my brand new carpet," Catherine had said, trying to sound stern but failing so miserably that both she and Sams burst out in hysterical laughter.

But he was allowed to take it outside right after breakfast and, while the other three pedaled up and down Oleander Place, occasionally joined by other small riders on other pristine bicycles, Sams drove his Vette in tight little circles on the driveway, beeping away and waving at Catherine every time he passed her standing by the garage door.

It had been a very good Christmas.

By early February, Sams was allowed to ride not only on the driveway but for three yard-lengths on each side of Oleander. At the end of the rose border on one side, he would dutifully turn around—staying carefully on the sidewalk—and ride back around, past his own driveway, and down the other side to where the white picket fence began, then turn around and repeat the process.

Left to himself, he would probably have been happy to putt around all day. Still, an hour or so in the afternoons usually satisfied him.

2.

Willard was in a hurry when he backed out of the garage early that Friday evening.

He had just gotten home—a couple of hours before usual, as it turned out, since his current project had been abruptly cancelled. He wasn't in a particularly good mood because of the interruption in his routine, but he was happy to be able to spend some more time with the kids. He wasn't generally around in the afternoons when they arrived home from school.

He was just settling in to work on a jigsaw puzzle in the family room with Will, Jr., Burt, and Suze, when he heard Catherine yelp from the kitchen.

Roaches was his first thought. But no elongated scream followed the short outburst, so he tentatively relaxed.

"Willard," Catherine called. No terror in her voice, just the everyday we've-got-a-minor-crisis pitch that any parent of small children might recognize.

He rose, careful not to disturb the scattered puzzle pieces, and made his way through a small disaster area of roll- and push-toys that Sams hadn't gotten around to putting away.

"What is it?" he called...just as he got the first whiff of smoke—thick, cloying, unmistakable. "What's wrong?" This time there was more urgency in his voice.

"Oh, nothing. Just this da...this stupid waffle iron. Again!"

The family-sized waffle iron was a virtual antique, the final fossilized relic of their wedding reception. It was a gift from one of Catherine's aunts, who gave one—identical in make and model—to each of her nine nephews and nieces as they married. Originally gleaming in chrome and black, the iron was now stained and streaked by spatters of ancient grease and the baked-on spilled-over remains of thousands of pancakes and waffles, all seemingly impervious to even Catherine's meticulous close-inspection cleaning.

Recently, it had begun taking forever for the heating element to get hot enough, and when the orange alert light finally went out, the resulting waffles were more often than not irregular, burned on one edge, half-raw on the other.

Now it sat on the countertop, its cord coiled sinuously over the tiles, its plug hanging like something dead over the edge of the stainless-steel sink, and the plastic cover of the outlet just above it blackened with a smear of greasy smoke.

"I just plugged it in, and the outlet sparked and then spurted flame. I yanked the plug and everything stopped. But I think the iron has finally shorted out."

"It's about time," Willard said. "It's old enough. Must have at least a hundred thousand miles on it by now." He leaned over the counter to give the offending appliance a cursory inspection. "What about spaghetti for dinner?"

"I've already promised the kids their favorite waffles. They've really been helpful today. And they like them so much. Everything's ready...except the iron."

The kids called Catherine's waffles *Super-waffles*. Willard glanced down the countertop and saw a row of little bowls already set out, filled with grated cheese, bacon bits, slivered walnuts, and chocolate chips. Each of the kids requested a special combination of ingredients, baked into the crispy waffles, then topped with maple syrup, raspberry jelly, or peanut butter and honey.

Some of their choices set Willard's teeth on edge, but the kids loved them.

"I guess I could run on down to Sav-on and see if they have an iron available," Willard said.

"They do," Catherine responded, perhaps a bit too quickly. "I saw one just the other day. I was going to buy it but hoped this one would last a little longer. I probably should have known better."

Willard sighed and shrugged. "Okay, let me get my coat and wallet. I won't be gone long."

"And while you're there, would you pick up some dessert," Catherine added as he disappeared down the hall.

She turned back to mixing the waffle batter.

Neither of them saw Sams standing in the kitchen doorway, listening intently.

3.

It took a couple of minutes for Willard to slip on his winter jacket, rummage through his suit pants for his wallet, convince the three children still seated around the jigsaw puzzle that they really would have more fun staying at home this time rather than tagging along to the store, and finally step into the garage.

Almost instantly, he felt a surge of anger flood through him.

He knew that he had lowered the double-sized garage door when he got home earlier. He distinctly remembered thumbing the remote and watching in the rear-view mirror as the heavy wooden panel slid down, then grabbing his briefcase from the passenger seat and climbing out.

He knew he had.

But now the door stood gaping open. Again. For the past few days, the automatic opener had been malfunctioning, erratically closing when the door was half open, opening unexpectedly when the door seemed firmly closed.

He'd have to get the motor fixed. And the back part of the foundation, he reminded himself furiously. The door was just one more thing to do. Shit.

He slid into the front seat of the car, buckled himself in, and turned the key.

At least the car started smoothly. No troubles there.

He began rolling out of the garage and down the driveway, gaining speed on the slight incline from the house to the street.

And suddenly slammed on the brake, jerking to a halt and jamming his chest painfully against the webbing of his seatbelt. For an instant he could not breathe and his vision went black.

Something red and silver had winked into sight in his side-view mirror, abruptly emerging from behind the dense, head-high shrubs that filled a small triangle between the driveway, the front sidewalk, and the side fence—virtually the only landscaping on the property that didn't look newly planted. Whatever it was had winked into sight, glimmered for an instant, and disappeared.

Behind the car!

Before he could even consciously register what he had seen, he knew—he *knew*—what it was.

Sams' new toy…with Sams' driving!

He had thrust the car into park, twisted the key in the ignition, released his seat-belt, and was halfway along the length of the car before his mind truly began functioning.

Those damned bushes. I knew they were too tall. I knew someone was going to get hurt some day. And now Sams!

Each beat of his heart clarified in his mind what he would see—what he *must* see…the small body lying crushed on the cracked concrete of the sidewalk, blood streaming from broken flesh to flow, dark and thick and cloying, into the crevices, into the earth beneath, sinking in deeper and deeper, to contaminate and corrupt….

As he reached the back fender and could see clearly behind the car—the empty sidewalk behind the car—he heard a long, high giggle from the passenger side, then saw Sams putting up the driveway and into the darkened garage. The boy executed a perfect circle with his tiny car, sliding with practiced ease into a spot next to the three parked bicycles.

As he climbed out, he lifted a small plastic bucket—his sand-castle bucket, Willard realized—now filled with half a dozen large, glossy oranges. He was grinning widely, proud of himself for helping.

"See, Daddy! I picked up dessert, too!"

4.

Almost before dawn the next morning, Willard stalked into the front yard, dressed in an old, thread-bare Pendleton shirt and a thick nylon vest, and began savagely slashing at the stand of bushes with a pair of long-handled, wickedly sharp, tree loppers.

It had taken Catherine the better part of an hour to calm Willard down the night before, so shaken was he at the realization that he could so easily have run over his son. First he blamed himself, then he blamed the bushes, then he blamed the previous owners who had planted the damned things where they would block the view like that. Then he blamed himself again, for buying the damned house in the first place, with its roaches and its cracked foundation.

The only person he didn't blame was Sams.

Dinner was a fiasco. Even though the kids intuited that something was wrong, that something had happened outside that Mom and Dad were studiously talking about only in hissed whispers, they were nonetheless upset when Catherine announced that, no, there wouldn't be any super waffles for dinner tonight.

"But you promised…."

"Mommm!"

And so on until Willard thundered, "Quiet!" and startled the kids so badly that Sams, who had no idea at all what was going on, started to cry.

Finally, though, dinner was over, the kids were settled for the night, Catherine and Willard were lying in bed talking quietly.

"Tomorrow, they go."

"Maybe we could call someone to take them out for us. You know, a professional gardner…."

"No. First thing in the morning. I'm not waiting another day."

So first thing in the morning, Willard began. His face tensed in an expression somewhere between concentration and obsession, he began.

At first the job wasn't so difficult. The plants were dense, woody, with leaves dusty green on one surface, a pale, rusty gold underneath. Even so, the newest growth was still tender, easy to cut.

As he worked his way down, however, the older shoots grew more thickly, intertwined so complexly that it was impossible to cut just one and pull it away from the rest. Again and again, he struggled to work the loppers through the woody heart of the shoots, until his shoulders and hands began to ache. His fingers throbbed from the strain, cramped when he took a moment for a break and loosened his grip on the handles.

Under his breath, without consciously realizing it, he began to curse, fluidly, angrily, letting words slip easily between his lips that he would normally never have even thought. Images flickered in and out of his mind, images of bloody bodies, and broken bones, and shattered skulls.

He slashed more violently at the plants.

In spite of the cool day, he began to sweat profusely. The thick flannel shirt hung along his back, sodden and sticky. Finally, he stripped out of his vest, removed the shirt and threw it on the ground behind him, slipped back into the vest, and, bare-armed, began again.

Hack. Slice. Wrench and pull.

And again.

"Dad, can I help?" Willard hadn't heard Will, Jr., approach, hadn't been aware that the sun was midway up in the cloudless sky and that he was panting and nearly shaking. He jumped in surprise...and anger at the interruption—even though a part of him welcomed a distraction from the directions his thoughts were carrying him.

"What?" He turned too quickly and for a moment felt dizzy. Then the disorientation passed. "What?"

"Can I help? I could...."

"No. I'm taking care of it. Thanks."

"But...."

"No. You heard me. No. Go away, Will."

Willard bent back to the task.

When Catherine came out some time later—he didn't know how long it had been—to hand him a glass of water, he barely acknowledged her. He took a long swallow, then poured the rest of the cool water over his head.

"Willard, you'll give yourself pneumonia if you don't...."

"I'm all right. Let me alone to work." Then hack. Slice. Wrench and pull.

It must have been mid-afternoon when he finally finished gutting the worst part of the bushes. He could almost see bare earth, and the bulk of the greenery lay thrown haphazardly behind him.

At ground level the stems were too thick for the loppers.

Instead, he had to get on his hands and knees and, using a small arced pruning saw, sever each one individually a foot or so from the hard-pan soil.

His back ached. His hands ached. His arms were covered with tiny scratches from sharp twigs, with a fine film of sweat mixed with loose dirt, flecks of sawdust, and a light, pale dust that must have rubbed off the undersides of the leaves. He was hungry. But he couldn't stop to eat. He had to get rid of these bushes.

They had nearly killed his son.

Abruptly, behind him, he heard small voices whispering, branches rustling. He glanced over his shoulder.

Catherine, Will, Burt, and Suze were bagging the greenery and dragging the packed black garbage bags along the side of the garage. Catherine cut the thicker stems into foot-long lengths with anvil shears, her hands encased in thick leather gloves, and then the kids picked up the short pieces and stuffed them into the bags.

For an instant, Willard felt an overwhelming urge to tell them to get the hell away from here, to leave the damned things alone, that he would take care of them because that was *his* job and *they had nearly killed his son*! He had even worked his way off his throbbing knees, using the loppers for support, and was half turned to face them when something in his brain went *snaaaap*! and, suddenly reeling for an instant with the same sense of disorientation that had struck him earlier, he shook his head and started to speak.

Catherine and the kids were standing in front of him, stock still. She still held the shears in one hand, an uncut branch in the other. Will had frozen in the act of lifting a filled bag. Burt and Suze dropped the bits of leafy detritus they had collected.

"Where's Sams?"

"Taking a nap." Catherine sounded cautious, unsure of whether to say anything more.

"Oh. Okay." Willard shuffled for a moment. Then: "Thanks, guys. For helping out, I mean. I guess I was a bit...uh...a bit short with you this morning, Will. And you, too, Catherine."

Catherine nodded. The kids remained like stones.

He was going to say something else, realized that he didn't quite know what, then knelt again and began sawing raggedly at the next stump. But he threw a quick glance over his shoulder and said "Thanks. Again."

With everyone helping—even Sams a short while later, after he emerged from the house, wiping sleep from his eyes and dragging his blanket across the filthy concrete until Catherine yelped in horror at the sight and set the grimy thing carefully on a folded garbage bag—with everyone working at cutting, trimming, bagging, and stacking, they finished by late afternoon.

As a thank you, Willard took the whole crew to the nearest McDonalds and let the kids have anything they wanted for dinner.

"Just this once," he said in answer to Catherine's reproachful glance. "I was a beast to everyone this morning, and they really did a great job when I finally came to my senses. They deserve it."

And they all enjoyed it.

By the time they returned home, however, Willard realized that he was in some discomfort. His hands and fingers seemed stiff, swollen, and the skin on his arms tingled painfully. Even though he had showered and changed before the family had gone out to eat, Catherine ordered him into the shower again.

"That looks like a rash coming," she said, pointing to a line of redness along the inside of his arm, a roughened patch of skin extending from elbow to wrist. "I'll bet there were some oils or something in those leaves, and you might be allergic. That might be why your fingers are swollen, too."

She handed him a small pill and a cup of cool water. "Antihistamine. Just in case."

He stood for a long while under the hot spray, soaping his arms and shoulders, washing his hands thoroughly, rinsing off, then soaping again. As he did, he felt knots in his muscles loosen, but even more importantly his mind—still vivid and fretful—eased as well. When he eventually emerged, he felt slightly weak, as wrinkled as a raisin, and finally, thoroughly clean. The redness along his arms was still there, but fainter. His fingers were swollen and stiff but he could almost make a fist when he tried.

He put on his heavy terry-cloth robe and wandered out into the family room.

It was empty.

"Catherine?"

"Back here." Her voice came from the bedrooms.

He sauntered down the hall, feeling pleasantly tired and relaxed. She met him outside the door to their bedroom and shunted him inside.

"The kids are down."

"Asleep already?"

"No, I told them they could play in the boys' room for a while...quietly." She reached behind her and carefully shut the door. "And they've been threatened with mayhem and dismemberment...all right, with spending tomorrow without any TV privileges," she emended at the look of surprise on Willard's face, "if they so much as step foot down the hall beyond Suze's doorway tonight."

She smiled, and with a couple of deft movements, slipped Willard's robe from his shoulders.

"Now it's your turn to be quiet." She turned him toward the bed and gave him a little push, just enough that he toppled face forward onto the covers. "You deserve something special tonight, something to make your poor, tired muscles relax."

She settled herself beside him and began kneading his shoulders and back, the length of his arms, then moved on to the long muscles of his thighs and legs.

From somewhere, he could smell a faint fragrance. Incense maybe. Or aromatic oils. Catherine liked both.

He sighed. He waited a long while before speaking.

"You know, Catherine, I...I think there might be something...wrong with me," he finally said, his voice little more than a whisper.

Her hands paused, then resumed their tender ministrations.

"What do you mean, sweetie?"

"All day, at least until you guys came out this afternoon, I felt...I don't know, *angry* isn't quite the right word. It went beyond anger. Red-hot fury, at least part of the time. Sometimes it felt as if I weren't cutting wood, as if I were tearing at flesh, or at least as if I *wanted* to."

Again her hands paused. Longer this time.

"Oh, Willard," she whispered. "I knew you were...you weren't really yourself this morning. You're never that short with Will, especially when he wants to give you a hand with something. When he came inside, he was...well, frightened. He said you looked really...different. Scary."

"I felt scary. And scared. Like all I wanted to do was lash out and hurt and kill." He shivered. Catherine began smoothing his skin again. Her hands were soft, and warm.

"Thank God those damned...sorry, those bushes were there. I could almost feel the need to hurt drain out of me as I snapped those loppers back and forth. Snap. Snap."

Catherine leaned over and kissed him on the back of the neck. "Shhh. Are you all right now?"

He rolled over to face her. And kissed her back.

"Yes."

"I can see," she whispered. And smiled.

The rest of the night passed...well, not quite uneventfully, but Willard didn't mind.

That was one of the last truly comfortable nights they spent for a long while.

The next day, the sky clouded over. The weatherman on the television predicted rain.

A lot of rain.

5.

Rain can be a rarity in Southern California. Particularly in the Los Angeles basin, where two, three, even four years of drought conditions are seldom enough to remind the floods of immigrants from less congenial states that the land their homes and condos and apartments and mobile homes rest on is essentially desert. In spite of seemingly endless vistas of meticulously landscaped emerald green lawns dotted by the false turquoise of ceramic pools, the basin is arid.

Some rainfall during the deep months of what passes for winter in the season-less sameness of Southern California is normal. A day or two, perhaps—three at the most—of light sprinkling is considered within the bounds of normal. More than that constitutes virtually apocalyptic flooding.

It began raining somewhere after midnight the next Thursday. On Friday, fully recovered from the stiffness in his hands, with the rash completely gone, Willard drove to work as usual. The freeways were mushy and slick with built-up grease released just enough by the rain to make conditions unpredictable, hazardous. Because of the slow traffic, he arrived at work forty minutes later than usual. That set the tone for the rest of the day. He arrived home nearly two hours late.

"Are you all right?" Catherine asked the moment he stomped through the front door, water dripping in sheets from his woefully inadequate excuse for raingear.

"Sure," he said as he shrugged out of the overcoat and shook it outside trying to remove as much moisture as possible before bringing the water-laden garment indoors.

"Let me take that," she said. She picked the coat up with two fingers and carried it to the first bathroom and hung it on a hanger over the shower curtain.

"Is it bad?" she asked, her voice muffled by the door.

"Worse," Willard muttered as he toed off his shoes. His socks were wet, the cuffs on his pants—his best suit pants— were wet for a foot or more up his legs. His shoulders were damp. He felt sodden, drenched inside and out.

Catherine reappeared from the bathroom carrying a vivid purple beach towel that had somehow slipped into the daily-use stack in the linen closet and was now unofficially "Daddy's" towel.

He scrubbed his face and hair with the coarse material.

"Get out of these clothes," Catherine said as she helped him out of his suit jacket. "You're a mess."

"And this is just from running from the driveway to the front door," he said, suppressing a shiver. "The garage door wouldn't open again. I don't know, maybe it's the remote. I'll have to get it checked. Soon."

"Honey, you're freezing," Catherine said as she felt his hand. "Hurry and change. I'll make some tea. That'll warm you up."

"Sounds good," he said, already halfway down the hall toward the bedroom.

The Levelor blinds were drawn, so the room was dark. Even with the furnace running, the room felt miserable, clammy and damp. He shivered again. He stripped his wet things off, dropping pants, shirt, socks, underwear in a heap on the floor.

No use hanging up the suit, he thought. It'll have to be dry cleaned after this, no matter what.

He rummaged naked through his closet, finally pulling out his thick terry-cloth robe and slipping it on. The action stirred memories—wonderfully pleasant memories. He smiled. He shoved his feet into slippers and, for the first time all day, began to feel warm. He felt his muscles relaxing.

He turned to leave the room, and as he did so, he noticed something.

In the dim light, he almost didn't see it. Perhaps if he had blinked at the wrong instant, he wouldn't have seen it at all. But there it was. In the corner, just below the line where textured ceiling joined wall, there was a jagged hairline crack, no more than two or three inches long. His stomach wrenched.

That's all I need, he thought. After this rain, after nearly getting drowned because the garage door is defective, to look up and see this.

He gritted his teeth.

Hair still damp from the rain, still wearing nothing but his bathrobe, he began padding slowly through the house, beginning with the back bedrooms, progressing to the bathrooms, the hall, the entry, the family room, the living room, ending up in the kitchen.

"Willard," Catherine said, a note of scolding in her voice. "What are you doing barefoot? You'll catch your death." She held out a bright red mug, steam coiling from the surface of its contents. "Here, this will help."

He ignored the mug and instead continued his slow, almost stalking survey of the kitchen, each wall, the ceiling, the floor tiles under the back window, several still ragged and broken from the night he punched through them with the paring knife to reveal the roach-filled rift.

"There's more of them," he said, almost absently.

"More of what?"

"Cracks."

Catherine glanced around. Now that he mentioned it, she could see tiny cracks in the angles where walls joined walls, where walls joined ceiling. She turned a slow circle. There was a thin shadow connecting one corner of the doorjamb to the ceiling. Another starting from the far corner of the window and spidering upward a foot or so.

"I hadn't really noticed them," she murmured.

"They're in every room. Every one," Willard said.

"Mom. Dad," came Burt's voice from the living room, just a few tones away from whining. "Will's cheating."

"What?" Catherine and Willard answered at the same time, turning to face their middle son.

"He's cheating!" This time the voice was sterner. Burt obviously felt more comfortable with his complaint now that he had his parents' attention.

"They've been playing Monopoly since they got home

from school," Catherine said. "They couldn't go out, and they were getting antsy, so I let them take the board into the boys' bedroom.

Catherine's father had introduced Will, Jr., and Burt to the wonders of high finance the previous Thanksgiving at her family's home in Santa Barbara, while she and her mother were cleaning up after the traditional family feast and Willard and Catherine's youngest brother sat transfixed by one football game or another.

Neither of the boys had quite grasped the subtleties of the game, but since Grandpa hadn't been too strict about the rules, they had gradually evolved their own version, one that was a bit faster, a bit wilder, a bit more cut-throat than a strict interpretation of game protocols might normally have allowed.

After several hours at the board, as they were putting the pieces away and carefully separating the play money into appropriate piles, Grandpa said, "Why don't you guys take this on home with you. Grandma and I don't play it anymore so you may as well."

Both boys went running into the kitchen. "Mom, can we, can we?"

It took a minute or two for Catherine to figure out what they were yelling about, since their voices overlapped so much that she couldn't quite understand the words, and her father just stood in the doorway, grinning, no help at all.

But in a few moments, the Huntley children were the proud owners of one well-used Monopoly set. It was a special-occasions-only treat for them, since they routinely became so engrossed that their games threatened to go on for hours. Rainy days frequently counted as special occasions.

"Okay, what's going on?" Willard spoke from the open doorway, Catherine behind him and Burt scuttling beneath his arm and squatting in his usual position by the board.

Will, Jr., sat there, looking owlishly up at his parents, his eyes wide with innocence but the trace of a grin—almost a gloat—hovering on his lips. Suze was across from Will, also her usual position, her face flushed and her eyes screwed up as if to keep from crying. Sams crouched along the side of the board between Suze and Will. He held a handful of play money in his chubby fists—he played Banker, holding out money when required so the others could take what they needed

Three voices answered Willard's question.

"Nothing!" A sharp treble with a hint of a crack in it.

"Will's cheating!" Burt's voice.

"Will's hiding money under the board! He knows he's not s'posed to hide money under the board." Suze was a stickler for rules, even if the kids had made them up themselves.

Willard held out his hand.

"All right! All right! Enough!"

Silence fell.

"You guys know what happens if you fight over a game."

"But, Dad...!" This time four voices tumbled over each other, Sams' joining the rest.

"No. You know what happens."

"Okay," Will, Jr., said. Shoulders slumped, he started picking up bills that had been scattered on the board and the surrounding carpet during the disagreement. Burt collected houses and hotels, dropping them into the proper slot in the box. Suze gathered up the tokens and put them away. Sams just sat there a few bills still grasped between his fingers. Will, Jr., had to pull them out of his hands before Sams finally gave up. Only then did he start to sniffle, prelude to a cry.

"Bedtime," Catherine said, stepping around Willard.

"But...." Again, all four chimed in.

"I know you haven't had any time with Daddy, but he was late because of the rain. And there's school tomorrow, so scoot, all of you."

None of them scooted, precisely. But under Catherine's and Willard's watchful eyes, they meandered through their evening rituals, finally settling themselves in their beds. Suze turned her light out without being asked.

Willard reached around the door jamb to flick the switch in

the boys' room.

"No!" Sams was sitting bolt upright in his box bed. He had his blanket pressed so tightly against his cheek that his knuckles glowed white in the overhead glare. "No! Light!"

Willard glanced at Catherine. This was new. None of their children—Sams included—had ever indicated any untoward fear of the darkness. Even Sams had slept without a night light since he was two.

Catherine knelt by his side.

"Come on, Sams. You know everything is all right, even with the light out."

"No!"

This time Catherine heard a touch of panic in his voice. She rubbed his back, trying to comfort him.

"Oh, let it be," Willard said from the hallway. "Just for tonight."

She shot him a sharp look. They had discussed this when Sams was first trying to sleep in a darkened room, and they had agreed that he was old enough. Anyway, his two brothers were in there with him, and he could crawl in with Burt if he woke in the middle of the night. And besides, they had a hard and fast rule—never disagree in front of the kids, especially when there was already a rule in place.

"Willard?" There was an unspoken question in the way she said his name.

He caught it.

"Just this once."

"Just this once," Sams piped in imitation. "Light?"

Catherine hesitated. To make an issue of it would probably reinforce whatever it was that was bothering Sams. But she didn't want to give in completely.

"All right. We'll leave the hall light on and the door open. That okay, Sams?"

He nodded, already relaxing under her touch.

She laid him back, tucked his covers around him—careful not to hide his blanket—and crossed to the door. Willard had already turned on the hall light. She snapped off the one in the boys' room.

"Good night."

"Night" came quietly from both bedrooms.

6.

"What were you thinking in there?" Catherine was almost whispering, even though she and Willard were at the opposite end of the house from the boys.

Willard shrugged and sipped his coffee. "I didn't think it really mattered that much. Just this once."

Catherine shook her head. "But after they were punished for fighting over the game...."

"Punished?"

"Having to put it away like that. We've never done that before. We've always given them at least one more chance. Then knuckling under to Sams...."

"Knuckling under?"

Catherine started. She heard anger in Willard's voice, not right at the surface yet, but there nonetheless.

She reached out and laid her hand on his.

"Willard, what's wrong? This isn't like...."

"Nothing," he said curtly. Then he took a deep breath and sighed. "Nothing, really. I guess I was just tired. First that horrendous trip home—the freeway was like glass, the rain was so hard that the wipers could barely keep up, and red lights kept flashing right and left like crazy. There were so many cars jammed together that it seemed like there had to be a roadblock or an accident somewhere up ahead, but there never was, just car after car after car creeping along like slugs.

"Then the garage door not working when I got home, and me getting drenched like that. And then the cracks...."

"Sweetie, don't...."

Willard's hand slammed against the table top. "Dammit, don't tell me to...."

Startled at the hurt expression in her eyes, he stopped, placed his hand over hers, and sighed.

"It's like all of a sudden everything is going wrong. The kids arguing like that, us arguing, the rain…and this house, falling apart and we haven't even been in it three months. And that creep Maxwell shrugging it off like it was nothing.

"We were *cheated*! And then he just blows us off like it was nothing. 'The house isn't going to fall in any time soon. Maybe in forty or fifty years, but not tomorrow.'

"Right. Only it isn't *his* kids that have to live in it, *his* wife that…. I feel like a total failure."

"Willard."

He looked at Catherine, suddenly realizing that he was holding his breath in…anger? No, *fury*. He had never felt this way in his life, so impotent, so helpless, so…so *cheated*! *Screwed*!

"It's not worth it, honey. Not tonight. There's nothing we can do right now. Tomorrow we'll call the county inspector or something, get someone out here who can help us. It will all work out. You know it will."

Willard took several deep breaths. "Okay. You're right. Maybe tomorrow everything will look better. Maybe the rain will stop."

7.

But the rain didn't stop.

If anything, it was pouring harder when Willard struggled awake at 5:00, showered and shaved, threw on his clothes, grabbed a left-over corn muffin from yesterday's breakfast, and shuffled off to work.

It was pouring even harder than that—solid sheets of water that almost obscured the world outside and left eerie dark patterns on the windows—a few hours later when Catherine finally had all of the kids up and seated at the breakfast, putting the finishing touches on their school lunches.

"I don't want peanut butter and jelly," Burt muttered. "I

always have peanut butter and jelly."

"But that's your favorite, isn't it?" Catherine knew that he insisted on the same thing every day for his lunch, had insisted on it since his first day in kindergarten.

"No. I hate it."

"Well, I'm sorry, but your lunch is already made and packed and you'll just have to eat it."

"No!"

Catherine turned to stare at him. Will, Jr., and Suze were staring at Burt as well. Sams ignored his bigger brother, intent on destroying his bowl of Sugar Crisps and drawing circles in spilled milk on the tray of his high chair.

"Burt!" Catherine's voice was sharper than she intended. "It's made and you'll eat it."

"But…."

"Don't argue with me." She glared at him, unsure herself why it was so important that she win this small tug-of-wills. Usually she wouldn't have minded, just made him a tuna sandwich like she made for Will and Suze. And peanut and butter *was* his favorite. The whole family knew that. Burt would almost rather have that than a bowl of chocolate fudge ice cream, his second favorite thing. But today….

"Okay," Burt muttered, lowering his gaze to his plate. He spooned fitfully at his own bowl of cereal, complete with milk, slopping soggy bits onto the table.

"Burt! Don't do that…." Catherine suddenly broke off.

With the part of her mind that mother's use to keep track of everything going on around her even while dealing with her children, she had heard something on the radio that she turned on each morning while setting breakfast out. The announcer's voice was low, almost inaudible, and rarely intruded into her conscious awareness.

"…reports the following school closures because of unexpected flooding in the…."

"What's wrong, Mom?" Will turned to look at the radio.

"Shhh."

"For the Newton Park area...."

"It sounds like they're closing some of the schools today. Too much rain. Shhh."

"...and for Tamarind Valley, Reagan Jr. High, Pitt Elementary, Redwood Heights Elementary, Greenwood Elementary, Charter Oaks Elementary...."

Hearing the name of their school, Burt and Suze broke out into spontaneous cheering. Will was quieter but a broad grin creased his face.

"No school, no school, no school...," the younger two chanted. Sams waved his arms up and down and joined the chorus. "No school, no school, no school...."

Will restrained himself.

Catherine sighed. No school today. Great.

8.

It wasn't half an hour after she had herded the four kids into the back bedroom to play and settled herself down to cleaning the kitchen and finally making herself some toast and tea when the front door opened, then slammed shut.

"Willard?" She jumped to her feet and started toward the entryway just in time to see him stamping his feet and dropping his sodden raincoat onto the tile.

Oh, no. The garage door opener again.

"What happened?" Somehow he looked different than he had when he got home last night, even though he was just as drenched. Did the car break down? Was he feeling ill? After all, last night had been difficult for him.

"You're not going to believe this." Willard looked as if wanted to laugh and curse at the same time. She'd never seen such an expression on his face before.

"What?"

The freeway's flooded. The *freeway*!"

Catherine didn't quite know what to say.

"Just before you get to the San Fernando Valley, you know

where the freeway takes that deep dip before the final hill? Well, apparently it's flooded there. All eight lanes. Traffic both directions is stopped completely! I couldn't believe it."

"But you've been gone for hours."

"Yeah." Now the odd look was replaced by a grimace. "It took nearly two hours for the highway patrol to funnel everyone off the freeway and onto that little, single-lane access road heading back toward Tamarind. You wouldn't believe the mess.

"And even that road was nearly flooded in a couple of places, so we had to slow down to ten miles an hour or so. It's unbelievable."

By this time, he and Catherine were back in the kitchen, sitting around the table. She was pouring Willard a cup of tea and refreshing her own.

"Then it took another hour or so to negotiate the surface roads. Half of them were either shut down completely or restricted to one-way traffic only because of mud slides along the hills. I didn't think I was ever going to make it home.

"But that's not even the worst of it," he said after taking a long sip and shivering slightly at the sudden warmth. "I was listening to the radio the whole time, trying to figure out what roads to take. The freeway is shut at the northern end of the valley as well, just before the Camarillo grade, right where the eight lanes narrow to six. No way out to the north.

"And the road at Norwegian grade has actually slid halfway down the hillside at one place. There's only part of one lane left, and the cops have shut it down completely as well.

"Basically, were cut off. There's no way out of Tamarind right now, at least not until the rain stops. Literally, no way out."

Catherine stirred her tea. "The schools are closed as well. Here and in Newton Park both. And a lot of the houses in the higher parts of Coastal Crest are in danger of sliding if the hills get any more unstable."

"All this after only a day and a night of this rain. What will happen if it continues as long as the forecasters predict?"

It did. The rain didn't ease for four days, when traffic

was finally allowed to travel north and south on the freeway. Norwegian grade wouldn't be usable for seven or eight months, depending on how long it would take to carve a new roadway out of the hillside. And in the lower parts of Tamarind Valley, some of the housing developments were cut off stores and businesses for almost a week.

Charter Oaks fared better.

It was built on a small rise, not quite a hill exactly but one of the higher parts of the valley. The Huntleys were not totally isolated. When they ran out of milk on the third day, Willard could negotiate the rain-sodden streets far enough to buy more— along with toilet paper, that other necessity for any household with multiple children. But for all intents and purposes, even they were housebound.

Two adults. Four children. Two hamsters. And a dog.

The rain continued to fall so hard for three of the four days that, except that single trip to the store, none of them left the house.

It was a big enough house. Everyone had a place to go for a moment of peace and quiet. But mostly they spent the days in the family. Willard watched TV, alternating between whatever sports events he could find and the incessant "Storm Watch" reports on half the channels. He missed going to work. He felt almost uncomfortable stranded in the house, with nothing purposeful he could do. He fidgeted, finding it increasingly difficult to concentrate on anything. Several times, when one of the kids raised a voice—whether in pique or even once when Sams abruptly shrieked with laughter at something Will, Jr., had done—he felt a deep irritation, something like the infant cousin of the fury the first night of the rains. A couple of times he couldn't keep himself from almost yelling at them to be quiet. He wasn't at all happy. He wanted to get out of the house.

Catherine watched with half an eye, mostly when reports on the "Storm-of-the-Decade" were on, and the rest of her attention on knitting scarves and sweaters for nieces and nephews that lived in colder climates. Although not an imperceptive wife, she noticed nothing particularly wrong with the way Willard was behaving.

The kids played Monopoly. One marathon game. The three oldest sat in their usual places around the board, rolling the dice and moving their tokens—there was an odd bit of squabbling at the beginning, when Burt grabbed the Boot, Suze's favorite, and Will took Burt's favorite piece in retaliation. It took an intervention by Catherine and a warning from Willard that the game would be put away for the duration if anything like that happened again to settle things.

Sams seemed perfectly happy to squat along the fourth side, holding out handfuls of money whenever it was needed. When he got tired, he simply rolled over and fell asleep on the floor, his blanket tucked securely along his cheek.

So they played, breaking only to eat and go to the bathroom and, somewhat later than usual, head unwillingly to bed. When Suze ran out of money on the first day, Will loaned her some. When Burt hit "Go Directly to Jail" three times in a row, Suze calmed him down.

And the rain continued. They could hear the constant drumming on the roof, and the splattering of drops on the picture window behind the couch. Oleander Place became a small river of runoff.

And the rain continued.

9.

When it came, the break in the monotonous routine was sudden and devastating.

On the morning of the fourth day, just before the rain tapered off, diminished to a restless drizzle, and finally stopped completely (although none of the Huntley family ever thought of that as the day the rain stopped), about an hour after breakfast and well into the never-ending monopoly game, Sams suddenly stood up and wandered down the hall.

No one paid any real attention.

A few minutes later, he returned carrying one of his favorite toys, a clear plastic ball in which either Yip or Yap, the boys' hamsters, could race around the floor, constantly delighting Sams as well as the rest of them. The short-nubbed carpeting in the family was just right for the ball—it slowed Yip or Yap sufficiently that Sams could keep up with whichever one was exercising at the moment, yet allowed the hamster to race along fast enough to keep everyone entertained.

Solemnly, Sams placed the ball on the floor by the game board. The he went to stand beside Burt.

"Help me?"

"What?" Burt kept looking at the board, intent on the fact that if Will threw a seven, his older brother would be confronted by the horrifying fact of landing on Park Palace…with three hotels. Burt waved his little brother away absently.

"Help me?"

"Burt," Willard said from the couch, barely removing his eyes from the television, "help your brother."

Burt finally glanced up, saw Sams, then saw the plastic ball sitting on the floor. He understood at once what was needed.

"Okay," he said with a sigh. "Don't roll until I get back," he instructed Will, Jr. He wanted to be there for the big moment.

The two boys disappeared down the hall.

They were gone for several minutes, longer than it should have taken to retrieve either Yip or Yap from its hiding place in the cedar chips.

Neither Willard nor Catherine noticed the time, although Will, Jr., wriggled in impatience at the wait.

Finally, Burt came down the hall, followed by Sams.

"Dad," Burt said quietly.

"Yeah."

"Dad, Yip won't play with us."

"Then bring Yap out," The boys could apparently tell the two hamsters apart, although to Willard's adult eyes they looked identical. "Maybe Yip's eating or something."

"No, he's just laying there. He won't get up to play with us."

This time Willard heard a note of anxiety in Burt's voice. He stood, casting a knowing—almost an accusatory—glance at Catherine. They had been waiting for this to happen ever since she had talked him into letting the kids have the things. Neither of them were particularly eager for what they both knew was coming. Catherine put aside her knitting and rose as well.

Will, Jr., and Suze simply sat at the game board, as if standing guard lest some errant breeze shift the playing pieces.

Willard led the way down the dark hallway toward the back bedroom. The room itself was cast into murky shadow by the cloud cover outside. The little Mickey Mouse lamp was on but not the ceiling light.

He walked over to the small table that held the hamsters' cage. One of them, it must be Yap, was running circles on the exercise wheel, spinning away as if his little life depended on it. The other one, Yip, lay half hidden in cedar chips at the back of the cage.

Willard reached in.

Yap ignored him and kept the wheel spinning at breakneck speed.

Yip didn't move, either. Willard closed his hand around the bit of fur.

Nothing.

He lifted the hamster out of the cage, glanced over his shoulder at Catherine, and nodded. They had both had small pets as children. Small pets, however much loved and however well cared for, often did not live long.

He led the small parade out of the bedroom and back into the family room.

"Will, put the ball away, will you?"

Will started to object, then took in the fact that his father—who almost never played with the hamsters—was standing quietly above him, holding something in his hand.

"Okay." He picked up the toy and disappeared down the hall. He reappeared only a moment or so later.

"Come here, guys," Willard said, voice softer, more gentle

than it had been for the past several days.

The children gathered around his knees, their eyes on the mound of fur. Will, Jr., already had tears forming in his eyes. He knew. Burt probably guessed but was still processing. Suze looked confused. And Sams seemed to wonder why Yip didn't get up and look at him.

"I'm afraid that Yip...well, that Yip has...gone away."

"No he hasn't, Daddy," Suze replied immediately. "He's right there. In your hand."

"Right there," Sams added, pointing.

"I know, but...." Willard looked up at Catherine.

"What Daddy is trying to say is that Yip has gone to sleep, and he is going to stay asleep for a long, long time," she said, her voice as gently as Willard's.

"You mean he's...*dead*?" Burt had finally accepted what he already intuited. "Dead for good?"

Before Willard could answer, Suze breathed a quick "No," and bust into tears. Perhaps she didn't truly understand death, but she watched enough television—even the children's programming that Willard and Catherine preferred—to know the word. And to know that it wasn't a good thing.

Sams stared at his sister, then his tears joined hers, even though he had no idea what was happening.

Will, Jr., took a moment, then said, "We'll have to have a funeral. Right away."

Willard looked up at Catherine, who started to shrug, then her head moved up and down so slightly that none of the kids would have noticed even if they had seen it. They hadn't. Their attention was fixed on Yip.

Willard felt again that momentary stab of irritation grate through him. All right for her to say it was okay, but *he* was the one who was going to have to trudge out into the rain, or at least into the rain-soaked yard, to officiate at the obsequies.

"Can we, Daddy?" Burt asked.

"I guess so."

"When?" Suze said. "Right now." For her, there never seemed

to be a future, just the now.

Willard sighed, "Yeah, I guess so."

"We'll need a box or something first," Catherine said. Suze scuttled away down the hall. A moment later, they all heard a drawer close, rather more loudly than necessary, and she reappeared in the doorway, cradling a small wooden box.

"Oh, Suze," Catherine said, "That's the redwood box Grandma and Grandpa gave you when they went to Monterrey. You don't want to…."

"Yes, I do. Yip was my friend. I loved him." The boys nodded their approval at her sacrifice.

Catherine went to her knitting and rummaged around in the bottom of the bag she used. Finally she stood up and carried a small irregular ball of dark purple yarn. She placed it on the fragrant cedar lining of the small box and tugged at the yarn until it made a kind of nest.

"Is that all right?"

All four children nodded this time.

"Willard?"

He opened his hand to set the tiny body in the makeshift casket. As he did so, he really noticed Yip for the first time. Something seemed odd. The hamster's head looks strange, as if it were slightly flattened on one side, as if someone had….

He stared at the four children. Will, Jr., with his red-rimmed eyes and carefully stoic expression. Burt, his eyes full of hurt and loss. Suze and Sams, their tears still streaking their cheeks even though they were no longer crying.

No. Impossible. None of them would have….

He began to lower the hamster into the box. Yip's body hung limply from his fingers. Too limply, it seemed. On an impulse Willard felt along the hamsters back with his index finger.

Nothing. No stiffness where the backbone should be. Not exactly mushy, but…giving, resilient.

He almost withdrew his hand, almost decided to question the kids to see if any of them had accidently hurt Yip, then didn't. They loved the hamster. They would have told him if anything had happened.

He laid Yip in the center of the tumble of yarn, then pulled a few strands over the body.

"All right?"

Again the children nodded in unison.

He closed the box and turned the tiny clasp.

10.

It really was too wet to be out, even if the rain had stopped. Willard stepped out of the side kitchen door, boots on his feet, jacket zipped close against the damp air, casket in his hands, rain hat on his head just in case, and a small shovel propped over his shoulder. Three similarly clad figures—minus the shovel—followed. Catherine had remained in the family room with Sams, who seemed exhausted by the whole thing and was nodding off. When they left she was cradling him in her arms and rocking him as if he were an infant again.

The small procession rounded the corner of the house.

"What the...?" Willard caught himself just in time. Little pitchers.

The entire back yard looked as if it were a lake. He had expected most of the rain to drain off along the sides of the house, down the front lawn and driveway, and into the over-filled gutters on Oleander. That what would have made sense for a house situated at the top of a rise.

No, that hadn't happened. Instead, water had pooled every-where, shallowly in some spots, so that the tips of winter-dead grass emerged like miniature reeds in an oversized black swamp, so deep in others that the faint breeze that had followed the storm created rows of ripples on the surface.

Water had puddle against the back of the house as well, flooding most of the concrete patio, up to perhaps six feet from the sliding doors. It wouldn't have taken much more for it to flow on into the living room. At the back of the yard, the fence seemed almost to lean into the pools, as if the posts were stark trees torn away at their roots, rotting but not yet willing to die.

"I'm sorry, kids," he said without looking down at them. "There's no place dry enough to…for a funeral."

"Will we have to wait until the water goes away?" Burt asked. "How long will that take?"

Too long, Willard said to himself. Too long unless Catherine is willing to store the Yipper here in the freezer.

"I'm afraid it would take way too long. We should just…."

"Throw Yip away?" Will, Jr., spoke as if accusing his father of murder. "Toss him in the garbage?"

"No!"

"No!"

Burt and Suze began screaming their sorrow.

Willard could have killed Will for piping up like that. He threw his eldest son a withering glance that made Will, Jr., stumble back a step.

"Stop that!"

The younger two suddenly stifled their sobs.

Willard sighed. "Maybe there's someplace dryer along the far side of the house."

The procession recommenced, punctuated by the slap of boots against water and an occasional sniffle.

They rounded the side of the house. It was almost as bad here. The six-foot-wide stretch between house and fence was spotted by standing pools, but up against the house, beneath the protection of the eaves on one side and the neighboring row of yews on the other, the ground, while still sodden, was at least visible.

It would have to be here.

He paced a dozen steps or so until he stood toward the end of the long wall—right outside the windowless wall of the master bedroom. Where he could slip out some dark night after the kids were asleep and play grave-digger to the Yipper's final resting place. By then the thing would probably be little more than a repulsive mass of goo inside a stained and worm-eaten box. Then he could throw the whole thing away and the kids would never know. That way if he ever decided to cultivate a small garden in the bare stretch, he wouldn't unearth a nasty surprise.

"This all right?"

"Okay, Dad."

Again, the nods from the others.

He handed the box to Burt and began digging. The soil was marginally dryer closest to the house, so that's where he began. Shovel in. Shovel out. Shovel in. Shovel out.

Until....

"Those bas....!"

"What's wrong, Dad?" Will, Jr., looked thoroughly scared of something. Burt and Suze weren't far behind.

"Shut up," Willard snapped.

They shut.

He removed another shovelful of dirt from the edge of the concrete foundation.

About five inches beneath the top of the soil, a half-inch-wide crack snaked parallel to the ground.

"I don't bel...."

This time none of the children spoke. Willard had almost forgotten they were standing there, a couple of feet behind him, halfway to the fence, ankle deep in mud and water.

He scraped the shovel along the side of the house, revealing more of the wall between where he had begun and the front corner. The crack continued. If anything it grew wider, blacker, deeper. Ominous. Threatening, at least to Willard.

He reached the corner. There, the lower portion of the foundation had separated by nearly an inch from the upper, a couple of inches below where the stucco started. The bottom of the stucco—painted an ugly shade of yellow instead of the neutral brown of the rest of the house—was *beneath* the level of the soil.

He stood back, winded although he didn't notice that, and leaned against the shovel handle, forcing it gradually deeper into the muck. His shoulders and back throbbed, and his fingers ached.

He already knew that the back wall had separated from the foundation. Now *this*.

The whole damned house must be simply sitting on top of the slab—or next to it—with *nothing* pinning the two together!

He looked up under the eaves.

Those shitty builders!

He groaned.

"Dad," Will, Jr., whispered.

"Get into the house. Now. All of you!"

They got.

Willard scraped more dirt away from the stucco, this time retracing his steps toward the back corner. The crack followed his digging.

After about six feet he stopped and just stood there staring… and getting more furious by the moment.

Everything they owned invested in this place, everything they had hoped for, even their very *lives* maybe…and now *this*.

Finally he trudged his way back to the kitchen door and stalked in. Catherine stood there. The kids were gone. He couldn't hear them anywhere.

"Take off your boots, please."

"Huh?" He looked down as if surprised to see that he had feet.

"Your boots. You're muddying up the floor."

He toed the boots off, then in a moment of rage, kicked them out the open door. They splashed into a puddle about where he had planned to plant a peach tree come spring.

"What's wrong."

He didn't answer. He didn't trust himself to answer. He took several deep breaths. Then several more.

"The kids came back into the house. They were frightened. terrified. Of you, I think. They said that something happened back there. Burt still had the box clutched in his hand. What was it?"

Willard ran his fingers through his hair and slumped onto a

chair.

"A crack. A huge, gaping, monster of a f... of a crack."

"Where?"

"Along the whole bedroom side of the house, I think. A big one. A couple of inches below the stucco line." His mind hadn't registered the full meaning of the different colors down there, not yet, so he didn't mention that.

Catherine's eyes widened in shock.

"And another one under the eaves where the wall joins the roof. There's some uneven patching that no one would notice on a quick glance...maybe not even on a careful glance. We didn't walk along that part of the wall before we bought the place. Maxwell stood with us at the corner and talked but didn't go any further. We...I just assumed...."

"Anyway, it looks like the entire wall slumps from corner to corner. I think its separated from the roof by an inch or two in the middle, just above Suze's window."

He laughed bitterly.

"I'm surprised the window hasn't cracked. Yet."

Catherine remained silent. For a long time.

Then she touched Willard's hand. He didn't move.

"Is there anything we can do about it right now?"

He shook his head. "We'll have to call the city engineer's office to have them send someone out, but that can't happen until the soil is a lot dryer than it is. Without more rain, or at least nothing like the last four days, maybe three weeks, a month."

"Is there any danger?"

"I suppose not. Like Maxwell said, the place has lasted nearly thirty years. The roof isn't bowing anywhere, so it's supported all right. I think. We'll just have to see what the city inspector says when he comes."

She nodded.

Outside, the clouds began to break up, signaling the official end of the worst storm in a decade. If they had looked carefully, the might even have seen some blue sky peeking through.

They didn't look.

From the *Tamarind Valley Times*, 30 October 1991:

LOCAL BUSINESSMAN SOUGHT
ON CHARGES OF FRAUD

Charges of real estate fraud and criminal negligence were formally brought against Andrew "Ace" McCall, sole owner of Ace-High Construction and McCall/Sidney Realty in Tamarind Valley early this morning.

State Real Estate Board investigators have provided evidence that McCall was personally involved in several schemes to defraud contractors, suppliers, and buyers of recently constructed homes in two subdivisions in the Valley.

Sunset Hills, located in the far eastern end of the Valley, and Charter Oaks, the newer of the two, located just west of the 101 Freeway, have both been under investigation for several months, although no actions have been taken against McCall until today. Charges range from using substandard materials to willfully subverting the local and state building codes, potentially endangering residents in both subdivisions.

A warrant was issued for McCall, although when contacted, the police indicated that he has not been located.

No clues have been found in relation to a second case apparently involving McCall, the mysterious disappearance two years ago of his former senior partner in Ace-High Construction and McCall/Sidney Realty, Bryan Sidney.

Sidney was last seen exactly two years ago today. No traces of him have been found to date. McCall was considered a subject of interest in the case but due to a lack of any substantive evidence no charges were ever filed.

If found guilty of the fraud and negligence charges as specified, McCall could face....

From the *Cactus Spine* (Newsletter of the Bureau of Land Management, Reno District), 24 December 1997:

GOOD TO SEE YOU GO—
(NOT REALLY!)

Farewell and best wishes to one of the stalwarts here at the Reno District. After forty-five years of government service, over thirty of them with the BLM, Abraham Morris—known affectionately as "Abe," "The Old Man," "That Old Fart," and "Hey, You" (among other names, mostly unprintable)—has finally decided to call it quits, hang up his compass and canteen, and re-join the human race. Most people call it "retiring." Abe calls it "recovering his lost humanity."

Abe first joined the BLM in 1962 after serving in the Army and later in the Forest Service. During his more than three decades with us, he has worked throughout the Western States. His retirements goals include....

CHAPTER EIGHT
ABRAHAM MORRIS, FEBRUARY 1998-NOVEMBER 2005

The Joys of Retirement

1.

From the first moment he saw it outlined on the crest of the low hill, Abraham Morris knew that the house on Oleander was a perfect investment for him. He might be old, he thought ruefully as the realtor's sleek car nosed into the driveway, they might figure him to be too decrepit to work for the federal government any longer, but he wasn't senile. He had always had a nose for such things. He knew a good deal when he saw one.

Nothing happened to change his mind until after he had finished a walk-through of the house and the sorely neglected backyard. On the whole, he liked what he saw, liked especially the potential in the way the place was set on the property, the sense of roominess and openness. It kind of reminded him of Nevada…only green. Yes, there was a lot a good green thumb could do in the yard, and the house was larger than he had figured on getting for his money.

By the time he had finished with the showing, his mind was almost made up.

The realtor had three locks to check before leaving, so while she was finishing, Abe walked a short way down the front sidewalk, primarily to get a better view of the lot as a whole.

"That's a death-house!"

His head jerked around sharply at the hoarsely whispered sound. For a moment, it was as if the voice had come from thin air, a disembodied sound that echoed strangely across the open yards. Then, squinting against the bright light, he finally spotted an woman next door, huddling in the shadow of a garage bearing the number 1042 in cracked wood cutouts desperately in need of a new paint job. She was staring directly at him.

He glanced over his shoulder. The realtor had just completed locking up and emerged from the shadow beneath the eaves of 1066 into the sunlight to join him.

"It's a murder house," the woman continued as if there had been no seconds-long interruption.

Abe could make out no details of her face—it was little more than a pale oval in the shadows. She was a large woman, almost grossly large, although that sense might have been due largely to the play of light and dark across her figure. He had the sense as well that she was old, perhaps ancient. In other times she might have passed for a witch, or at least a hag, given the vehemence—and distinct if perverse pleasure—that echoed through her voice.

She did not speak again right away but simply hunched there, seemingly oblivious to the look of pained annoyance that flitted across the realtor's face in the split second it took for her to take in the scene, cross the remaining yards of sidewalk, slip her arm into Abraham's and ease him back toward the car.

"People die in that house," the old woman called after him from the shadows. He realized with an odd pang that had never seen her face clearly. Her cracked, warbling voice was eerily strained, as if she simultaneously wanted to yell out a warning and was afraid to raise her voice above a raspy whisper.

"They die."

He glanced over his shoulder once more, just in time to catch a muted shimmer of yellow polyester pants as she disappeared around the corner of her garage.

At the car, he turned to face the realtor—a pretty young thing named Rebecca Cantwell, who was pretty enough and young enough that she should have been at home caring for her man and her little ones, not strutting around showing houses to old farts like himself. Not for the first time, Abraham Morris admitted to himself that he was indeed getting old. Everything he believed in and valued and knew to be inviolable and unalterable was shifting like sands beneath his feet. And lately the tide had been going out faster and faster. The reality of mortality struck him at that moment, as it had so often and so unexpectedly in the four years since Matty had died—struck him full in the face and for a moment he was blinded and made breathless by its power.

"Mr. Morris?" Rebecca asked, "are you all right? Do you want to sit down?"

"No, I'm fine." He paused for a second to catch his breath. "Is it true?"

"Is what true, Mr. Morris?"

He was mildly amused to notice that she was lying to him... well, to be generous, not precisely lying, since she hadn't exactly answered him, but she sure as hell didn't want to talk about something.

Toying with him was perhaps closer. As if he wouldn't notice when she turned the snow-job machine on full tilt.

"What that old woman was talking about," he said patiently. *Old* indeed. Who knew, he might even have a decade or two on her. He couldn't really tell, not with her hidden in the shadows like that.

"About this being a 'death-house.'"

There was a long silence as Rebecca Cantwell rummaged through her purse for her car keys. Abe thought the movement curiously stereotyped, verging on deliberate. She's stalling, he thought. Why?

The young realtor glanced up and saw him staring at her. She flushed embarrassedly and jerked the key ring out of the depths of her large bag.

"Uh...well," she said, slipping the key into the door lock, "Uh, to be frank, Mr. Morris...."

Uh-oh, Abe thought. Here it comes. Beware realtors when they decide to "be frank." He waited, not giving the woman any clues as to how she should proceed to save a once-sure sale that might suddenly be in jeopardy.

"There was...uh...some...unpleasantness here a couple of months ago."

He opened his car door and slid in. He waited patiently while Rebecca fumbled with ignition and finally started the car. His glance was firm and his face unexpressive.

"The previous owner...a businessman here in the valley, respected, really an exceptional man. Uh, his stepson went... well, Mr. Morris, to be blunt, the kid flipped out completely."

Behind the unmoving muscles of his face, Abe grinned at Cantwell's lapse into slang.

Lost his marbles, his generation might have said, or *wigged out*, *blew his gaskets*. But the result would be the same, whatever you called it.

"The boy killed his stepfather?" he asked gently. "In the house?"

Cantwell looked momentarily surprised. "Yes, in the master bedroom. And his mother afterward. With a knife."

Abe winced. That was a bit more than he had anticipated. "How old was he?"

"Fourteen or fifteen, I don't remember exactly." Her face was now pale, as if she were the senior citizen who needed to sit down and catch her breath before she fainted.

"What happened to him?"

"He's dead, too."

Abraham raised one eye brow quizzically.

"Not here," the woman rushed to add. "Not in the house. He tried to get away in his step-father's car. It went off the road a couple of miles from here. There was...an explosion."

Abe nodded. Then he turned slightly away from where the woman leaned against the door of her powder-blue Cadillac

Eldorado, and he studied the house again. Not that the deaths made any difference, of course, not to him at least. It was a shame that things like that happened. The boy was probably on drugs or drunk and just couldn't handle life. He had heard of such things before, although never quite this tragically. Three people dead. He shifted his position.

The house.

In spite of what might have happened inside a couple of months ago, the house was still a good buy. The inside had been completely renovated: new carpeting in every room; new hardwood doors hung in each room; new paint throughout.

He squinted against the bright sunlight. The mildly angled roof sloped down from each side of a central gable, giving the house a deceptive profile. It looked smaller, closer to the ground than it really was; the fourteen-foot, open-beam cathedral ceiling in the living room had surprised him, as had the fact there were five bedrooms. The place just didn't look that large. From where he sat, he could see the crisp lines of white-rocked shingles. The roof was in good shape, he decided, and the exterior had recently been repainted as well.

The plants close to the house itself were all young—obviously newly planted. They weren't doing all that well, but a spot of good fertilizer would fix that. Most of them would probably come out, anyway, since Abraham Morris had very definite ideas as to what was appropriate and not appropriate for front yards and flower beds. Roses, irises, gladiolus, geraniums—that sort of thing. Old fashioned cut flowers like Mattie so much enjoyed. He glanced disapprovingly at the straggling junipers and juvenile jade plants that promised nothing but unending, unchanging, year-round green.

Boring.

He noted with somewhat greater pleasure that the lawn had been re-sodded as well. Vaguely, Abraham wondered what the house must have looked like at the time of the...incident. From all he could see, everything replaceable had been replaced.

But, taken all in all, the place was obviously a good buy. It was perhaps a bit larger than he had originally intended, but that would mean all the more room for the two most important things in his life now that Mattie was gone: his grandchildren, and his collections—definitely in that order. And there was a lot of room for gardening, both in the front and in the deep back yard.

All in all, he repeated, a good buy.

Sold, he said to himself.

He turned to face the realtor, catching the flicker of uncertainty in her eyes—uncertainty coupled with a hungry eagerness to make a sale that he couldn't miss.

"Well let's get going," he said brusquely. "Don't you have anything else," he added, knowing full well that any further showings would serve primarily to give him leverage when it came time to bargain for the house on Oleander.

The engine roared as the car backed out of the driveway and negotiated the turn. As they pulled away Abe glanced in the rearview mirror and caught a final glimpse of the house, *his* house, as he had already started to think of it.

Now for the fun part, he mused silently. Just how hard will this realtor lady bargain to get rid of a *death house*?

It was going to be entertaining finding out. And then his new life would begin. A new life in a new place, with a new house. He figured he had ten or fifteen good years in front of him.

Even though escrow on the house closed a little over a month and a half later and he moved in two weeks after that, he never saw the woman in yellow again.

2.

Abraham Morris had developed diabetes just after his forty-ninth birthday.

"A mild case," Dr. Sideko said as unconcernedly as if he had been diagnosing a hangnail or an ingrown body hair. "Should be no trouble at all controlling it."

For the next eighteen years, Abe Morris religiously followed the prescription for Diabinese. And for eighteen years, the medication did in fact control the disease.

When Abe turned sixty-seven, however, the new doctor in California recommended that he change medication.

"The diabetes has worsened slightly," he said, his youthful face twisted into what he no doubt considered an appropriate expression of concern for the health of his old-timer patient. Abe snorted to himself and caught himself thinking *whipper-snapper*, a word his grandfather had always applied to wet-behind-the-ears doctors that thought they knew everything. "We could go to insulin," the kid continued.

We, Abraham thought contemptuously. Yeah, right. You and me shooting up together, sliding needles into our thighs on cue. Junkies in tandem. Junkies on parade. *We. Right.*

"But I think this will work just as well." The kid-disguised-as-a-doctor handed Abe a prescription for a different drug, Glucotrol, that would take care of everything. He promised.

3.

Abe knew that blood disease ran in his family. His father and grandfather had died in their early sixties from heart attacks. He hadn't really figured on being immune to it, but when his first attack came in the spring of 2003, it was more of a shock than he cared to admit.

It was a relatively mild attack. Within six months, the doctor assured him, he would be right back to normal. With care— proper diet, moderate exercise—no one would even know he had suffered the attack.

But still, Abe knew.

4.

The Parkinson's Disease developed gradually and unobtrusively at first, then finally afflicted his every movement.

The still-a-kid-disguised-as-a-doctor sent him to a neurologist, who prescribed Artane.

"No problem," Abe said. "Just what the doctor ordered." He simpered at his own feeble joke.

5.

As the years slowly rumbled past, the house became more of a burden than Abe had anticipated. He never quite got around to many of the surface repairs he had promised himself he would take care of when he first saw the house. Ruefully, he acknowledged to himself early in 2005 that he was probably going to have to sell the place. He just couldn't take care of everything himself.

6.

"It's Grandpa," Elizabeth Morris called, cupping her hand over the telephone as she yelled the message across the family room to where her father was immersed in a 2,000-piece Big Ben puzzle he and Mom had been working on now for weeks with little overt signs of progress. The thing still looked like the jagged skeleton of a picture. So far they had only managed to fit the edges together, with random bits of connected pieces scattered through the center.

"Just a minute," Jay said, beginning the complex process of extricating himself from behind the wobbly card table without disturbing any of the pieces so carefully laid out around the promised-but-not-yet-emerging representation of a crumbling European castle surrounded by unbelievable emerald forests and plastic turquoise skies.

"Hi, Grandpa," Elizabeth said, removing her hand and speaking directly into the phone. "How are you?"

"I'm fine, sugar-plum. And how is everything there?"

"Fine. I won the spelling-bee in school today. I spelled *cantankerous*." She giggled.

"That's just great."

For an instant, Elizabeth caught an undercurrent in Grandpa's voice that worried her. She was about to ask again how he was feeling, when Jay finally made it across the room to the telephone. He took it from her, ruffled her hair (which he knew she hated), and spoke to his father.

"Hi, Dad."

"Jay, how's everything."

"Just great. How about you?"

"Can't complain."

"You're sure. No problems?"

"Just the usual," Abraham said, his voice coming heavily through the telephone. "I'm falling apart and no one can do a damn thing about it but other than that everything's fine. How's Linda and the girls?"

They continued in this vein for a few minutes, Abe catching up on events in his son's household, then sharing the most recent news of Jay's sister Ellen, her husband Sam, and their three kids. Pretending that Jay actually cared. Finally, though, he came to the meat of the conversation.

"Jay, how about you and the ladies coming out here for Thanksgiving this year?"

"But Dad, that would be too much trouble for you. All that work. Having us all descend on you like that. We couldn't."

"Now you listen to me, young man. I'm old and retired, but I can still whip up a turkey dinner like you wouldn't believe—I had the world's best teacher, remember? And besides"—here his voice took an edge of seriousness—"besides, you've had me out there so many times that I'm beginning to feel guilty. I'd really like to have my children home for the holiday this year. All my children."

Jay thought for a moment. Dad was right, he realized suddenly. It had been, what...almost two years since Jay and his family had made the four-hour trip from Palm Springs to Tamarind Valley. It hadn't been that long since they'd seen Abe, of course. He came out for a weekend or so at least three or four times a year. But for the last while, instead of them visiting him on holidays, they'd paid his round-trip bus fare, convincing themselves that the ride in an air conditioned bus would be more comfortable for the old man than having the four of them descending like marauding locusts. Besides, to be honest, there wasn't really that much to do at Dad's place.

Jay sighed, thinking of how bored his girls had been the last time they had been there—almost a week at Christmas, 2003, and both Elizabeth and Anna had nearly gone out of their minds with not having anything to do. No friends, no toys, no nothing except walking up and down the street and watching TV. Dad had been recovering from his attack, so even short sight-seeing trips had been out.

No, Jay decided, no matter what, that house would never mean as much to his kids as Jay's own grandparents' farmhouse had meant to him when he was that age. There they had dogs and cows and horses and pigs and chickens to watch and feed and play with, attics to explore, creepy dark corners of the cellar to dare, alfalfa fields full of was-that-a-snake! remnants of dried hay to wander. There had even been a swaying, single-board bridge over a rippling creek that threatened to spill him into the water each time he crossed. That had been a *real* Grandpa-house.

Grandpa Abe's was just another tract house in an older part of a typical southern California suburban complex.

Still....

"Let me check with Linda, Dad," Jay said. "I'll get back to you later tonight or tomorrow. Okay?"

"Sure, but Jay...," Abe's voice crackled into a surge of static that startled Jay.

"What? I didn't get that. We must have a bad connection."

"I just said," Abe repeated, his voice enunciating every sound carefully, "that I really want you folks to come out. It's real important to me. Okay?"

"Okay. Sure."

"Fine. Now let me talk to that other princess you got out there."

"Here, Anna," Jay said, handing the receiver down to his younger daughter. "Grandpa wants to talk to you."

She began a murmured chatter that Jay hoped would carry across the bad connection.

He looked at his wife and mouthed his question, "What about it?"

She shrugged, her eyebrows tugging up in concern—for his father, Jay knew, not for herself. "If it means that much to him," she whispered, "Okay."

Jay nodded. As soon as Anna finished telling Grandpa Abe about her new goldfish, he would get back on the line and tell the old man it was a Go for Thanksgiving.

He remembered how frail his father had looked when he came out for the Fourth of July weekend. His eyes had been persistently slightly bloodshot, the lids wider open than usual. At times Abe had a faintly frantic, faintly crazed expression. He had occasional trouble speaking as well. His words sometimes slurred, and more frequently than usual his voice cracked upward into treble like an adolescent suffering through puberty in reverse. The Parkinson's was visibly worse. His fingers and hands shook so hard that at dinner the first night, he could barely feed himself. Jay noticed how translucent his father's fingers and lips had become. The flesh seemed almost bloodless.

That weekend had seemed to help. By the time Abe caught the bus into Los Angeles on Wednesday, he looked and sounded much more like the old Abraham Morris. Jay remembered wishing that they lived closer to him, but Abe had reassured his son that he was doing fine, that everything was going well. Jay had believed him.

But now, listening to his father's voice over the telephone, he wasn't so sure. There was something in the sound that bothered him. He shook his head.

Quit borrowing trouble. Dad wasn't one of those parents who waited until after they were dead to let their kids know that they had a problem. He'd kept Jay and Ellen posted on every change in his health. He'd called at least once a week. He wrote as often

as he could, although the Parkinson's did make that more difficult recently.

Jay shrugged. Nothing he could do about his father right
now, anyway. He'd wait until Thanksgiving, only four weeks
away. Then he'd see.

7.

Ellen Cameron, her husband Mitch, and her three children—
Thad, Josh, and Colin—were already at Abe's place when Jay
and his family arrived just after noon on the Wednesday before
Thanksgiving. Their brass-toned Ford van squatted dead center
in the two-car driveway, forcing Jay to angle alongside the curb.

"Look's like it's going to be a family reunion, after all," Jay
said to Linda in what he hoped would come across as a light,
optimistic tone. Linda and Ellen did not get along that well.
Linda and Mitch in one house were even worse. And those three
kids of Ellen's—it would help if someone had bothered to teach
them discipline and self-control somewhere along the way. Most
of the time they behaved like what Linda referred to as a bunch
of wild-eyed, foul-mouthed hooligans. *Jackanapes*, would have
been Abe's word, Jay thought, although Dad would never have
applied it to his grandsons. Still, Jay had no trouble agreeing
with Linda on the point. He sighed. He already wondered if
agreeing to get together as a family had been a big mistake.

"We're here," he called over the seat to where Elizabeth and
Anna cuddled together asleep. He reached back and gently
shook Elizabeth's knee. "We're at Grandpa Abe's."

Elizabeth sat up and began the more lengthy process of
waking Anna. Jay killed the engine and glanced up at the house.
The hair on the back of his neck prickled.

It was a shambles.

Abraham Morris had always been a proud man, but more than
anything (except perhaps his collections), he consistently prided
himself on one thing—having the neatest yard in the neighborhood. Mattie and he had loved kneeling side by side, working

with rich black soil. They loved plants and flowers and shrubs and trees, loved neatness and growing things. Jay remembered summer after summer, his bare back baking to a golden brown in the heat as he and Ellen had bent over weeding in gardens, trimmed lawns twice weekly, raked, swept, pruned—whatever was needed to make the place neat (whatever place it was— because of Abe's job they had moved far more frequently than Jay had found comfortable).

But this....

Except for a ragged fringe of green along the edge closest to the sidewalk, there was no lawn. As the yard sloped slightly upward to the foundations of the house, the desolation became worse. The few straggling clumps of St. Augustine grass and Bermuda grass—normally impervious to almost all attempts to eradicate them—quickly died away completely. In the middle of the yard, the ground was bare, naked earth packed to concrete-hardness. The cold shadow cast by the house obscured skeletal remains of what had once been roses. The canes might have been bare simply because it was November and because the weather had been unusually cold for this part of Southern California, but Jay knew at once that he was looking at more than just normal winter kill. Those plants were dead. No amount of judicious pruning and feeding and watering would bring them to bloom the next spring.

In what should have been narrow borders of color along the sidewalk there was more desolation. Irises were nothing more than clumps of wilted, brittle brown and yellow spears, and the chrysanthemums, short stubs of blackened growth without leaves or greenery.

Along one edge of the driveway, a ragged clump of dense shrubs covered in unattractive grey-green leaves provided the only break from the sense of utter devastation.

Jay shook his head wonderingly. The house was in bad shape, too. This close he could see the paint peeling from the stucco wall as well as from the hardwood trim around the eaves, the windows, and the doors. A hairline crack started four or five inches above the foundation line, midway beneath the front bedroom window and jagged continuously for six feet or so to the corner.

Jay whistled under his breath.

"What's wrong," Linda asked, shooting him a worried, questioning look.

"That," he said, nodding toward the yard and house.

"I know," she said. To herself she wondered what Mattie would have thought about the state of the house and gardens. She was probably spinning in her grave like a top, Linda decided.

By that time, though, the girls had unwound their tangle of coats and books and toys and were piling pell-mell out of the car. They pounded down the sidewalk, oblivious to the deadness around them. They skirted a leafless bougainvillea that should have overhung the entryway with masses of scarlet brilliance but now grew more like the wall of thorns from Grimm's Sleeping Beauty than anything else. They were knocking excitedly on the front door before Jay and Linda were even out of the car.

Ellen's oldest, Thad, opened the door. He's grown up, Jay thought as he glanced up and saw the fifteen-year-old towering over his girls, his hair long and greasy and blond and unkempt, and the glint of something gold dangling from his left earlobe.

"Hey, it's the insects," the boy called over his shoulder, his voice a vibrant bass.

He's only grown up physically, Jay amended. Mentally he's as immature as always. A nasty little boy squashed in an almost-a-man's body.

The girls filed by their cousin, their enthusiasm dampened by his crude welcome. The incident didn't bode well for a pleasant Thanksgiving weekend.

8.

Abraham Morris met his younger child and the boy's family with a slow smile. He spoke little, beyond a soft, "Good to see you, Jay." He gave Linda a brief peck on the cheek, but seemed unusually aloof around the girls. Elizabeth looked worried and disappointed when Grandpa virtually ignored her, but Anna squatted in a corner and watched Ellen's two younger boys fighting over a PlayStation console that couldn't have been out of its box for more than a couple of hours. The Styrofoam packing material lay scattered across the living room like stark white bones in a desecrated graveyard.

Jay shuddered at the image.

Josh and Colin tugged simultaneously at one joystick; a second lay unnoticed in the middle of the floor. Jay picked up the joystick and held it out.

"You don't need to fight over that one. There's another one right here." He thought nothing of the action, but Ellen shot him a vicious glance that clearly said *keep out of my family affairs, I don't tell your kids what to do, do I?*

Jay and Ellen hadn't gotten along well for a long while now, but even he was startled by the vehemence implicit in her expression. He dropped the joystick and turned away from the squabbling boys.

The rest of the day quickly disintegrated into family quarrels over trivialities that left Jay exhausted by the time he finally got to bed late Wednesday evening. He and Linda shared a three-quarters width roll-away bed Abe kept in the closet of the back corner bedroom. Ellen and Mitch had apparently decided—as always—to act on a first-come, first-served basis. Jay had not been the least surprised to see their suitcases already laid open on the queen-size bed in the middle bedroom, between Abe's and the one Jay and Linda inherited by default. Jay's girls were sleeping in the first bedroom, just across from the master bath and next to their Grandfather's room. Ellen's three boys had finally sacked out in the family room, their bulky sleeping bags and stacks of clothing cluttering most of the floor space.

The remaining bedroom—tucked between the corner room and the living room—was too tightly packed with the bulkiest and most cumbersome of Grandpa Abe's books and collecting equipment for anyone to sleep there. Jay had glanced in earlier that evening and noticed with increasing alarm the thick coating of dust on the dead-grey filing cabinets, on the microscope, on the taxidermy table, on the ends of the thick books that had served his father for a lifetime of identifying the specimens of rocks and plants and animals and insects he had collected from nearly every part of the Western United States.

The sight of that thick layer of dust had bothered Jay much more deeply than the usual snips and quips from his brother-in-law, whose law practice in San Diego was admittedly far more lucrative than Jay's work with Compu-Corps, or from Ellen's usual (but this time unusually flawless) impersonation of the massive iceberg that gutted the *Titanic*.

"Are you feeling all right?" Linda asked, abruptly breaking him out of his dark silence.

"I'm fine."

"You don't act like it."

He glanced at her and smiled. "It's just...it's just that I don't really like sleeping in here. I always feel half-dizzy when I walk in." He gestured with one hand around the room that was originally designed as a bedroom but was now functioning more like a branch specimen room of the Ventura County Museum of Natural history.

Birds of all sizes—ranging from tiny hummingbirds to a huge Great Horned Owl—clung with needle-sharp claws to stumps of wood that seemed to jut from the very substance of the sandy tan walls. Small birds like wrens and sparrows seemed to flutter on invisible wires hooked into the ceiling. Abe's collection of western birds created a sensation that Jay found intensely claustrophobic. There were too many birds, too close together, their arced wings almost touching, their glass eyes sharp and too reflective, their beaks and claws angled threateningly.

Most of the floor space around the edge of the room was filled with glass-fronted display cases and small, narrow tables containing collections of pinned butterflies and insects, minerals and rocks, and mounted samples of the smaller wildlife of

Montana, Nevada, Arizona—including ground squirrels, chipmunks, two skunks, a mole, and a full-sized rattlesnake coiled like an oversized ashtray on the top shelf of the bookcase just inside the door. Hundreds of leaves and seedpods and blossoms lay desiccated and crumbling and pressed beneath protective plastic sheets collected in thick ring-binders that stood blackly along the desk top underneath the window.

Even the closet was open and crowded with parts of Abe's collections. The original hard-wood folding doors had been removed, and on homemade shelves rising above the blank space where the rollaway had been stored—now eerily apparent as the only empty, uncluttered stretch of wall in the entire room— were stacked case after case of slide carousels that Jay knew contained the life history of the Morrises as well as a pictorial, encyclopedic natural history of every area Abe had worked in during his decades with the Bureau of Land Management.

The room was reasonably large, Jay thought, especially for the fifth bedroom in a five-bedroom tract house. But it was so crammed with boxes and files and specimens along every wall and in every corner that it seemed crowded, breathlessly cramped. He felt as if the walls were inching nearer, as if the birds and animals were not dead and stuffed but merely caught helplessly in some weird half-living stasis, waiting for the right moment to break loose and flutter creep scuttle crawl insinuate themselves into his life.

"This stuff always gave me the creeps," he said finally, "even when I was a kid. I hated show-and-tell because Dad always insisted that I take one of those." He gestured toward the birds. He shuddered. "I hated them."

Linda reached across the low bed and touched his hand with hers. "I know. I don't especially like it in here, either. But the girls would have absolute screaming fits."

He nodded. Then he grinned. "I'd like to see those three little heathens in the family room stay in here for a night. Maybe I could rig up something with flashlights and batteries and a few wires, so the hawk and eagle would appear to attack...."

"Jay!"

"He shrugged, the grin lingering on his face. "Hey, everyone's entitled to a fantasy. After the way those boys treated Anna and Elizabeth...."

"I don't think the girls ever got to play with the video games, not once," Linda said, tacitly agreeing with Jay. The evening had been rough on the girls.

And it was even rougher, Jay knew, because Grandpa Abe had spent most of the time sitting silently in the old bentwood rocker Grandma Matty had bought as a young mother. He hadn't even rocked very much; he spent the evening staring at a spot on the wall opposite, six inches under the faded, antique-framed photograph of his own grand-parents—Jay's great-grandparents—stiffly postured for a formal wedding portrait. He had sat and stared and spoken very little

Jay sighed. Obviously things weren't going as well here as he had been led to believe through Abe's telephone calls. He reached over and flicked the light off. Moonlight streamed through the curtainless window, striking him full on the face. The light cast the stuffed animals and birds into sharp relief. He rolled away, covering his eyes with his forearm.

Linda nestled close against his back, her arm over his side. "Try to get some sleep," she whispered in his ear. "Tomorrow will be better."

9.

It wasn't.

The girls woke at seven, before anyone else was awake, and crept into the family room and turned the television on. They dialed the volume knob so far down that the sound emerged as little more than a blurring murmur. They sat three or four feet from the screen, neither moving, neither making a sound. But something woke Thad up anyway, and when he sat up in his bag and saw the two girls staring intently at a cartoon he had grown tired of when he was ten, he yelled, "Hey, get out of here, bugs! We're sleeping." Thad yelling full-voiced was in itself an interesting phenomenon, one capable of waking everyone else in the house.

It did. It jerked Jay from a tangle of hateful dreams that had kept him tossing and turning all night on the narrow bed. For her part, Linda had not dreamed, but Jay's restlessness had perforce communicated itself to her. Jay was up and out the door before Linda was fully awake.

Within five minutes, the only person still asleep was Grandpa Abe. The door to his bedroom was closed, and Jay heard no movements behind it as he hurried down the hall to see why the girls were crying. He rounded the entryway only a few steps in front of Linda, who was followed closely by Ellen. Elizabeth was whimpering, but Anna was screaming full volume. Thad had her by the upper arm, his fingers gripping so tightly that even Jay could see the bloodless white of the boy's knuckles. Anna was almost off the ground, only one toe brushing the carpeting. The television screen was black, and Thad clutched the on-off button in his other hand.

"*Hey!*" Jay yelled, forgetting for an instant that the six-foot-one, straggly-haired ape wearing only a pair of drooping boxers hanging from his bony hips was his own nephew. "What's going on?"

Thad let go of Anna instantly—so fast, in fact, that the girl almost fell. Elizabeth grabbed her and steadied her. Thad spun around to face Jay.

"Uh, Uncle Jay," he said, as if that flicker of recognition were deserving of special notice. "Uh...we were sleepin' and the bu… the girls came in and turned the TV on and woke us up and...."

Jay crossed the room, stepping deliberately over the cocoon-like lumps that were Josh and Colin—both of them sitting up breathless, wide-eyed, and tousled. When he was less than a foot from his nephew, he spoke in a voice that was so low and calm and controlled that he barely recognized it as his own. "You touch her again, punk, and I'll break every bone in your body."

Thad stared down at his five-foot-nine uncle and started to say something.

"I mean it," Jay said before the boy could speak. "Every bone in your fucking body."

"Jay!" Linda's voice registered disbelief. Jay *never* cursed.

Jay whirled to see Linda at the entry to the family room, Ellen pressed close behind. For an instant, it was as if a thick red curtain had parted from before his eyes.

He blinked.

When he looked back at Thad, he was shocked. There wasn't a wild-eye, hippie-type hulk towering over him. It was his nephew, the boy he had dandled on his knee. A skinny, fifteen-year-old boy whose emotional growth had not yet caught up with his body. Jay remembered vaguely his own teenage years, how difficult and rare it was to wake feeling like anything other than a temperamental grizzly on the constant prowl for mayhem.

"Uh, listen, Thad, I'm sorry," Jay began.

"Get away from him!" Ellen jerked at Jay's arm, forcing him to turn and face her. "Get your filthy mouth away from my son!"

Jay was so stunned at what he had said and at the unreasoning fury he had experienced, at what he felt—*knew*—he would have done to the boy in another moment or two, that he couldn't speak. He strode past Linda, who was crouching by Elizabeth and Anna to reassure them. He walked past Mitch, who was cinching up his robe in the entryway and obviously wondering what he had missed.

Jay continued on to the back bedroom. He entered and shut the door behind himself, meticulously careful not to slam it. He dimly heard Ellen's raucous voice, interrupted and punctuated here and there by Mitch's deeper, grating bass. Once or twice Linda's voice came through as well. Thad didn't appear to be saying much.

Finally, even the dim rustle of voices died away, and Jay was left with silence and turmoil. What the hell had he been doing? Okay, so the kid shouldn't have grabbed Anna like that, but did that make it all right for Jay to come on like gangbusters. And what in *hell* made him spit out language like that. He rarely used it, never to family, especially not in front of Linda and the girls. He shook his head and sat staring at the floor.

A long while later, Linda cracked the door open and slipped in.

"Ellen and Mitch and the boys have gone out to get something to eat. Your Dad's still asleep. The girls are reading."

Jay nodded numbly. Linda rested her hand on his hands, where they lay limply across his thighs and loosely clasped.

"I talked with Ellen. I know you didn't get much sleep last night. You must have been having a humdinger series of nightmares. You were moaning and tossing and turning all night long."

Jay touched her cheek. "You didn't get much more, did you?"

She flushed. "Anyway, I think Ellen understands. You were just overtired, worried about Grandpa Abe, upset. And Thad apologized for losing his temper and breaking the television knob and grabbing Anna like that. He was pretty shook."

"I guess. I would have been if it happened to me," Jay said softly.

"So the upshot is that I think everything is pretty well smoothed over."

They sat quietly for a long time, just the two of them, side by side on the edge of a narrow, lumpy rollaway.

10.

When Abe Morris woke at ten-twenty, the house was deathly quiet. He stared around him curiously, as if he were seeing the room for the first time. Then something in the back of his brain shifted, and the familiar furniture and pictures and clothing snapped into place and he knew where he was and who he was.

But aren't Ellen and Jay here? he wondered briefly. *I was sure they came here.*

He got up, feeling every savage bite of pain in his joints and bones. He dressed slowly, wishing that he could just remain in bed and sleep and dream, but knowing that for some reason he had to get up.

That's it, Jay and Ellen are coming today for dinner. For... what was it, yes, Thanksgiving. The family all together for Thanksgiving.

He smiled.

Then the smiled faded. He looked down at the unruffled quilts and pillow on the far side of the bed.

Not the whole family. Sweet Mattie had been with him all night, but now he remembered that she was dead. Not the whole family.

Finally dressed, he opened the door and stepped into the hall. There was no one there.

Better hurry, he reminded himself. Lot's to do before the kids get here.

He shuffled across the hall to the bathroom. Without noticing the crack of light beneath the closed door, he swung the door open.

"Grandpa!" a thin, high voice shrieked. The door slammed, almost catching Abe's toe as it shut.

What who I thought they weren't coming until later today that wasn't Ellen who was that?

An arm surrounded him, enclosing him in a firm, tight grasp.

He looked up into Jay's eyes.

Jay's not that old Jay's only twelve and Mattie's not feeling well and I'm going to cook the Thanksgiving turkey myself this year why is Jay looking at me like that....

"Dad," Jay said gently. "Dad, are you all right?"

Abe couldn't find any words. Oh he knew well enough what he wanted to say: Why are you here and why are you so old looking and who is that little girl brushing her teeth in my bathroom and why did she slam the door in my face and call me Grandpa.

He knew what he wanted to say, but he simply couldn't find the right sounds to say them.

"Nnnhh," he began. His voice frightened him. It wasn't his.

The tongue pressing against teeth wasn't his. The too-old Jay led Abe down the hall to the family room and started to help him settle onto the couch.

Click.

Everything slid into focus.

"Jay?"

"Dad, are you all right?"

"I'm...of course I'm all right." And he was. Now he was, although he vaguely recalled being disoriented only moments before. Or was that part of the dreams? He wasn't sure. But now he remembered Jay and Ellen coming yesterday, remembered sitting in the rocker and watching his sweet, lovely granddaughters and his fine, handsome young grandsons playing together, thinking how proud Mattie would be of all of them.

"I'm fine," he repeated. He glanced around at the room, taking in the clumps of sleeping bags tossed in the corner. His eyes swept across the clock face.

"Oh no," he said. "It can't be that late. I was going to get up early and start cooking...."

"No you don't," Jay said firmly. "You sit right here."

Abe melted back into the couch. It felt nice. A woman entered the room. He looked up at her curiously. She seemed familiar. She was.... Damn, he had almost had it there for a moment. He looked more closely at her. She was...she was *Linda*. Of course. Linda. Jay's wife. Abe shook his head and sighed. It was so hard to remember things anymore. Everything seemed to get all mixed up some days. Other days, he was fine. Those were the days he when he would call Jay and Ellen and the grandkids on the telephone—no use getting them all worried because he was occasionally forgetful.

"...Not another word about it." Linda's voice.

"Huh," Abe said. He caught Linda's expression as she glanced quickly over to Jay.

"Dad, you're not cooking anything. You're just going to relax. We'll pull the turkey out of the oven after Linda makes reservations for us all at a restaurant this afternoon. That'll be nice, Thanksgiving dinner without any dishes to do or mess to clear up. Right?"

Abe was going to answer, was going to insist that he felt fine, that he could cook up a dinner like Jay wouldn't believe—but just then the front door swung open and Ellen and Mitch and the boys trooped in. Abe thought there was a long moment of cold silence when Ellen's eyes met Jay's. Too bad the kids never really learned to get along, he thought. Matty was always disappointed about that.

Jay crossed over and said something to Ellen, then stood in front of Thad for a long while. Abe could see Jay's lips moving, could even hear his voice, but the sounds didn't make any sense. The boy listened intently, his ears and cheeks suddenly flaming. He nodded once, then Jay reached out and gave the boy a hug. At first, the boy seemed horribly stiff, almost frightened, as if terrified of his own uncle. *Why?* After a moment, though, Thad raised his arms and hugged his uncle in return.

That's more like it, Abe thought. A family that really loves each other.

11.

Jay had hoped for a full reconciliation, but by late morning on Thanksgiving Day, he knew that Ellen wouldn't let that happen. Mitch was able to repair the television set, so everyone crowded into the family room to watch snatches of parades and football games.

To an outsider, it might have seemed like a perfectly normal family gathering, but Jay knew better. He felt an undercurrent of hostility that bothered him. He couldn't quite place it. Ellen talked and laughed and joked enough; she didn't seem to be any angrier than usual. And Thad, though he studiously avoided even approaching either Elizabeth or Anna, was soon immersed in the intricacies of football, his newly discovered basso rumbling over the rest of the hubbub of noise. Neither seemed particularly upset over the morning's debacle. Mitch ignored Jay. That was all right by Jay. Dad seemed better as well. His eyes were not as staring, not as wild. And the moments of vagueness that had worried Jay earlier that day had disappeared. Abe sounded normal, his mind clear, his words appropriate and understandable. Maybe it was just waking up that made him sound so... distant, Jay decided.

No, everyone seemed normal.

But still there was a persistent feeling, a heaviness in his mind like a headache about to descend and ravage him, that made it impossible for him to enjoy the day.

Thanksgiving dinner passed without any incidents. The combined families took up three tables in a Baker's Square seven miles down the freeway. The food was hot and good, the service excellent, the wait for available tables marginal (thanks to Linda's foresight in making reservations). Abe presided over one table, quietly and rather distractedly, to Jay's way of thinking. The kids sat at the other one, and for once Jay heard no squabbling at all from them. Once or twice, in fact, Thad or Josh said something and both of his girls would hide their faces in their hands and giggle. They were having fun together. Every element of the day was as it should have been, more subdued than usual perhaps, but nothing to suggest that anything was wrong.

Still, as Jay dressed for bed that night beneath the watchful eyes of the stuffed specimens on the walls, he felt oddly tense. His head swam, his heart raced, and for a time he was so short of breath that he had to sit on the mattress and force himself to relax. Linda came in a few moments later and rubbed his shoulders. Even that helped only marginally. His sleep that night was even more ragged, more disrupted than before.

12.

"Aw, do we have to?"

Thad's voice edged into a whine. Ellen's harsh soprano all but drowned out the boy's complaints.

"Yes, you do. We all do. It's the least we can do for Grandpa Abe." She looked around the gathered family members as if daring anyone to contradict her. She's in her element, Jay thought with a flood of realization that startled him. She's the matriarch, now that Mom's gone. She's taken full charge, telling everyone what to do and when to do it and where to go. Even Dad.

He glanced over to a patio glider that squawked thinly as Abe's weight shifted. The old man sat silently in the shadows, his eyes downcast. Jay wondered if his father saw any of them, or whether the old man was really aware of where he was. Since the episode on Thanksgiving, Jay had been watching his father closely, not at all pleased with what he was seeing. At regular intervals, Abe seemed to phase out—almost, Jay thought, as if he were drugged. Jay had toyed with the idea of checking to see if his father's medications were interacting but decided to wait a bit before mentioning his concerns. After all, no one else seemed to have noticed anything untoward.

That morning had started well enough, with everyone sleeping in until eight or nine. Then, right after breakfast, Ellen had hustled everyone into the back yard—including Abe, bundled in three layers of sweaters and jackets in case the crisp November air should be too much for him.

"He needs the fresh air," Ellen insisted. "And besides, you know how much he loved to garden."

Loved. Ellen had that one right. She herded the kids like a general marshalling troops, handing out rakes and hoes and shovels, directing her boys to one part of the overgrown yard, Jay and his girls to another. Linda had opted to stay inside and clean up in the kitchen. Mitch was out front, puttering around with his engine.

Apparently, Jay thought, it's all right for my wife to work to straighten up her father-in-law's place, but Mitch is somehow immune to the same obligation. He was surprised at the anger that realization kindled in him.

He turned to the job at hand—hacking down brambles of dead

and dying plants that clotted the foundation line of the house. He showed Elizabeth and Anna how to grab the stiff, blackened passion-plant vines and twist them into small bundles and stuff them into thick brown lawn-and-leaf bags. He actually didn't mind them working in the yard with him; in fact, he enjoyed it more than he would have cared to admit. It reminded him of his own childhood, when his was the small hand struggling to control a recalcitrant branch, and Abe's the larger reaching over and with a single deft touch putting things to right.

If only Ellen weren't acting like the Her Untouchable Highness, the Queen of the May.

They broke at noon, and after lunch—superbly cooked and served up by Linda, who had managed to make second-day turkey taste like a rare treat—the kids stayed inside. Ellen's three began arguing almost immediately about the PlayStation. Anna and Elizabeth settled themselves onto the couch and began leafing through old picture albums Grandma Mattie had accumulated over fifty or sixty years. Jay could remember thumbing through them himself on rainy days when he was a child. The adults returned outside. This time Mitch deigned to join.

"Still a lot to do," Mitch said judiciously, as he surveyed the line of fifteen or so brown bags, stuffed to the top, secured with metal twist-ties, and set waiting to be hauled out for the garbage on Monday. They had already arranged for a neighbor boy to take care of the bags, since neither Mitch nor Jay could stay beyond Saturday evening.

"Looks like everything he planted died."

It was a simple statement, but it took Jay by surprise. Thus far, in spite of his initial impressions as he had arrived the other day, he had been working on the assumption that they were essentially cleaning up old growth. But Mitch's words forced Jay to look again, more closely.

Mitch was an arrogant, self-centered, conceited blowhard most of the time, but this time he was right. Abe's place was a graveyard of unburied plants. Everything Jay saw was dead or dying. The branches of a two- or three-year dwarf peach standing forlornly in one corner were brittle and shattered when he bent them to test for sap. Roses, wisteria, pyracantha, even two palms set out at the far corners of the patio—everything was dead. Along the foundation, not even the hardiest weeds survived. Jay knelt and pulled up handfuls of dry, flaking Bermuda grass. The roots—usually almost impossible to remove from the soil—ripped up in brown, rotting masses.

Without saying anything more to either Ellen or Mitch, Jay made a circuit of the place, front yard as well as back. He wasn't a professional gardener or horticulturist or anything—at home, he barely touched his own place, relying on the twice monthly services of a Japanese gardener who worked diligently and competently and could speak no English and write little more than the date and amount due in the appropriate spaces on the bill he slipped once a month into Jay's screen door. But even with his narrow expertise, Jay knew enough from his childhood to know that something was wrong.

Nothing seemed alive.

He wondered worriedly what the house must have looked like during the spring and summer, when every other house on the street would have been a riot of Southern California colors—the vibrant scarlets and oranges and purples of bougainvillea, the delicate lavenders of wisteria and jacaranda and blue hibiscus, the fluorescent pinks and violets of geraniums. But here, at the house on the top of the hill, there would only have been brown and grey and the dingy black of dead and dying vegetation. Even the elm overhanging the corner of the yard looked diseased and rotted, its trunk seamed and twisted.

"What's going on here?" Jay asked himself as he crumbled dry leaves between his fingers. It looked like more than just neglect contingent upon failing health. It looked as if Abe had deliberately poisoned every plant in the place.

Jay started for the garage, intending to pull out a shovel and test the hard-pack soil in the front yard when a shriek from inside the house drove any such ideas from his mind.

Elizabeth!

He recognized her voice, recognized her cry as one of pain and fear, not just the petulance of a ten year old. He slammed through the front door. Elizabeth stood in the center of the family room. One hand cupped her chin, from which blood was flowing in a steady stream.

"She's dying, she's dying," Anna whimpered from her corner on the couch. Jay took in the scene at once. Thad was not in the room. Thirteen-year-old Josh stood defiantly with his back to the television screen, on which an electronic Mario whistled and burbled unnoticed. A heavy glass ashtray was clenched in his fist. One edge was starred and stained with deep red.

"Shit!" Jay said, "Now what." Even as spoke he was lifting Elizabeth and rushing her down the hall to the front bathroom. He heard the back door slam as he disappeared around the corner—that would be Linda and Ellen and Mitch. They could take care of the kids in the family room.

He set Elizabeth on the toilet seat and gently pried her fingers away from her chin. The skin was sliced, shallowly and neatly, for perhaps an inch just to the right of her mouth. Jay dabbed at it with a hand cloth from the rack next to the sink. It was bleeding heavily, but it looked like the blood was more superficial than serious.

A hand touched his shoulder. It was Linda.

"How is she?" Linda did not try to keep the fear from her voice.

"All right, I think," he answered. He held a clean hand cloth to the cut and pressed. Elizabeth winced but didn't say anything. Her eyes were still clouded with tears, but she was no longer screaming.

"More frightened than anything."

"Let me see," Linda said. Jay gently released the pressure on the cut. He pulled the cloth away. The wound was now a thin red line, oozing lightly but no longer flowing.

"Where are the band-aids?" Linda asked.

"Up there," Jay said, motioning with his head toward the medicine cabinet. Linda opened the mirrored door and rummaged for a few seconds in the depths. She took out a box of band-aids and small pair of scissors. With the deftness honed by years of motherhood and family crises she snipped at the band-aid until it was butterfly shaped.

"Move a minute."

Jay shifted away from Elizabeth. Linda carefully positioned the butterfly band-aid on the cut, then lifted Elizabeth and sat down on the toilet seat, her daughter securely on her lap.

"It's all right, honey," Linda murmured. "It's okay. You're going to be okay."

Jay reached out and touched his daughter's forehead. As he moved, he noticed that Abe was standing in the hallway, watching the proceedings intently.

"She's fine, Dad," Jay said in an attempt to reassure the old man. "Just an accident."

"Huh-uh," Elizabeth said. "Josh hit me."

"What!" Jay swung his attention back to the small, pale face pressed against his wife's shoulder.

"Josh hit me."

"Why?"

"I wanted to play. With the video game. He didn't want me to, and he grabbed that glass thing and hit me."

Jay surged to his feet. Linda grabbed his arm and held him tightly.

"Jay, please, try to stay calm and find out what happened."

"Calm! Stay calm! That little bastard nearly kills your daughter and you tell me to stay calm."

Linda blanched at the anger in his voice, then her face flushed red and hot.

Jay was out the door in an instant. He shouldered past his father, not noticing the distanced, glazed expression in the old man's eyes, not noticing that as he passed his father Jay almost knocked him off balance. The old man slumped against the wall. Already Jay was in the family room yelling. But Mitch was there also, running interference, hunched aggressively between his son and Jay.

Jay accused. Mitch defended. Josh burst into tears and threw the glass ashtray. It spun in the bright winter light, catching sunlight and refracting it in rainbow spirals as it shattered the family room window and disappeared into the dead yard.

The crash of glass startled both Mitch and Jay, enough at any rate for the nearly crazed fathers to catch their breaths. They stared at each other, realizing with a unanimity that was itself breathtaking how close they had come to blows. Mitch's fists were clenched at his sides. Jay's breath was ragged and shallow, and his voice shook as he spoke.

"Anna, come here." She came. Without a word, she slipped across the room and stood behind her father. Jay took her by the hand and led her down the hall. As he passed the bathroom, he looked in at Linda and Elizabeth.

"We're leaving. Now," he announced. "Anna, pack your things and Elizabeth's."

"Yes, Daddy." She disappeared into the bedroom the girls had shared.

"You stay here with Elizabeth," Jay said to his stunned wife. He rushed down the hallway and threw his and Linda's things into their still-open suitcases, hammered the Samsonites shut, and yanked them up. Without speaking to anyone, he stalked through the hall and out the front door. He thrust the unoffending cases into the trunk of the car, slamming the lid hard enough to jostle his key ring loose. The keys dropped to the pavement with a harsh, raucous clatter. Blood throbbed in his temples as he leaned over to retrieve them.

He re-entered the house, carefully avoiding any words with Ellen, who now fluttered protectively around her boys. Thad was in the family room as well, Jay noted, his long frame slouched in Mattie's favorite chair, his feet hooked over the arm. The boy's shoes were filthy.

He helped Anna close her bag and Elizabeth's, then took them outside as well and, moving like an automaton in spite of his mounting fury, went inside for a final time. By then Linda and Elizabeth were on their feet, standing together in the bathroom doorway.

"Jay," Linda began. "Don't you think...."

"Think, nothing. I'm leaving. Now."

He swept Elizabeth into his arms and carried her outside. Anna followed, her eyes dark with unwept tears. Jay sat Elizabeth on the back seat, then held the door open for Anna and waited until both girls were securely seat-belted in. He looked up. Linda was on the door-step. He could see Abe's silver hair glistening in the darkness behind his wife.

For a moment, Jay faltered. This is absurd, he heard himself argue. You haven't even talked to the boy; you don't know what really happened. Elizabeth is fine; she probably won't even have a scar in a couple of weeks—shallow cuts like that bleed like hell but don't really do much damage. Why are you acting like this, like Attila the Hun with raging hemorrhoids, setting out to rape and ravage and slaughter.

For a moment, he almost turned back to the girls and unbuckled their seatbelts and helped them from the car. Part of him wanted to. But that part was weaker than the part that repeated incessantly *Get out get out get out*. Even that part knew that Elizabeth's injury had little to do with the need to be away—away from obsessive Ellen and her obnoxious brood, away from Mitch's unfeeling superciliousness, away from....

Away from this house!

Admit it, Jay old boy, that's the real thing. Away from this house. He swallowed convulsively and gestured for Linda to get into the car. As she passed him, she reached out for his arm again, as if she were his mother trying to help him realize for himself the enormity of his mistake before things went too far.

He shook his head. "I know what I'm doing, hon." He waited until she was in the car, then he returned alone to the front door.

Ellen and Mitch were still in the family room. They were not speaking; they were watching him with an intensity that unnerved him. The boys were gone—whether out back or into the bedroom Ellen and Mitch were using, Jay didn't know. He didn't care, either. After the way Thad had acted the first day, after Josh injuring Elizabeth today, he didn't give a damn if he never spoke to his sister again. He focused his attention on his father.

Abraham Morris looked old and frail in the filtered light. His skin hung loosely from his face, his lips trembled even though he was not speaking, and his eyes darted back and forth, as if he were trying to discover who this stranger was standing in front of him.

"Dad," Jay said as gently as he could. "Dad, Linda and I have to leave. You understand?"

Abe nodded.

Jay wasn't sure that the movement meant; there was something about it that suggested his father did *not* understand anything that had happened in the past few minutes.

"Look," Jay continued, "I'll call you as soon as we get home. We'll have you out to our place soon. Maybe later this week. You can come out and stay until New Years if you want. Longer. We've got the room. And I don't like the idea of you staying here in this house...alone."

Abe's eyes cleared. His lips stopped their nervous tremors, and when he spoke, Jay heard his father's voice the way he remembered it from years before.

"I'm fine, Jay. I'll be fine. You just take care of Lizzy-Bizzy and Anna-banana and Linda, and let me worry about me."

Jay swallowed. He hadn't heard his father use those pet names for years.

"Okay, Dad." He paused, unsure what to say next. "Look, tell Ellen that...tell her I'm...I'm sorry and I'll call her later, too. When I've had a chance to cool down."

Abe nodded. "That would be wise. I'll talk to her."

Jay looked at his father and—on an impulse he would never quite understand but for which he was grateful for the rest of his life—reached out abruptly and threw his arms around his father. He felt the angularity of bone beneath the bulk of Abe's clothing, and realized anew that his father was old and frail and thin. He hugged Abe with all the strength he could muster, and when the two men finally broke their embrace, both had tears in their eyes.

"Okay, Dad. And...thanks."

"You drive careful, now. You hear?"

"Sure, Dad." Jay left. Abe followed a few steps out onto the porch and waved at his daughter-in-law and granddaughters in the car. Then he turned and went inside and shut the door.

"Jay?" Linda's voice was calm but subdued.

"I'm okay."

"Should we...?"

"I told him we'd call. We'd have him out soon. For a long visit." He cranked at the engine, relived that it turned over right away. "For a real long visit."

13.

Ellen's family spent that night at her father's house. Not a word was spoken abut Jay or Elizabeth or Anna. Neither Thad nor Josh was punished in any way, but all three boys were un- usually quiet for the rest of the day.

Thad slept alone on the rollaway in the back bedroom. Twice Ellen made her sleepy way down the dark hall to check on noises that had awakened her, coming from that direction. The first time, just before she opened the door, she thought she heard Thad—who *never* talked in his sleep, who always slept like a corpse, barely even shifting his body during the night—cry out. She thought he was speaking, rather than just groaning from too many turkey left-overs at dinner time. But by the time she opened the door, he was silent and still.

The second time came much later, just before the first glim- merings of dawn. This time, for some reason, she woke a few seconds before the sounds filtered through her closed door.

She was up and heading toward Thad's room before the muffled cries stopped, and this time she was able to step inside just as he fell silent.

"No, leave me alone," the boy muttered, his new-found bass

crackling unpleasantly into a childish treble. "I don't want to. No!"

When her hand grazed his, he fell silent.

She spent the rest of the night perched on the edge of the roll-away, her hand stroking his long hair. He did not move under her touch.

He did not cry out again.

Later, at breakfast, she asked, "Did you sleep all right, Thad."

"Yeah," he answered, almost sullenly. That, at any rate was normal. Thad was a hard waker.

"No bad dreams or anything?"

He stared long enough at her to make her slightly uncomfortable. The rest of the table fell silent, as if waiting for his answer.

"No, nothing like that," the boy finally said. "It was just…. It…. Sorry Gramps, but, Mom, those stuffed birds are *creepy*."

Everyone, including Grandpa Abe, laughed at the intensity in Thad's voice. After a tense moment, during which it seemed as if he might lose his temper—not an unusual occurrence for the teenager—even Thad joined in.

"I mean, every time I opened my eyes, there they were, hanging there, looking like they were about to pounce on me or something. Totally, totally *creepy!*"

The Camerons left before noon. Ellen promised to call her father later that week. They would talk things over, she promised. Maybe he could come down to San Diego for a long visit. A real long visit.

"We'll see," Abe said quietly. "We'll see."

14.

The Saturday after Thanksgiving, 2005, started out unseasonably warm, but by early afternoon the ocean-driven clouds had invaded the valleys, bringing high winds and the threat of rain. The air was damp, charged with heaviness.

Abe noted the cloud cover as he closed the front door. A car had just pulled out of his driveway, but right at the moment, he couldn't quite remember whose. It was important to remember; he new that much, but the names, the faces just wouldn't come.

He leaned against the door. His face was flushed and hot. He shuffled into the kitchen and drew a cooling drink of water from the tap. He crossed to the cupboard and carefully took down a small revolving stand that supported ten or twelve amber plastic medicine bottles, all imprinted with his name. His hand hovered over several as he tried to concentrate.

This one, for sure. He knew that he had to take the little white one. His hand dropped to another bottle. The six-sided red ones? Were they once a day? Or twice? He couldn't remember for certain, and even when he squinted at the tiny print on the label, he couldn't be sure. He took one anyway. He took four others as well, washing them down with the cool water. He opened the refrigerator and took a thin slice of turkey from a plastic-wrap-covered tray.

Turkey. It tasted good.

And it reminded him...reminded him...reminded him.... Yes, he would have to get the turkey out of the freezer in the garage soon. Wouldn't do to have the Thanksgiving turkey still cold and frozen and dead when the kids got there. Ellen should be pulling up any time now, and Jay, with their kids. I'm gonna cook them a dinner they won't soon forget, Abe reminded himself.

Just to be on the safe side, he took a pad from the kitchen drawer and carefully wrote a note to himself: "Kids coming— Thanksgiving tomorrow."

He slid the pad back into the drawer and closed it. He looked around. For a moment, he wasn't sure where he was. He felt dizzy, and his breath was painful as he drew air into his lungs. His arm and shoulder ached. He would lie down.

He went down the hallway, but instead of turning into his bedroom, he continued on to the specimen room. The rollaway was open in the middle of the floor, sheets and covers rumpled at the foot. One pillow lay like something lost on the floor, mostly hidden by the metal framework of the bed. The roll-away. That surprised him. He didn't remember putting it down, but then he didn't remember many things nowadays. He sighed. He removed the sheets and pillows, folding them carefully and setting them momentarily on the top of the bookshelf near the door.

It was a chore for him to close the bed by himself, but he finally got the metal hasps on each side locked. After that, rolling the bed back into the closet was easy. He placed the sheets and pillows on top of the metal frame.

Finished, he turned and looked over the specimen room. He enjoyed the room. It brought back memories. Everything here was as it should be. Everything in place, just as always.

No, not quite everything.

A scrap of white cloth jutted out from beneath the desk opposite the closet.

Can't have that, Abe thought. Got to get this place spick and span. I think I'll have Ellen and...and...whatshisname...sleep in here this time. Let Jay and Linda have the good bed.

Still puzzled as to what the bit of cloth might be, Abe leaned over and picked it up. The movement made his ears buzz and a wave of dizziness made him stumble. He nearly struck his head against the sharp edge of the desk, but caught himself just in time.

He held the cloth out, studying it, turning it over and over in his hands until he finally recognized it—and felt embarrassed when he realized how puzzled he had been by something so simple as a pair of undershorts.

Probably one of the boys' from last time they came.

But that was months ago. Abe was certain that he'd cleaned up since then. Why had he missed them all that time?

His hand closed over the material. It was oddly stiff in places, and for an instant Abe fluttered on the verge of remembering something more, something from his own youth so far back that he rarely ventured to visit there, even in memory.

He held the underwear in his hand and stared out the window for a long, long time.

Then he heard a sound. Two sounds, actually.

He turned toward the closet. The girls were sitting in there, sitting on the rollaway that he was sure he had closed up just moments before—but now their faces glowed with the vivid scarlet of a cloudy November sunset where the light poured through the window behind him.

Abe stiffened in horror.

The girls were naked. Sitting naked on the bed and crying, as if he had done something to them *how could he have done anything he just came inhere to clean a minute ago then how come it's dark outside old man, and how come they're crying and cringing from you in terror in horror but he'd never even considered even thought of touching them not once not ever may God strike me dead this instant if I ever even thought but they were crying* and the buzzing and the pain and the dizziness struck again with so much force that Abe stumbled backward, striking his back sharply against a filing cabinet. No *no no no* he wailed silently as the girls suddenly turned to face him, their eyes accusing and bright with hatred, their heads crowned with haloes of blood that ran slowly down their cheeks and dripped onto their bodies.

"No no no no no," he wailed, but this time out loud as the buzzing increased until it was no longer inside his head but outside, in the room with him. His eyes darted around the room. Everything was moving. Wings fluttering, beaks clacking viciously, eyes opening and closing, talons stretching, paws extruding needle-sharp claws. The walls were a wash of movement, silent and threatening and angular. Shadow struggled with light, and even the once-familiar forms of ground squirrels and robins and sparrows enlarged and rustled toward him.

He tried to whirl away, but the pain and the dizziness came a third time. The last time.

This pain was an explosion that rocked his chest and hammered the breath from his body. He thrust his hand out to steady himself on the bookshelf. His fingers touched something hard and cold and ridged. The buzzing increased, only now it concentrated itself in a single focus.

As the rattlesnake struck—once, viciously, pumping poison from its glittering fangs into the old man's frail wrist—Abe heard shrieks of laughter from the darkness that was the closet. He struggled to penetrate the darkness, to see whether the girls were gone, but he could not. Instead, the darkness reached out and touched him, penetrated his confusion and his terror and his loneliness.

And then there was only darkness.

And silence.

From the ***The Sun—San Bernardino and the Inland Empire,***
1 November 1994:

YOUTH FOUND DEAD IN HOME,
FOUL PLAY NOT SUSPECTED

The body of Brady Wilton, 12, was found in his Redlands home late last night by his parents, Frank and Julia Wilton, shortly after they returned from a costume party at Wilton's company, Alexander and Wilton Electronics, in nearby Mentone.

"They were only away for an hour or so," a neighbor, Benjamin Morely, revealed. "Frank owns the place, you know, and they really had to be there." Brady was a careful and responsible young man, Morely added, fully capable of taking care of himself.

Another neighbor and a classmate of young Wilton's, Roland Elkins, also 12, said, "He was moody sometimes, withdrawn. He could get angry easy, too, especially the last few weeks. He wouldn't even go Trick-or-Treating with kids from the neighborhood."

Preliminary reports from the coroner's office suggest young Wilton may have died from a stroke. "It's quite rare in children this young," a county representative revealed, "but it does happen."

The Wiltons, who moved with Brady to Redlands three years ago from Tamarind Valley, near Los Angeles, are not currently under investigation for any....

CHAPTER NINE

THE HUNTLEYS, MARCH 2010

Further Complications

1.

As matters turned out, Willard's estimate of somewhere around a month before any action could be taken on the house was dead on.

After three weeks of abruptly summer-like weather, typical of the typically Quixotic California climate, the ground finally dried sufficiently to allow any sort of testing. Catherine called and made an appointment to have one of the city engineers come out and examine the slab. But before he could arrive, another, seemingly unrelated, crisis struck.

It began simply enough.

Midday Saturday was a lazy time, school work done for the week, chores done, and nothing much to do. The four children were playing in the back bedroom, immersed in their own fantasy worlds of toys and books.

Willard was watching football in the family room. Catherine was puttering around in the kitchen.

In the middle of a particularly exciting play, Willard glanced toward the door from the entry way, almost as if he had been called. Burt was standing there, expectantly, as if he had something to say.

"What?" Willard was irritated at the interruption, even though the boy had said nothing yet. His voice was sharp, his expression almost angry. "What?"

Burt remained silent for a second, then faded back into the duskiness as he slipped into the living room. Willard watched until his son disappeared, his forehead creased and his eyes narrowed, even though he was not aware of it.

That was his usual expression nowadays.

A moment or so later, he heard Burt's thin voice in the kitchen. He couldn't catch the words. Catherine responded, then Burt.

Willard settled back into the couch again, intent on the game.

Catherine came to the door between the kitchen and the family room.

"Burt says he can hear a funny noise."

"Hmmm," Willard said.

"He says it's coming from the bathroom. Maybe you should…."

In the recesses of the house, Suze screamed, Will, Jr., yelped as if in surprise, and Sams, not to be outdone, started crying.

"Oh, for…! What's going on now!" Willard was up and striding toward the hallway before Catherine even left the kitchen.

"It better be something important," Willard muttered as he turned the corner in the hall and glanced toward the back bedroom doors.

The bathroom door, situated on the opposite side of the hall, midway between the open doors to Suze's room and the boys' room, was closed. The hall was dimly lit, as usual, but it seemed like the carpet at the end of the hall was far darker than it should be.

And Willard could hear a distinctive gurgling from the bath-room.

"Oh shit!" He stamped down the hall, his footsteps echoing his incipient anger. It couldn't be….

It was.

He shoved the bathroom door open, but already he had heard

the *squish* of water beneath his feet as he crossed the sodden carpet, so he wasn't surprised when he flicked the light on to see water spilling over the top of the toilet bowl. The floor tiles were an inch deep in the stuff, and the runoff was apparently following the path of least resistance, out the door, across the hall, and into the boy's room.

The toilet was spewing gallons of water, it seemed, fortunately clear enough but tinged faintly with not-quite green, not-quite brown against the white porcelain He sniffed reflexively, testing the air. Something…faint, but unidentifiable. Repellent in its own way, but definitely not sewage.

Willard ran over to the toilet, knelt on the flooded floor, cursed under his breath as his knees went suddenly cold and wet, and struggled to twist the ball valve and shut off the flow. It resisted for a couple of moments, while time the water continued to gush over the toilet rim, onto him, onto the floor.

"Catherine," he yelled, still fighting the valve. "Catherine! Towels. Quick!"

Behind him, he could hear the linen closet door screak open, then shut, then the soft *thump* as Catherine threw towels over the threshold in a futile attempt to hold back the flood. Too little, too late, Willard thought.

Finally, with a thick, unpleasant squeal, the valve turned and the water slowly tapered off, then stopped completely.

He stood, dripping from the knees down, hands chilled to the bone, face flushed with anger and frustration. What next?

"The boys' carpet is wet about halfway across the room, but the other bedrooms are dry," Catherine reported while laying another layer of towels in the hall.

Willard stood in the boys' doorway. The dark brown carpet was almost black in a quarter circle that extended from the door as far as the closet. The boy's bunk beds stood partially in the circle, as did their dresser. Sams' little box bed seemed dry, and there didn't seem to be any problem with the low table underneath the window that held a scattering of their toys, Yap's cage, and assorted detritus of cast-off clothing.

"Okay, guys," Willard said, sighing. "Let's get busy."

While Catherine mopped up the bathroom and the younger kids were relegated to the family room to watch a DVD, Willard, Will, Jr., and Burt began the tedious task of moving everything out of the bedroom—Sams' bed; the dresser drawers, one by one; the toys and clothing that had been lying on the floor and were now either sopping wet or still dry but to Catherine's mind contaminated and therefore to be removed. With a curl of his lip, as if he smelled something extremely distasteful, Burt dumped wet things into a plastic laundry basket just beyond the damp edge of the hall carpet. Will, Jr., stripped all of the beds and, careful not to let any edges trail, hauled the bedding by the armful into the family room to toss it in a corner behind the couch.

The only problem came when he entered the family room carrying Sams' blanket, crossed the room, and tossed the grubby, smelly thing into the washer.

"Nooo," Sams screamed, and Catherine had to race in from the back and comfort him, reassuring him that the blanket was only going to be gone a little while.

"Gone away, like Yip, forever?" Sams demanded.

"No, sweetie, not like Yip. You'll have it back fresh and clean before the movie's over."

It helped, but Sams spent the rest of the hour standing guard over the washer, then the dryer, until finally his blanket emerged safe and sound. He curled up on the corner of the couch, sating edging in his mouth, and promptly fell asleep.

That was probably for the best, since tempers were rapidly becoming shorter and shorter, and he was out of the way, at least.

A sharp yelp came from the back bedroom.

Catherine raced back to find Willard standing in the center of the room, water squishing out around the soles of his shoes. He was nursing a bloody finger, his good hand holding the injured one away from his body to keep his shirt from getting stained. The wound had already bled profusely enough to stain his hand red and drip onto the floor. Sodden as it was with the over-flowing water, the carpet seemed to absorb the drops almost immediately, as if drinking them.

"What happened?" Catherine took one look and turned around to retrieve the first aid kit from the top shelf of the linen closet. She grabbed a dry hand towel as well—all of the larger ones were spread on the floor to draw up the water.

"I caught my finger between the bedpost and the tip of the screwdriver when I tried to loosen the back bolts on Will's bunk, and sliced myself all to hell." He extended his hands so Catherine could see the injury better. "I'm going to have to dismantle the whole bed to get it out of here. We're going to have to take the carpet and the padding out as well. They're too wet to dry back here without molding or something."

Catherine muttered soothing non-words as she worked on his finger, wiping away the blood and cleaning the slash.

"It's not too deep, it just bled like crazy," Willard assured her absently while scanning the floor. Finally she finished wrapping the wound in a thick gauze bandage. Actually, the injury looked fairly serious. They might have to get Willard to the hospital, she thought.

"Come on out and sit down," Catherine said, tugging gently at his sleeve. "You can't do this alone, and Will's too little to be much good at moving the heavier furniture. I'll see if any of the neighbors can help."

2.

Even though the Huntleys had only lived on Oleander Place for a couple of months, they were well enough known and well enough liked that it didn't take long for a crew of half a dozen men to show up and start work, with a couple of their wives to assist in the cleanup. Piece by piece, the men hauled mattresses, box springs, the wooden frame of the dresser, the low table, then bits and pieces of the bunk beds through the family room and into the garage, stacking everything neatly along the wall.

Willard tried to help, but his hand really was starting to throb and he felt dizzy every time he went into the bedroom, so finally he took Catherine's advice—all the while glum, grudging, and frustrated—and remained in the family room. It grated on his nerves, though, whenever one of the men carried another piece through to the garage.

I should be helping them. It's my damned house. I should be able to take care of it. I shouldn't have to call on neighbors and then sit here like a cripple while they do all the work.

Finally, the men reported that, except for the clothing hanging in the closet and the pictures on the wall, the room was empty.

"Want us to rip up the carpet as well?" Ned Wilcox asked. "I used to work as a carpet layer to pay for college. It shouldn't take long."

"Let me come back and see," Willard said. He could help with that at least.

At the threshold of the bedroom, he surveyed the damage.

The faint odor he had detected earlier in the bathroom seemed stronger now, even though most of the overflow had been sopped up in the hall and the bedroom.

He wrinkled his nose and took a deep breath. The air was damp, musty, almost dank, as if it belonged in a old earth-floored, spider-web encrusted cellar. The odor was sharp, acidic, not quite strong enough to draw attention to itself but easily noticeable if one concentrated.

The most obvious result of the spill, however, was clearly evident, now that the carpet had been removed.

Arcing from the corner diagonal to the door to midway along the closet wall, a jagged crack showed stark and black against the concrete. On the far side of the break, the floor was stone dry, the typical grey of cement, with occasional dark brown rough spots where the padding had been glued down. Nothing unusual there, except for an inch-wide fissure along the back wall, perhaps two inches in from the floorboards—the extension of the crack Willard had first noticed in the living room and traced further in the kitchen. Now it was evident that the crack continued the entire length of the back wall. If he removed the carpet in the fifth bedroom—Willard's office—he would no doubt find the same condition along the wall there.

On the near side of the break, however, the floor was still damp, almost black, with an odd sheen that suggested that it would be slippery. It looked miasmal, unhealthy.

Willard stepped into the room.

The floor wasn't slippery at all, he was surprised to discover, but he could tell that it would take a while longer for it to dry completely. The kids would have to camp out in the family room for a couple of days, he realized.

Wilcox and one of the other men—Willard thought his last name was Kemp—stepped into the room after him.

"That's some crack you got," Wilcox said.

"Kind of reminds me of the Grand Canyon," Kemp added. "Just not quite as wide or as deep."

Willard nodded.

Wilcox moved past Willard and Kemp, toward the far corner where the crack began. He seemed to be pacing, measuring something.

He turned and looked at each of the other corners in turn, then at Willard and Kemp.

"You've got a bit of a slope in here, too," he said. "I figure a good three, four inches difference between the door over there and this corner." He gestured at the crack. "If it weren't for that, the water would probably have run clear across the room, under the wall, and up into the studs. Could have been a real problem."

Willard nodded.

Wilcox pointed along the back wall. "And you got another problem there," indicating where the wall had separated from the foundation. "Never seen anything like that before."

Then he brushed his hands against the sides of his pants, as if getting rid of a layer of dust or something, and said, "Anything else we can do for you, Huntley?"

Willard shook his head. For some reason, he couldn't bring himself to speak. Perhaps because actually seeing the fissure running across the entire width of the room had startled him, perhaps because he was already fuming—yet again—at the incredible ineptitude, or worse, of the builders. And perhaps because he understood that whatever was happening here, whatever would be needed to make this place livable for him and his family might just be beyond his ability to fix.

3.

The city engineer arrived the next Wednesday.

The boys were still sleeping in the family room—they had constructed a make-shift tent of chairs, quilts, and sheets in one corner and sheets and seemed perfectly happy to stay there for the rest of their lives. Sams was especially pleased with the arrangements. He would sit just under the front flap of the tent, blanket in hand, and watch the television, giggling to himself at some secret joke.

Yap seemed equally content in his new place on the wide window sill. He spent hours, it seemed, whirling around in the exercise wheel, the small *whirr* becoming an integral part of the atmosphere in the room.

The carpet and padding were still laid out in the garage. Thanks to the unusual weather, the garage was overheated for this time of year, hot and stuffy. The padding seemed dry, but the carpet retained an unpleasant stickiness when touched. Perhaps a couple more days would be enough, then it could be re-laid.

Willard answered the doorbell with a sense both of anticipation and of incipient foreboding. Whatever was going on with the house, at least the inspector would know.

"Mr. Huntley? I'm Edgar Sai, from the city inspector's office. I hear you have some questions." The man was short, official looking, with a calculator in one shirt pocket and a clipboard in his hand. He glanced down, as if to re-check his data.

"A few," Willard responded. "A few."

In a couple of minutes—after the introductions were made

and Catherine went into the family room to keep herd on the kids—Willard and Sai were walking along the back of the house. Sai kept his head down, studying the earth along the foundations of the house, the way the concrete patio slab canted toward the grass, the surface of the yard itself. Occasionally he would nod. He did not speak.

They turned the corner and stood at the end of the narrow strip along the side.

"Here's where I found it," Willard said. He pointed to the shallow excavation that paralleled the wall, but the action was unnecessary. Sai was already on his knees, one finger tracing the exposed crack. He stood.

"Do you have a shovel?"

Willard indicated the one leaning against the fence.

It took Sai only a couple of minutes to continue the trench the length of the wall. He was more proficient with the tool than Willard had been.

"Okay," he said when both of them could see that the crack extended from corner to corner, never less than half an inch wide, sometimes as much as two inches. "It's pretty clear what happened. We've seen this often enough here."

"What do you mean, *here*?"

Sai straightened and leaned the shovel back against the fence.

"Here, in Charter Oaks, as well as in Sunset Hills, over there toward the hills. There were a lot of problems when the subdivisions were built, improper materials, inadequate compaction of the soil, even some outright illegalities in construction. Happened, oh, twenty, thirty years ago or so."

"But what...?"

"Basically, the builders failed to meet most of the codes then in place, and the houses started to fall apart within a couple of years."

"Weren't there laws...?"

Sai had apparently had this conversation many times before. He seemed to know what Willard was about to ask and had no compunctions about interrupting.

"Sure. But laws only work when you catch the bad guys breaking them. This guy—McCall—was too canny. It wasn't until two years after this subdivision was finished, almost five years after Sunset Hills was finished, that the inspectors finally started to close in on him."

"Did they get him? Put him in jail or something?"

"Actually, it was sort of ironic. About the time the indictments came down and the law finally got in motion, he…died."

"Died? How?"

"Well, as a matter of fact, some kids found him…." Sai suddenly stopped. His eyes dropped to the clipboard in his hands. He took a second or two to read something, the looked up at Willard. For another couple of seconds his eyes widened and he just stared. "Uh, they found his body on Halloween night. Gave them quite a scare. Still a bit of a mystery as to how he died."

Sai seemed unwilling to say more. He made a few notes on the form on the clipboard.

"From what I see here," he said finally, "it's pretty clear what happened. This McCall had a nasty habit of cutting corners wherever he could, regardless of what it meant to the integrity of the structures.

"One of his favorite tactics was supremely simple. He would set the foundation boards and lay the steel rebar, everything ready to pour the slab. The inspector would come out and find everything perfectly within code. He'd sign off on the house, then leave.

"And McCall would pull up the rebar, pour the slab immediately, and use the same rebar in the next house. Saved a lot of money that way. No one knows which houses, if any, finally got to keep the rebar."

"So the concrete would just give way after a while," Willard said, almost to himself.

Sai nodded.

"That in itself would have been enough of a problem. But he had another trick as well."

Sai knelt down and caught a clod of dirt in his had, then stood, crumbling it as he did so. Both men watched the dust filter to the ground.

"The soil here, and at Sunset Hills, is unusually expansive. It captures moisture when it rains, and...well, *swells* is a good non-technical term. Then when it gets dry, it shrinks. Up and down.

"That's why rebar is so crucial around here. It helps stabilize the slab to minimize the effects of the recurrent movement. In addition, construction permits in the Valley specify a particular compaction technique on a property before any building can begin. It takes a fair amount of time, some expensive heavy equipment, and specially trained operators for the technique to work properly.

"Unfortunately, there's no real way to test the soil before construction to make sure it's been compacted sufficiently."

"Let me guess." Willard knew what was coming. "McCall skimped on it."

"Yeah, most of the places around here are still sitting on pretty loose ground, and when we have a wet winter followed by a dry summer...."

"Up and down. Up and down."

"Right. And this is what happens. The walls separate here," Sai pointed to the foundation. "And there." He pointed up to the jointure of wall and roof. "You can see where...."

"Yeah, I noticed."

Willard stood silently for a minute.

"Wasn't anything done about the houses, I mean, after the city found out what was happening?"

"Not much. By that time McCall was dead. The other partner in the business had disappeared a couple of years before— everyone figures he guessed what was coming and took off for parts unknown. There weren't any laws like the first-year guar-antee back then, so buyers were on their own.

"A couple of insurance companies made good on claims for the first year or two. Then, when it became obvious that probably every house in both subdivisions was defective, they got together and set up a deadline. They honored claims up to that date. Afterward…. Well, *caveat emptor*, as they say."

"But…" Willard was feeling more than a bit of the rage that had been with him since the roach experience weeks before. "But what about now? Isn't there anything like an inspection that would let new buyers know?"

"Sure. But there are ways around that as well. Look here." He knelt again and indicated the place where the stucco showed at least three paint jobs.

"This"—pointing to the lower color, sickly yellow showing here and there where a more recent slate blue had been abraded away—"this was probably the original paint job. From the looks of it, it was probably the only one for twenty years or so, then the house was repainted with this blue. See how the coats of paint extend a couple of inches below the soil level."

Willard nodded.

"This"—now running his finger along the earth-tone paint just above—"is new, probably less than a year old."

He surveyed the wall more closely.

"Yeah, it looks like the last owners realized how difficult it would be to sell the place, so they fixed it up. First, they hauled in enough topsoil to cover the foundations for six inches or so. See how the side here and the front part of the back yard slope away from the house?"

"Sure, but I thought that was normal."

"Some slope is. Not that much. And the fact that they completely covered the crack here, then repainted the house to hide any additional cosmetic treatments," he paused and jerked his thumb toward the eaves, "like plastering the break up there, tells me that they knew exactly what was going on and decided to hide everything."

Willard was livid by now, almost unable to speak. He kicked savagely at the leaning shovel. The fence shivered threateningly as the impact vibrated through the handle.

"Those bastards! I knew that something…." He took a deep

breath. "But aren't there inspections before sales, don't houses have to meet some kind of standards? Aren't there disclosure laws?"

"Can you show me your contract?"

By the way Sai asked, Willard knew that worse was coming.

4.

Five minutes later they were sitting in the living room. Catherine had just returned from the master bedroom, where they kept important papers in a small lockbox tucked away at the top of their closet.

She settled herself next to Willard on the couch. Sai faced them in the matching armchair.

Without speaking, she handed the sheaf of legal-sized papers over to Sai.

He shuffled through them, muttering here and there as if keeping tabs on what he had seen and what he had not. He was apparently looking for a particular sheet.

"Ah," he said finally. The silence had begun to grate uncomfortably on both Catherine and Willard. They could hear the kids playing quietly in the family room. No interruptions. Thanks for that, at least.

"Here we are." He leaned across to hand the papers to Willard. He had folded the top sheets back and under at the place he had been looking for, and indicated a short paragraph which his finger. "Read that."

It was only a line or two on the inspector's report.

Willard read it aloud: "Structure shows signs of some foundation issues, notably minor cracking of the external surfaces and additional soil at the base, above anticipated grade level."

He looked at Catherine. She looked back. They both shook their heads and shrugged, nonplussed.

"What does *that* mean?" Catherine handed the papers back to Sai. "Sure, we saw a couple of small cracks here and here outside, especially at the corners of the windows, but isn't that common with stucco houses?"

"Yes, it is. But that is not what this sentence is talking about. What you have here is realtor-speak for 'Beware—there's something wrong with the foundation, otherwise the current owners would not have gone to the expense of hauling in dirt and hiding the base.'"

"It doesn't say a word about...!" Willard was on his feet.

"Sit down, Mr. Huntley. Please." Sai leaned back in his armchair and looked sympathetically at the pair. "You're right. It doesn't. But what it *does* say is sufficient in a court of law to indicate that there were fundamental problems with the slab. I've seen this sentence—or others like it—on enough contracts here in the Valley to recognize legalese that basically says 'You haven't got a leg to stand on. You were warned.'"

"But we didn't even *see* that!" Willard was standing again, gesturing angrily as if he wanted to strike out at someone—Sai, since there was no one else available.

"You initialed the bottom of the page," Sai said quietly.

That stopped Willard for a second. He examined the paper again. When he spoke his voice was cold, his rage under control for the moment but waiting to explode.

"When we signed the papers," he said carefully, biting off each word, "they took us through them so quick that we didn't get a chance to read everything. And Chuck said...."

"Chuck?"

"Chuck Maxwell, the real estate agent." Willard's teeth were clenched now, his body perfectly rigid.

"He offered to accompany us to the signing. To help us if there was anything...." Catherine fell silent.

She understood now.

"Maxwell." It was a low murmur, redolent with emotion.

Sai shook his head sadly. "Even so, everything done was— from the court's point of view—legal. Punctiliously so." He seemed to enjoy the word. He had probably used it before in just this context.

He let the Huntleys have a couple of moments before he

spoke again.

"I would venture to guess that you've seen more than just the foundation problem."

Willard looked startled, shaken from an angry reverie.

"Uh, yeah. You could say that."

He stalked to the sliding doors that led to the patio and jerked back the carpet and padding, not difficult to do since there was no longer any tack-strip holding them down. He pointed to the break.

"This goes from the far corner of the kitchen all the way along the back of the house."

He gestured widely with one hand.

"There are cracks in nearly every joining—walls, ceilings, floor." He motioned for Sai to follow.

"You can see where the slab's broken under the tiles here in the entry way." Sai nodded. Willard did not give him time to respond any other way.

"But here's the best. Oh yes, here's the really fun part." He laughed bitterly as he led Sai down the hall. Catherine did not follow. She went into the family room to be with the children. She could hear small sounds of discomfort coming from them. They had heard their daddy's tone of voice before, and they did not like it.

5.

They stood in the doorway of the back bedroom, Willard fuming and speechless, Sai calm and dispassionate.

Willard didn't need to say anything.

It was all there. The sinuous crack nearly bisecting the room, disappearing beneath the baseboard with the clear intention of continuing on into Suze's bedroom and, who knew, on from there into the master bedroom.

The rough fissure fully exposed along the back wall, inches wide and black as hell, who knew how deep.

The odor, even though faint, still cloying and oppressive five full days after the spill. Suggestive of rot and decay and suppuration, suggestive of many things but *not* of sewage.

Sai merely stood there, impassive.

When he finally spoke, it was with a certain amount of sympathy in his voice. "I've see this before. House after house. There's one place in Sunset Hills where the living room floor is so displaced along one side that there is a four-inch differential. It's like the owners have half a sunken room. They are one of the unlucky ones. It didn't slip that much until after the insurance deadline passed."

Willard stared at him, speechless.

"I would guess that the side wall here probably shifts as much as a couple of inches between winter and summer." He studied the line where ceiling and wall met. "See there, in the closet, where the new plaster is already cracking. You'll probably have that in all three rooms along this wall. On family with a problem like this told me that in the summer, they can see stars between the wall and the ceiling."

He turned to face Willard.

"At least this house has wide eaves. Probably you won't have any rain coming directly inside unless the wind is especially strong."

He paced over to the back wall and knelt beside the break. He crumbled a bit of the concrete between his fingers. Then he took a pencil-like implement, extended it to a couple of feet, and worked it into the crack. Inch after inch of the thin metal disappeared. He wiggled it back and forth. Willard could hear concrete scraping against the metal.

Sai pulled the shaft out and studied it.

"See here," he said, pointing to a clump of damp brown caught on the end. "The crack extends completely through the foundation slab, more than a foot. This"—indicating the clump—"is soil from beneath the house."

He ran his hand up and down the back wall.

"Most likely, this wall will continue to pull away from the slab, a bit at a time. The patio out there is slowing the movement a fair amount, but even that is being pushed gradually toward the back of the yard.

"I wouldn't worry too much though," he said, facing Willard again. "It will probably take a couple of decades more before the place threatens to collapse." He shrugged as if to say, wish I could tell you something else, but facts are facts.

"What can we do," Willard whispered, stunned beyond anger.

"The house is about 1600 square feet, right?"

Willard nodded.

Sai pulled out his calculator and began working it. His fingers flew from key to key, *tap tap tap*, faster than Willard's eyes could follow. Then Sai made a few notes on his clipboard.

"Okay. First, you'll need a geologic survey. Figure about $10,000."

"Didn't they do a survey when they built...."

"Sure, but surprise, surprise, the original reports for these two subdivisions disappeared years ago. You'll need a new one.

"Then permits from the city. Considering what has to be done, another couple of thousand."

"But we don't...."

Sai continued inexorably. He had long since realized that it was more merciful to get all of the bad news out at once.

"Then you have a choice. The easy way would be to dig a trench, say three feet deep, all around the house. Install pneumatic jacks every three or four feet and gradually raise the house sufficiently to drill horizontally into the existing slab and insert as much rebar as possible. Then force a layer of cement across the top of the slab to fill in the cracks. That will have to cure for a couple of months, probably, then the house can be let back down into almost its original position.

"Of course, that will create a host of new problems inside, which will have to be repaired. Tearing down a fair amount of the drywall, retiling and recarpeting, repainting the whole shebang."

"How much would that cost?"

"Conservatively, figure seventy-five to a hundred thousand.

Plus loss of living space for several months."

"But…" Willard began to feel as if he were simply a machine stalled on one word. "But…."

"That would be the easiest way, but probably would end up being only a temporary solution. The ground would continue to expand and contract and the slab, still fractured in places no matter how well supported and repaired, would keep shifting.

"Isn't there a…what's the *hard* way."

"Oh, that would cost you may be three, four hundred thousand."

Willard gulped audibly."

Sai looked around the room.

"Tear the whole place down, start over, and do the thing right."

From the *Malibu Times,* 15 May 2003:

SMALL TEMBLOR FELT, NO DAMAGE REPORTED

A 3.5 earthquake was reported yesterday, its epicenter five miles off the Malibu coast. Although windows rattled and floors shook slightly, no damage has been reported.

The quake was not an unusual occurrence for this part of the California coastline, since....

CHAPTER TEN
THE MERRICKS, JUNE
2006-DECEMBER 2009

Retreat

1.

Moving's a real bitch.

Jack Merrick wiped the sweat from his forehead with his loose shirttail—already sodden in the June heat—hoisted the box from the back of the mid-sized U-haul van onto his shoulder, and began his umpteenth trip up the driveway, into the garage, and from there into the kitchen.

The movers had already taken care of the heavy stuff—refrigerator, washer and dryer, living room furniture, beds, bureaus, dressers, that sort of thing. Most of the rest of the larger pieces had been sold off, anyway, in a massive yard sale just before they left Oregon—the, the boat, the trailer, and the motorcycle. Jack figured that it would be cheaper to buy new things than to move a truckload of this and that, most of which was junk anyway.

That left just the single van, which he had driven to California, accompanied by his younger son Clark, while Ariel and Mark followed in the Saturn. Most of what was in the van was the personal shit that accumulates, even though they had only lived in Oregon for three years, and in two cities during that time.

Dishes, pots and pans, clothes, the kids' toys—Jack had wanted to sell the bicycles but Mark and Clark had raised hell at the suggestion and, good father that he was, he had given in—a few books, Ariel's sewing supplies, and on and on.

All neatly packed in cardboard boxes.

That now *he* had to lug into the new house.

Ariel tried to help, but her hip was still too sore to bear much more than her own weight, so she was puttering around inside, putting this away here and that away there, emptying boxes in the kitchen and bathrooms.

Mark was making himself useful enough, Jack thought, bringing in some of the smaller boxes and breaking down the empties and stacking them in a corner of the garage. They cost enough, and the family might need them again. Who knew?

Clark was probably sitting on his bed in his room. The cast was due to come off sometime next week, and the kid was pretty good at swinging himself along on the crutches, but he wasn't worth crap as a worker. Even when he didn't have a broken leg. Lazy shit. Eleven was old enough to pull his weight—Jack knew that from his own experiences as a kid. A broken leg wouldn't have been much of an excuse for him back then. The old man would have made him tuck stuff under his arms and swing away, or balance boxes on his head. Clark was lucky to have *him* as a father, rather than Grandpa Merrick.

"Hey! Watch it!"

"Sorry, Dad." Mark peeped around the corner of the box he was carrying. It was big enough and awkward enough that the kid couldn't see over it or around it, so he was following the line of the driveway. Came this close to bumping Jack. That wouldn't do.

"Well, be more careful next time."

"Okay."

Jack dropped his burden to the sidewalk and swiped at his forehead again. He watched his son struggle his way into the house, heard him yelling at Ariel, "Mom, where does this go?" Jack couldn't hear Ariel's response. She was pretty soft spoke, rarely raised her voice above a whisper. Made for a quiet home, something Jack valued.

He shouldered the box again and made his way into the shade of the garage—it must be ten degrees cooler in there—and then into the house. The air conditioner was running full blast but the place didn't feel any cooler than the garage. The AC unit sticking up on the roof like a blister was as old as the house itself, nearly twenty years old, Slick Maxwell had said on the final walk-through yesterday. Maybe they'd have to replace it. Maybe not. Who knew?

Jack continued through the house, down the hallway, around the corner, and on to the back bedroom, *his* room. His *sanctum sanctorum*. The place where he would go when the kids got to be too much, when Ariel got on his nerves and he started to lose it.

The room wasn't large enough to be a proper *den*, but it would hold a couple of streamlined leather armchairs, his flat screen, his antique liquor cabinet, and the few personal items he carried with him wherever they moved. Mostly mementos from college, a couple of trophies, a football signed by the team the year they went to state and he was voted MVP for the playoff game, that kind of thing. What he needed to make him feel like the man he was…or at least used to be.

He dropped the box and fell into one of the armchairs. He threw his head back against the cool leather and closed his eyes. He'd worked up quite a sweat. It was pleasant to sit back and take a well-earned rest.

"Jack?" Ariel's voice barely carried the length of the hallway but it was enough to interrupt his short breathing space. "Jack, where did you put the box with the curtains for the living room?"

"How the hell should I know," he grumbled to himself. "It probably looks just like all the rest." But he pushed himself out of the chair and headed down the dark hallway. Might as well get this over with. "Coming," he yelled. "Get me a cold one from the fridge, will ya?"

Yeah, moving sure was a bitch.

2.

The first few months in Tamarind Valley went smoothly, like they always did just after a move.

The new job went like jobs went. Jack was good at what he did and no one ever complained about the results. Which was good, since it made work easy to find wherever they moved.

He took the money they had put away when they got rid of the place in Oregon and bought pretty much the same things he had sold up there. First a camper. Southern California summers were everything the travel brochures promised, and almost from the first the Merricks spent every weekend on the road, traveling to the ocean or the desert or the mountains. It was always good to get away from things, and anyway, the great outdoors was healthy for the kids, wasn't it? They certainly enjoyed the freedom to wander around from dawn to dusk without having to be shepherded every moment.

They enjoyed the trips even more after Jack bought three off-road motor bikes, one full-sized for him, two used, cut-down models for the boys. Ariel didn't like bikes, which was just as well. She preferred to spend the time in the camper, reading or napping. Just as well. Saved some money there.

Once Jack found out about Lake Cachuma, a couple of hours to the north, he decided that the family had to have a boat. Something small enough to haul behind the camper but big enough for fishing and water skiing. A week later a trim little craft was parked in half the driveway, safely sheltered by an electric blue tarp.

Yeah, the Merricks were a with-it, mobile family, all right. Jack liked it that way.

The boys settled into their school routines easily when fall came. Slick had pointed out the advantages of having schools near enough that the kids could walk there and back. Be good for them. Build them up. Build character.

There were the occasional rough spots, of course, but Ariel knew well enough how to handle them.

No one questioned Mark's injured knee. Ariel write a bullshit note about him tumbling down some stairs and bruising it. It got him out of running in P.E., which was all the kid cared about. Ariel only had to drive him and pick him up a couple of days before he could limp his way to school.

Clark stayed home every now and then, but the school seemed to understand that kids that age sometimes just wore themselves out playing and needed an occasional day to recuperate.

And, on the whole, they performed well. Mark's grades were just above average in most subjects. Clarks dipped below now and again but he always managed to pull them up. Both boys came home with report cards bearing teachers' notes that indicated the boys were shy and perhaps a bit socially backward—but that came with moving so often, didn't it? They both excelled in P.E, though, and that counted for something.

After the blazing heat of summer passed, Ariel was more comfortable, too. She had rarely left the house, not even to work in the yard, which was Jack's self-proclaimed bailiwick. When she did, it was to drive the second-hand Kia Jack bought for her to go to the store and back. Stores were air-conditioned, so no one ever said anything about her long-sleeved shirts or full-length pants.

And everyone in Southern California wore shades in the summer.

On the whole, Jack was satisfied with life on Oleander Place. Since they were on the end of the street and, in spite of what he might tell Ariel, he only infrequently actually worked in the front yard—mowing and a bit of weeding now and then—they made few close friends among the neighbors.

That was all right. Jack liked his family to be self-sufficient.

3.

By the beginning of June, 2009, however, Jack was getting a bit worried. He knew the signs well enough.

Then it happened.

For once, he was glad that what seemed like every kid in the neighborhood was hanging around their back yard. For some reason, a bunch of boys had tagged home with Mark after school on Friday, and Ariel had let them stay to play. She had whipped up some lemonade, even though she knew that Jack would disapprove. When Mark lost his handhold on one of the top branches in the disease-ravaged elm in the corner, and the branch beneath gave way under his weight, there must have been ten kids standing around.

Great.

Witnesses.

This time, when he took Mark into the ER at Oak Glen Hospital, none of those goddamn know-it-alls would look at him that way. This time, he had witnesses that would swear that he hadn't laid a hand on the kid, that he wasn't even in the yard when it happened.

He was, in fact, sitting in the recently converted garage that now served as a family room, watching a replay of a Lakers' game on the tube, drinking a cool one and wondering if this was the summer that he would finally break down and get rid of the old thirty-six incher and go for broke and buy a window-sized flat screen. The Lakers were even ahead for a change when he heard Mark's piercing shriek.

Shit, it would have to happen right now—whatever the hell was going on out there. Right in the middle of a game. And with Ariel out gallivanting somewhere, God knows where that woman gets to even though she always claimed it is only to Albertsons or Sav-on, so he would have to take care of whatever was wrong. Probably just a squabble among the brats and Mark had lost. Jack got up and hitched his pants to his waist and made his way through the kitchen—not too fast, don't let the kid think he can control you, even if he is still screaming bloody murder.

But even Jack knew with one glance that there was more wrong here than just a backyard fight. The bone stuck maybe an inch through Mark's forearm, white and gleaming and stained with red. The boy was on his feet, but wobbly and white and looking like shit warmed over.

Okay, hospital time.

By the time Jack had buckled in and cranked the ignition, Mark was seated on the passenger side. Jack had grabbed a towel in the kitchen as they rushed through and wrapped it around Mark's arm, so there shouldn't be any blood on the seat.

"Hang on, kid."

Mark didn't answer. Jack glanced over. The kid's eyes were squeezed shut and he was sweating like a pig.

Jack floored the accelerator.

He knew the way to Oak Glen, so it wasn't more than a few minutes before they screeched to a halt outside the ER. An attendant was right there with a wheelchair, and Mark disappeared into the urgent-care rooms before Jack had time to follow.

When he got to the admissions desk, the receptionist glanced up. Her eyes narrowed and her lips pursed.

"Mr. Merrick?"

"Yeah, it's my son."

"Mark or Clark."

"Mark. He fell out of a tree. Broke his arm."

She nodded. "We've got him inside. You can go on back when you finish signing this." She slid a form toward him.

"Yeah, him and a bunch of kids were playing out back and Mark fell. I was watching TV."

She nodded again but still didn't speak.

"A Lakers' game."

He slid the paper back to her.

She barely glanced at it. "Go on back. You know the way."

He was told which examining room they had taken Mark to. When he entered, there was Mark, laying back on the bed, eyes still closed and breathing heavily. The doctor was there— what was his name, Raja-badda-bing-bang or something foreign like that. They always seemed to be foreign any more. Like the hospital couldn't afford to hire a good old American doc. And there was another person, a grim-looking heavy-set woman in a business suit standing just inside the door.

Jack crossed the room and laid one hand on Mark's other arm.

"How's he doing."

"Compound fracture. But you probably guessed that. Doesn't look terribly serious but we'll have to keep him here at least over night to stitch him up and set the arm. Then keep him under observation. Infection, you know."

At least they got the one that was fairly easy to understand, Jack thought. Spoke decent English.

The doctor had not looked up but kept his attention riveted on what he was doing.

"He fell out of a tree," Jack said. "Bunch of kids were out back playing in the tree. He fell." Jack ended weakly. He'd already said that. Enough.

The doctor shook his head slightly, up and down just sufficiently to indicate that he'd heard but not enough to invite further discussion.

"Mark?" the doctor said. "How does it feel now. I've given you a shot that should help."

The boy still kept his eyes closed. "Okay, I guess. Numb now."

"Mark, what happened?"

"I just told…," Jack began.

The doctor held up one hand. Jack shut up.

"What happened?"

"I was up in the top of the old tree and slipped. Fell onto another branch. It broke and I fell all the way down. It hurt."

"Mr. Merrick?" The voice came from behind Jack.

He stood and turned to face the woman. Hatchet-faced old broad.

"Would you step out into the hall with me, please?"

"Who the hell are you?"

"Please step outside, Mr. Merrick. We can talk more freely there."

Jack patted Mark's good arm, then stalked out of the room.

"Okay, what the hell is this about? Who are you?"

"Orinda Washington. Hospital liaison with County Child Services."

"Child… I don't have to talk to you." Jack turned and began opening the door to Mark's room.

"Yes, I'm afraid you do, Mr. Merrick. Here and alone with me, or in my office with a security officer."

Jack stared.

"What do you mean. Mark *fell*! A dozen kids saw it!"

"That's what the boy said. Before you came in. It's what we expected him to say, that he fell from something. Of course, we'll have an officer at your home shortly to verify what happened."

"Then what…!"

She held up a hand, not to placate him but to stop him.

"Your son's file was flagged, Mr. Merrick. Both your sons' files, as a matter of fact. And your wife's. In fact, you are the only member of your family whose file in the ER is *not* flagged."

"This was an *accident*! How many times do I have to tell you people that. Mark is clumsy, he climbed too high, and he fell. End of story."

"This time, perhaps. But we've established a…what shall we call it…a cut-off point, where the signals become too obvious to be missed. This time might have been an accident. The last time also. But so many times in less than three years? That worries us."

"Worries *you*? What the hell have you got to be worried about?"

"Actually, Mr. Merrick, perhaps *you* are the one that should be worried."

"Are you threatening me? Because if you are, I'll sic my lawyer on you—and this dipshit hospital—so fast that…."

"Not a threat, Mr. Merrick. Not even a warning. Just a word of advice. We are worried about Mark and Clark…and Ariel, as well. We just wanted to know that their files are flagged."

"Yeah, well you're not the only hospital that…."

"There are only two hospitals in Tamarind Valley. Oak Glen and County. We share information about certain cases. *All* of our information. It would be wise if we never saw...."

Jack turned his back on the woman and slammed through the door.

"When can he go home, doc?"

4.

When Jack stomped into the house a few hours after he left with Mark, Ariel knew the look on his face. She had seen it before. Her heart fell. *Not again.*

She started to ask about Mark.

"Not a word," Jack growled. "Not a word from you."

He strode down the hall and disappeared around the corner. An instant later Ariel heard the door to his den smash against the jamb.

Clark looked up from where he was half-laying on the floor, doing his homework while stealing glances at the TV screen.

"Is Mark all right?"

"He's still at the hospital. They will probably keep him there for a day or two."

"Like last time?"

"Yes. Like last time. But I'm sure he will be all right."

"Mom, are we going to move again?"

Ariel swallowed. She knew the signs. There had been sufficient...episodes...in the sixteen years their marriage had endured. She knew the sequence—move to get a fresh start, stagger along as if they were a normal family for a while, then the excuses and the yelling would begin again. She could almost write out a time-table. But somehow, she felt that this time things were different. Frightening. Moving at a much faster pace than ever before. Deteriorating almost day by day. Jack seemed... different here, in this house. Sometimes when he emerged from his den after a...difficult evening, she almost didn't recognize him.

She smiled wanly at her younger son. She couldn't find it in her heart to answer him.

5.

"Slick, this is Jack."

Jack winced at the undercurrent of static coming through his cell phone. The thing was the newest model, only a couple of weeks old. The interference only happened back here in his den, and that sure as hell made him mad. Every other place in the house, clear as crystal—back here in his den, *hisssss buzzzzz sssssssh.*

"Jack," the voice answered. "Good to hear from you, buddy. How they hangin'?"

"Not so good. That's why I'm calling."

"Well, you know, nothing too good for an old roomie. What can I do you for?"

"It's…well…I've been thinking of selling this place and moving."

"Going upscale on us, huh?"

"Not exactly. More like moving away. Out of state."

Hissss, buzzzz, ssssssh. The static surged more loudly as the voice on the other end momentarily fell silent.

"Like that, huh?"

"Yeah, afraid so. Anyway, you know how much I appreciate your getting us into this place. Bargain-basement price and all."

"No problemo. After the old fart that used to live there died, his two kids couldn't get rid of it fast enough. Funny, though, the deal almost fell through there at the end. I couldn't even get them together in the same town long enough to sign the papers. Not a family I'd like to know better. They didn't so much as speak to each other the whole time. But that's neither here nor there. How can I help?"

"I know the market's pretty soft right now…."

"That's the understatement of the year!"

"Yeah, but it's…I…can you help me dump this place? Fast?"

"Sounds serious."

"It kinda is. Look, you and I know the condition the house is in. Will that make it too hard to get rid of?"

"You made any improvements."

"Just the room conversion. The old garage is the family room now, and I had them build an adjoining garage. The property was just wide enough between the house and the fence to fit."

"Umm. That will add a good bit to the square footage. Any more…uh…complications?"

"Not really. Just what you know about. Cracks along the foundation. Cracks on the inside walls. Seems to have slowed, though. Not much new recently."

"Okay, Jack. I think we can work with this. It'll take a little of money, though, not as much as a major re-build but a bit."

"Whatever."

"Okay, buddy, here's what we're going to do…."

6.

Jack had a bitch of a headache. It started at his temples and shot across his forehead, *throb throb throb throb.* His eyes watered from the pain.

He settled deeper into his armchair, grateful once more that his den had turned out to be the quietest room in the house. Ariel and the kids were probably in the family room watching TV. From back here he could hear nothing.

Except the *throb* of blood rushing through his veins and pounding against his temples.

He took a long pull on his beer.

Cold. Thank god for the mini-fridge back here. He didn't think he could stand to walk as far as the kitchen right now.

The headache had begun during the drive home. That had happened more than once in the five months since he had placed the call to Maxwell. The call for help.

Five months.

An eternity.

There had been a few nibbles on the house almost as soon as it was ready to show. Two prospects had even tendered offers, but for some reason they had been withdrawn shortly after the marks had made a careful walkthrough. Slick hadn't been too concerned.

"That's the way the market is right now. Mostly lookie-loos. Don't worry. Things will probably pick up after school opens."

Easy enough for him to say, Jack thought bitterly. He didn't have to come home to Ariel and the kids and these damned headaches.

He rolled the cold can against his forehead.

He knew that he sometimes had…problems. He tried to keep control, and most of the time he could. But every once in a while, situations arose and he just…let go.

But for the last few months, it had been worse. Much worse. Much harder to manage…things.

He knew from past experience what the red rages felt like, the need to lash out and *hurt* someone. He was careful, though. Never too much. Never too often. And usually he didn't have to make an ER run.

But now.

He shuddered.

Hurting didn't seem to be enough. A slap across the cheek. A punch to the shoulder. A good solid whack on a naked rear end. A belt on the back of the legs—high, where it wouldn't show. Those didn't work.

Now he wanted, *needed* more. When the mood was on him, he could close his eyes and easily—oh, so very easily—envision smashing his fist into Clark's face, breaking a jaw and spilling teeth all over the floor like kernels of bright-red rice. Or crushing Mark's nose with his elbow, feeling the sudden, almost orgasmic heat of blood flowing across the flesh of his arm. Shattering Ariel's arm the next time she tried to restrain him, feeling the bones crumble into fragments, like the slab beneath his chair. Beating them all…all of them at once. Pounding them bloody. *Destroying them.*

When he was in control, that seemed bad enough. But it wasn't the worst.

He took another long drink.

He probably should get up and turn on the light. It was already dark, even though daylight-savings time wouldn't end for a week or two. His den was shrouded in shadows…and sometimes the shadows seemed to flicker, to *move*.

Sometimes they whispered to him to…to do *things…horrible, terrifying things…not to Ariel or the boys but to* himself.

It was the memory of *those* urges that utterly froze him. His headache geared up a notch or two.

Shit. How much more of this could he take.

Rap. Rap.

Small, tentative knocks sounded on his closed—and carefully locked—door. Anger flooded through him.

The *knew* that the weren't supposed to disturb him when he was in here.

Rap. Rap.

"What!"

There was a short pause, then a faint voice. It was Clark. Jack could almost see the brat's face, pale and drawn at the prospect of what he knew must be coming.

"Dad?"

"I told you not to…!"

"There's a man here to see you."

Jack sat bolt upright. The movement sent spikes through his brain.

"Cops?"

Another pause.

"No. Just a man. He says his name is Maxwell."

Jack released his breath explosively and settled back into the chair. He upended his beer and drank the rest in a single long swallow.

He rose, thumbed the lock, and pulled the door open.

What the hell!

He jerked back convulsively, almost slammed the door closed, then blinked.

A phantom *something* seemed to be floating chest-high in the dimness of the hallway. Green glowing eyes, green glowing teeth, splotches of red glowing like baleful, fevered eruptions on dead skin. Everything else black, dead black. Black so deep it seemed to swallow what little light there was.

"Dad?" Clark sounded worried...and terrified.

"What are you...?" Jack hit the switch beside the door and the den light flared, casting stark shadows everywhere but emitting enough light into the hall to illuminate the figure that stood before him.

It was a fifteen-year-old vampire, Dracula-cape and all, its hair blackened for the occasion and slicked back.

Clark in costume.

Clark must have figured out what was going on in his father's mind. "It's my costume," he said hurriedly. He backed a step toward the wall behind him. "For the Halloween party at school day after tomorrow. Mom was finishing it for me when the doorbell...."

Jack swept past his son, unaware of brushing the boy's shoulder hard enough to force Clark further back into the wall. Clark groaned, but only a bit and mostly under his breath. He knew better.

Jack nearly ran down the hall. Now that the shock of seeing that damned costume was receding, excitement flooding through him in its place.

Slick was here. It *had* to be good news.

Five minutes later, the two of them were seated comfortably in the armchairs in Jack's den. The overhead lights were on, as were the desk lamp on the top of the liquor cabinet and another on the small table he used as a make-shift desk. The room was harsh, stark, uncompromising in its brightness. Right now, Jack needed it that way.

"Yeah, this time the deal's going through. No problemo," Slick said, chuckling softly. "I gave them a sob story about how you had bid on a custom-built place in Newton Park and if you didn't close on this house soon, you would lose it. They're first-time buyers, excited by the prospect, eager, and above all gullible."

"But you're sure."

"Positive. I took them through last weekend while you were in Palm Springs, and they burbled all the way about how perfect it was, what they were going to do with this room, who was going to sleep in that room. You could see her running up curtains in her mind and planning on ordering throw pillows to match the color of the living room walls."

"They didn't notice anything?"

"Nah. Oh, they tried to look nonchalant, even slightly disinterested, but you can't kid a kidder. They're hooked and they didn't bother to check out anything too closely."

"What happens if they find out about, you know, the *real* problems."

Maxwell leaned over and slapped his old roommate's knee. "Come on, Jack, have some faith in me. I've handled enough of these places, here and in Sunset Hills, to know how to protect myself…and, of course, you as well.

"I recommended an 'outside inspector' when they first got interested, even said I'd pay his fee. They took me up on the deal. Fred's a good friend…and a good *silent* partner, emphasis on 'silent.'" He chuckled. "He knows exactly how to word the reports. After all these years, and all the lawsuits, he's a past master at saying things without actually saying them at all. Don't worry about that."

Jack relaxed into his chair. He grabbed another beer out of the fridge next to the chair, then grabbed a second and tossed it to Chuck Maxwell.

It wasn't for nothing that his old friend had earned his nickname as far back as college.

"Slick," indeed!

The two men clicked rims of their beers in a toast and laughed together.

From the *Tamarind Valley Times,* 25 April 2009:

LA COUNTY RUNS DRILL FOR "THE BIG ONE"

LA officials reported today that the recent county-wide earthquake-preparation drill was largely successful in increasing residents' awareness of the importance of being ready should "the Big One" strike.

Volunteers at stations across the county arrived at "emergency centers," to be made-up as victims of a major earthquake, such as could occur in Southern California at any time.

Scientists have warned for....

CHAPTER ELEVEN
THE HUNTLEYS, MARCH-JULY, 2010

The Frog and the Cauldron

1.

It was like the old winter's-tale of the frog and the cauldron.

If one were to place a living frog in a cauldron of boiling water, it would reflexively jump out, thus saving itself.

If, however, one were to place the same frog in a cauldron of cool water, then gradually increase the temperature, degree by degree, the frog would remain content to paddle in small circles until, without ever realizing what was happening, it died.

Boiled to death.

Gradually. Gradually.

Thus it was with the Huntleys. Gradually. Gradually.

And they would regret to their dying days that they did not truly notice it coming.

2.

The remaining weeks of March were frustrating and difficult for the entire family. Willard finally calmed down enough to realize that, while long-term solutions might seem—indeed might *be*—impossible given the family's financial situation, there were some immediate, short term responses he could take.

First order of business, he had to dry the back bedroom floor completely. As soon as Sai left that afternoon, he hustled around the neighborhood and borrowed five high-powered box fans. It was lucky that the weather remained so warm, because he could open the window, set three fans up in the room and the hall to keep the air moving. Slowly, the dark sludge-like stain dissipated, although even after three or four days, the concrete was still several shades darker there than on the far side of the crack.

The fans helped a bit with the odor as well. Even though it never disappeared completely, it faded—gradually—until Willard had to focus his attention to detect it. Curiously, he thought several times, there was still no distinctly sewer-like smell. What he could smell seemed odd. He never could quite place it.

The carpet and padding were drying out fairly well in the nearly stifling garage, so it took only a day or two more with the remaining two fans to complete the job. The padding seemed fine, but there was still that unpleasant stiffness to the carpet nap. A couple of rounds with the vacuum should take care of that though.

Catherine was Catherine. Pretty much impossible to faze—except for roaches and such-like vermin. She was the primary stabilizing force in the family, even after Willard returned almost to normal. The only real difference in her actions during this interim was to grow gradually more protective about the children, watching them closely when they were in the house or playing in the yard, checking on them more frequently than usual after they went to sleep.

Suze was like her mother, solid and resilient.

The boys…ah, the boys. They was a different story.

Almost immediately after the carpet was re-laid and Willard had moved the boys back into their bedroom, they began fussing more and more about little, inconsequential things.

First it was Sams' tantrum when Catherine began dismantling the make-shift tent in the family room.

"No!" Sams screamed when she pulled off the first sheet. "No" seemed to be his favorite word recently, and he used it with full force this time. "No! I want the tent!" He went so far as to drop his blanket unheeded on the floor and race across the room to start a lopsided tug-of-war with Catherine, grabbing the tail of the sheet, wrapping it around his waist, and struggling to pull it out of her hand.

"Sams!" Catherine sounded almost as upset as he was. "Let go of that. You're a big boy now. You know you sleep in your bedroom, in your own bed. This was only a...a just-for-now."

The tussle lasted for several moments before Willard finally showed up at the doorway, took the problem in at a glance, gritted his teeth, swept Sams off his feet, and literally unrolled the sheet from his waist. He kept a kicking and screaming Sams pinned tightly in his arms until Catherine had finished putting away the sheets, blankets, and chairs, and nothing at all was left of the tent but a bare spot on the carpet.

"No," Sams wailed, but this time it was a soft moan, almost a whimper, as if he had used up all of his strength. "I want the tent."

"Come on, Sams," Willard urged. "Your bed's all set up for you and waiting. Just the way you like it."

Sams shook his head. "No." This time it *was* a whisper.

Willard leaned over and retrieved Sams' blanket. To his surprise, the boy stared at it for a long moment, as if he didn't recognize what it was. Even when Willard held it up to Sams' cheek, the boy still wouldn't take it.

Willard looked to Catherine for an explanation. This had *never* happened before. She shrugged.

It wasn't until Willard actually laid Sams in the little box bed and settled the blanket next to him that Sams reached out for it, touched it several times as if to remind himself of what it was, and pulled it toward his face.

When Willard left the room, the baby was half asleep, worn out by the intense emotions of the past half hour.

Later that night, long after Willard and Catherine figured the children should be asleep, they heard an odd, snuffling sound from the back of the house. Catherine went to check.

By the time she reached the end of the hall, the noise had stopped.

She looked first in Suze's room. Nothing. Suze was curled up, a sweet smile on her lips, deeply asleep.

Catherine continued on into the boys' room. Sams was asleep as well, his face covered by his blanket. As usual, the satin edging was again sodden and sour-smelling, but beneath it his chest was moving up and down with clock-like regularity. She felt his cheek. Warm, but not too warm. He was fine.

She turned toward the bunk beds.

"Don't...don't...leave me alone. No...."

It was Will, Jr., in the top bunk, talking in his sleep so quietly that the sounds came out more like an extended moan than meaningful, articulate words.

"Will," Catherine whispered, shaking him gently by the shoulder. "Will, honey, wake up. You're having a bad dream."

"Leave me alone...alone.... What?" He sat up so suddenly that he nearly struck Catherine's nose with his forehead. "What do you ...?"

"Will," she whispered again.

"Mommy?"

Catherine was startled. Will hadn't called her that for a couple of years. He considered the word the ultimate in baby-talk and refused to use anything but *Mom*.

"You're all right, sweetie."

Mommy.... Mom...bad dream. There was a...man... bloody...."

"Shhhhh." She laid a hand on his chest and gently pressed back. His heart was thudding like a captive bird's, throbbing more rapidly than she had ever felt it. Still, he settled without further murmuring into his bed again, asleep before his head even touched the pillow.

Catherine leaned down to check on Burt. Stomach and legs bare as usual, covers swathing his head as usual. She straightened the sheet and tucked it around him. He didn't move, beyond a small twitch with one hand when she touched it.

"Everything all right back there?" Willard was engrossed in the paper and barely looked up as she entered the room.

"I…I think so."

He looked closely at her. "Think?"

"Will…. No, everything's fine. Will was just mumbling in his sleep. A dream, probably. It's been a stressful few days around here."

Willard nodded absently and kept on reading.

3.

The next days and weeks proved that things were indeed not fine.

Catherine figured that things would settle down. But by the beginning of April, she admitted to herself that she was becoming concerned.

First, Sams seemed to end up sleeping on the floor every night, almost in the middle of the room. She would go in first thing in the morning to get the older boys up for school, and there he would be, nose pressed to the carpet, blanket resting on his cheek, with no covers over him at all, fast asleep.

Then both Will, Jr., and Burt began having bouts of sleeplessness. Initially, it was only Burt. Catherine would wake suddenly, frequently from unusually vivid dreams that, while they seemed to carry over for a few moments into the waking world, she could never recall. Her eyes would abruptly open, she would undergo a few seconds of utter confusion as to who she was and where she was, then she would roll over, her back to Willard, to face the wall.

And see Burt standing there, silent, eyes wide and fearful.

"I woke up," he would say.

When she checked the clock on the night stand, it would read

2:00, or 3: 23, or 4:05—never quite the same time but always in the deepest, darkest part of the night.

"Go back to bed, honey, and you'll go back to sleep."

"Can't."

"Can't get to sleep?"

"Can't go back to bed."

When Burt said this the first time, so softly that she had trouble hearing him, she sat up and half-lifted him up to the bed with her. "What's the matter?"

"I been trying to sleep for a long, long time. But I can't. Now I can't go back to bed either."

"Why not?"

But already his eyes were fluttering, his head nodding. And before she could say anything else, he was asleep.

She carried him to his bed and tucked him in, conscious of how heavy and how tall he was becoming. His feet thumped lightly against her shins as she walked, and she could barely manage to lean over and lay him on the lower bunk.

The next time she woke to see him standing beside her—it was only a day or two later—she didn't invite him up. She let him talk for a couple of minutes, mostly repetitions of "I can't sleep" or "I can't go to bed," then she would gently say, "All right, Burt. Everything is all right. You can go to bed now."

And—amazingly, considering how adamant he had seemed the first night—he would toddle off. She followed him once or twice to make sure he got in bed all right. Then she would pick Sams up off the floor and settle him into his bed as well, and return to her own.

Sometimes, she went right to sleep herself. Sometimes she was still awake when the alarm jangled and Willard stumbled up at 5:00 to get ready for work.

After a week or so of that, she woke up in the middle of the night, rolled onto her side and saw...Will, Jr.

"Can't you sleep, either?" she whispered.

He shook his head solemnly.

She let him sit on the edge of the bed for a few moments,

stroking her hand up and down his arm, soothing him in the way that had worked so well when he was younger.

Then he stood, leaned over and kissed her, and went on his own back to bed.

That continued for a few more days, with Burt and Will alternating their deep night visits. They never came at the same time or on the same night.

4.

That phase came to a head at the beginning of the third week in April.

For four days in a row, all three boys visited their parent's bedroom. Only this time, they did more than just stand by Catherine's side until she woke.

"Mom! Mom!" Will was half-whispering, half-shouting in her ear, his voice urgent with fear and need. "Mom, wake up!"

She sat bold upright.

"Shhh. Don't wake your father."

"Too late," Willard rumbled from the other side of the bed. "What's going on?" He felt for his own alarm clock next to his side of the bed, and lifted it up close to his face. "Two-fifteen? What...?"

"It's all right, Willard. Will just had a bad dream or something."

"No, it wasn't that," Will whispered, as if afraid that someone else, someone not his father or his mother would hear. "I thought I saw...something...someone in my bedroom. A shadow by the closet. It moved. I'm scared."

By this time Willard was sitting up as well. "There's no one there, son, you must have been dreaming or...."

"No, I wasn't asleep. I haven't been asleep for...for the longest time now. I was just laying my bed looking up at the ceiling. Sometimes I see birds up there, I think. And I like to watch them fly in little circles. In little circles." His voice too on a dreamy, muffled quality that Catherine found unsettling.

"Then that was it," Willard said, laying back down and hunching under the covers. "You were dreaming. Go back to bed. I've got to get to sleep now."

"Mom," Will whispered again. "It wasn't a dream. It wasn't like before, with the birds"—at the mention of the phantom birds, Catherine felt a chill along her spine—"this time there was *something* in there."

"All right." Catherine got out of bed, threw on her robe, and stepped into her slippers. "Let's go see."

As the two of them left the bedroom, she carefully, quietly closed the door. Willard really did need his sleep. The drive into L.A. was hard enough without doing it half-awake.

In the boys' room, she picked up Sams and put him back in his bed, then flicked on the Mickey Mouse lamp. The dim light cast shadows across the room, shadows that danced with each movement she or Will made. She padded to the closet—there hadn't been a door on the closet when they moved into the house and, in spite of his promises, Willard hadn't yet installed a new one. She slid the row of shirts and coats back and forth, showing Will that there was nothing behind them. She even lifted some of the fallen clothing from the floor and stacked them onto the upper shelves.

"Nothing here."

"No. Not now."

"All right, then. Up you go." She waited for Will to climb into the upper bunk and settle himself, then returned to her own bed.

She was still awake when she heard another whisper in her ear.

"Mommy?"

It was Burt this time, standing so close to her that she could smell his warmth and the slightly acrid sweat on his pajamas.

"Yes?"

"I saw something in my room. A monster, I think."

Catherine sighed. It much be contagious. Monster-itis, or Something-spooky-in-the-dark-itis. And both boys had caught it.

"Catherine." Willard didn't move or say anything else, but she understood his message. Get him back to bed and let me sleep!

"Come on, Burt."

Together they walked the length of the hallway and entered the back bedroom. Then she went through the same routine. Pick up Sams and put him in his bed. Turn on the light. Check the closet. Reassure Burt that everything was okay. Get him bundled into his bed. Check on Will, Jr., retrace her steps to the master bedroom. Slide into bed as quietly as possible so she didn't disturb Willard again.

This time she had slipped into sleep, had even begun to dream—another of those vivid, surrealistically realistic, unmemorable dreams, even though she didn't realize it, since the dream seemed merely an extension of the night's alarms—when her eyes opened yet again.

Sams.

He didn't speak

He didn't even wait.

As soon as he saw that she was awake, he crawled onto the bed, over her, and under the covers between her and Willard.

"What the hell…!" Willard shot out of bed, brushing frantically at the front of the well-worn Lakers T-shirt that was part of his night wear. That and his boxers. Winter or summer, never anything else.

Catherine sat up just as abruptly.

"Willard!"

"He's *wet*! *Soaked*! Just feel."

She did. She hadn't noticed it when Sams crawled over her into the bed, but he was drenched, sopping, the front of his pajamas stained shades darker than the back.

Sams had been wearing extra-thick pull-up night diapers for a couple of months now. He had *never* had an accident before. He was almost completely potty-trained. Both Catherine and Willard were proud of how well he had managed the transition.

But now, he lay curled up on the bed, deeply asleep in spite of having just come into their room seconds before, and smelling pungently of urine. There was a dark spot spreading on the sheet beneath him, and a matching dark spot across most of Willard's chest.

"Okay, Willard. You change. I'll take care of Sams. And the bed."

By the time she had picked the baby up, he was awake. He started to whimper.

"You're all right," she began. Then: "Willard, he's shaking like a leaf. Trembling all over."

Now that he was over the shock of awakening to the feel of wet-baby against him, Willard seemed more in control. He had stripped out of the T-shirt and, since they were damp as well, out of his boxers.

Naked, he circled the bed and put his hand on Sams' back.

It felt like he was touching an electric vibrator set on 'high.'

Willard rummaged in the closet for an old sweat shirt while Catherine removed Sams' pajamas and the diaper. Urine dripped from the plastic lining, ran glistening down the back of Sams' legs.

Willard grabbed him and wrapped him in the sweat shirt, holding him close while Catherine pulled sheets and blankets off the bed and threw a new set onto the top of the dresser.

She had just tucked the last corner of the fitted bottom sheet around the mattress when: "Daddy, why aren't you wearing any clothes?"

Will, Jr., stood in the doorway, his eyes riveted on his father.

Willard grabbed one of the cast-off blankets—fortunately mostly dry—and whipped it around his waist, never letting go of Sams.

"Will, what are you …?"

"Daddy didn't have any clothes on?" That was Burt, coming up just behind his brother to stand in the doorway.

"It's okay," Catherine said, hurrying over to the two. "Sams just wet himself in our bed and Daddy's clothes got all wet, too."

"Oh." Both boys nodded. Curious mystery of nature

explained.

"Why does Daddy…?"

"That's enough." Willard let more than a little of his impatience—and embarrassment—show in his tone. "What are you guys doing up. It's"—he glanced at the clock—"3:15."

"We couldn't sleep." Will answered for both of them.

"And we can't go back to bed." That was Burt.

"There's something in…."

"Oh, for…." Still wrapped in the blanked, still clutching Sams to his chest. Willard led the boys back down the hall. Catherine had told him about the frequent night-time visits over the past days, and Willard had thanked her for taking care of things and letting him sleep. She had also told him about the putting-which-ever-boy-it-was-to-bed routine.

He didn't have to put Sams in bed. The baby was still shaking, although not as much, and was fast asleep. Willard didn't want to disturb him. And anyway the kid didn't have a diaper on yet.

But he could turn on the Mickey Mouse lamp, check the closet and with one hand shift the hangers around to reassure Will and Burt that nothing lurked behind them. He watched Burt crawl into his bunk and Willard climb up the end of his, then stretch out and pull the sheets up. He switched off the lamp, called a quiet "Good night," and left before either of the boys could answer him.

"Catherine, what in hell is going on?" He was whispering but his voice carried over the soft rustling of bedclothes being smoothed.

"Let me have Sams. And you put something on."

She laid the sleeping Sams onto the bed and deftly dressed him in a dry diaper and fresh pajamas. She had already tossed the wet things in the hamper in the bathroom, but the air still carried an ammoniac tinge. Willard wrinkled his nose in distaste.

He dressed in fresh boxers and a different—but just as faded—Lakers T-shirt and crawled into his side of the bed. Catherine laid Sams between them and settled herself.

"Are you going to let him sleep in here? I thought we agreed that he was old enough...."

"Just this once. I think the poor baby was really frightened. He felt like a nestling that has dropped to the ground, terrified and shaking and.... And I want him to stay with me tonight."

Willard stared for a moment.

"Okay. Now let me get to sleep." He grunted and rolled over, his back to Sams. Catherine noted that he left a small space between his body and his son's. Just in case.

The rest of the night—what was left of it—passed undisturbed. Willard managed to pull himself out of bed when the alarm clanged, changed quietly enough that Catherine and Sams never stirred. When he left, he carefully closed the door, although something inside of him wanted, oh so badly *needed*, to slam the door.

Let them see what it was like to get wakened from a sound sleep.

That morning at breakfast, the boys were subdued, even more than they had been for the past little while. Suze was fine; she chattered and ate and got ready for school with no problem.

Sams was sleepier than usual but that was perhaps to be expected. And—Catherine noted with no little surprise—he didn't bring his blanket with him to the table. As soon as he had eaten, though, he disappeared for a minute, then came wandering back into the kitchen with the wretched thing dragging behind him. Okay, so he was all right.

Will spoke very little. He didn't remember why he had come into his parent's room that late. He didn't remember dreaming, or thinking he had seen anything. Neither did Burt.

Both boys did remember seeing their father without any clothes. Willard was fairly modest—except, of course, when he and Catherine were alone...they did have four children, after all. So none of the children had ever seen him naked.

The boys started to ask questions, but Catherine simply shook her head. No, this is not the time.

They both seemed unduly fascinated by what they had seen.

5.

The same thing happened over the next three nights, Tuesday through Thursday.

Well, not the same thing, exactly, but for one reason or another all three of the boys found themselves, singly, in pairs, or as a triad—standing by Catherine's bed in the middle of the night. Each night there was enough commotion to rouse Willard. Each night he handled the interruption of his sleep with less and less patience.

"What is this," he bellowed at Will, Jr., when the boy was leaving for his own bed at 4:15 on Thursday night, "a damned tag-team performance?"

"Willard," said Catherine, laying a hand on his arm.

He shrugged it off, perhaps more vigorously that she expected.

"Well," he said, not modulating his voice at all out of deference to Suze, who was still asleep in the next room and hadn't caused any problems all week. "It might as well be. It if isn't one of them, it's the other. If it's not that one it's the third. Or all three of them."

To be fair, Catherine thought, he has a point. Not all of the nightly visits had been quiet, or easily resolved. More than once, Sams had been in tears. Burt came in on Tuesday night sobbing as if his best friend had died. Will, Jr., was generally quieter, but as Willard's anger grew, he took to glaring at his father, as if trying to stare him down. Twice, it had been enough for Catherine to traipse down the hall with the wanderer—or wanderers—and go through what had become an established ritual. The other times, it took either Willard or both of them to persuade the boys to return.

"Can't."

"Won't"

"Don't want to."

"Scared."

"Birds."

"Someone...something...in the closet."

At breakfast on Wednesday, long after Willard had departed for work, just as Will, Jr., was stepping out the front door to walk to school, he turned to Catherine.

"Mom, there really was someone in the closet."

"Okay, Will." She was distracted, trying to watch Burt and Suze as they made their way down Oleander.

"Really. He was like Dad was the other night?"

"What" Again absently.

"You know. He wasn't wearing anything/"

She turned to stare down at her eldest son. "He.... Why on earth would you say something like that? We both know there was no one in the bedroom, there never has been anyone in the bedroom. The door are all locked at night, the windows are locked, we don't even have a fireplace for Santa to come down on Christmas Eve. And we both know Santa wears a big red suit with white fur trim." This last in an attempt to wrest a smile from Will.

It worked...a bit.

"But...okay. Bye, Mom. See you this afternoon."

And so went the remainder of the week.

Until Friday night.

6.

"Okay, kids. Bedtime. Kiss your Daddy good night and come with me."

It was Friday evening. Catherine stood in the doorway between the front entry and the family room. The rest of the family was scattered in ones and two around the room, reading, playing, or—in Willard's case—intently watching the evening news.

His attention barely broke as each of the children leaned over his chair and kissed him on the cheek.

"'Night," he repeated four times.

One by one the children clustered in front of Catherine. She led them down the hall and into the back bedroom, where she hunched on the edge of the lower bunks and they dropped to the floor, squatting or half-laying.

"You all know what tomorrow is."

"Saturday," Burt responded before the others could say anything. Burt and Suze nodded gravely, their expression matching Catherine's. Sams just sat on the floor, cuddling his blanket in his arms and watching his mother.

"That's right. Saturday. Daddy's day to sleep in."

She paused, and they all nodded again.

"Daddy's really, really tired right now. You've all had really rough nights this week, and he hasn't gotten very much sleep. And you know he has to get up very, very early, even before the sun comes up, to get to work on time."

Again, they nodded.

"So tomorrow, I want you to remember to be very, very quiet when you get up. Let's let Daddy sleep as long as he can. All right?"

Nods around.

"When you wake up, I want you to play quietly in here until I have breakfast ready. Then we will all go very quietly into the kitchen and eat, and then you may watch T.V. in the family room."

"Can we all sleep in here?" Suze actually raised her hand before speaking, as if she were in school, and spoke in a soft, modulated, answering-the-teacher voice.

Catherine considered for a moment. She wanted for Suze to be as independent as possible, to grow up self-sufficient, so even though the three boys were now crowded into this one room, Suze had always had her own. But this was an unusual night.

"Okay. But you will all have to be quiet."

"Can I sleep on the bunk with Burt?" Suze again. Sometimes during the day, she and Burt—and occasionally Sams—would play on Burt's bed, tucking his blanket under the edge of the mattress on Will's bed and letting the rest of it hang down, making a kind of tent. At times they would play with Suze's dolls, at other times with Burt's small plastic army guys, using the rumpled bedding as hills and valleys and marching the toys across one by one. Sams usually just sat in one corner watching them, giggling along with them at some unspoken joke. Will rarely joined the fun, considering it too 'baby' for a twelve-year-old.

Catherine had never let them do it at night.

But tonight.

"All right. But you have to be very quiet. You can't shoot off cannons or anything like that. And no giggling and staying up until the middle of the night."

Nods again.

"Can I leave the night light on and read?" For Will, that would count as a special occasion.

"Yes."

"I promise I won't turn the pages too loud," he added, a quick grin crossing his face.

Catherine laughed lightly.

"See that you don't, buster-boy, or I'll have to come in and confiscate your book." She grinned back.

"Con-fi-scate," Suze said carefully, as if tasting each sound as it crossed her lips. "That's a funny word."

Everyone laughed...quietly. They were already practicing for tomorrow morning.

"Okay, guys, get ready for bed. Here, give me kisses."

She waited until all four of the kids were settled—making sure that Sams' night-time diaper was still clean and dry—then stepped into the hall and shut the door until only a crack of light showed from the Mickey Mouse lamp. Already she heard the rustling of bedding being arranged into a bunk-bed-tent.

Someone on the other side of the door laughed again...quietly.

She went on down the hall to join Willard in the family room.

7.

That Friday, no one woke up in the middle of the night.

8.

"Daddy! Mommy!"

Two young male trebles, high-pitched and full of terror.

A single, drawn-out shriek from a small girl.

"Yaaaap!" That was Sams's voice, breaking into tears.

Catherine sat bolt upright in bed.

Daylight struck her eyes. As she always did now, she reflexively glanced to the far corner of the room, where the patching plaster had been inexorably drawing away from the popcorn-textured ceiling. It was a dry year. The soil was compacting. She caught a glimpse of sunlight through the small slit that had formed.

Then she was on her feet and grabbing for her robe.

Willard threw himself onto his side, facing the far wall, and grunted angrily, "Damn those kids…." Then he, too was on his feet and racing around the end of the bed. He was out the door before Catherine. She heard his bare feet slapping against the hall floor.

A door opened, slamming against the wall.

A beat.

"Catherine! Get in here!"

She ran down the hall.

What now?

When she shot through the open doorway, Willard was standing by the low table beneath the window. All four kids were huddled together by the closet, tears either streaking their cheeks or still streaming from their eyes. None of them was speaking, although Sams—pressed against Will, Jr., whose hand curled protectively around his little brother's shoulder—was whimpering softly.

"Look!" Willard stabbed one finger toward the table top.

Toward the cage where, now solitary, the single remaining hamster lay crushed against the side. The wire door hung open along the front. A few cedar chips lay strewn on the table top, looking in their roughly rectangular shapes like tiny, toppled tombstones.

Catherine crossed the room.

"Willard, why are you yelling at me?" she started to whisper. After all, they had just gone through this a short while ago with Yip—another small, dead hamster, one of the expected traumas of childhood, given the average lifespan of the little creatures. This shouldn't be *that* unexpected. She felt her blood pressure rise. Willard had been angry before—now she was too.

Until she drew close enough to see clearly into the cage.

The little thing was, indeed, dead. Anyone could see that.

Including, unfortunately, the children.

Its fur, rather than being fluffy and full, even in death as Yip's had been, clumped matted against its body, stiff and crusted with russet brown that could only be dried blood. Blood had spattered all over the cedar chips lining the floor of the cage, all over the plastic exercise wheel now silent and still at the back, all over the thin wire of the cage itself.

It was even spattered on the desk top for several inches beyond the cage.

Catherine stared at the cage, then at Willard. His eyes were already fixed on her, dark with anger and fear.

"What happened?" Catherine's voice emerged thin and shaky.

"He was like that when we woke up," Will, Jr., answered from behind her. "We all saw him like that, then Sams started crying and Suze yelled and...."

"Shut up!" Willard roared, not even bothering to turn to look at his children. "Not another word!"

He grabbed the cage, twisted the wire door closed, and lifted the whole thing. Below, a clean square showed where it had been sitting—all around the square was a rough circle of dark brown splotches.

"Clean that up," he ordered as he passed Catherine.

The door slammed behind him.

"Okay, kids," she said, as calmly as she could. "I want you all to sit right here on Burt's bed"—she noticed that the blanket tent-wall had been pulled down—"until I get back."

She ran to the bathroom, drenched an old wash cloth with a spurt from the faucet and, water dripping from her hands, returned to the bedroom.

White-faced and frightened, the children were sitting on the bunk, arranged in age and size from Will at the farther end to Sams at the nearer. Catherine crossed in front of them, and with a few judicious swipes of her hand scraped the brown crust from the table top. She wadded the cloth and dropped it in the waste basket by the table.

"Mom," Will began. Suze and Burt had opened their mouths to speak, as well. Sams sat stonily on the edge of the bunk, his blanket jammed against his cheek.

"I…I don't think we should say anything until Daddy gets back. He…I…. Let's just wait for him."

The next few minutes passed in painful, devastating silence.

9.

"Now," Willard said, half-sitting on the table, precisely where the cage had stood. "Let's have the truth."

Catherine noticed that the back of the jeans he was now wearing was darker than the rest. The table top must still have been wet. Willard either didn't feel the dampness or he didn't care.

It took a moment for what he had just said to filter through her mind. When it did, she stared at him in disbelief.

"Willard, you can't…."

"The truth now. *All* of it." With one hand he sliced at the air between him and Catherine—peremptorily, she thought—meaning *Stay out of this.*

The four children hadn't moved.

They hadn't spoken either, neither to Catherine while Willard was gone nor to him when he stalked back into the room.

"I'm waiting."

"Daddy, where's Yap?" That from Burt—he was probably the

closest thing to a "master" the hamsters had had. Will, Jr., had his dog, Crud; Suze had her dolls; and Sams had his blanket.

"Gone." Willard's jaws clenched with the word.

"Gone? Where? We haven't had his funer…."

"There won't be a funeral for him, for *it*." His eyes flashed, cutting off whatever Burt—and Will and Suze—was about to say. Sams disappeared further behind his blanket. Even he could tell that Daddy was mad, madder than ever before.

"There won't be a funeral, and there won't ever be another hamster in this house. That I can promise you. Maybe never even another pet."

"But Crud…."

"Be quiet."

Will, Jr., closed his mouth and bit his lips.

Catherine tried again. "Willard…."

"Be quiet, all of you. There's something I'm going to say, and I want you all to listen to it. Very carefully. Understand?"

The children nodded. Catherine started to speak but a glance from her husband warned her that this was not the time to disagree with him.

"Something happened here last night. To that hamster. I want to know what it was," Willard said.

Silence. A long silence.

"I'm not going away until I find out. Nobody leaves this room until I find out. First Yip, and now this.

"What the hell happened?"

The kids exchanged terrified glances—it seemed that they were as frightened of speaking up to their father as they were about what had happened during the night…who or what had killed the hamster.

"I was asleep the whole night," Burt finally said.

"And so was I," Suze added. "I was asleep right here"—she patted Burt's bed—"and I don't know anything about it."

"Asleep," Sams' added timidly. "Asleep the whole night."

Willard swiveled his head to face his eldest. "I guess that leaves you, Will, unless one of the others is lying. Are they?"

"I, uh…." Three sets of eyes were riveted on him. He could see how close the younger kids were to tears. Yap was dead, and now Daddy was acting like *this*. Daddy *never* acted like this.

"You, uh, what?"

"I didn't see anything, either. I slept through the night, too. When I got up this morning, I went over to feed Yap and saw… and saw…him. I didn't know what to do. We promised Mom last night that we would be quiet when we got up this morning so you could sleep late."

"Thanks." The sarcasm in the word was so heavy that even Suze seemed to know something was wrong. Will, Jr., visibly flinched. Only Sams seemed oblivious.

"Um, I stood there watching for a long time, then Suze came over, and Burt. And then Sams, and he started crying, and then we were all crying and…and we couldn't help it, we wanted you guys to come in and…and help us…and make everything right."

By then tears were streaming down Will, Jr., cheeks.

"Make everything right? And how in the hell was I supposed to do that!"

Will winced, swallowed, and tried to continue. "I think…I think it was him. You know…the man."

Burt and Suze nodded slowly in agreement. Sams said, "The man. The man in the dark."

Willard's hand slammed against the table. The crack startled everyone, perhaps even Willard, since he raised his hand almost immediately and seemed to study it for a moment.

When he spoke again, his voice was tight, controlled, as frosty as an iceberg.

"The man you see at night? The naked man?"

The children nodded. They had no words at this point.

"*There is no man in here!*" Willard stomped to the closet and tore armful after armful of shirts and coats and school pants from their hangers and flung them onto the floor. "*There's nothing in here!* There never was!

"Now I want to know which one of you killed that hamster!"

"Willard!" Catherine's voice cut through his like a saber, quick and sharp to his bludgeoning broadsword. "Willard Huntley, I want to talk to you. Now!"

She grabbed his arm with a strength she didn't know she possessed—certainly Willard had never felt anything like it in their entire married life—and pulled him so hard that he almost lost his footing.

"Outside. Now! And you four stay in here. Don't any of you move."

Catherine and Willard disappeared through the door and down the hall.

Behind them came the soft sounds of sobbing. Sounds that grew louder and louder.

10.

She finally stopped yanking on his arm when they stood at the corner of the back yard, behind the garage and right below the eight-foot slump-stone fence that separated their yard from their neighbor's.

"I can't believe that. I *don't* believe that. You just accused your own children of killing their pet!"

"Let go of my arm." Every word slow, carefully enunciated. "Now."

"I don't know what you're thinking, but let me tell you...."

Craaack!

With his free hand Willard swung furiously and struck Catherine sharply, viciously across the face. For a moment she froze, not even breathing, uncomprehending, unbelieving.

"Let...go...of...my...arm." Not a syllable had changed tone or pitch.

She dropped her hand. Without a word, she spun on her heels and strode into the house, slamming the door behind her. Willard heard the lock *click*.

Stunned, he crumpled against the garage wall.

What had he done?

He had *never* struck Catherine, never struck any of the children. Certainly not in anger.

Certainly not in the rage of fury that had overwhelmed him while talking with the children.

His head throbbed.

And his hand hurt, stung, burned like he had thrust it into an open flame.

He slumped to the ground.

What was happening to him? To them?

The house.

Everything had begun to go to hell when they bought this damned house, with its shattered foundation and its disintegrating slab and its web-work of cracks crisscrossing every damned wall in the place.

And now it was shattering him.

Him and his marriage.

Catherine would never talk to him again. Would never love him again.

11.

Nothing was easy.

It wasn't easy to get back into the house. Every door, every window he tried was locked, solidly, as if barred by solid oak instead of cheap tract-home plywood. He stood by the front door for perhaps five minutes, then turned and trudged down the drive.

It took two hours and a long walk through the Charter Oaks subdivision, following one twining street after another, before he even began to feel a bit like himself. Before his breath calmed and he realized with even greater clarity the horrendous step he had just taken.

In an instant, everything in his life seemed to have changed.

Changed, nothing! It was a full-out train wreck!

He had struck his wife.

As he walked, however, he gradually began noticing things.

Perhaps it was his obsession revealing itself to the rational part of is mind. Perhaps it was just that his eyes were finally opened.

Everywhere—*everywhere*—in almost every house, across almost every stretch of sidewalk, every length of drive, he spotted flaws. The corner of one house was literally crumbling away a few inches above the ground, the cement flaking off like layers of too-thick make-up peeling from the cheeks of some ancient hag. In another, every window had thin, spidering lines like age-wrinkles fanning from each corner, some masked by meandering splotches of plaster, others fresh and jagged, painfully black against the stucco. This one had a long front eave that sagged in the center, making the entire place look off-kilter. That one was as sway-backed as an aging nag, its roof line slumping tiredly, as if weighed down by the decades.

It came as a shock. It wasn't just *their* house. It was every house on every block.

It wasn't just *him.*

When he finally returned to the house at the end of Oleander Place, he found the front door unlocked. That was a good sign, at least.

He moved quietly down the hallway until he stood in front of the back bedroom. The door was closed but he could hear the subdued murmuring of voices inside. He couldn't understand any of the words—it sounded like ghosts whispering through the labyrinth of dead branches in some midnight cemetery. Rising, falling, rising, falling, but never quite emerging into articulated speech.

He didn't try opening the door. He tapped with one finger on the smooth surface. *Click. Click. Click.*

The sounds inside ceased. He felt that he could almost hear five hearts thrumming just on the other side, could share the ache of hot, pent-up breath in five waiting breasts.

"Catherine." Barely audible—but shatteringly loud in the silence. "I...I'm sorry. Please. Can we talk."

Nothing from inside the room.

"Please."

Not even the rustle of bed clothing shifting beneath the fragile weight of a child's body.

"I'll be in the family room." That way, if she wanted to, or if one of the children needed something, she could skirt him completely and still go to the kitchen and back.

"I'll wait as long as you want."

It was nearly an hour later when she appeared in the doorway from the front entry. One second the space was empty and cold—the next, there she was, stock-still…and cold.

He stood up but did not move toward her. He started to speak, then halted. He would wait for her to make the first move.

"If you ever speak like that about my children"—*my* children, not *our* children—"or so much as threaten to strike me, or them, you will never see any of us again. Ever." Cold, dispassionate yet resonant with anger and hurt and, even now, disbelief. "Believe it."

"I know."

They remained like that for several long minutes.

Finally, he felt like he could break the silence. "Saying 'sorry' isn't enough. Not nearly enough. If I could take back everything, run the clock back to this morning when the kids' needed me, I would. I would do anything to change what happened."

She waited.

"I don't know what got into me. You know I'm not like that, I'm not that person. It was…it was like someone else was talking through my mouth, acting through my body."

"Like *something* in the dark terrifying our children?" At least it was *our children* again.

"Yeah. I guess."

Catherine hesitated, then crossed the room and sat stiffly on one end of the sofa.

Willard sat on the other.

After a silence that was still uncomfortable but no longer inhibiting, they talked.

12.

Later, Catherine brought the children into the kitchen, where she laid out chocolate milk and cookies for each of them while Willard sat in his usual place at the head of the table and, speaking carefully to each of them in turn, apologized for what had happened that morning.

Then the entire family got into the car and went to the park for the rest of the afternoon.

No one ever mentioned the episode again. No one ever mentioned Yap, either.

13.

For a few days, the atmosphere in the house lightened, ever so slightly. While the kids remained aloof from their father, they didn't go out of their way to avoid him, either. But they were clearly more comfortable when their mother was around as well, to act as a buffer if….

Catherine and Willard were still demonstrably cool around each other, as well, neither forgetting but neither indulging in further recriminations. Theirs was a patient, hopeful truce. With time, this rift could heal. Maybe.

Until early on the morning of the last Saturday in July.

The kids had gone to bed earlier than usual, for some reason subdued and restrained during the evening, even in their play. They went right to sleep.

Catherine and Willard stayed up until just before midnight, occasionally talking, more often simply sitting next to each other on the family room couch and watching-not-watching television. One might reach out and touch the other's knee and receive a small pat on the hand. One might lean into the other for a second, then straighten and resume watching whatever program happened to be on.

It felt as if everything would be all right, sooner rather than later.

They went to bed at around midnight, made love for the first time in more days than either could remember—quietly, tenderly, their words of repentance and forgiveness translated into touch and feel and breath and warmth.

Then they slept, facing each other, arms entwined

Catherine woke. She did not jerk into awareness, nor was she startled from sleep—as she had so often been during the past weeks—by the intrusion of one of her children. No one stood by her bed waiting patiently for her to open her eyes. No one cried out in the darkness for her help or her love.

She woke gradually. It was deep night; she could feel that by the stillness in the air, the darkness all around her, the almost oppressive silence of the house.

She lay unmoving in her bed, waiting for sleep to resume, for whatever dream that had carried her away only moments before to return and reclaim her. She heard Willard breathing next to her, lightly, comfortably. She felt his warmth radiating from him and smoothing against her flesh.

But she did not fall asleep. If anything, she grew more awake, more aware. She found herself tensing, listening for... something....

Finally, she rolled out of bed, careful not to disturb Willard. She felt around at the foot of the bed and located her robe, pulled it on and cinched the belt around her waist. She stepped into her slippers.

Without turning on any lights, feeling secure with her sense of feel as she trailed one hand along the wall, she moved down the hall to Suze's room. There was enough light filtering through the window for her to see Suze fast asleep, one arm thrown around her favorite stuffed animal, a grey-striped cat that she had had for so long that it was now flattened and out-of-shape from being used as a pillow. Flat Cat, Catherine called it.

She stepped out and moved on to the back bedroom.

Again, the light from the window was sufficient for her to see, even though the shadows in this room were much darker, blacker than they had been in Suze's room.

She glanced to the left. Both boys were asleep on the bunks. Will, Jr., was bundled up, almost invisible in the layers of sheet and blanket that muffled him like a cocoon. Burt was, as always, nearly naked, his pajama bottoms pulled up to his thighs and his tops wrinkled just under his armpits. But his head was, also as always, snuggled into his pillow beneath a layer of blanket.

She shrugged. It was a warm night. She wouldn't bother tucking him in, since he would probably look just like this in the morning.

Sams was curled up on the floor, halfway between the older boys' bunks and his box bed. His blanket lay across his face.

She stepped over to him and leaned down to pick him up.

The scream of anguish and terror blasted through Willard's dream, exploding him into the night. For an instant, he couldn't breathe.

Then the scream repeated, and he was on his feet and flying down the hall toward the back bedroom and Catherine's hideous, gasping cries.

He spun around the door jamb.

Burt and Will, Jr., sat bolt upright in their beds, their faces screwed up in fright. Both seemed on the verge of shrieking but neither had yet found his voice.

Catherine stood in the middle of the room, cradling Sams' tightly in her arms.

She turned to Willard. Her face was as white as death, and her voice shook so badly he could barely understand her. When he did, he felt the blood plummet from his face as well.

"Sams is dead! He's dead! My baby is dead!"

From the *Tamarind Valley Times,* 5 November 1995:

OFFICIAL END TO VALLEY MYSTERY

The courts moved earlier today to declare Bryan Sydney, the Tamarind Valley real estate executive missing since October, 1989, legally dead. Members of Sidney's immediate family gathered in the chambers of Judge Martha Feldmann to hear the official declaration which put an end to a seven-year investigation into his mysterious disappearance.

With the ruling, legal claims levied against the now defunct Ace-High Construction and the equally defunct McCall/Sidney Realty will advance to a more abstract level as attorneys for sixteen families....

CHAPTER TWELVE
THE HUNTLEYS, LAST
WEEK IN AUGUST 2010

Final Reckoning

1.

August passed.

Each member of the Huntley family tried to deal with the fact of death privately, individually.

Suze spent much of her time at home in the far corner of her room, the farthest from the boys' bedroom, moving her dolls in complex, repeated patterns on the carpet and speaking to them in a voice so faint and fragile that, standing in the doorway and watching her daughter, Catherine could never understand any of the imagined conversations. Suze would retreat to her room as soon as she arrived home from school on weekdays, and frequently not leave it for longer periods than to eat and go to the bathroom on the weekends. Catherine and Willard might try to entice her out—even demand that she join the rest in some activity in the family room, a game or a particular television program—but as soon as their attention strayed from her, she quietly disappeared.

Burt didn't seem quite so badly troubled. He was willing enough to spent time in the front of the house—perhaps too willing. He would clear a space on the family room floor and play for hours with his army figures, the same ones that Sams had so enjoyed watching in the make-shift tent on Burt's bunk. He would send army against army, silently destroying formations with a single swipe of his arm or leg, and knocking individual soldiers over by striking them with the base of whichever one he held in his hand.

Will, Jr., preferred the armchair next to the couch in the family room, where he would sit with his dog, Crud, for hours on end, ruffling the dog's fur or scratching its ears. Sometimes he would simply hold onto the animal, cradling it tightly in his arms. Often, he would almost cry.

Willard became more an automaton rather than a person. He woke at 5:00 AM on work days, got ready to leave and let himself out of the house without saying a word, without making any extraneous sounds that might disturb the others. He never called home from work. He never spoke about his work while at home. He began arriving home later and later, sometimes an hour later than usual, sometimes two hours or more, always explaining curtly that "Traffic was bad." Those words, exactly, never an alteration. "Traffic was bad."

On week ends he puttered around the house, futilely spattering plaster on the ubiquitous cracks that kept extending themselves in corners, on new ones that spread like narrow cancers in window corners. He never repainted any of the repairs. Occasionally he would work outside, doing what was required to keep the place presentable—mowing the front yard but rarely the back; sweeping the front sidewalk and drive when blowing leaves accumulated along the foundations of the house; trimming the hedges separating his house from those on both sides, but ignoring the overgrown shrubs along the back fence.

Catherine responded worst of all to Sams' death. She barely registered what the coroner's representative meant when he said, in abstracted, formal officialese that nearly left her breathless: "If the child hadn't been so old, I would call it SIDS—as it is, all we can say is that he suffered an ALTE that ultimately proved fatal."

"ALTE," Willard had asked humbly.

"An apparently life-threatening event. We found no other definable cause of death."

And, as far as the authorities were concerned, that was it. Dead child. So sorry. Nothing more to say.

She wouldn't let Willard remove the little box bed from the back room. He had wanted to carry it out to the back yard and take a sledge hammer to it, pound it until nothing remained but infinitesimal fragments that would blow away with the faintest breeze…but he never told Catherine. About a week after she had found Sams' body, he made one effort to pick the bed up, then noticed that she had changed the bedding that morning, left the room, and rarely entered it again.

Catherine did, though. She would perch on the edge of the box, its pine frame cutting painfully into the back of her legs, and stare blankly at the floor…and the place where he had been laying that morning, where the faint line of the shattered slab created a ripple in the other-wise smooth carpet.

She also carried Sams' blanket with her almost everywhere. It was still filthy—she had actually intended to wash it later that Saturday with the rest of the sheets and pillowcases from the children's rooms but obviously hadn't. The satin edging was ragged, stained, stiff where normally it would have been damp. It stank. But she either held it in her hand or tucked it under her arm or squeezed it between the waistband of her pants and her skin, where the touch of it made her flesh chill and shiver.

There was no family anymore. Merely five people of varying ages quietly inhabiting the same space…the same house.

Certain times of the day proved more difficult than others.

Suze seemed to have no trouble falling asleep in her own bed, although the number of stuffed animals keeping Flat Cat company on top of her coverlet increased dramatically, until there was almost no room for the girls' body. Still, once she burrowed her way under the layers of plush and politically correct, non-flammable, hypoallergenic filling, she slept deeply, rarely waking until well past dawn.

But the boys….

The boys' categorically refused to sleep in the back room.

It didn't matter how much Willard blustered or wheedled, how often he led them by the hand back to their bunks and warned them to stay there or else…no matter how resolutely he carried out the motions of preserving the sense of a normal bedtime, the boys always woke the next morning twined together on the family room couch, sometimes covered by one of Burt's blankets, sometimes completely uncovered.

On week days, Willard never looked into the family room to see if they were there. He ignored them, moving through the darkened kitchen and living room and entry and out the door like a phantom. On weekends, if it was a good day, the boys were up and dressed before either Willard or Catherine roused, and things went…well, placidly. If it was a bad day, Willard would find them asleep, and stomp out of the house without eating and spend most of the rest of the morning in mindless, useless chores.

Beyond that, the boys spent as little time as possible during the day in their room. If they needed to change, they whipped in, grabbed whatever clothes they needed, and locked themselves in the back bathroom until they were fully dressed. If Burt wanted a particular set of army figures, he would halt outside the door, take a deep breath as if he were about to dive into shark-infested waters, and race in and out as fast as possible. If Will left his homework or his school books in the room, he was more than willing to take whatever punishment his teacher might mete out for his lapse, rather than walk down the hall and retrieve them before heading out to school.

In all, one could fairly say that the Huntleys were at a stalemate, neither openly—and perhaps healthily—grieving for loss nor taking any steps to move beyond it.

Until late in the afternoon of Sunday, the twenty-ninth of August.

2.

Willard was, as usual, immersed in the television—some football game or another, essentially identical to any other he had stared at over the past month except for the colors of each team's uniforms, and even those were almost indistinguishable beneath their crusts of mud and swampy-green grass stains. There was a score, the teams were something to something, of course, but he couldn't have told anyone what it was. The game was busyness, something to do, something to keep from thinking.

Catherine was sitting at the other end of the family room couch, pretending to watch the game as well, but in reality paying more attention to her hands as they slid aimlessly up and down the nap of the bit of blanket on her lap.

Neither looked toward the kitchen door as Will, Jr., entered, carrying something.

He didn't speak. He simply stood there, motionless, deathly pale and breathing so shallowly the rise and fall of his chest barely fluttered his shirt.

Finally, Willard glanced up.

Then stood up, urgently, in one swift motion. Catherine caught the movement out of the corner of her eye, then rose to her feet as well.

In a breath, both were at Will's side.

"What's wrong?" They spoke at the same instant.

Will didn't answer. Instead, he raised his eyes—hollow, bruised, red-rimmed—to meet theirs. Then he dropped them to the object he held in his hands.

When they saw what it was, their faces abruptly drained of color until they were as pale, as ashen-white as their son.

It was just a dog-food bowl, Crud's dented aluminum bowl that usually held crusted remnants of the morning's helping of kibble.

Today, it held that…and something more.

The edges were caked with flecks of rust-brown, some

distinct, round spots, others ragged smears that stained the metal as well as the remains of Crud's food.

Blood.

Dried blood.

"Will...?" Catherine could get no further with her question. It was as if she already knew the answer.

Willard dropped to one knee and placed his hand over Will's. "Where's Crud?"

"I don't know, Dad." Tears filled his eyes. "I've looked for him all over the house and the back yard. Then, when I went to re-fill his dish...."

No one had to say what they were all thinking.

Yip and Yap.

Dead.

Willard stood and circled his son with his arms. Catherine took the dish gingerly from Will and started into the kitchen to clean it.

"Let's go out and look for him again," Willard said. "Maybe he's just...."

But he never finished his sentence.

3.

It began as a distant rumble, a freight-train-bowling-down-the-tracks growl that escalated into an ear-drum shattering roar before the three of them quite registered what they were hearing.

Then the walls shimmered, the shade on the floor lamp beside the armchair began swinging back and forth, slightly at first, then more and more rapidly, until it was vibrating so rapidly that it seemed more likely to disintegrate than to stop. The lamp itself began rocking, swiveling on its base until with a clattering of smashing bulbs it crashed against the floor.

"Earthquake!" Catherine yelled.

In the kitchen, cabinet doors flew open and plates, saucers, glasses cascaded onto the floor, shattering into glistening fragments.

From the back of the house they heard two children screaming.

Willard spun Catherine and Will around, almost shoving them as he yelled, "Outside! Get in the middle of the yard. I'll get the others."

Before they began moving, before he finished speaking, he was running toward the hall, struggling to keep his footing as the floor quivered and thrust beneath him.

He bounced once off the walls, stumbled around the corner that led to the back bedrooms The house was still trembling as if it were itself terrified of what was happening. The roar became even more menacing.

Suze and Burt were huddled in the doorway to Suze's room. All of the other doors were closed but shaking so violently in their frames that they threatened to burst open.

"Daddy!" they screamed in unison.

He grabbed Suze up in one arm and gripped Burt's hand.

Behind him, shards of drywall from the ceiling clattered to the floor, breaking and bouncing as if they had a life of their own. Somewhere, a window shattered.

"We can't stay here," Willard yelled above the booming of the quake. "This place is falling apart."

Hauling Burt behind him so rapidly that the boy's feet barely touched the roiling floor, he crossed Suze's room in two strides, let go of Burt—who nearly tripped but managed not to—and opened her window with a single thrust, then popped the screen out with a second. Before it struck the ground, he had lowered Suze out the window until she was on her feet, then yelled, "Meet Mom out back!" and grasped Burt's arm and began boosting him out the window as well. By then Suze was beyond the corner of the house and out of sight, and Burt was halfway there when Willard crawled out the opening and ran alongside the house, grabbing Burt up as he ran.

Bits of stucco flaked off the side of the house as they passed, a dust-brown scuff of snow that caught in their hair and settled on their clothes.

The ground was still shaking when the five of them clustered in the center of the back yard, far from trees, power lines, anything that could crash down upon them and injure or kill them.

The ground still jerked back and forth as if it were electrified.

Perhaps sixty, perhaps as many as ninety seconds had passed.

A whining howl rose, banshee-like, from somewhere inside the house, just as the window of the boys' bedroom exploded, frosting the ground below with fragments of glass.

"Crud! Cruuud!" Will shook off his mother's grasp and bounded toward the house. Willard reached him before the boy could cover more than a few yards, threw his arms around Will's chest, and began pulling him back toward the others.

"No, Will. You can't!"

"But it's...."

Another sound rose behind Willard. One even more horrifying that the dog's cry.

"Mommmy! Daddy!"

Staggered by the voice, Willard caught Catherine's eyes just as she started forward, whispering, "Sams!"

Even as he shook his head, even as he gestured for her to stay with Burt and Suze, even as he shoved Will, Jr., toward her, even as one part of his mind screamed "Sams is dead! You know he's dead! It *can't* be him!" another part—a stronger, more desperate part—responded to his child's cry instinctively, impulsively, and he raced toward the house, unconscious of the fact that the ground beneath his feet was abruptly solid and unmoving, and threw himself through the open window frame, impervious to the savage pain as broken shards sliced his arms and thighs.

4.

Catherine *knew* Sams was dead, had seen his tiny body in the horribly white coffin as they had closed the lid and hidden him forever from her sight. She *knew* that she had seen the coffin lowered into the gashed earth and knew that whatever was left of her baby lay there, unmoving, unbreathing, unable to love her or call to her.

She *knew* all of that.

She knew it, and *knew* that Sams could not possibly be inside the house...and *knew* that Willard had to find him, bring him out, rescue him and return him to her.

She sank to her knees and clutched feverishly at her older children. The pulled closer to her, trembling and crying in hope and terror and confusion and despair.

"Willard!" she screamed. Then: "No, Willard!" just as somewhere within the bowels of the house, beneath the remains of slab that had shattered and disintegrated under the force of the earthquake, a gas line ruptured, two bits of metal collided with sudden violence, struck a spark, and—even as the side wall of the house began crumbling and sloughing away, detached from the rest of the structure by the earthquake's fury—sheets of fire erupted from every window, every doorway, every crack, and the house burst into flames.

From the *Tamarind Valley Times*, 30 August 2010:

TEMBLOR STRIKES VALLEY;
SEVERAL INJURED, ONE DEAD

The 4.5 quake that rumbled across Tamarind Valley yesterday left minor structural damage behind, although several injuries were reported and one death resulted.

Willard Huntley, 38, was killed when the gas line beneath his home burst, presumably as a result of the temblor, and exploded, destroying the house. He is survived by his wife, Catherine, and three children.

The Huntley home was the only one seriously damaged in the quake which, though mild according to the Richter scale, nevertheless continued for over a minute, causing pictures to fall from walls and items to tumble from shelves in stores across the Valley. Authorities are unsure why the Huntley home was so severely effected when others nearby were not. In one home not a block away, a single vase fell unbroken from a piano, the only result of the quake.

Tragically, the Huntleys were still recovering from the sudden death of their youngest child a month earlier. Samuel 'Sams' Huntley, 2 ½, was found....

EPILOGUE
THE DAY AFTER, 30 AUGUST 2010

If Only....

1.

Catherine and the children were not present the next day when investigative units from police, fire, and county inspectors' departments sifted through the wreckage of 1066 Oleander Place. The family had been driven away a few hours after the quake by her parents, Howard and Eleanor Prinz, and were now in her childhood home in Santa Barbara, physically unharmed but in deep shock. Two physicians remained in the house rest of that afternoon and well into the evening.

The police team, led by forensic specialist Emily Naples, arrived first on Monday morning. A short time later, Jorge Garces and his group, representing the Tamarind Valley Fire Department, drove up Oleander Place and, watched by small clusters of neighbors in front yards along the way, parked behind the police vehicle.

As luck would have it, Edgar Sai was assigned by the city engineers' department to represent them. He parked several housed further down Oleander and walked slowly up the hill toward the remains of 1066. He stood for a moment just outside the police tape surrounding the front yard, then shook his head sadly, sighed, lifted up the tape, and moved toward the blackened skeleton of wood and ashes.

"How's it going Em?" he asked as he was greeted by Naples.

"Not much left of the place, is there?" she gestured to the fire scorched concrete and the scattered clumps of what once were roof beams, interior wall supports, and outer walls. "Fire department says it was a gas leak but it sure must have burned hot. Nearly everything inside's destroyed."

"They got Huntley out yet?"

"Just left in the coroner's van. What was left of him. A few bones mostly. It must have been like an incinerator in there."

"What about the others?"

"What…?" Naples, shook her head as if to clear a moment of confusion. "Oh, yeah, the child."

"And the dog."

"That was the first report," Naples said, "immediately after the first squad arrived yesterday. Mrs. Huntley was nearly hysterical—which makes perfect sense, considering what had just happened—and rambled on for a while, something about a child. And the oldest kid was crying about his dog, said he knew the dog was trapped in the house."

Sai shook his head sadly. "Must have been tough."

"Yeah, anyway, the squad found the husband right away, he must have gotten trapped in the back of the house. They searched but didn't find any other remains.

"Then it turns out that the family had lost a kid about a month ago, SIDS or something, so apparently Mrs. Huntley imagined that she heard the child's cry, or hallucinated it in the fear of the moment. Something like that.

"The kid's dog will probably turn up. It must have been terrified by the earthquake and ran away. Someone will track it down."

Sai didn't answer, except to say, "Let's get on with it, all right?"

They shuffled through what had been the family room, observing, measuring, picking up a bit of litter here and there and sniffing it.

"Morning, Em, Ed," Garces said as he ducked under a couple of charred beams and approached them.

They returned his greeting. Tamarind Valley was a small place. The various investigators knew each other well enough from meeting at scenes of fires, murders, burglaries, and the rest.

"Found anything unusual?" Em asked, mostly *pro forma*, since it was pretty clear already that the true culprit behind the death and the conflagration had been Nature in the form of an earthquake.

"Actually, yes. I was just coming out to see if Ed had arrived yet. You both should see this."

The trio threaded their way down the burned-out shell of the hallway, careful not to stumble where the concrete slab had twisted and buckled from the force of the temblor. They could see into remains of a bathroom, two bedrooms—all gutted. Carpet, drywall and most of the wooden structural supports, everything of the furniture except the metal bits and pieces left over from bed frames and dressers, melted, twisted, scored and blackened.

"Hell of a fire," Garces said. "Though from the bits and pieces of wiring I've seen, this place should have gone up years ago. Looks like the builder jury-rigged all of the wiring in the house, connecting whatever scraps he had on hand. So far, we've found no single piece longer than a couple of feet. And they vary in gauge as well.

"If it hadn't been the gas line, an electrical spark in the studs would have done the trick.

"The people that lived here all these years, whoever they were, those people don't know how lucky they were."

There was nothing more in the third bedroom or the back bathroom. In the back corner room, however, they found half a dozen police and fire personnel blocking the shattered doorway.

"Make way," Garces ordered. The uniformed figures parted, letting the trio enter.

If the rest of the house had been burned beyond recognition, this room was devastated. Even though the plans indicated that the gas line had run beneath the converted garage/family room and into the kitchen, it looked as if the focus of the blast area had been the middle of this room.

The side wall had been forced outward from the bottom, crushed against the slump-stone fence that separated this property from the neighbors'—and which, miraculously, had not fallen over when the fragments of wood, plaster, and stucco had struck it. The roof—what was left of it—lay piled on top of the wall, heaped as neatly as if some monstrous hand had positioned it there.

In the room itself, the concrete slab had erupted. It looked as if some gigantic behemoth had shouldered its way from underground, lifting wide portions of the slab up and outward, leaving a pit in the center of the room. Two men were in the pit, bent over something.

"Find anything more?" Garces called out to them.

One of the men straightened, swiped at his brow with an ash-blackened hand.

"You're not going to believe this, sir."

He motioned the trio closer.

They stood as near the pit as they could get, behind a buckled hunk of scarred concrete. The upper edges were jagged and worn, almost eroded, suggesting that this break had occurred long before the earthquake had forced this portion of the foundation upward.

The other man hauled himself out of the hole.

Revealing...on the far side of the break, a long, rounded extrusion of concrete that arced beneath the rest of the slab. Originally, it must have been a solid structure, eight feet long, four feet across, three feet deep, where the original excavation for the house had been deepened before the concrete was poured. In shape, it looked almost like a roughened mummy case, slightly wider at one end, narrowing at the other.

The quake had lifted it almost level with the rest of the slab, canted it until its entire length was visible from where the trio stood, and shattered portions of it. Where the old cement had blistered away, bones protruded into the open air.

"I think there's a complete skeleton in there, sir. Must be as old as the house, though. It's certainly not fresh."

2.

It took only a short while to photograph the remains *in situ*, then carefully remove the bones, reconstructing their original open-air arrangement on a blue-black tarp spread over the nearest nearly level bit of floor. One by one the stained, fire-blackened bones emerged into the light.

Little else was found. Whatever clothes the unknown victim might have been wearing had decayed or dissolved or other-wise deteriorated to little more than patches of muck along the bottom of the case. There was a belt buckle, unadorned and functional. A watch face but no band—perhaps the band had been leather, since a small buckle lay beneath the corroded watch. Some indefinable sludge that must have been shoes, since it still covered portions of the feet.

"No idea what would have cause this kind of damage," one of the investigators ventured. "Usually, even after decades, more would survive. Leather. Synthetics. It looks almost as if some kind of acid or something had been poured over everything. But there's no trace of any damage from corrosives on the bones themselves. Other than having not a trace of flesh on them, they are almost pristine." He shook his head. "No idea at all."

Finally, at the bottom of the concrete tomb, they located a single clue. Two bits of metal, thin and rectangular, that looked like a set of dog-tags, or a pair of medic-alert pendants.

It took some cleaning and a strong magnifying glass to read anything through the accumulated layers of grime, sludge, and almost rock-hard sediment.

Medic-alert tags.

The name on one of them was still legible, although any

mention of medical disorders had been totally eradicated.

"Bryan Sidney."

"I know that name from somewhere," Edgar Sai said. "Give me a minute." He placed a call on his cell phone, stepped away from the small group for several minutes, then returned.

His face was pale, and he looked shaken.

"Bryan Sidney. Disappeared November, 1989. Police figure he'd skipped town. He and a partner built this original subdivision, then got caught cutting to many corners. Talk was they were both in deep shit, probably were going to be arrested, maybe serve some time in jail.

"Then Sidney disappeared. No trace. The talk settled down for a while.

"The it re-surfaced a two years later, stronger. More evidence, I guess, or something. Indictment actually came down.

"The night before he would have been arrested, Sidney's partner, Andrew McCall was found murdered."

Sai stared around at the wreckage from the fire, the gutted rooms, the shattered foundation slab, the black pit lying open and revealed just a few feet away.

"He was found murdered," he continued, "in *this* house."

3.

Later, after most of the official presence had departed, and he was alone with two men from the coroner's office and the recovered bones, Edgar Sai stared down at the remains of Bryan Sidney, hidden for over two decades in a silent sarcophagus of cold concrete.

"If only," he muttered, "if only these walls could talk...."

From the *Tamarind Valley Times,* 12 June, 2012

NEIGHBORHOOD PARK ANNOUNCED

The Tamarind Valley Planning Commission publicly announced today the planned construction of a small neighborhood park in the Charter Oaks Subdivision.

The property, which has stood vacant since September of 2010, defaulted to the city after a legal contest in which the previous owners relinquished all claims of ownership.

In an arrangement with the family, the new park will be named the Willard and Samuel Huntley Memorial Park, after Willard Huntley, a valley resident who perished in the fire that consumed the home during a small earthquake that rattled the valley on August 29, 2010. A freak gas-line fire lead to Huntley's death. The remainder of the family survived.

A month earlier, Huntley's 2 ½ year old son Samuel died suddenly of a SIDS-like event.

The Planning Commission intends to dedicate the park on August 29 of this year, in memory of….

ABOUT THE AUTHOR

Michael R. Collings is an Emeritus Professor of English at Seaver College, Pepperdine University, where he directed the Creative Writing Program for over two decades. He has published multiple volumes of poetry, novels, short fiction, and scholarly studies of such contemporary writers as Stephen King, Orson Scott Card, Dean R. Koontz, and Piers Anthony. Recent works include *The Art and Craft of Poetry*; *In the Void: Poems of Science Fiction, Myth and Fantasy, and Horror;* and a Book of Mormon epic, *The Nephiad*.

His previous fiction, also published through Wildside, includes: *The House Beyond the Hill: A Novel of Fear*; *Wordsmith, Volume One: The Thousand Eyes of Flame* and *Wordsmith, Volume Two: The Veil of Heaven*; *Singer of Lies*; Wer *Means* Man, *and Other Tales of Wonder and Terror*; and *Three Tales of Omne: A Companion to* Wordsmith.

He is now retired and lives in his native state of Idaho.